Peggy Diedrichs

About the Author

GARY DIEDRICHS was born in Ohio, schooled in New Jersey and New York, and lives in a Sausalito houseboat.

As a journalist, he once asked a man on his way to becoming one of the FBI's Ten Most Wanted, "Tony, is it true you bomb people?" In that same spirit of honest inquiry, he interrogated porn pioneer Marilyn Chambers regarding her favorite fantasy. And as a magazine editor, he prevailed upon presidential aspirant Dennis Kucinich to judge a pizza-eating contest. Kucinich, then a city councilman, declared the winner to be a very hungry German Shepherd. (The dog also ate the pizza box.)

Diedrichs was a radio newsman, a newspaper reporter, has written travel guides and scores of magazine articles, and edited magazines in Los Angeles, Detroit, and Cleveland. THE EARTHQUAKE SHACK is his first novel.

GARY DIEDRICHS'S
THE EARTHQUAKE SHACK

Earthquake Shack habitat which a series of dramatic events
are set to destroy."
—Susan Trott,
author of CRANE SPREADS WINGS

"This is a terrific tale about one of the great chapters in San
Francisco's extraordinary history, the story of about a small
community sprung up from the ashes of the great earthquake and fire. In a city of great neighborhoods—North
Beach, Nob Hill, the Haight-Ashbury—these 'temporary'
homes should find a permanent spot in our hearts."
—James Dalessandro,
author/screenwriter, 1906

"A page-turning ride across time and history, THE EARTH-
QUAKE SHACK is a mystical romp that paints a picture of
times gone by with a bright brush. Infused with quirky
characters and zany plot twists, you end up pleased, satisfied, and hungry for more. I put off reading the end of the
book to hold onto its deliciousness."
—Linda Joy Myers,
author of DON'T CALL ME MOTHER

The
Earthquake
Shack

A SAUSALITO\LOVE STORY

To Donna —
Water Rats, Unite

G A R Y D I E D R I C H S

TWO BRIDGES PRESS
San Francisco

Library of Congress Control Number: 2006906110
ISBN 10: 0-9723947-9-6
ISBN 13: 978-0-9723947-9-6
Printed in the United States of America.

AUTHOR'S NOTE

I BECAME A Sausalito Water Rat the moment I settled into the beachfront earthquake shack (barged across the bay sometime around 1907) that inspired me to imagine this work and become a serious fan of San Francisco earthquake history and Sausalito's tangy and spirited past. This is a work of fiction, but I have tried to respect history and geography throughout—with the exception of mostly minor instances where it did not suit my design or fancy. Any character's resemblance to persons living or dead, except for well-known historical figures such as Jack London, Sally Stanford, Alan Watts, Sterling Hayden, Jack Kerouac, and Jean Varda, is purely coincidental.

Enjoy.

For
my beautiful Peggy,
who gave me
the two great gifts
of her love
and time
to write as well
as I am able

Prologue

IT LANDED HERE EVEN BEFORE A BRIDGE SPANNED THE destroyed city where it was raised and the tide-swept beach where it was dumped. It came by sea. An ark without paired beasts but with a past.

An earthquake refugee shack, so the thousands like it that sprang up in tidy mushroom rows overnight were called, identical, painted sylvan green, conceived as temporary shelter for the homeless majority after nature gave San Francisco its worst last call so far. (The party in the smoldering city was over, at least for a little while.) These makeshift villages built of old growth redwood soon had hand-lettered signs marking their "streets" on the blowsy park meadows, and they spawned neighborhood associations and whore houses and Sunday worship, and their inhabitants lived life and died death in their spare new quarters, added homey touches to them, made improvised improvements to their simple design, settled in not as squatters but permanent settlers of precursory subdivisions.

This, of course, would not do.

When the ruined city was restored sufficiently for authorities to turn their gaze to this unbridled roosting on the saw grass, they right smartly determined that the public parks must be reclaimed from said public. They offered the inducement of letting the squatters keep their shacks, indeed of paying the drayage, if they were hauled away forthwith—move along now, no dawdling, see?

Threatening, despite severe shortage of housing still, to otherwise pull them down. Reduce them to splinters. Flatten them as though another natural disaster had rolled through the cornrows of refuge like giant stones.

So these shacks were sledged to the top of Telegraph Hill, to the flats of Cow Hollow. Others were loaded onto barges and ferried across the bay. This one ending up here, in Old Town Sausalito, on a curl of inlet where for eons Miwoks dug clams and pounded acorns and purified their spirits in sweat lodges before being shoved out by whites. An exile within sight of its homeland across the rippling water, snugly wedged between much grander structures on the rough brown sand.

There it has sat, on a short stretch of exclusive beachfront bounded by Castle by the Sea, a saloon and transient residence where Jack London is said to have written the opening salvo to one of his best tales, and the rowdy beer hall called Valhalla.

The nesting instinct in us being very strong, and something about this funny little place—its very modesty perhaps, or because it literally sprang from the embers of destruction and thus fires man's will to forge and recast his surroundings until they please and protect again—has inspired successive occupants over the decades since to add their own imprints to our Earthquake Shack.

Most noticeably, a tiny shotgun cottage from just up the hill was lifted and urged to the beach, joined to the shack's south face, roofed over, with a new hallway between the halves from stem to stern. To this addition a later tenant, a shipwright's assistant from Old Town's boat works, contributed lintels of scrap teak and other exotic hardwoods above interior doorways, no two alike. Someone else, exactly whom nobody recalls, enclosed the open-air porch across the shack's front; it became the narrow slice of front sitting room with views to

Angel Island, Alcatraz, Belvedere, East Bay, and the City.

Thereafter arrived the pastry chef just fled from a harpy wife. He saw the unadorned walls with a cake decorator's eye. He needed a project to ease an anguished mind. Loading his muslin icing bag with plaster of paris, he set to piping—loopy swirls and floral flourishes here, escallops there, his masterpiece the elaborate filigree he gave a pair of closet doors. Thanks to this chef's fitful artistry, they became like twin sheet cakes upended.

The tinkerings and added touches did not end there. But you get the idea. Like a periwinkle's home, the shack changed and grew in presence and personality year by year.

One room, though, does demand special mention. Through all the shack's accretions and transformations, it remains, always, the showstopper. The epicenter. Where so much life has been lived, borne of such tragic circumstances. Once the all-purpose living-eating-sleeping area, all who enter the Earthquake Shack are arrested by these four walls. This room, more than the rest, also having a distinctly nautical air. Naturally enough, since arrive by sea it did. But truly the oddest aspect is that entry to this cozy ship's cabin can be gained from any of *five* hatches—*seven* if you count those twin doors tarted up like cakes, apparent passageways below decks that lead only to hanging garments and a jumble of shoes. Upon entering or leaving each time, a choice must be made: this way? or that? or that? This is a room ready-made for that silent movie gag where the jerky buffoons search frantically for one another by yanking open and rushing through door after door.

Such a porous captain's quarters might prove dangerous in a storm. But a seaside room they make ripe with possibility! For letting in salt air and light—completely, partially, or not at all. For opening yourself up or closing yourself off. A room you won't soon forget. And one you may not want to leave—maybe ever.

And is it true? More than a few uneasy occupants have sworn this particular room, raised from the ashes of the Great San Francisco Earthquake and Fire of 1906, is haunted. Yes, indeed they have said so. Have sworn that a ghost or spirit or entire gaggle of spooks is responsible for the sudden slamming of the many doors—though it could easily just be the fog wind roiling like a tsunami over the coastal headlands and down though Old Town, which has the well deserved nickname of Hurricane Gulch. But they have also pointed to ghostly creakings and groanings and to flashes of eerie light (no, not the sweep of Alcatraz's powerful beam that travels the boardwalk every half-dozen seconds through the night) ... and to that dream-invading racket on the roof, especially when the moon is fat and full.

Are these things easily explained away? Of course they are.

Or, like all matters spiritual, is faith in the existence of these shack spirits more powerful for their quick dismissal by others as childish nonsense?

Of course it is.

After all, what better playground could a spirit ask for? Or any human, for that matter, desirous of multiple means of ingress and egress, entry and escape.

January 1960

1.
Another Herring in Paradise

IS THAT YOU, MALACKY?

'Tis, Mi-Wash. Did you see him? Dead as a jellyfish on our beach?

Yes. White. Swollen.

Like dough for soda bread.

I do not know this soda bread. No day is bad for dying, that is the teaching of the Spirit Coyote of the Miwok people.

Aach … Holy Mother Church taught me to fear the hellfire even more than the private parts of an eighty-year-old nun!

But now we know. We know what waits over the Great Divide. Is that not good, Malacky?

'Tis a blessed relief, that's for certain sure.

It is sad.

Damn right—we're dead as the soda bread man.

It is sad we cannot open the eyes of those who still breathe the cool sea air. I would help this one—the one who found the swollen white man. His pain is great, he suffers more.

More than the peacock who made the fancy pies and sweets from dawn to dusk? Or the widow who sobbed through the night?

Yes, more than all before him who made their cooking fires at this place of my family's lodge and in your people's … how do you call it?

Refugee housing, that's what they called it. Must I tell you again? To me, 'twas just "the shack." But wouldn't *he* turn the color of soda bread dough if we meddled in his misery....

EXCERPT FROM *A letter (never mailed) from Will Dumont to Ariel Dumont, his daughter:* I knew by the wind and tides he might wash up on my beach—I'd studied the damn currents enough, the bay's patterns and flows. Like a 'coon, the bay craps pretty much in the same old locations, time after time. And come morning there he was.

That was it, the final straw.

My girlfriend, who thinks I'm a loser, lies there lifeless as a wax dummy. You, my daughter and only child—fast in the clutches of the Wicked Bitch of the Midwest—think I'm dead and buried. And now this.

Why didn't I report what really happened? You'd have thought I would, my job and all. I could have, and then spent the rest of the night telling and retelling my story, how it was I was there in the first place, how it happened so fast, how I knew he was a certain goner. Maybe the cops would believe me. But they sure as hell wouldn't let me go organize a search and recovery. More likely, they would turn their suspicious gazes straight in my direction. Their cop minds would tell them it didn't add up, that I must have had something to do with it—which of course I did.

Just not the way they would think.

Matter of fact, it *was* pretty much my fault—again. And I hadn't done a damn thing to keep it from happening. Again.

So why didn't I report it? Dearest daughter, your old man couldn't handle it, I just couldn't, that's all. It was too much.

I'm confessing that much. Finally.

Instead I went a little nuts, I guess. That fish tank was the most beautiful, the most Zen thing, and I loved my poor, poor little pets. And it was one huge conch shell. Your Aunt Grace

sent it to me years ago. You wouldn't believe the mess. High
tide in my home sweet shack. Water *everywhere.*

MORNING APPEARED OVER water smoothed like a mother's apron
and flushed the crimson of keen embarrassment over the soft
shoulders of the hills beyond the bay. A cottony shawl of fog
draped across Angel Island, trailed out of sight past Lime Point,
the Potato Patch, out to open ocean. Seabirds untucked heads
from under wings with eyes alert for the morning's first silvery
herring or some scrap tossed aside by ferrygoers as they gaped
across the expanse. A lone figure in a dark sliver of rowing shell
pulled against the current, silhouetted in sunrise.

In the small park across the road from the riprap—scut-
tling ground to orange-clawed crabs alert to passing shadows
that might foretell an imminent reduction in the crustacean
census—one of our chief practitioners of petty theft of public
property crouched over his work.

Name was Bel, short for Belmont. Bel's momma, a horse
player, had a hunch she had a winner with this entry, when in
fact he turned out to be a dark horse, immense and tar-col-
ored and none too quick out of the gate. On this morning, Bel
was on guard for approaching enemies of his own; namely,
any officer of the law or flap-jawed flunky who oversaw these
grounds. "Hafta git these … and prolly these, pay attention,
Bel," he reminded himself while nudging clumps of lilies and
marigolds from their municipally maintained beds. These liberated blossoms he would sell on the houseboats, to replenish
the window boxes and marine-flotsam planters.

In nearby Old Town, Mephisto, our defrocked professor
of higher learning in the yellow Thomas-tumbledown cottage
choked in wisteria vine, was preparing a morning meal for
Marilyn the macaw from overripe fruit pilfered with a gleaner's
eye from the "you buy now" box at Willie Yee's market. Then

they would mount the gleaming Indian Chief and take their habitual cobweb-clearing run—to drink strong coffee and plot who-knew-what questionable deeds with Jake the Anchor Out and possibly others in their loose knot of miscreants. And what of Maggie, our lovely Maggie of the kelp forest hair? She was deep in her dreams in Galilee Harbor after a night of typhoon-force creative gales, and she would remain asleep until the sun sat high above Point Bonita.

All in all, another fine day in the paradise asylum of Sausalito.

But this was not, in fact, just an ordinary day. Inside the Earthquake Shack, on this particular day, Will was making one hell of a racket. Making such boomings and bangings that it woke the exhausted sexual Olympians Putty and Princess next door. They briefly feared for their lives as the ornately framed mirror five feet above their heads shook and threatened to flatten them like ecdysiasts under glass; they both bolted upright, bedcovers flung off, wide-eyed and disoriented. Then, recognizing Will's voice behind the noise, fell back into their pillows like a pair of synchronized swimmers.

Soon all of the boardwalk, and all of Old Town, was awake. The sirens screamed as they turned a sharp right and then left and left again, coming to a halt where Main meets the bay. The rescue squad, followed by a conga line of tan-uniformed police, scurried down the low sea wall, onto the brown beach, and between the toredo-pocked pilings beneath the Valhalla. By this time Will was waiting beside the white-faced, bloated figure in dull green curled into a fetal crouch. Officer Mack, displaying his lavish gift for the obvious, knelt next to this unexpected morning visitor and deduced—quite correctly, it turned out—"Jumpsuit. Must be a jumper."

"Godammit, Mack," Will blurted back with startling fury. Pointing out that, of the multitudes who choose this famous exit of high drama, none was required by fashion or logic to crawl into a jumpsuit to hurl himself from the Golden Gate Bridge. Declaring he knew exactly whereof he spoke, given his line of work. Telling Mack that when first he spotted the patch of color, he thought another marina anchor ball had worked loose and floated in with the tide. Coming for a closer look, saw it was a dead man in institutional coveralls.

Mack held his ground. "Been no report of an escape from San Q. Look at him. He ain't fresh. Been in the water more than an hour or two. Either jumped, fell out a boat in that getup, or—"

"Or what?" demanded Will.

"Or he didn't," Mack retorted. "You seem awful worked up about this, if you don't mind me saying so, Will."

Will didn't appear to like hearing that, and he seemed on the edge of saying something you don't say to law enforcement, even if it's Mack.

"Didn't know this fella, did you?" Mack asked with casual interest, fishing in the corpse's pockets for an ID. Will said nothing, causing Mack to pause and look up from his search. "No," replied Will in a low voice. At this point Mack gave Will an odd look and thanked him for his professional opinion and for doing his duty as a citizen and said this was a police matter now.

But Will wasn't quite done. "Don't like jumpers is all … if that's what he is." Mack was ignoring him, signaling at the coroner's transport unit that had arrived to begin work. "Something incredibly … selfish … showy…." He didn't seem to care Mack wasn't listening. "Not saying it isn't sad, Mack, course it's sad, if he wasn't already on his way out from something, that is. But it's not like popping pills or opening a vein in the privacy of your own home." Mack was rising heavily to his feet, brushing coarse dark sand from his uniform trousers. "Someone who ends it with a swan dive, Mack, out in public, right in front of the damn toll takers, people passing by, total strangers

... family maybe ... like he's flipping us all the bird...."

Then, to no one in particular, "And why? Why?"

Will fumed a little more before leaving the green-clad floater to the authorities, which surprised his friends and neighbors hearing about it afterwards at The Glad Hand and the No Name. When calm again reigned on the boardwalk, only One-Eyed George, the brown pelican who adopted Will after he freed him from a fisherman's hook, noticed he was not his usual self. That he was still shaken. George cocked his head and fastened his good brown eye on his friend, uncertain how to read what he saw in this man whose natural bond with all creatures of the sea, birds and mammals included, was a subject of local conversation and wonder. Hopping quickly aside as Will passed on the boardwalk when normally he would extend his head for a soothing scratch.

Perhaps it was only natural we failed to see something was weighing heavily on Will. He just let off some steam, went the talk around town afterwards. Shock over the morning's events, that's all. But what was that ruckus in Will's place about? That had happened even before the sun blinked awake, before Will had even made his grisly beach discovery. This bafflement lingered. And it was not to be answered the next day or next week— for such questions take time to consider fully, take a look back over a most unusual year, take even more than that.

March 1959

2.
Monster in the Cellar

WILL BECAME A WATER RAT EARLY THAT SPRING, when he moved into the Earthquake Shack after old Mrs. Farquehar died. The place an ungodly mess. At ninety-two, she barely swept the blowing sand and seagull mess anymore, let along take her broom to the 'coons as they nosed in the garbage, chattering away like it was their holiday picnic by the sea. Arriving one achingly clear morning, Will proceeded to make the rundown shack clad in mossy brown shingles his own. Piling Farquehar refuse onto its sagging front deck. Scrubbing. Daubing paint. Hammering.

Another new life for the old place smack dab at the midway point of the rickety boardwalk.

Folks here liked him right off. He was friendly, not pushy. He called his manners Midwestern, did not elaborate. When someone asked, usually a stranger making small talk over a steam beer, he would always reply, "How about you?" Whatever the stranger answered, Will picked somewhere else. We overheard this routine often enough we stopped being curious about the real answer.

Why, you might ask. Well, our little town is a kind of refuge for people with pasts they would rather forget and presents they have recently invented. We pick up clues about a person as they are revealed, and over time put a semblance of the puzzle together. Will, when he got going, could ramble on about places he had been and people he had met, yet in matters of personal history and his feelings about them, he was ... selective.

But he made no bones about not giving a rat's rear end for the Hillclimbers and their palaces piled like match-boxes on our picturesque hillsides, high and mighty above us Water Rats. And so, from the first day he was one of us.

We knew one more thing for sure. He loved that ramshackle cottage. "Suits me like a tailor took my measure, elbow to asshole," he would joke.

THINGS ABOUT WILL no one here knew back then, maybe not even Maggie.

Nothing criminal. Not that kind of past.

William Ellis Dumont: pre-war baby. Born on the shores of the Great Lakes. Circumcised at birth. (As is the practice in this modern era, robbed of half his penile nerve endings in the name of progress and hygiene, by complete strangers.) Full effect of this jolt, as with others to follow, failing to register immediately.

Mother and child in hospital his first week, respective sex organs in recovery. Total bill at discharge—room and board, meds, nursing care, the works—sixty-four bucks. (Fact known due to hoarding instinct of mother, an uncontrollable pack rat.)

Reared in nondescript rural town. Nowhere, Ohio.

Mother, high cheek-boned Slav, rigid by nature. One-quarter teaspoon means one-quarter teaspoon. Whole note means four beats, no more nor less. Her prescription for successful child rearing, closely monitored, the daily bowel movement. Always immediately upon rising, without delay.

Father, descendent of draft-dodging Bavarians who fled the bellicose adventures of the Kaiser. (In 1916, the family surname was changed from Dinkelspiel to Dumont, to evade this

nation's mounting anti-Hun frenzy.) He was handy, a regular
Mr. Fix-It, who knew from tin snips and augers and awls. Able
to make or repair anything, excepting himself: damaged goods.
Anger was the most well-worn tool in his toolbox.

A brooder, he appeared to possess the emotional range of
an ill-treated rottweiler, an invisible choke collar restraining
whatever tenderness was trapped inside.

Will was their first born. Taking up residence in his first
earthquake shack at age eight days. Unaware of this unhappy
fact at the time, painfully aware by the time brother Ben was
born; sister Grace was still years off.

Bawled through his first two months, until Mr. Fix-It
reached into the toolbox.

"Nadine, if you don't give that kid more damn tit…"

"But Leo, the pediatrician said every four hours."

"Pediatrician, my ass! All that college boy sonuvabitch
knows is sending the bill."

Father employed by a remote outpost of The General Electric Company in a small glazed brick building of a single story
a few blocks from the Dumont residence. Fabricating fila-
ments for electric light bulbs. Tiny coils brilliant in the night
like miniature skylines until that unannounced instant—then
only spent silvery ash, a metaphor waiting to be exploited if
there ever was one.

With Will barely out of diapers, Mr. Fix-It took it upon
himself to "modernize" their turn-of-the-century home on
the mild-mannered street called Uselma that was shaded with
red maples, sidewalks heaved by tree root. Off came Midwestern Victoriana edging eaves and porches and tall double-
hung windows. Off, the screened door of scrolled wood that
slammed, replaced by a bland modern door with an automatic
closer that hissed.

An ordinary house with a modicum of period charm transformed into a big ugly box with a metal door. The Uselma box

house: domestic earthquake refugee housing.

Mr. Fix-It not content yet. No cellar under the house. Perhaps as defense against his wife's detested saving of every artifact of the family, Will's father decides "cellar" was a Dumont's inalienable right. So one Saturday in June, he stripped off shirt and ribbed undershirt, grabbed for a shovel. Started burrowing. One shovelful at a time. Like a crab tunneling the world's biggest crab hole, but into grayish Ohio clay.

Excavation from under the house piled up. The pile mounded into an imposing hill. (Will became the King of Mount Dumont, perfect for snow sledding and showing off a Tarzan cry, and a position of no little standing in the pancake-flat neighborhood.) Father dug and dug, every spare daylight hour, until a commodious void lurked beneath. Finishing in August, heat and humidity like boiling in oil.

Will not remembering much of this clearly. Having his mother to thank for documentation as usual: shoe boxes crammed with Kodak Brownie snapshots, a mother lode, if you will, discovered in the airless attic. "Before" and "after" photos of the Uselma box house, labeled in her cramped hand, and one of his father, bare-chested and glistening in sweat, a conqueror's smile on his face, shovel in hand, standing at the gaping entryway to his handiwork:

"Leo, Finished At Last, August 1941."

Cellar becoming the father's haven. His bear cave. His vampire coffin. Will remembering this clearly—refusing to go into that dark and dank place, afraid of monsters waiting to pounce. Monster did. Father reaching often for the well-worn tool. Will's world repeatedly shaken like a sock in a dog's mouth. (Oddly, no Richter Scale readings were given on the radio's evening news.) Mother standing by. Knowing she would likely be next.

A presaging. Young Will's favorite toy was a frogman. A Post Toasties box prize of red plastic. Propelled by bubbling baking soda jammed into a flipper that was outsized and deformed, giving the diminuitive diver the appearance of having an advanced case of the gout.

Hours of tub play alarming Will's mother. "Get out right this instant, you'll be a prune!" Will ignoring her, staging mock battles between his frogman and the creature in the cave that shot stinky bubbles.

Will "happy" as a child for lack of a basis for comparison. "I love you" not in either parent's vocabulary.

3.
The Curse of Kane

IWAS THE FIRST, YOU KNOW. THE VERY FIRST CALLING IT
home sweet home.

How can you claim this? The Miwok have lived here since
Coyote and Falcon created the people.

The shack. I'm talking about the shack. I was first to hang
my hat in it after the Big Shake.... I swear, Mi-Wash, me
and the clientele of the Red Rooster got to know each quicker
than this. Coyote and Falcon ... you yammering to animal
spirits too?

Falcon told Coyote to create us.

That so? Took my Creator six days, so they say, and the
seventh He spent licking His wounds.

Coyote was too wise ... or too lazy ... even to begin,
Malacky. Too much work, he said. But Falcon insisted that it
be done. So Coyote went out and threw himself on the ground
like a dead creature. Crows and buzzards pecked at Coyote but
he kept still until they had eaten a large hole in his rump and
crawled inside. Suddenly he caused the hole to close. Many were
caught. Falcon plucked them all. "Now," said Coyote, "we will
put these feathers in every direction." On each hill they placed
one buzzard and one crow feather. The crow feathers became
the common people and the buzzard feathers, the chiefs. The
feathers he placed here, on this sand beside the stream, they
became our Miwok people. Here we were content for more

moons than anyone can count. Until the barbarians—

That barbarian blarney again! Will I never convince you of the innately civilized nature of my fair race?

We saw their great rush boats from far away, and listened to stories told by visiting Miwok people who came to warm at our fire. They told of those from across the great waters who were here. They said, "They cook the same as we do. They smoke after meals, they talk, laugh, and sing, as we do. They have five fingers and toes, only their skin can be light as a fish belly, not dark as us. But they bleed. And they bring a kind of poison, a sickness." These kinsmen told us not to trust these men, who already had many of their people as slaves. We listened, but our village had never seen any of these strangers—until the one called Ebekanezer Kane. He was chief of the tallest rush boat we ever saw, and he brought the first of your people to our beach ... and caused my sister Tachi to bleed the same place the crows and buzzards pecked Coyote.

In the arse?

Yes.

Hah! Holy savior!

She was coupling with a young man of her age. When this Kane came upon them, he shot thunder from a long stick, a terrifying weapon we never saw before. Tachi ran screaming, her blood spilling onto the sand and berry bushes—

Poor soul, was her backside left with disfiguring scars?

We shot our arrows at Kane's boat but it was too late. He left behind other barbarians with many such long sticks and also short ones that shoot just the same, too many for us to defeat. Our shamans, even the poison shaman, failed to find the magic to cause these invaders to go away. Their magic was stronger than our magic. So my father, as chief, ordered the only sensible thing. We left our ancient home by the stream that joined the great waters and moved up into the hills. When we were gone, the barbarians destroyed our living lodges and sweat lodge and our entire village. They made their own village on the ashes, right here, where your shack came one day.

INDULGE A DIGRESSION. It will be brief and to the point. Imagine a baritone voiceover on some documentary sponsored by, say, Mutual of Omaha. The voice intones, "To understand our more recent past, you should know a bit more of our history...."

Sausalito's first white resident of note was William Antonio Richardson. Twenty-seven years of age when he arrived, in 1822, in what would be San Francisco Bay. Sent ashore from his whaler because he spoke *espan-yole*, to bargain for water and supplies from the Mexicans at the Presidio's garrison.

With a glint in his eye, he jumped ship and married the *commandante*'s daughter. He began calling himself Guillermo. The governor of Alta California, Don José Figueroa, soon appointed him captain of the port and ordered him to establish a permanent *pueblo*, a civilian settlement. Surveyors laid out a grid for streets, then *Señor* Richardson claimed the first home for himself, in Yerba Buena Cove. And thus this intrepid deserter became founding father of San Francisco too.

Where Tony Bennett would one day leave his heart little fresh water was to be found, so Richardson's eye roamed next across the bay, where sweet water gushed. As port captain, he directed incoming ships to the shores of Whaler's Cove, where the Earthquake Shack would be beached and Old Town Sausalito grew. There these ships resupplied, and he collected duties and anchorage fees on behalf of the Mexican government. The histories noting he performed his duties in the way of a child picking bush berries—for every one into the bucket, eating two.

In February 1838, Richardson was rewarded for selfless service with clear title to 19,571 coastal acres, from today's Marin headlands to Stinson Beach, to "enjoy freely and exclusively";

he called his prize *El Rancho del Sausalito.* Here he oversaw his waterworks and anchorage, provisioning visiting ships with foodstuffs, wood, leather, tallow. He chose an agreeable spot slightly north, later called Pine Street, for his hacienda. He farmed and planned a cattle empire, worked by Miwoks and his sons.

Then came the Bear Flag Revolt, and so did a ragtag cadre of *yanqui* guerillas led by Kit Carson, who murdered unarmed Mexicans in San Rafael before galloping through Rancho del Sausalito to capture the Presidio and help win California for the Union. The following year, 1847, shortly after Richardson's Yerba Buena was renamed for St. Francis, a brushfire nearly wiped out its fifty-three shanties and twenty-six adobes. Two years more and the Gold Rush was on, spiking San Francisco to fifty thousand residents by 1853.

Our announcer voice would say something phonily profound at this point. Like, "But in those heady days of the Gold Rush, as many dreams were dashed to bits as came true...."

But it *was* true. Richardson figured to be wealthy beyond measure by then, from a flourishing rancho and provisioning trade. Instead, due to bad speculations and worse luck, he was drowning in debt. And his Sausalito lay untouched by the boom across the bay. In fact, it shrank.

Gold made everything more expensive, including lumber. So at the height of gold fever, in a strong indicator of the state of civic boosterism in our nascent town, Sausalito was dismantled and hauled away: most of our wooden buildings were sold to Sacramento, to replace those consumed by fire on the delta city's riverfront.

Except for the Richardson homestead, a sawmill, a few lean-tos, and a small hotel, we were all dream, no rush. While San Francisco crowed lustily fewer than three miles away, we languished. Visited only by sailors at anchor in what by then was called Richardson's Bay.

Our jilted fortunes proved to be every inch the proverbial double-edged sword. The expanse of water dividing us, as it had from the arrival of the first colonizers across the Golden Gate, into our separate histories. We missed out on the riches, but never fell under the thrall of the largest, most self-important metropolis of the American West. To a large extent, we went our separate ways.

And, at length, we even began to show the promise Richardson foresaw. The man himself, after selling off most of his land grant to erase his indebtedness, died in 1856 of mercury poisoning. Maybe it was suicide. His family signed over nearly all their remaining holdings to a slick lawyer named Throckmorton for a few thousand dollars, prompting the sour observation from one heir, "Thus we parted with a principality for a beggarly pittance." But after the Civil War local developers graded waterfront streets for businesses and laid out modest lots for workers and shop keepers in the flats; in the hills they earmarked prime views for villas, many of them for aloof English aristocrats, "second sons" attracted to overseer positions in the burgeoning financial whirl of San Francisco.

Then, in 1875, the railroad came to town, a narrow-gauge line from Tomales. Ever more felled redwoods began rolling southward to connect by ship to the city. Northbound travelers transferred from ferry to parlor car at our new ferry landing and railroad wharf. Sausalito became the railhead for all passengers and goods linking San Francisco to points north.

The town awakened at last like a spring bulb, in a growth spurt contained only by topography—our steep hillsides posing challenges for builders but also bestowing upon us the admirable comparisons to the stepped villages of the Azores and Mediterranean.

With prosperity came more settlers to work as conductors and brakemen on the railroad, ferrymen, maritime workers and fishermen, shop owners, and servants for the wealthy.

These transplants were lured from around the nation but also from working-class Europe and Asia, especially Portugal, Italy, Ireland, and China.

Eventually we came to lump together those who lived close to sea level, calling them our Water Rats. Those higher up, the Hillclimbers.

The Hill looked down on us. We blew our fish breath right back at them. Both camps in eyeshot, yet apart. So it has been, pretty much, ever since.

4.
Air Apparent

ONLY A FEW DAYS AFTER WILL FIRST ARRIVED IN TOWN, he began to earn our admiration, betraying no hint of troubles of his own, when Jake the Anchor Out accused the Turban Woman of breathing too much air. According to Jake, this selfish act inflicting upon him the foulest imaginable headache. Everyone knowing, even Jake, that the Turban Woman was a harmless and pathetic soul, a mother gone batty years before, after her children were snatched away by pitiless bureaucrats. She was a poor dear a more decent society would wrap in a big hug and lead to a warm place so she did not wander our streets in a shapeless cloth coat and a blue towel wrapped high around her head like she was just stepping out of the shower or joined to a cult from the Indian subcontinent. A high wheezing noise escaped from her as she breathed, the bronchial gasp of many damp nights on the waterfront—and this was what Jake, on that day, chose to object to.

Of course, he was being chased by his own customary demons, a condition easily aggravated when your world consists of a partially submerged yawl, THE SQUIRTLE, tethered to the mud two hundred yards offshore, and a leaky dinghy on which to maintain a tenuous umbilical to solid footing. On the kindest day, Jake was foul weather.

When Will came upon them, near the Cass Marina, Jake was looming over the Turban Woman with a splintery oar cocked above his shoulder, seemingly on the verge of bashing her repeatedly on the head and towel. Cursing and carrying on about lack of oxygen, while the Turban Woman wheezed in frightened pants even more loudly than usual.

Will asking, quietly, "I know I'm about as welcome as a fart in bed right now, but did you read the paper this morning?"

Naturally, this aroused Jake's curiosity, even in his agitated state. "Wathsit?" he replied. Dentistry, like many a trade among Water Rats like Jake, was a homegrown pursuit. Results were mixed. With the exception of ceremonial occasions, and so far there had been none, Jake refused to wear the ill-fitting set of choppers he swapped at a Chinatown pawn shop for an oyster sack full of ill-gotten chickens. And as a result, Jake's words leaked air. His favorite eatery advertised with the slogan: *You don't need teef to eat Uncle Jim's beef!*

"Air's thicker today," Will continuing. "Thicker. So it's harder to breathe."

Jake glowering and lowering the oar a little. "Nawwwwf—"

Will persisting in this explanation. "That's right. A fact." Had Jake's attention now. "Really," Will said just as quietly. "Now let her be." Reaching down and helping the Turban Woman to her feet.

Her eyes were big as salad plates, and Will noticed a dark wet stain on the back of her heavy coat but pretended not to, out of courtesy.

In the face of Will's fresh breeze of rationalization, Jake eased his main and let his sails luff. Lowering the oar, muttering something under his breath, he trudged off toward his beached dinghy. Even in his diminished capacity, somehow instinctively respecting Will's authority in matters such as the relative abundance of air available for breathing at any given moment.

Although Jake did not know it yet, it's time you did. Will

was an actual expert in this area. Oxygen, for him, was not to be taken for granted like with most of us.

By trade, he was a rescue and recovery diver. A professional frogman. On call twenty-four hours a day to plunge feet first into our frigid waters, where an unprotected man would last exactly twenty-two minutes before hypothermic death—if not drowned in deadly currents and undertow first. Will's survival depending on tanks of life-sustaining air, two plies of a diver's wet suit, gloves and booties, sometimes a woolly bear vest, while bringing up whatever thing or person had attracted the attention of state authorities.

Asked point blank, he would also admit to having studied literature and marine biology. At an institution of higher learning back East, folks would confide out of his hearing. Cornell, or maybe it was Princeton. As usual we did not pry. We got the feeling he did not want to feel boxed in by the notions people held about such things.

WANTED: PROFESSIONAL SEARCH & RESCUE DIVER. MUST BREATHE RARIFIED IVY LEAGUE AIR. NOSE TO LOOK DOWN A NECESSITY.

5.
The Nose Knows

TELL ME AGAIN. TELL ME HOW IT HAPPENED.

Give it a rest, lass. When first we happened upon this odd cohabitation of ours, 'twas fine. But by now you've heard it more times than a whore makes the mattress sing.

No. Tell me. I have a thirst I have not known since I hid from my sister in the sweat lodge. So much I missed, Malachy, so much I do not know, even if it is a story of your people. Begin ... begin with the day before.

Aach, as you wish. It's April seventeenth, nineteen ought six, a Tuesday. I was working as usual at my piano, banging out tune after tune at The Sign of the Red Rooster. Bassity's place. Indeed, the most famous brothel on the Barbary Coast. The place packed to the rafters, the wait for favorite whores longer than an Irishman's whistle. But on that night the true center of attention was the world's greatest opera singer, Mr. Enrico Caruso. The famous tenor was buying drinks for the house and raining greenbacks on the likes of me, in a grand humor. More than his triumph for the city's swells, as Don Jose in *Carmen*, was he celebrating. To anyone who'd listen to his tortured king's English, he were crowing like a cock who'd escaped the very hounds of hell. The volcano Vesuvius had blown its top back in Italy, incinerating a heap of Neapolitans, and he had dodged an engagement there by warbling in our own opera house. Hah! Had he only known, and in just a few hours! Of course, over at his usual table sat Himself, Mr. Jerome Bassity—brocaded waistcoat, fat neck swaddled in silk, diamonds flashing, always the spectacle befitting the richest pimp in San Francisco, which meant in all the West. You could see him already counting the night's receipts in his head. And by his flinty grin you knew he was getting good reports from all his other houses too. Surrounded by this cacophony of his success, the dirty bastard was holding court. The good-looking young actor Barrymore was with him, along with a tipsy female in opera finery. One of those magical nights, 'twas. Like New Year's Eve and July Fourth and St. Patrick's all rolled up into one—

My people would be awake to the signs.

Signs?

Did not the dogs howl? The horses cry and pound their hooves?

'Tis true. I would hear that the cur belonging to my boarding house neighbor ran in crazed circles just before it started, then leapt out an open window. This was on the third floor. When it began I saw cats rushing wildly about, their tails all puffed out, and afterwards, the cows wouldn't give milk and hens wouldn't lay.

You lived to see the sun.

Merciful Lord, barely ... by the fateful moment I was on my way home from supper at the Oyster Loaf. Six bits for all the food, wine, and god-knows-who doing the bunny hug a man can take. Just after five it was, the morning of the eighteenth. First I heard the rumbling and roaring, like a locomotive running you down at full speed. Then the cobblestones in the streets came alive, jumping and dancing, and I saw the sidewalk in front of me open like a passageway to the underworld, then close up again. The ground rolled like waves on the sea, and with it everything in its path—streetlamps, trees, wagons, whole buildings, people bobbing like corks. I was knocked to the ground and I bumped and slid like everything else.

You must have offered many gifts to your Great Spirit when it ended.

He weren't done with His sport, not yet! Next came the conflagration. The Big Shake lasted a minute, though scores of smaller jolts plagued us after, but the city of San Francisco burned three days and three nights. Fires so bright you could read Hearst's *Examiner* at midnight, if there'd been an *Examiner* to read. Neighborhood after neighborhood ablaze. Chinatown. Russian Hill. Telegraph Hill. The Barbary Coast itself—pleasing those who condemned it as the haunt of the vile and low. I'll vouchsafe a living hell it became ... as close to it as ever was witnessed by these eyes.

Hell is not known to my people. The beliefs of barbarians are—

Enough! To think I'm made to keep company in my own house with another who's passed on, but with a heathen spirit at that!

Have you not wondered.

Eh? Wondered?

Why we are here.

Here. Well ...

Where is your lord, Malacky, your heaven and hell? And where is my Spirit World, my ancestors?

Bit odd, isn't it? Two spooks and not another soul in sight.

It is good we have the living to make us laugh.

I wish I had my piano.

I wish I could smell the sea.

IT WAS HIS SMELL. To Maggie he smelled like what we later called comfort food.

Maggie was Will's girl. Or at least that's how she saw

it. From the second moment she encountered the stranger in town that memorable springtime, she wanted him. (We'll get to that first meeting in a moment.) It wasn't his looks, for they were only slightly above average. Wasn't his money, he did not seem to have much. Wasn't his skills as a lover, they were underdeveloped, which she didn't find out until later. It was his smell. Passing her on the sidewalk near the No Name, her nostrils filled with a buttery, pleasantly pungent aroma. She recognized the smell immediately. A toasted cheese sandwich. She loved toasted cheese sandwiches. She wanted to eat Will up on the spot.

All omens of an olfactory nature Maggie took very seriously. Her mother's family was Swiss, a people noted for an attuned sense of smell. They use their noses like armaments of homeland defense. By her teenaged years, Maggie outgrew the embarrassment of being ushered out of roadside cafés and other unfamiliar eating-places even as her family was being led to a table, her mother murmuring in dialect an odious comparison to shitty rear-ends or sweaty armpits. She became accustomed to picking the perfect picnic spot not for its sun or shade but for being upwind or down. For by then she, too, had come to trust her mother's adage: "The *nase* knows." Every one of us, Maggie realizing, possessed a scent as individual as a fingerprint and as inescapable as the protuberance of ears or pudginess of feet. And she learned to read scents the way others read auras.

Having inherited her mother's gift, a simple walk for Maggie became a stew of smells that could sometimes be overwhelming, always enlightening. With eyes shut, recognizing friends and neighbors at fifteen feet, the wind blowing right. Her nose sorting and cataloguing multiple smells from multiple sources simultaneously, and even layers of smell, peeled back like an onion: the *eau de toilette*, the cotton-alpaca blend, the skin. The skin was the test. In her experience good people smelled good. Not a sweet or floral note necessarily, for she equally appreciated the earthy musk of a morel, the barn-yard stench of strong ripe cheese, the herbaceous tang of a lit reefer. Smells she couldn't tolerate tending toward the spoiled and the industrial—sour milk and dirty crankcase oil, rotten meat and chemical contamination. Even an Adonis, redolent of dirty socks, could not hope to get close to Maggie, who was convinced scent was released from the soul.

She believed, in fact, in relying on all her senses. Certainly over any process of logic or reason. Maggie was an artist. For grocery money and the company of others, she worked a few nights and weekends at the No Name. Occasionally she baited hooks and untangled lines on Captain Roy's fishing charter. But it was on her houseboat in Galilee Harbor that she did her heartfelt work, except when working in metal or stone, in which case her friend Arvie Engstrom always made room at his boat repair off Gate Five in Marinship.

Our Maggie, she was a native Water Rat. Now, Rats in general are not fashion-shoot material. At maturity they aren't pretty. These are weathered people. Lined and furrowed. Prac-titioners of home health remedies and home haircuts, they could be a clan in Appalachia. She was the exception. Born beautiful, she stayed that way. Gray eyes flecked in green that turned smoky when the light was just so. A nose that grew strong and proud as she did. Skin as smooth and unblemished as the lining of an oyster shell. But her hair, this was her most arresting attribute—thick, tangly, a glistening dark mass, like King Neptune's own royal preserve of undulating underwater forest. A kelp forest of hair.

She was delivered by a midwife who quoted Margaret Sanger. "When motherhood becomes the fruit of a deep yearn-ing, not the result of ignorance or accident, its children will become the foundation of a new race!" exulted the woman as Maggie crowned like a hairy wet coconut on the abandoned ferry ISSAQUAH, where she grew up with five other families. Her mom and pop, impressed by the event and the proclamation, naming her for the patron saint of family planning. Whether she was truly the parade marshal of something brand-new or not, she found it as natural to be around Sausalito's cast of characters as 1920s Harlem did with young Duke and Cab and scat-singing Ella.

When the out-of-town famous and locally infamous came looking for the Water Rat party, usually at Grover Boaz's, she'd barely look up from her hand-me-down tarot cards, sweet little face in a tousle of hair, to say, "See the naked ladies on the swing?" While the party bongos boomed, she'd happily chicken-neck for crabs with Grover's two boys, Hieronymous and Tahoe.

By the way, this is the same Grover Boaz responsible for the famous bohemian artistry of the Trident, the Kingston Trio's place on the pier across from the old volunteer firehouse. Even the other famous musical types who stopped by, for instance that skinny English kid named Mick whom nobody recognized, were at least briefly distracted by Grover's carpentry and away from the joint's chief attraction, the mesh peek-a-boob tops of the Trident girls.

Maggie never waited tables at the Trident. Her own heavenly "C" cups could have easily passed muster—in an indiscreet moment Will once said they were sweet as Santa Rosa plums in June and Sheralyn melons in August, and in size somewhere just between. Her entire womanly form, in fact, would have flared the groin of Trident goers, male and many a female, like an exploding seed in a bottom-of-the-bag roach. Yet even as a youngster she was beyond being the bait but not the brains, the cigarette girl denied entry to the smoke-filled room. In that way maybe she was part of a new race, a prototype. Everyone in town said the only way a man would ever get to feast his eyes on Maggie's unblemished fruit was to deal with her as Maggie first, today's dessert special second. (Little did *we* know, but there's no sense getting ahead of ourselves.)

Will, however, was one of the lucky ones. Or is it no girl's safe from the perfect approach? That special serendipity. In this case, by sea.

A DROWSY SUN flooded her houseboat that morning before the westerlies began to stir and cool the air. The fluffy web of feathers on the pelicans and cormorants perched on channel markers offshore were still and unruffled. Amazing how quiet it is on the waterfront, though these floating homes were packed in like the hold of a fishing trawler squirming with catch. An occasional peal of laughter or stomp of feet or pedaling of a squeaky bike in a hurry toward town. Intermittent insect drone. The growl of an outboard, splash of an oar.

But mostly, only the periodic squawk of gull and trill of tern and bicycle-horn honk of duck. And, of course, the soothing water lap against the logjam of human habitation.

Maggie was working on her DHARMA. Her True Meaning in thirty-eight feet of plate-steel, an infantry landing craft reincarnated into a cheery yellow with lavender trim. A triumph of arc welder and art. Atop the hull she and Arvie Angstrom having affixed an abandoned railway boxcar, remolded at one end to match the swoop of the hull and to give the roofline a graceful nautical curve. A window cut at the bow was outfitted with leaded stained glass (courtesy of a fellow Water Rat artist), hinged at the top to admit sea breeze and give Fifa, Maggie's cat, the purr-fect vantage point. Replacing the sliding doors of the boxcar was an entryway with a gabled roof, approached from a gangplank that rose and fell with the tides. French doors filled the big opening cut at the stern and led to the floating dock where Maggie met the glory of dawn, once in a while, and the moiré of sky at dusk.

The overall impression from this considerable effort was

a waterborne alpine chalet ... *Hansel und Gretel* afloat ... and thus, ultimately, a creation of Maggie's alone.

Yes—Maggie was up unusually early that morning. Gessoing the hell out of new canvases stretched the day before. Heated by her labors and the still, radiant air, she'd thrown open the double doors to her rear deck and the barely crenulated bay. Too warm yet, doing what she often did working in the solitude of her gently swaying home. She stripped. Freedom from clothing uncorking her creative juices. Making movements of her brush more fluid, adding unfettered body language to her strokes. Even if spreading gesso didn't require any art at all, she felt good doing it *au naturel*.

Now, it happened that Will, too, was at work at this hour. Still new to town, he was getting familiar with the currents and general conditions of the bay. In a few days he would begin his job as a state frogman. This was a reminiscence he told better after a few steam beers.

"A personal orientation drill," he would begin. "Tide heading out, depth of about a fathom near the shoreline to four or so in the boat channel. Even in my wet suit, a hood, gloves, so damn cold. That's the big shocker. Sun can be simmering your stew up top, but in you go and the cold hits you like an ice floe." Taking a swallow of suds about then, a pause for effect. "Murky, too—barely see your hand in front of your face. Unfortunate. You have no idea how much stuff is in the muck. They used to call this the Boneyard, so many ships laid up here during the Gold Rush."

He lectured on, as if to a class of scuba babies. "It was a semi-circular search pattern, a guide tied to a piling. Now, success or failure of any underwater search is affected by a whole bunch of factors. Surface conditions, visibility, depth, bottom topography and composition, vegetation, accessibility, surge, tides and currents, accuracy of bearings, water temperature, obstacles, hazards, et cetera. Only one thing down there's really truly under my control—organization. Most often it's just that, or the lack of it, makes all the difference."

We hung in. He was getting there.

"Your semi-circular search works just like it sounds. Hunting in concentric half circles along a fixed line as reference, good for a diver working alone. I do maybe three sweeps and find a barnacle-encrusted hunk of metal that bears further investigation. Up I come to mark my bearings. As I surface, I see something I can't place"—pausing again—"this blurry vision through my mask. In living watercolor"—yet another pause—"of sublime feminine pulchritude."

Fifa, the houseboat cat, awoke from her dream, no doubt of mousies in cream, and sprang to the back deck, mewing the alarm. For that frozen first moment of meeting, the two staring at each other. The *au naturel* gal daubed with gesso and the creature from the black lagoon.

Neither certain of what was being seen.

Then the creature showed a toothy grin and disappeared in a froth of foam. A mote of toasted cheese hanging briefly in the air, undetected. The *au naturel* gal angrily throwing the double doors shut.

They had met. Luckily for them, it got better after that.

6.
One Small Step For Anarchy

HAVE NO FEAR, MY SIBILANT SIDEKICK. THE IMMU-table laws of quantum mechanics are at play. This is no jive metaphysical phenomenon we're about to perpetrate."

"Arwkk," agreed Marilyn Macaw, rocking on the handle-bar of Mephisto's Indian Chief and looking extremely dashing in her tiny black storm trooper helmet.

Jake the Anchor Out was crouched beside the passenger side rear of Officer Mack's parked patrol vehicle. The heavy sedan slowly listing to starboard. Moments thereafter right-ing itself again, sunken by several inches.

Jake rising and stepping back to admire his handiwork. Multiple puncture wounds, four flats. Then he crept to the rear of the car and jammed an object into the vehicle's exhaust pipe before gingerly prying up the hood and slashing hoses and cut-ting wires and splattering a fistful of rotten eggs onto the V-8's manifold. His head rolled back from the sulfurous stench.

"Ride!" cried Mephisto, stomping on the starter, his machine spewing flatulence. Jake barely managing to hop into the Softtail's sidecar as it began popping gravel. The bike abruptly gathered speed, the sudden rush of air pushing back Marilyn Macaw's helmeted head; grimly, she tightened her talons' grasp on the chrome.

It was a sight to behold (and to put a bemused grin on

Will's face, had he seen it). Mephisto, in the grown-up version of his bird's head gear, a black leather vest, washed-out Levi's, scuffed engineer boots; Jake, soft cheeks sprouted in stubble, greasy black hat pulled tight over a mane of rusty brown and gray fluttering in a pony tail. The indigo Indian Chief with I LIVE TO RIDE emblazoned on the fuel tank. And the bird clinging gamely to its handlebar, beak to the wind.

Our head anarchist, his pet, and his crony on their way to celebrate this latest, if patently otiose, victory over The Man. Even if the Establishment stooge in question was merely a paunchy cop caught with his pants down, so to speak.

"FLACCID FIRESTONES. AN apt metaphor for the *politzei* penis, wouldn't you say, Jake?" asked Mephisto, who drew freely upon the Deutsch of his childhood, even though—more likely because—all Germans except Einstein and Wernher von Braun were highly unpopular since the war. If he'd let it be known he was also a Jew, that would have put a wholly different slant on things. But of course he didn't. He was crowing now at Juanita's Galley on Gate Five Road over a cup of steaming Joe.

Juanita's opened at two in the morning and did not close until midnight, and for most of those hours was presided over by Juanita herself, three hundred pounds of sourdough, crusty as hell on the outside, soft in the middle. She kept a deer and turkey as pets, and you had to keep an eye on them or they'd cage food off your plate.

The grub at Juanita's was moderately good. Service was notoriously lousy. Juanita's temper, just notorious. On the walls and hanging from the rafters were all kinds of junk and mementos, like the framed photo of the "lady" herself brandishing a rolling pin the size of a Yule log. Yet for every story of her skillet-hot temper, there were more of her warming-oven heart. Ask any kid—she doted on them like her pets.

Mephisto could hear Juanita banging pots in the kitchen about then, and complaining to her cook about some stranger who escaped before she could act out her credo of *eat it or wear it.* He swept a glance around the dirt-floor café, noting that morning's roll call of fellow masochists, alighting for a long moment on two others who, along with Jake, often followed in his own perfidious shadow. In particular Belmont, the park flower snatcher, and another unmistakable local we called Bunny. The pair was huddled in hushed conversation at a nearby table.

When it came to lost sheep, especially of the black variety, Mephisto was our shepherd. This was not news around town. But not so widely known was this: of all those in this sorry flock, only Bel had gotten seriously gypped in original equipment. His story was simple, like him. He was born the sweet loser. Bunny, on the other hand, was anything but simple. He had a cranial switch askew—the one powering sexual polarity.

Bunny didn't *want* a Playboy bunny, he wanted to *be* one. (Though not as a full-fledged female. It gave him the creeps to think what Christine Jorgensen had done.) And so he habitually wore silken pink ears that sprouted adorably from wildly ratty hair, secured under unshaven jowls with a baby blue bow. Even more, though, Bunny wanted *Mr.* Playboy—that is to say, none other than Hugh M. Hefner himself. He wanted him more than a tick wants a dog. We saw Bunny as Hef's worst nightmare, but Bunny figured he knew exactly what it took to make that man happy. Wasn't he a natural blond? Didn't he like to stay up late and didn't he adore pipe-puffing sophisticates in their smoking jackets and peejays? Besides, he could execute the famous Bunny Dip to perfection and figure the tab on umbrella drinks better than any of those pneumatic bitches in Hef's hutch.

And so Bunny figured it was only a matter of time until the world's best known swinging bachelor, so unfettered by middlebrow mores, would see that his path to happiness was not between the thighs of Janet Pilgrim.

And then there was Jake. You had to feel sorry for Jake, at least a little. Instead of a life of dry rot and decay aboard THE SQUIRTLE, he had been earmarked for prominence and ease. Son of a bayou wholesaler, he was heir to a Louisiana shrimping empire. Until most of his Cajun savvy was lost in the service of his country. But it wasn't the Reds in Korea or imperial MacArthur that ruined Jake, it was the boyfriend of a Seoul bargirl. The beating he took rendered him unfit to grow large in the shrimp world. (And left him with a deeply ingrained distrust of the female gender.) When, rather than embrace the sociopath returned to them, Jake's family disowned him, his fortunes were reduced to a lifetime of headaches and bad disposition. If this black sheep could steal from you, he would. If he could sell you some bad weed or a filched wristwatch, he'd do that too. There was almost nothing he wouldn't do, in fact, to augment his meagre disability check and settle his score against humankind.

"Or is it the *politzei* prick, a redundancy if ever I heard one," Mephisto said to Jake, who nodded agreement.

"Only neth time don leef tho goddamn fasth. I almos drot my brefist...."

Marilyn Macaw jumped to her master's shoulder and picked at his ear, waggling her tongue, a bird in love. Jake retrieved a flattened cruller from inside his hat and broke off a piece to feed Marilyn, who airily rejected his offering. Testily, he dunked it instead into his raven-dark coffee.

"Whore's breakfast!" Mephisto crowed, sending the bird flapping to the far end of the table. "Six inches and sweet."

Indeed. Salvaged from the trash bin behind the Valhalla, where Jake also found the rotting mango that now plugged the tail pipe of Mack's cruiser, this very same stale pastry might have been meant to impart a sugary burst of stamina to one of the Valhalla's hardworking girls. Perhaps to one of the hard-working girl's hard-breathing customers.

AT THE OPPOSITE end of town, Sally Stanford peered up from her bookkeeping over pince-nez specs. "I trust you found everything in order, Mack," she said. The flushed officer of the law emerged from the stairwell and was heading for the door. Grunting in reply, hitching up his trousers as he walked.

You see, when it came to females who can thrive in a man's world, we were doubly blessed. Juanita ran her place like an Old West hanging judge while her arch rival, "that awful Stanford woman," was the gimlet-eyed dance hall queen who got her way with wit and wile.

Sally ruled like the madam she was—for decades, the most famous in San Francisco. Best houses, best girls, best clientele. Buying the Valhalla, she announced she was going legit. Knowing full well that those thin-lipped Hillclimber wives hectoring their husbands to steer clear of her place would only add to its reputation and trade. She also knew a thing or two about courting, and buffaloing, the constabulary. At her invitation Mack and his fellow officers "inspected" her establishment weekly.

"A first-class road house, boys," she'd say in a voice that rasped like a fish scaler. "Only things got laid in here are the farm fresh eggs."

Sally turned to smack a mackerel stare on a waitress setting tables for lunch. "Charge that rich bastard Cazneau for plucking my carnation off the table and handing it to his lady friend last night?"

"Like you said, Miss Stanford. Buck-fifty."

"Drive careful," Sally called sweetly after Officer Mack. "And don't forget to give the working man a break!" Watching as the heavy door swung shut.

A busboy was arranging glasses on the back bar.

"Frankie, be a dear and run a fifth of Scotch over to that cottage at Fourth and Main, the one all covered in wisteria and about to fall down any sec. Leave it by the back door. The house label, f'crissakes, not the top shelf."

Sally Stanford, smiling.

Mephisto and Jake were both chortling, imagining Mack was done spending his seed and had learned of their handiwork. Seeing his splenetic fit over the deflated, out-of-commission squad car. Vowing to roll it right into the bay next time.

Juanita, yelling. Another regular could pipe down and wait—couldn't he see she was making smiley-face hotcakes for the Spurgeon boy, junior tool wrangler for the day at Vern's machine shop?

Bunny sweet-talking Bel into applying for a job on the peek-a-boob crew at the Trident. Grazing Bel with his droopy silken ears as he bent close to practice his pitch: "Then I say, 'Leland, you call yourself a manager? Can't you see how me and Bel take you off the charts on the hip scale?'" Righting himself to declare, "Why, when Mr. Hefner hears of this, he'll put it in 'Playboy After Dark.' We'll all be famous! *Sooooo* ring-a-ding-ding, eh, Bel?"

Bel grinning like a lap dog.

Mack having the imagined fit.

7.
Fire-Brewed Daddy

AKING IN THE SHADOWED GAP BETWEEN NIGHT and day, Will let the shack talk to him. The hated Uselma box house, for all it memories, never spoke to him, nor was it ever a party to his well-being. The shack he found altogether new and different. Though it demanded nothing of him, he recognized a "presence" in its breathing and its sighs. This had already become important to him, needed even, although he could not put this need into well-chosen words. The shack felt good, he ventured. Reliable. Safe. As if being sheltered within its walls was his one smart move, measured against the others which were not.

Most mornings, even waking from unsettled dreams or jolted into consciousness once again by mama raccoon passing beneath his windows while scolding her kids at precisely quarter past four, he greeted the new day ... unaccountably renewed. Part of this, he reasoned, must be the bay—the rhythmic reassurance of the waves, keening sea birds, the lowing of foghorns. But it was also this swoop-ceiling room in which he slept, created expressly as a place of refuge. It had harbored the man who looped the cake decor, the one who hammered up the mismatched lintels, the others who loved it enough to leave something of themselves.

Is it not possible, he fleetingly wondered, that all of us have been drawn to this room through a force mere mortals do not comprehend? Something unseen and unheard?

An auspicious thought, for Will was not particularly super-stitious or at all religious. Lying in bed, watching water reflec-tions dance where the sweep of light from Alcatraz had visited through the night, he would yawn and scratch a sudden insis-tent itch and laugh at himself.

And yet, there also were times when he sensed more than the shack's past in the room. He swore he could smell it, too. Catching a whiff as if prying open a seafarer's ancient chest. For only an instant, the odor escaping and filling his nostrils with what he could only liken to ... a very musty human. Curi-ously, no one else smelled it (not even the *nase*-ily endowed Maggie, after she and Will got to know each better). Failing in any plausible explanation, his thoughts wandered to his long-dead grandpa—an Ohio farmer who planted by the lunar cycle and had an affinity for woodland critters as strong as Will's for life from the sea.

Will remembering grandpa standing astride the seat of his old Oliver tractor and taking in the stench of a dead ani-mal, saying, "Poor thing just gave up the ghost, that's all that is, boy."

Will had never seen a ghost, and he didn't plan on seeing one. He sure never figured to smell one.

But what does the past smell like?

And why can't we living humans shed the malodorous baggage of our past lives as easily as, say, suitcases abandoned on the tarmac?

MORE ABOUT WILL. More nobody here knew before the ... incident.

Fact: his past was why Will showed up in our town, a stranger and not knowing a soul. Will was on the run. He was someone with a stench in his nostrils so strong of what's done, he couldn't pick up the scent of what's yet to do. A man with the claim check to some mighty weighty baggage who had lost the key. From the moment of his arrival in Sausalito, though, Will knew there could not be a place more laugh-out-loud perfect, given where he'd come from and who he was—a refugee fleeing the earthquakes of a lifetime.

As a man in flight from what he'd come to think of as the toxic normalcy of his personal history and his native Midwest—both posed as ordinary but were deadly, a child's playground straddling an undetected fault line—it was hardly surprising him finding refuge in sweetly screwed up and openly abnormal Sausalito. Gratefully, he sought his sanctuary. Hoping like the others in the Earthquake Shack before him for a world that would be upended no more.

The wounded seek healing wherever they can find it. But Will was not naïve. By the time we came to know him, he understood with a painful clarity that he was—much as he had hoped otherwise—his father's son after all.

Granted, unlike his father, he hadn't known actual declared war. Especially Leo Dumont's ignoble kind of war. Will's father had enlisted for military service two days after Pearl Harbor, when Will was barely four. Signing on with the U.S. Marine Corps because going gung-ho *semper*-fucking-*fi* was the strongest screw-you Leo could give to his own father. (Funny, isn't it, how often it is that scarred baggage gets handed down the generations, a sorry, unwanted heirloom.)

For Leo Dumont recalled his childhood with bitterness, too. The rutted back roads of the Deep South, his uprooted family living in the sun-baked Studebaker. Far from home and Yankee doctors, in the name of a merciful Almighty. Rather than blame Him for plucking the wings off his creations for idle amusement, Leo held his old man responsible for the death of their mother. That generation of the Dumont family disintegrated somewhere in Alabama. Leo was twelve. And he held that pain and anger within himself all his days. Even as his older brother Ellis sat out the war in a federal prison cell, a conscientious objector and faithful witness to their father's Jehovah. The third brother, Lyle, was too young for military service but not to exhibit the hairline cracks in his psyche which would later lead to institutionalization.

Leo going to war. God knows he saw it about as bad as it got. Marine-made into a radioman, the most sought-after sniper target in the infantry. Grazed in the head by a sharpshooter at Guadalcanal. For good measure, also seized by malaria (which Will witnessed as nightmarish reoccurrences in the Uselma box house, his father quaking uncontrollably and milky-eyed).

When his wounds mended, Corporal Dumont was sent to learn how to intercept Tojo's messages and tap them out on a Jap typewriter. This time the malaria saved his life—sign of a just if jaded Divinity after all?—when it launched another attack just as he was about to be ordered behind enemy lines.

Will knowing all this because Leo told his war stories until his son was old enough to remember them, then suddenly they just stopped. This was when Will was in the fifth or sixth grade, at about the same time the other father-son things fell away, like playing pitch and catch on the street and helping out with school science projects.

Instead, Leo retreated into himself, and increasingly into his hand-made cellar. He was darker in his moods, withdrawn from Will, Ben, and baby Grace. Much later, Will heard the hidden truth about the most serious war wound—the "nervous breakdown" which led to electroshocks and experimental drugs in military hospitals. Which led to, instead of a repaired Leo, relapse in civilian life.

Will's mother blamed the horrors of the Pacific. The ailing, partial husband and father returned to the family, confided Nadine Dumont to her eldest son as if revealing a marital infidelity, bore scant resemblance to her apple-cheeked high school sweetheart.

Ex-Corporal Dumont was haunted by his failing. Traumatized war vets overflowed the asylums of America by late 1945 (nearly half the beds in public hospitals were filled with psychiatric patients), yet this Marine patched over his feelings of disgrace by putting on a show. Will watched with escalating horror as his father was pulled off the neighbors, his Scout leader, the doltish guard at the town beach who objected to Nadine sunbathing in a swim suit that revealed the shocking female midriff.

Leo the onetime Marine never backing down. Never giving ground. Erupting—with words, with fists. And not only to assail neighbors and strangers. The Uselma box house rocked, rocked on its foundation.

Time after time, Will was shaken awake, sensing the fury roiling outside the door to his darkened bedroom and about to billow up onto the cowboys and Indians wallpaper, the framed snapshots atop his dresser—Will as smiling baby, as solemn toddler, as a fierce, midget Hopalong Cassidy with cap pistols blazing.

He grew to become a firstborn who shut his heart to his father. And, fair or not, to his mother too—for taking it, and for taking back this man Will barely remembered when he reappeared. Hating the Uselma box house, which Will came to think of as his father's house: its stripped and straightforward walls implying a solid family fortress but hiding instead a rubble field from the neighbors' view.

Concealing the domestic devastation within.

"MOM, CAN'T UNCLE Lyle be my dad?"

"Will, don't dare say such things! Your dad is your dad and always will be."

He saw that look, saw her try to hide it from him.

Uncle Lyle, not in the war; not like his older brother. "Thank heavens," said Nadine Dumont more often than necessary. "Lyle's such a dear to us." Though not yet seventeen, pale and fragile, Uncle Lyle was who she leaned on during those lonely wartime years. He lived just around the corner and was around a great deal. When Leo finally came back, Lyle moved a few miles farther away but continued dropping in on the Dumonts of Uselma.

Will idolized his uncle, his feline and even mysterious presence. Where his brother Leo's outlook was blunt and bunker-like, Uncle Lyle was a deft idea man. He had what he called Dumont-o-vision. "You can have it too. Think big, kid," he'd say, tugging at Will's ear and pulling him close. "Why waste your dreaming?" Will would gaze up at those eyes of palest blue, the color of high summer sky. Uncle Lyle's eyes were twin memorials to his dead mother—in fact, they were girl's eyes, almond-shaped with long lashes.

Nadine Dumont was too obvious in her affection for this gentler brother. Leo was bound to notice. Once, Will overheard his parents arguing over his beloved Uncle Lyle.

"Buncha hooey, Nadine. Him and his damn schemes. He don't listen, of course. Thinks he's got it all figured out, a real hot shot."

"All he's asking, Leo, is five hundred dollars."

"Five hundred bucks! Christ, what do I look like? A Rockefeller?"

"Leo ..."

"So you fucked him, that it, Nadine? Me halfway across the world getting my ass shot at and you and him—"

"How could you, Leo! Your own brother."

"Well?"

"Leo!"

"You think I'm stupid, Nadine? Think I don't see? I'm warning you—"

"Stop, Leo. Please stop!"

It got worse, but it was Uncle Lyle who stopped. Not showing up again for a very long time. Will sensing from his mother's reaction to his questions that something had happened to him, something was wrong. She saying only he was away on business. Maybe he was making his big dreams come true. Maybe he'll come back and take me with him, Will told himself.

He did come back one time. Three years had passed. Will had grown up a lot in the meantime, but he would never forget Uncle Lyle's last surprise appearance at the Uselma box house. His father's funny reaction to his brother's arrival—he didn't seem happy about it at all. Instead Leo turned edgy and quiet. Will not understanding this because seeing his uncle again was thrilling to him. After supper all of them gathered in the living room, in their customary places. Will, Ben and their mother—a squirming Grace on her lap—sat on the slip-covered davenport. Leo in his armchair next to the ashtray mounded with crushed Chesterfield butts. Uncle Lyle, as the visitor, on the straight-backed chair with the needlepoint cushion rimmed in tarnished upholstery tacks.

"So I guess you won't need to borrow my winter overcoat too," Will's father said to break the strained silence.

"Guess not," said Uncle Lyle.

"Take a warm sweater at least, for on the way," Will's mother said.

"Where you going, Uncle Lyle?" Six-year-old Ben asking.

Lyle smiling wanly. Leo and Nadine exchanging looks.

Will learning years later his uncle was an escaped mental patient. He had walked off the grounds of Lima State Hospital and then thumbed rides the hundred and fifty miles. He came to beg his brother for "a loan," so he could keep running all the way out to California, where he wanted to start over. Unbelievably, this time Leo said yes. When Will learned about this, as usual from his mother, he wondered if his old man's guilt over putting his younger brother away made him part with the incredible sum of fifteen hundred dollars.

The morning following Uncle Lyle's arrival, Will rode along when his father drove his brother to the Trailways station. The cold air held the threat of winter, and their breath froze until the heater kicked in and filled the car with the stench of singed carpeting. Nothing much was said, and Will, in the back seat, watched the two brothers stare straight ahead through the fogged windshield. At the bus station Lyle promised to write, promised again to repay the money; he gave Will a gentle hug and a tug of the ear. Will's father stiffly shook his brother's hand. Will watching as his uncle boarded the motor coach bound for Chicago and points west.

Then the bus door closed and Uncle Lyle was gone. Will and his father walking in silence back to the car across a crunch of gravel. In the front seat next to his father on the drive home, Will noted with amazement a glistening of his father's eyes.

After a few letters, one postmarked Albuquerque, the other San Juan Capistrano, they never heard from Uncle Lyle again. Will was eleven when he left, and soon his favorite uncle was a blurry memory. Yet when Will himself first came to California, he made a point of making his own pilgrimage to seaside San Juan, stopping at the local newspaper, the public library, the police station, looking for a clue, finding none.

Will carried on as that boy back in the Uselma box house, coping best he could. Escaping in his own way, just like Uncle Lyle. He learned to detach and float free. Recoiling equally from his father's fury and what he, from a boy's perspective, saw as his mother's willingness to endure it. Creeping out of bed to the top of the stairs in a pathetic heap of pajamas to hear it all.

By the time Will grew to near manhood—and was more than able, ironically, to stand up to his father—his detachment was in place. Will maintained a constant space between his father and him, but also between himself and his own receded landscape of emotion. With others, from this vantage point, becoming the one with no skin in the game, the neutral go-between to smooth the ground and extinguish the flame. With himself, becoming the great escape artist, refusing to be trapped. Or touched.

Yet at the same time, not unlike Leo, despising his own failure—for not rescuing his brother and sister and his mother; for not standing up to the old man and beating him at his own game. (As later he would reproach himself for allowing his wife to win an equally grim contest of wills, their daughter the prize in the balance.) In truth, Leo Dumont's son was afraid, of course. As his father was in his war, he had been at the receiving end. Not yet in his teens and he'd learned to watch closely for the lurking threat, especially near bedtime. If his father was not in the cellar but in his living room armchair. If his stare, usually unfocused, lost on things unseen, turned suddenly in his direction. He knew then to stop immediately what he was doing. He knew at such moments never, ever to look the old man directly in the eye (a simian signal of aggression, he discovered to some dismay, during a school field trip to the zoo). He knew to retreat from the room quickly and quietly.

Except that one time. Ben and Grace got the stare and both had been slapped to tears for playing "gymnasium" on the davenport. Their father's arm was ready to deal a more punishing blow when Will, heart in his throat, put his body between them and their aggressor and yelled in a voice he barely recognized as his own, "Dad, cut it out! Dad! Don't!"

His father, startled, recovered quickly. "That so, buddy boy? You want some now?" But like a predator cat daring his prey to escape, he only shoved him aside to stalk heavily into the kitchen for another beer.

"You're—gonna—get—killed," a wide-eyed Ben whispered. "Scram!"

Will racing out of the house and into the night. Though it was black as a priest's cassock under a starless sky and mosquitoes feasted on his flesh, he hid out in the underground fort he'd help to cover over in cardboard and scrap wood in the weedy lot down the block. Hiding out until well past eleven, hearing his mother call his name from the street.

Above all, of course, vowing never to be like him. Swearing to it.

"WILL."

"What?"

Ben creeping into his brother's room, the floorboards of the Uselma box house complaining under his small bare feet.

"How come he's like that?"

"Go back to bed, Toad."

"You known him longer. How come?"

"I don't know." Will, sitting up in bed to face his brother, a vague shape in the darkness. "I just know I won't ever be like him."

Ben, a sufferer of countless allergies, snuffled. "Me neither."

Reaching out to find his brother's shoulder, Will grabbed hold. "Swear," he said.

"I swear."

"Me too."

Both of them were too young to understand the cumulative effect of the nightly six-pack on already shorted-out synapses. The father drank Stroh's, AMERICA'S ONLY FIRE-BREWED BEER.

8.
The First Time

I-WASH? YOU THERE?
Malacky.
I was wondering—

Yes?

Do you miss it?

It. What is this "it"?

You know—the carnal pleasures. The mystery of passion ... the dying of little deaths and the miraculous resurrections.

I wish I had knowledge of this, Malacky.

For pity's sake, tell me you're joking.

I do not joke. My time with my people ended before I ... I was not ready to pull a child from between my thighs.

Well, for sure I done too much of the gabbing. I figured you was grown when you—why, what calamity could befall the daughter of an injun chief?

Your barbarian sickness. Many, many of the people died. My father and my mother gave me warning. Do not to come to your people's village, they said. But I was too full of the foolishness of the young. One day I crawled along the edge of the stream, just over there, where my people lived before and where you came to place this lodge. I was quiet as a snake. I hid in the thick fennel, breathing in its sweet smell, and I watched the barbarians from my hiding place.

Don't be thinking I'm not noticing the disgraceful name

calling again. But go on.

I heard the small barbarian.

A wee one.

No larger than a baby seal. A boy child. He wore only a loose shirt of elk skin, and he was sitting cross-legged near the edge of the stream very close to where I hid.

Heard, you say.

He was holding in his hands a box. It shone like a wet stone, and when he opened this box the most beautiful sound I ever heard filled the air. My mouth fell open. I was put under a spell. I did not hear anything but this magic music until there came a deep growl and the boy cried out and I heard a sharp crack as the mountain lion broke his neck. And the small boy was gone and only the beautiful music was left behind.

By Christ! Did you run?

Not until I grabbed up this box and raced with it back to my lodge. I would not let it out of my hands, and it was full of the sickness. The next day I lay down with terrible fever. My father at first believed my suffering was the evil spirit of the young barbarian. He paid a dancing and singing shaman to chase it away. When that did not make me well, he decided the barbarians got a poison shaman to shoot the pain into me. He paid a different shaman to use her magic to find the poison.

This witch doctor, you said "her." It were a female of the species?

Yes. They were many, and they had great magic. Some ate glowing coals or caused whales to flee the sea. They could change themselves into wild animals and make the skies fill with flashes of light.

Good God, shades of the Old Testament....

I know only this—a shaman's path is long and hard. Seven moons she must gather wood up on the ridge to burn each night while dancing in the sweat lodge. Not eating or drinking until falling into a death-like sleep. She also inhales the smoke of burning angelica root and cuts herself and rubs her wounds with young fern fronds. The creature who lives in the tooth shells, which our people use as payment for her magic, eat angelica leaves and live in the ferns, and in this way she dreams about the riches she will have—giving her strength to dance. She does these things until she wins control of her pains. She can take them out of herself and lay them in a basket. Only then can she see all the pains flying about the heads of other people, and drive them away.

Fascinating malarkey. This shaman, she saw your pain cavorting about in the air, did she?

More than that. She placed her mouth on mine. She sucked and pulled with her teeth. My pain came out of my mouth like a salmon liver, dripping blood. My mother and my father were happy I was cured. They thanked the shaman and gave her many tooth shells. But I was not cured. Three days after, I left my family and the living. Until I fell into the sleep that did not end, I would not give up my music box. My father wanted to destroy it, but my mother begged him to let me listen as long as I wanted. They placed the box in the burial basket with my body and buried it by moonlight in the soft sand near where I found it. When the end is near, we hold onto what we love with the fierceness of the owl, do we not, Malacky?

Aye.

THE NO NAME became Will's hangout. He liked its name, or lack of one, bestowed by the man named Davis who opened this Sausalito drinking establishment. Will, when he wasn't rattling around the shack or expelling bubbles five fathoms under, especially favoring the No Name's trellised-over patio for sipping a beer undisturbed. If in the mood for company, he moved inside; there it was dark even at midday, a clubby hideaway like all good saloons. Like the Log Cabin, the squat, seedy tavern his father sometimes let him tag along to as a boy; he barely noticed Leo ordering his "regular"—a shot of Seagram's, a longneck Stroh's—for all his wide-eyed gaping at the amber, dark caramel, and crayon-colored liquors mirrored in the back bar. His young imagination was in thrall to these vessels of mystery, wondering what magic each must hold. Now that he knew, or enough to be no longer curious about the rest, he still found a dark barroom edged in the circus colors of cool neon as comforting as an old pair of shoes.

Will was occupying a No Name stool one evening not long after his fateful first meeting with Maggie. She was tending the elbowed bar that night. He knew her instantly by the amazing tangle of hair; she did not recognize him as the peeping-tom frogman, but was all but overwhelmed by the aroma of toasted cheese wafting across the shellacked wood. This was the same mouthwatering sandwich that had turned her head as he passed on the street only the day before—that much she did know. It was an unusual dead calm at the No Name, and the two of them were alone. Will asked for another steam beer, she pulled it, setting it on a coaster and sliding away, busying herself with wiping and tidying. He introduced himself finally as she wandered back to stack clean glasses.

"Maggie," she replied, extending her hand.

Will noticed a residue of oil paint in the notch between her forefinger and thumb, and looking into her eyes saw they were turned smoky—appreciating what he was seeing now after admiring all of her revealed at their first encounter.

"Visiting?" she asked then, situating herself downwind from him and the freshets of air from the windows off the street. Billie Holliday was dead since summer, but her soulful cooings were alive in the jukebox.

"Moved here. I'm in Mrs. Farquehar's old place."

"The cute little Earthquake Shack on the boardwalk. I used to be scared to death of it."

"Did it smell haunted?"

She gave him a mystified look. "Not that I recall—and, believe me, I would."

"A musty dead stink?"

"No, but me and my friends did swear it was haunted. Mrs. Farquehar looked like a witch. When I was seven or eight maybe. She got even more dried up after that, but then I thought ghosts were cool. Say, you been hearing chains dragging around or something?"

Will gently edged his empty glass a few inches toward her and she tucked it under the bar, finding a fresh pint and deftly pulling him a refill.

"So that's it," he said. "I thought it was just the two next door."

"You mean Putty and Princess? Big guy and a platinum blonde with—"

"Yeah, the boardwalk sex show, if you don't count the pros at the Valhalla."

That made her laugh. He felt himself lowering his guard a notch. Maybe it was the beers.

They kept it going till closing. A few customers interrupting but mostly they had the No Name to themselves. Just the two of them doing the first slow dance of the mutually attracted: tentative at first, also a little daring; more moves as it went along, but still holding back hints of future intent. Will parrying questions he wasn't ready to answer but letting her know he was unattached. He was tempted to say more than he did, if only to let on they had met before.

"So how do you like our odd little town?" she asked at one point. Bobby Darin swinging now. *"Oh the shark has such teeth, dear. And he shows them ... pearly white...."*

"What's not to like?"

"Not much. But we do have our blemishes, like anywhere, I suppose."

"Such as?"

"Well. You got your Hillclimbers—that's what we call them. The rich and mighty up on the hillsides, think they own the world."

"Just a jack knife has old MacHeath, dear. And he keeps it ..."

"Know the type."

"Mostly good for local entertainment."

"... out of sight...."

A truck was belching thunderheads, and she made a sour face and glanced toward the street. "You know San Simeon? Down the coast?"

"You mean the Hearst castle?" Newly arrived in California and working his way up Highway One, Will had taken the dollar tour of the fifty-six bedrooms and sixty-one bathrooms. The property was now a state park. "What about it?"

"Hearst wanted to build it here, on our scenic slopes."

"William Randolph Hearst?" He knew the name, if not the man's excesses, before his tour. But he hadn't brought up his own stint of newspapering, which could lead to scabs he didn't want picked. Now, instead, he heard for the first time the famous Sausalito tale of the wealthy publisher and the massive foundation he laid on the hill just up from Old Town. How he just abandoned it one day.

"Can you believe it? Just for carrying on with an actress? Like their shit don't stink. Hearst got pissed at the stiff necks, so he left," she told him. It was his turn to laugh now, and she felt prickles of heat color the pale indentation at the base of her throat. She had long since decided to have a few beers herself.

He screwed up the courage to ask point blank, "There a boyfriend, Maggie?" She didn't say yes and didn't say no but made her situation clear by replying, "I don't believe in having a man just for the sake of having one." Failing to mention that any man of hers must also smell mighty fine. Will was relieved, despite himself. "You don't get lonely?" A question he would ordinarily not risk.

Maggie moved closer, her expression matter-of-fact. "Sure. If I'm that needy, I just do it myself."

The jukebox was quiet now. Leaning back on his bar chair, Will let out a low whistle. *You're not in Ohio anymore, Toto.* He faked interest in a fly circling the cocktail garnishes by the beer taps. Breaking the silence after a long moment to reply, "I can't believe you said that."

"Why not? Women can have urges." She was wiping circles with a rag.

It was like he was seeing her naked a second time except he wasn't in a rubber suit, which accounted for the hairs on his neck rising in imitation of elsewhere. Emboldened, he told her, "Girls say they remember their first kiss. But boys, well—I'll never forget the first time I, um—I can't believe we're having this conversation."

Maggie was steady in her gaze, her nostrils full of him. "Where were you?"

"I know exactly. I was on a lumpy bed in the sunroom of the farmhouse where my mother grew up. It had a crocheted bedspread."

"And?"

"My buddy Darryl shamed me into it. He couldn't believe I hadn't done it yet. I mean, I knew it felt good, but he swore that if you rubbed long enough, it would be like you hit a home run or found an Indian arrowhead. I didn't buy it."

She giggled. "Go on."

"It was barely light, and I was in that floaty place just after sleep. My grandma and grandpa were doing chores." He raised his eyebrows into twin caterpillars of suspense. "So I, uh, reached into my pajama bottoms and tried it. Nothing. I kept at it, seemed like forever, until I was getting kinda sore. I was going to give up and tell Darryl he was a dickwad as usual."

Maggie was still wiping up imaginary spills, tracing figure eights on the bar. "I can figure out what happened next."

"To say the least, I was aghast and agape."

That giggle again, a musical trill that reminded him of a dolphin squeak. She pulled him another beer without being asked. "On me."

"Trying to pry more loose?"

"Right." Inhaling him. Will sensing her magnetic pull.

"Well," he said. "Since we're on the subject."

"What?"

"I've never told *anybody* this." He raised his right hand like a star witness ready to be sworn in. "In my teens, this palm should've looked like a fur mitten."

"You and every other boy I've met, apparently."

"No, wait. It gets better. Would you mind putting that rag down? There's not a drop of spilled beer left on the planet."

"Go on." She edged even closer.

Will lowered his voice to divulge the terrible secret. "I discovered my dad's *Playboy*. Do you think he whacked off with it? Naw, you'd have to know my father. Anyhow, he'd hidden it at the bottom of his sock drawer."

"Perfect," she said.

"It was the one with Jayne Mansfield on the cover. Remember how Jack Paar introduced her?" He affected his bullfrog at the bottom of the well voice. *"And now, ladies and gentlemen,* here they are ... *Jayne Mansfield."* A deep swallow of beer. "I lent myself that *Playboy* about a million times."

Maggie laughed this time but also feigned shock. "That all you got for me? Here I was thinking there was an exciting new man in town."

"Okay, okay. Jeezus, I *really* never told anybody this—underneath Jayne Mansfield and some old letters, I found a photo. An eight-by-ten."

"Cheesecake."

"No, arty."

"So?"

"My mom."

"Get out!"

"I kid you not. My mom, naked as a jaybird. He must have taken it before the war, before I was born even. I can't imagine how the hell he got her to do it."

"Now I'm mildly impressed."

Will stared into his beer. Maggie marked time again, fiddling with a stack of beer coasters. Will saying finally, "You want to know."

"Not if you don't want to. Really."

More silence.

"I learned something," he said. She stopped her neatening as Will grinned. "No Oedipal hang-ups."

"So what did you do?"

"My naked mother I took to my room. I stared at her. I stared for a long time. I mean, you just don't think of your own mother as a ... a ..."

"Jayne Mansfield?"

"Oh, Christ, no, nothing like her. Much smaller—but—but very nice, I thought. Hell, I couldn't even remember what they looked like. I hadn't seen them since she nursed me." He looked sheepishly at Maggie, who was clearly waiting for more. "Okay. Sure. I got hard. At that age you get hard over a donut hole. But I couldn't go through with it."

"Again I ask, what did you do?"

"Snuck back into their bedroom. Tucked the photo back under Jayne Mansfield and rearranged the argyles. Then I tiptoed back to my room, sat on the edge of my bed and said Hail Marys till I was sure no one could hear my heart exploding in my chest." He looked over toward her. "Satisfied?"

Maggie took his empty glass and five-dollar bill, and she said, "Best story I've heard all night."

Will waited while she punched the keys on the big National cash register. The Schlitz sign was buzzing but neither of them paid any attention.

"I got one more."

Maggie looked at him over her shoulder. "Nothing else you might say can shock me, Mr. Dumont."

"Fair enough," said Will. "Then you won't mind me saying I saw you naked too."

9.
Man Bites Dog

L OCAL MAN DUG OWN GRAVE" IS HOW THE OBITUARY headline read in the local newspaper when Will's father went. At this juncture of our tale, that memorable, if rather mordant, one-liner becoms relevant—even if telling the whole story of Leo's demise would get ahead of things and so, has to wait. For it might surprise you to know that if Will was still employed by that same newspaper, he would have taken it upon himself to wipe the self-satisfied smirk off the face of the headline's author. Father-son relationships can be complicated as the plot of a Russian novel, everyone knows that.

This was the same assistant night city editor who challenged Will to a rumble the first week Will was on the job, after first making snide remarks about cub reporters from "pansy Eastern schools." It happened at Ike's, a dive where reporters, rewrite men, and low-level editors drank in their off hours. So did bail bondsmen, just-released thugs and hookers, and off-duty homicide detectives, because Ike's was conveniently across from the downtown cop shop, as the reporter called police headquarters. Will, never suspecting this aforementioned editor would later bestow his smug sign-off to Leo Dumont's life, ignored him. Besides, at ten-thirty at night the man was on "lunch break" and therefore drunk.

Will was drinking too, yet was not drunk enough.

To drink, of course, was the thing to do. Will began this

rite of passage in college. During those formative years, he built up his capacity, stamina of the bent elbow, even as he joked, "It's not how many it takes it, it's how few." He viewed this affinity for drink in a wholly different category from his father's—didn't he get happy, not mean? Up to and including the moment he passed out.

At his male-only university, partying was confined to weekends, which encompassed Thursday through Sunday afternoon. This was also when women were present, adding exponentially to thirst. Will was graduated an accomplished drinker and failed lover. A technical virgin, he learned that intense groping leads to intense frustration. And to seeking solace in the flask or bottle.

Will's college immersed him in the sciences, but he found equal interest in the human condition. Observing people was as interesting to him as a Skinner box rat avoiding electric shock. (His thoughts turning inevitably to the Dumonts in the Uselma box house.) That he veered into journalism was an accident. After summers working as a fill-in worker at an axle factory—watching with fascination and no little horror as his fellow time-clock punchers tossed down whiskies at noon in the taphouse that cashed their paychecks—he lucked into a job at an Ohio metropolitan daily.

He was a copyboy. His boss that summer was a middle-aged Czech who shouldered twin boulders of responsibility as copyboy chief and comics editor. This dour czar of the funny papers was anything but funny. With barely a word for anyone, he slouched at his desk in the bustling city room, nose to the afternoon editions, flinching only when an editor in the slot barked, "Boy!"

But Will fell in love with newspapering. After graduation he applied for a full-time job, eager to distance himself from his classmates, whom he saw mainly as inert trust-fund types bound for the gentlemanly professions in greed. Comforting the afflicted and afflicting the comfortable rang to him of a higher calling.

In fact, he was also attracted to the "official observer" stance affected by the press. Not unlike the lab-coated scientist! As though a well-chosen modifier on page one could not make a stranger's life a living hell! Journalism was another way of playing God and certainly much more fun than straining your eyes squinting at X-rays or obscure case law. For this was also before reporters and editors thought of themselves as white-collar professionals. A newspaper office in those days was more like a safe house for sociopaths, a gypsy encampment. A city room then was populated by closet poets, street-corner philosophers, bottle-in-the-bottom-drawer drunks and odd ducks of every stripe.

Will, in wide-eyed wonder, soaked it all in. The obit writer who slept in a casket. The journeyman reporter whose byline had wandered a dozen states and who habitually peed on the editor's potted palm. The big breasted, big hearted "women's editor" who claimed to have balled FDR on his private train to Hyde Park and who took the prep school sports reporter, a genuine dwarf, into the newspaper's test kitchen and locked the door.

Oh, and then there were the war stories. These were not like Leo's. They were more like Norse legends celebrating the prized traits of the newspaper hero: tenacity, calm under pressure, accuracy and, most of all, getting the *whole story*. Thus ... the World's Greatest Rewrite Man. A rewrite man is unknown to newspaper readers. He labors anonymously, never leaving the newspaper offices, never interviewing a crime victim or local politician. He takes dictation—from, say, the theater critic phoning in an opening night review. More often he assembles and writes stories from raw details gathered at the scene by reporters. Minutes from deadline for the next edition, this can be nerve-wracking work. The heralded rewrite men are like smooth-running vacuum cleaners sucking up facts. And every reporter prides himself on being ready to feed a rewrite man every scrap he could possibly need to make his story supremely tragic, hilarious, uplifting, or off-beat.

> WGRM : Whaddya got?
> REPORTER (*on the phone*): It's the classic, you'll love it. "Man bites dog."
> WGRM: Yeah? Go....
> REPORTER: Okay, one Herman normal spelling middle initial V Gerkowski G-E-R-K-O-W-S-K-I age thirty-eight address three eight eight Beulah Ave. father of six approximately four-thirty this p.m. attacked a brown and white spaniel name of Sport ... (*continuing in this vein, an exhaustive recounting of every possible detail*).
> WGRM: (*still typing fast*): Um-hmm. That it?
> REPORTER (*jubilant, sure he has covered every conceivable angle*): Yeah, that's it. Great stuff, huh?
> WGRM: (*pause*) I got one question.
> REPORTER (*suddenly alarmed*): You do?
> WGRM: Uh-huh.
> REPORTER: Okay. What?
> WGRM: The man have false teeth?

Stories like these were the currency at Ike's, the long-neck beers sliding across the scuffed bar like pawns in a chess game. The same bar the bony barmaid danced on naked while Will and the others continued boozing and feeding the jukebox after hours, with Ike's blessing. Will, at such moments, fighting double vision; and wondering what his father would think.

Hey, you tough old Marine who cracked like an egg. Look, your boy doesn't pick fights, he only sees two of everything....

Will was assigned to the police beat. The Parris Island for

reporters. The dark side of the moon, where the night city editor, before agreeing to "four inches" or "six inches" about man's latest inhumanity to man, would ask, "White on white, black on white, or black on black?" On these distinctions hung the difference between a front-page byline above the fold, getting buried in the metro section, or the spike.

It was not long before Will also discovered the real sport of police reporting. Being first to the victim's family. Beating the other papers, beating the cops if you're lucky, thanks to a tip or alert monitoring of the police radio band. Then it was a race to some neighborhood of moldy divans on the front porch, rusted junk in the yard. Pounding on the door until the shouting began inside and dirty-faced kids appeared; and then the mother with wounded eyes, pregnant again by that no-good son of a bitch. At such moments it fell to Will to break the news.

Will Dumont from the Press, ma'am, awfully sorry, but your son was just butterflied by a fast-moving freight ... pulverized in a head-on ... stabbed in the kidney at a motorcycle gang war over on Kosciuszko.

Express sympathy. Absorb the anguish and shock. Get a few quotes. But, above all, *get the photos*—beg, borrow, or steal them all, framed or in family albums—of the newly deceased. Thereby skunking the competition and bringing glory to one's self with yet another saga to unveil at Ike's. Thus were careers and heroes of local journalism made. And thus did he learn a bitter truth: he afflicted the afflicted much more often than the comfortable.

Will's mother saved his every bylined article, a personal clipping service. Will wondering after there were dozens why he hated re-reading them. Why he began smoking Camels in the pea-green press room at the cop shop, tucked around the corner from the candy stand run by a blind man who smiled and rolled up opaque eyes when he heard coins drop onto his counter. Why, on more and more nights, his fingertips turned numb and he could hear the blood pounding in his ears. Was he cracking like an egg too?

One day he marched into the editor's office and quit. Will found himself standing before the head editor, a man who had covered *wars and revolutions*. Why, he was asked. Will hesitating. Finally, he returned the editor's penetrating gaze and said, "It's all too close." The man exhaled a cloud of smoke and pulled a pipe from his mouth. He looked as if he needed a translator.

Will's newspapering came to an end after a routine "ten-sixteen": police code for a domestic disturbance. Ask any cop. This is the workaday call they dread most. A male beating the pulp out of his female, a neighbor phoning for help. And then when the police arrive, a victim who suddenly sides with her tormentor. The two of them closing ranks, aiming their accumulated fury at the uniformed intruders. Always have back-up in a ten-sixteen, the cops will tell you.

Will was returning from the first traffic fatality of the night in a light rain, the scanner in the police beat car spewing the usual static. He heard the dispatcher's flat voice announce the code and give a nearby address, heard a squad car's "ten-four." Not bothering to detour because an ordinary ten-sixteen is not news. If his paper printed every case of domestic mayhem, no space would be left for sports scores, horoscopes, or the comics.

"Shots fired," crackled the radio then, repeating the ten-sixteen address. Two more squad cars responded. Will, doing a stuntman U-turn, spun out on the wet pavement. As he raced past darkened businesses with bars on the windows and iron grates across their doors, past mean-looking neighborhood bars where beer signs smeared their colors across his windshield, he heard excitement for the first time in the voice of the dispatcher. "Officer down. All units, officer down!"

Will radioed the city desk and said to send a photog. He

stopped paying attention to stop signs and floored it through intersections. A cop shooting was page one, every reporter knew that—if he got it in before the final edition went to bed.

He found the address just ahead of half-a-dozen black-and-whites, their lights flashing and sirens wailing behind him. Pulling onto the sidewalk and running full tilt toward the two-story house with peeling white pillars framing a front door thrown wide open. Hearing the neighborhood dogs barking wildly in the distance, and then, as he was on the walkway bordered in baby's breath, he heard human sounds from inside, unintelligible.

Cries of anger, cries of terror.

He stopped suddenly. Frozen. Why had he almost run into the middle of it? What was he doing? Reporting ... or rescuing? Heart stampeding, body quaking—convulsions he had not known in a long time—since he was a small boy—at the top of the stairs.

"Get the fuck away, Dumont!" screamed a police sergeant he knew, shoving past with his service revolver drawn and held out with both hands.

Will's future rescuing would be from the murky depths. And at a greater emotional distance.

And Pickle would prove that even from there, he would not be safe.

10.
In a Terrible Pickle

CROSSING OVER ...
Yes.
What was it like for you?
It only was.
You felt nothing—no pain, no pleasure?
Only a new journey, a new path.
Surely you missed the family dearly. Your injun chums.
I could see them weeping, and I called to them to tell them I was safe, but I gave up. My name was gone from their lips even with the ashes and pitch of mourning on their faces. And I too began to forget.
Forget you was dead?
I forgot to worry about my mother digging clams and gathering acorns without me, or when my sister Tachi would marry.
So you was never sad. I'm asking because sadness is of profound interest to an Irishman. 'Tis the Irish inheritance. Some claim we invented it.
I was not sad.
Never. Not even a wee bit?
Malachy, I laughed at my own mourning ceremony. But the clown was very funny.
A clown. At your funeral?
Yes.

By my soul, you're one of us! Sadness comes natural to us as the stations of the cross, so we joke and laugh like lunatics. Ever been to an Irish wake? I'd wager not.

The mourning ceremony is when we say our last words to those who died the twelve moons past. Guests from other villages come to feast, dance, and sing—and for the burning of the dead's likeness that is our custom. On my day, I watched my father, as chief, call to my village to get ready.

> *Get up! Get up! Get up!*
> *Wake up! Wake up! Wake up!*
> *Visitors are coming, visitors are coming.*
> *Strike out together!*
> *Hunt deer, squirrels!*
> *And you women, strike out, gather wild onions,*
> *wild potatoes!*
> *Gather all you can! Gather all you can!*
> *Pound acorns, pound acorns, pound acorns!*
> *Cook, cook!*
> *Make some bread, make some bread!*
> *Make acorn soup so the people will eat it!*
> *Eat! Eat! Eat! Eat!*
> *So we can get ready to cry.*

Eating and crying, now there's a stew an Irishman can belly up to.

It was strange, Malachy. For the first time I did not know hunger or tears. But I saw my family and guests shout out their grief, until Woochi stood up.

Woochi? The clown is called Woochi?

He is named for his shouts of "Woo! Woo!" His body is painted white. He stands before everyone, and first he mocks my father. His gestures are hilarious and obscene. He is tricky, greedy, lewd, like Coyote, whose sacred powers give him courage to scorn even the poison shaman.

A comic melodrama to rival the fighting Flanagans!

Then the poison shaman appears. I see her behind the clown, hunting him. They leap at each other, they shoot with bow and arrow, dancing as they go. The shaman scatters earth and throws it at the clown. She makes him bleed at the nose and mouth, makes him die. When the sun is low, she draws him back with her cane, back across the Great Divide to the living world again. Woochi coughs up the poison. The shaman laughs. Woochi laughs too, as he returns to life. The two are then partners and friends.

WILL, PARTNERED WITH Pickle. Partners who became enemies. Once, in school, Will wrote an essay his teacher returned with the word "marital" circled in red. In the margin the teacher wrote "martial," with the prophetic notation, "In practice, the two meanings are often interchangeable."

They met by chance on a sticky July day just over the Pennsylvania line—at the Pymatuning Dam, feeding the carp. Hundreds of these scaly creatures with Louis Armstrong lips roiled in the brown water of a cement pit. Someone's brilliant idea of a tourist attraction: buy loaves of stale bread, four for a buck, watch the riotous brawling over crusts of Wonder Bread. BUILDS STRONG BODIES EIGHT WAYS. All day, every day. The spectacle drew crowds from the nearby farms and mill towns of Ohio and Pennsylvania.

The sad fate of these fish made Will sick, but he was there because his grandmother loved carp feeding; it was her birthday, and so this was the entertainment following the warmed-over buffet at a historic Pennsy country inn decorated in lacy doilies and patent medicine bottles.

Pickle—a childhood nickname that stuck—was there with her sister. She was pretty and fawn-like, with thin long legs and arms that put her on the edge of gawky; her cheeks were covered in blond fuzz. She wore pink shorts and a halter top. Nervously animated, she drew Will's attention as she elbowed her way to prime carp feeding, even as her sister hung back. Reaching far out over the railing to skim a slice of Wonder Bread, it whirled like a flying saucer—trailed by a bracelet that glinted silvery sunlight, flung from Pickle's slender wrist.

She let out a cry of anguish. There was a frenzy of over-carboed carp.

Will, not knowing why, as if apart from himself and merely observing, jumped the rail. He dove headlong into the pit, splashing brown water and fish feces onto open-mouthed onlookers. Crazed carp fled in all directions. Acting on pure instinct, he groped in the unspeakable scum. He found coins and beer bottles and a Super 8 camera, but no silver bracelet.

Coming up for air, oozing muck, he dove yet again.

PICKLE VISITED HIS bedside while he was still woozy on medication and his doctors worried about a litany of disease and infection. She had tracked him down from the story in *The Erie Call.*

MAN HOSPITALIZED AFTER CARP DIVE

She brought him a loaf of Wonder Bread, gift-wrapped, as a joke.

Six weeks later they were married in the back yard of Pickle's parents. She asking him to ask her. He wanted a civil ceremony, but she insisted on a minister, and they settled for the non-denominational chaplain from the hospital where Will recovered. His white blood cell count was still too high. Antibiotics battled against bronchial complications. The drugs, however, did not deter him from alcohol, and he woke the morning after the ceremony with scant memory of his inauguration into married life.

There was no honeymoon. Will, finishing his scuba certification in a chlorine-reeking "Y," began training with the Water Search and Rescue Unit of the Cuyahoga County Sheriff's Department instead. The WSRU worked storm-prone Lake Erie and miles of inland waterways, including the serpentine Cuyahoga. This was the river that became internationally infamous for catching fire, and in Will's day it was already a chemical stew that made the carp pit a kiddy pool by comparison.

Pickle was junior marketing manager at Bargain Barn, where she dressed as Scrooge McDuck and handed out helium balloons and candy suckers to mewling children. She stayed at her job during Will's training and for another seven months—allowing her to claim afterwards that her career was sacrificed for the sake of family and happy home. Nine months to the day after the wedding, Pickle underwent an emergency caesarian.

Daughter Ariel was born in acute fetal distress, the umbilical cord cinching her neck. Will was feeling a rapidly tightening noose of his own.

Months before, it had begun to become clear to him. Marrying Pickle was as hasty and foolhardy as his plunge into the carp. A mistake of major proportions. In the face of his realization, Will met Pickle's news of her pregnancy with anguish, not joy. It was much too early to begin a family, he told her, leaving the "with you" unsaid. Initially Pickle agreed. She hunted down an abortionist, made the appointment, but then abruptly relented.

And seeing his doubt about her and their union, she hardened. Her anger grew as her belly did. She would fix things, she decided, so this man would never be rid of her. Chain-smoking and gulping cheap sherry, she knew the satisfaction of the child who would bind them forever kicking in her womb.

Will's response you can guess at. He surrounded himself with his bubble of detachment, thinking he was safe there and could not be touched. This of course enraged Pickle all the more, but he did not care. The bubble worked like a heat shield. It was subzero inside. But then his bubble burst with the force of the Hindenburg—the moment the nurse handed him tiny Ariel, wrapped like a cabbage roll in a thin green blanket.

In disbelief he stared at his daughter's perfect face, roseate and shiny, with astonishingly long eyelashes. His heart fell open, and he loved her immediately and unconditionally. "For you," he whispered to the sleeping infant. "For you." He promised himself and her. He would make it work with Pickle.

Swearing to it.

It did not work. And so Pickle's fury at her husband's love for their child and feigned affection for her grew like crabgrass, and she set about single-mindedly piercing his shell. Jab, jab, jab. Needle, needle, needle. Attacking his measured response. His forced good humor. His floating game. Will was a fly in her noxious web. He could not run away. He could not hide.

He knew it. He knew he was outmatched. Even as he struggled to remain indifferent to her thrusts. And he also recognized, with increasing alarm, the familiar terrain of his childhood, and so he feared being swallowed into the crevasse that might swallow their subdivision.

Pickle, seeing that she was winning the battle but not the war for her husband's heart, went instead for the kill. Relentlessly, she hunted his Achilles' heel. In retreat, he turned for succor where he had always found it before—with trusty companion John Barleycorn. But his old barroom buddy, this time, turned on him too.

Will was a fire-brewed daddy.

Crash bang! Fight. Fight back. Stop her!

Pickle collapsing to the floor, a rag doll triumphant. An elegant flow of red from her nostril. Smiling her fiercest smile.

"Come here, Ariel honey, come to Mommy. See what Daddy did!" she said with perfect calm.

11.
Eye Yi Yi

LIFE GOES ON, EVEN FOR THE REFUGEE. IT WAS ANOTHER seasonally fair morning after Will's arrival in town, long before his discovery of the corpse under the Valhalla. He was settling in, feeling lucky to be in our midst. Missing Ariel, of course. Lecturing himself not to dwell on that: the only way, for a long while, was learning to live without her. But maybe his luck was changing for the better. Maybe he could get on with his life. Why not?

Will dragged his new dory onto the beach and secured the painter to a piling under the Earthquake Shack. The pastel morning reflected off a mess of herring at the bottom of his boat—freshly netted for the pelican he'd named One-Eyed George. Brown pelicans, as Will could tell you, spot their meals from thirty feet up and drop like stones to scoop up seawater with their catch. But they lose a lot before gulping whole what's left. This one was struggling against both the ordinary odds and a missing eye.

George had been part of Will's life for a week now. Walking along Bridgeway on a similar morning, he noticed a crowd gathered around a pair of fishermen. A stringy Chinese in a billowy shirt and trousers had managed to snag the unfortunate bird, the hook lodging deeply in an eye socket. Both man and bird were panicky but exhausted and the unwanted catch flopped listlessly on the rip-rap. The man's companion, another Chinese, was motioning for him to cut the line and be done with this unwieldy creature showering them with salt spray and feathers. A young Hillclimber mother had appointed herself spokesperson for the crowd, and she berated them both for not helping the suffering pelican.

"Mommy, is the bird crying?" asked her wide-eyed daughter.

"Coming through," announced Will in the next instant, shouldering quickly past the onlookers and kneeling by the bird, holding his neck down while softly stroking his head; leaning closer, he spoke in a low voice, drawing out the calming vowels, until the pelican stopped struggling and merely fixed him with a stare from the good eye.

"You," he said, looking up at the other fisherman. "We've got to get him turned over, to get at the hook."

The fisherman shrugged and answered in Cantonese.

"Okay, then you." Will nodded toward a man in a greasy black cap who had edged to the front of the crowd.

Will looked directly into the pelican's eye. "Easy now, big guy. We're not going to hurt you." He kept a firm hold and continued talking in the same reassuring way as the two men gingerly turned the bird to expose the injured eye.

"Good," said Will. "Now help me keep him still."

"Thiiiiit —," muttered Jake the Anchor Out, the man in the greasy cap. He knelt with obvious reluctance.

Glancing up again, Will addressed the young Hillclimber mother. "In the tackle box. Find me the needle-nosed pliers."

"The what?"

"Just like it sounds," he said evenly. "Pliers with pointy ends. Hurry." The pelican was becoming restive and trying to flap his wings despite the hands on him. The woman pawed noisily through the tackle box, prompting a protest from one of the fishermen.

"Take it easy, lady," Will admonished her.

"I—sorry." Her voice was more indignant than embarrassed as she found the pliers and handed them over.

"Will the bird get glasses now?" her daughter wanted to know.

"No, sweetheart," Will said. "Maybe a little black eye patch, like a pirate." The girl frowned. "Nuh-uh." She burrowed a forefinger into her nostril.

Taking hold of the pelican's beak, Will whispered other soothing words before grabbing the shaft of the hook in the pliers and, in a single motion, pushing the barbed end through the eye and out; the bird shuddered but did not struggle. Then, effortlessly, Will clipped the barb in the pliers' cutter, guided the barb-less hook back through again and nudged it free. He waved the hook and line above his head and grinned.

"Neat," said the little girl. Others murmured approval and gave claps of applause.

A final time, Will spoke to the bird. Then he said to Jake, "When I count three, let go and back away. Let him adjust to the eye. Ready?" They released their hold, and the pelican rose unsteadily to his feet, unhurt except for a smudge of bright red under the destroyed orb. He stamped on the rocks a few times and briefly cocked his head to look at Will before flying off in a blur.

And that was the start of their friendship. One-Eyed George began hanging around the boardwalk like a rescued puppy. Will said the downy-headed bird reminded him of the comedian George Gobel—"he winks a lot too, ever notice?"—and thus he got his name.

Now, as Will finished tying up, George swooped to his breakfast in the dory; he hoovered up the herring, throwing back his head and working them down, then hopped over to Will, nudging him for a postprandial scratch. "Hey, George," Will said. The pelican peered up with his good eye. Will smiled wearily, then made his way doggedly toward the shack. He deserved to feel beat. A two a.m. report of "man overboard" had rousted him from a warm bed. There ensued five frustrating hours of searching in the treacherous currents of the Raccoon Straits off Tiburon, without a trace.

This morning he would skip his usual early walk through Old Town. Nodding greetings to his neighbors (though never at that hour to Putty and Princess, whose libidos recharged until midmorning), to Sally Stanford chain-smoking Luckys while auditing the previous night's take; pausing to glance at how the sloop was taking shape in the boat yard just down the cove from the Valhalla, crossing Second Street and taking quick strides up the hill.

Instead, Will slept the dead sleep of the truly tired. And so not witnessing yet another sortie for the Water Rat Revolution: missing a chance, perhaps, to head off another statistic in our town's rising rate of crime against public property.

LET'S SEE WHAT we got."

"Not tho fasth. I haf to pee firth."

"Go out back. The *scheisser* is *kaput.*"

"Worf than my boat," groused Jake, turning to make his way along the narrow corridors of Mephisto's cottage, chockablock with bins of dusty books and yellowed academic journals next to stolen goods of every sort. Bel nearly toppled a stack of scholarly treatises as he fumbled deep into his coat pockets before spilling out dozens of small boxes with stenciled markings on each one.

TOP SECRET

PROPERTY OF U.S. GOVERNMENT

"No one saw you?" Mephisto demanded, examining the boxes with care. Opening one, he found a cluster of brown bottles inside, their typed labels reading "Benzodiazepine." He unscrewed a cap, put his nose to the bottle and inhaled, then spilled its contents onto his palm: dozens of tiny pills.

"Bunny?"

Bunny was preoccupied with modeling a tatty chinchilla wrap; his silken ears danced a rumba as he turned to face Mephisto. "Truck was down the way from the Glad Hand, dear one," he assured Mephisto with an impish grin. "Not a soul in sight." Bel grunted his agreement.

"*Zehr interessant,*" said Mephisto in a satisfied way. "Here we have uncovered our own Manchurian Candidate."

"Wath tha?" Jake was back from his mission of biological urgency.

"Brainwashing," Mephisto replied matter-of-factly, continuing to examine the pink pills in his hand. "In Korea." Jake backed a step at mention of his personal Waterloo, colliding into Bel. The gentle giant put his huge paw on Jake's shoulder, and Jake brushed it off.

Mephisto was suspicious of anything perpetrated by the government, knowing too well what happened when *that* bunch got behind closed doors and not believing for a minute the Chinks and Ruskies were the only ones playing mind-altering games. These goodies in his palm were destined for some secret Army lab at Fort Baker in the Headlands, he was certain.

"Could be Bennies mayhaps," offered Bunny.

"They ain't speed," Mephisto said. In his younger days, back East, he had snorted or swallowed plenty of Benzedrine to induce days of crazed sleeplessness. Despite the similarity in name, these didn't look or smell the same.

"Shom kinda supa-bennie," Jake suggested. "We should peddle 'em to the Rats."

Mephisto wasn't listening. He pronounced to no one in particular, "Once, I was a teacher. That made me a builder—of minds. Since they took that away, I am in demolition. I tear down the established order. And I will not stand idly by while their thought police does its dirty work."

"Come on," said Jake with impatience. "Dollah a hit."

Mephisto carefully returned all but one of the tablets to their container and the bottle to its box. He stacked the boxes in neat rows and laid a protective hand on top of them. Looking at Jake with eyes sharp as arrowheads, he shook his matted mane.

"They're too hot. And I think we should reserve them for some far better purpose."

"Like what?" Jake wanted to know.

Not answering, Mephisto held the remaining tablet between his thumb and forefinger. And he wondered just what it would do to a human brain.

12.
Mama d'leau

ELL, LASS ... YOU WERE UNWILLING TO GIVE UP what pleases most. Aren't we all? Let me tell you what I clung to in the wee hours of that fateful April morning in nineteen-ought-six.

Yes, and do not forget any part of it.

Right then. After the earth stopped trembling, I ran like the Maria wind through the screaming hordes, the streets and grand avenues of San Francisco awash with rubble, the dead and the dying, till I found myself back on the two blocks of Morton Street, off Union Square. Utterly transformed our little Babylon was. Gone, the raucous music and the laughter of drunken men, the brazen women at the windows selling their titties for ten cents for a squeezing, fifteen the pair. Gone, Bassity's stable of whores he rented at twenty-five cents for a Mexican, half-buck for a nigger, Chink or Jap, and one solid greenback for a fine white girl. All gone, gone. Instead, the debris was so heavy there was barely a passageway on the paving stones.

Malacky, you were not afraid?

Course I was! But I would not give up what I wanted most.

A pale barbarian girl?

Heaven help me, no!

Who then?

The luck of the Irish was with me. In complete ruin was the house of Rotary Rosie, who loved book learning more than whoring, and Iodoform Kate's, where the blue plate special, so to speak, was a heaping serving of fiery Jewess. But at my Rooster—it were a miracle! I stumbled in the gloaming into the parlor and to my utter delight, there stood my darling! Covered in plaster dust and bits of tin ceiling but unharmed there she was ... my piano....

I have seen this music box! In your lodge ... it is so large!

That ain't the same one, but you are correct—'twas a mighty thing indeed. Three hundred pounds, for sure. A Schumann upright with lovely scrollwork on polished oak. Technically, she were the property of that bastard Bassity, but he would lose her in a few hours anyhow. Ah, yet here was the rub—with no castors on her, I couldn't begin to budge the thing.

Did you seek others of your tribe to help?

No. Auld Sod ingenuity, that was the ticket.

I do not know—

'Tis of no consequence. This is what I did: using every last ounce of muscle, I levered her up with a busted-off table leg and onto a truly wondrous find ... shoe skates! Belonged to two dyke whores they did, who liked rolling over to Union Square when business was slow. I slid a skate under the Schumann at each of her four corners and tied them tight with rope we kept for certain customer requests. Bless me, then I cleared a path and proceeded to roll out! Out on the street, though, my real challenge waited. What route of escape? Toward the Ferry Building? That would take me far from my lodging, which I hoped might still be standing. Heading west was out—I seen the chaos and the rousted hotel guests thronging Union Square. North was uphill. So I turned south towards Market, where the going was mostly downhill or flat. Keeping myself and my precious treasure upright while dodging debris and overturned conveyances, dead horses and the torn-up cobblestone—'twas a mighty and arduous task. But that morning I were endowed with the brute strength and cunning of a chain gang.

Did you save your music box?

You ain't tired yet?

Tell me ... tell me to the end of your story, Malacky.

I'll tell what happened next—'cause that's the other point you put me in mind of. There I was, rolling my piano down Fifth, two hours since it all began. By now the great conflagration that started in the workingmen's ghetto was filling the air with smoke and cinders as thick as fog, and the sky were blood red tinged with lavender and yellow. At Mission Street, through the filthy half light, I saw a sight even yours truly, this old Bassity hand, could not believe.

What did you see?

Looming before me was the mighty fortress, the U.S. Mint—

Mint?

Where all the loot is, little one. Millions in gold bullion and coin.

Ah, you speak of money. Our people have money but it is beautiful.

Your people sold Manhattan Island for trinkets and beads.

I speak of the beautiful tooth shells ... our money ... made by a living creature, not from cold rock.

Sweet Jesus, you exhaust me. May I proceed? So I was saying, here I am at the grand structure of the Mint, a gigantic ghost ship in the smoke pall. Looking to the roof, towering above me, I seen smoldering, the embers streaking down like shooting stars. But, oh my Christ, what was that on the broad sweep of the front steps? A score of tarted-up whores, that's what! With their equally gaudy pimps. Escaped from the Tenderloin they was, hoping to save their sorry hides. Up and

down those marble stairs were men and their females naked
or nearly so, their attire strewn this way and that, and they
was screeching ribald songs at the top of their lungs, chasing
each other about, and piling up in heaps of limbs. Entwined
like bowls of noodles, they were, and plenty sauced from a
wagon load of commandeered booze. In the certainty the end
was at hand, these wastrels was hell-bent on finishing things
off with a bang.

Strong drink lead us to dancing and singing too—but only
our men. They take the potion of blackberry and honey to give
them courage and visions of the hunt, to outsmart Coyote or
ignore pains shot by the poison shaman.

'Twas oblivion these hooligans was hunting … till me and
my fine piano was spied.

They hunted you?

Aye. First to see me was a swarthy Mexican pimp I knew
as Pock Face Pedro. Well, he let out a war whoop, and soon a
dozen was fast closing in, screaming for my precious cargo.

Did you fight them, these barbarians?

Hah! For once you're on the mark, Mi-Wash. Barbarians
these were. Believe me, I was steeled to defend myself. Yet just
as the battle royal was about to begin, fate stepped in.

Spirit Coyote is a cunning trickster, Malacky. He wished
to taunt but not kill you.

Hogwash. 'Twas not the work of animal spirits nor any lep-
rechaun—no, it were the earth itself. Shaking again, another
terrific wave and roll, the last big one of that terrible day.
When it started, the drunkards froze in their tracks. Then they
turned tail and raced back to their debauchery. I wrapped my
arms round my piano tightly as she softly moaned. When the
ground got still, I swiveled Madame Schumann about face
and escorted her away fast as I could, back up Fifth, till all I
could hear was the distant shriek of the whores, from fright
or pleasure I know not.

―――――――

YES, WE SURELY love our fun. (Here comes that Mutual of Omaha announcer voice again....) Even in the last century Sausalito had its free-spirited reputation. Witness the *San Francisco Chronicle* ("SAUCY SAUSALITO, A MOTLEY COLONY OF ENGLISH AND PORTUGUESE," 1889):

"Undoubtedly there is a considerable amount of quiet dev-iltry carried on in the snug little cottages.... The Sausalito gossip would never dream it worthwhile to speak of little mistakes made with latchkeys by belated husbands returning from a club meeting in the wee small hours ... or why a new Phryne or Belladonna has taken up her quarters at one of the mansions on the hill."

In that same era, after both San Francisco and Oakland banned wagers on horses from saloons wired to the racetracks by Western Union, these "poolrooms" flourished here. And throughout Prohibition, getting a drink was as easy as patron-izing our several speakeasies or ordering directly from your favorite bootlegger. Why, down at Madden and Lewis's, they built the fast boats used by liquor agents *and* the fast boats used by the rumrunners. Herb Madden himself, the mayor of Sau-salito, was pinched for violating the Volstead Act.

But "sin" was a sideline compared to our true genius: cre-ating things almost magical out of nothing more than spare parts. Freestyle in found objects, the art of improvisation with odds and ends.

It began in Marinship, at the north end of town, where we were players on the world stage during the war, in case you didn't know. That's where we whipped the Axis practically sin-gle-handed while Maggie was still in pigtails and Will was nowhere near. Old-timers still shake their heads over Sausali-to's ragtag roll call to the war effort. The payrolls listed souls of every mongrel race and religion, color and citizenship—among them Annie Obedience and Cave Outlaw, Orange Mary Green and Empress Lovely, not to mention Early Pluck Buggs.

All of them hammering, riveting, and welding away at Liberty Ships and military craft at the unheard-of pace of a new christening every thirteen days. The war won, we Water Rats were left with acres and acres of Quonset huts, pilings and piers, mounds of abandoned metal and rusting odd-lot machinery.

What some saw as a godawful mess we saw as golden opportunity. Waterfront living for the taking, with the raw materials as plentiful as old growth redwood a century earlier. It may have started with that young couple and their baby who moved into the men's locker room of Building Number Three, near the launching quays. But before long others looked beyond the decommissioned shipyard to Richardson Bay itself. They simply took the next step—backwards, in evolutionary terms.

A homesteading rush to the sea. Anything that could float, or be floated, had potential.

As word got out that here in Sausalito was a cheap, easy, and accommodating life that rode the tides, our houseboat community was born. Joining those of us who fished, crabbed, oystered, clammed, gathered abalone, built boats, repaired boats, sewed sails, or worked in other maritime trades were … well … folks even more strange than those hired on during wartime. These new arrivals were free to do damn near anything they pleased. In no time at all, to the Hillclimbers' growing alarm, our Water Rat population swelled. Sausalito became the thriving artist colony it is to this day. We attracted bohemians and beats, drifters and tramps, free thinkers and fringe thinkers, homosexuals and Negroes, troubadours, musicians, poets.

And most of these found their place on the water. A kind of functional anarchy came to be, in which a natural order predominated. Normal rules need not apply. Electricity, for instance, was often a "borrowed" commodity, the tangle of patched wiring a tribute to the make-do. Boats splayed on the water with little rhyme or reason, in all shapes and sizes, built of scrap or scrapped themselves—erstwhile lifeboats and trawlers, ferries and tugs, abandoned military craft. Spacious enough for a family of six to spread out below the water line, or so small a solitary occupant developed a permanent slouch while enjoying the comforts of a castaway. Utilitarian, rough-hewn shelters, or elaborate statements of art and whimsy christened THE OWL, DRAGON DEN, or TRAIN WRECK.

Like floating Gold Rush camps, there was room for everyone with grit to stick it out.

It did not end there. Look beyond the waterfront, out onto the bay itself, and behold. The anchor outs. An existence reduced to a vessel too non-seaworthy to travel, too seaworthy to sink … just yet … today.

Each one of them testament, you might say, to the buoyancy of the human spirit—though most, like Jake's SQUIRTLE, were just pretty damn sad. We watched their inhabitants row in on battered dinghies. Faces hidden but for sun-scorched noses under beards and bushy mustaches or wild woman tresses. Caps pulled low, dungarees worn white over bony behinds. They wore woolen gloves with fingertips snipped for a surer hold to their tenuous existence, long sleeves to ward off the chill rising from the water even in the heat of day.

Ashore, they tied up slowly, uncertain on unmoving territory. Retrieving a rusty bicycle to pedal off for flour, beans, cheap wine. Tramps, some would say. Water gypsies.

The ultimate Water Rats.

UP AT ARVIE Engstrom's, Maggie was intent on smoothing a blemish under the right cheekbone. Awake since first light spilled over East Bay, and after prying open a Puss 'n Boots for Fifa and wincing from the stench of pulverized fish first thing in the morning, she had crawled into paint-spattered

coveralls, corralled her hair inside a faded bandana, and ped-
aled her Schwinn from Galilee to Marinship like a ten-year-
old on the last day of school.

Now, safety goggles on, she was striking sparks with the
wire disk. Work nearly finished: a human-sized figure cast in
scavenged bronze from military surplus shell casings, abandoned ship's fittings, other nautical trash. An excellent likeness of that most alluring, most mystical of sea creatures, distant cousins to the libidinous sirens who bedeviled the great
Ulysses. Maggie liked the way the French said it—this was her
mama d'leau. Her mermaid. Arms outstretched, hair thick and
entwined like Maggie's own, tail curling delicately on a ped-
estal that mimicked the sea floor, while at her side an octopus
extended a shy tentacle toward a hand mirror resting on a small
treasure chest, apparently in need of a makeup check.

"How's she looking, Arv?" Goggles lifted to her forehead,
Maggie stepping back for an appraising once-over. Eyes glow-
ing even in the dust and dimness of Engstrom's workshop.
"Arv?"

The ginger-haired boat builder finally turned away from
the keel he was planing to cast a glance in the mermaid's direction. The bronze beauty did not look any different compared
to the last dozen times he was asked to pass judgment. Engstrom knew Maggie was stalling long past the time her creation should be launched. "Like a dime in a room fulla nick-
kels," came his dry reply.

"Oh, c'mon, Arv." Maggie persisted. "Put down that tool,
come take a real look. Your honest opinion."

The old man, creased as mud flats at low tide, aimed puckery
eyes in Maggie's direction. They reminded her of twin chicken
butts. Ambling over to the *mama d'leau,* he pretended to look
her up and down, a hand appraisingly stroking his billy goat's
whiskers. He made thinking noises. He leaned in, as if to inspect
the detail. Stepping back finally, he said not a word.

"Well ...?"

"*Ja*, by d'soul of my mother who brung me into da world, you caught 'er, Mag. But what's dat?" A bony finger pointing.

Maggie beamed. "Her birthmark!"

Engstrom eyes widened to reveal crescents like milky new moons.

"At the No Name, she leaned in real close over the bar and she giggled and told me about it, told me it was right there where you see it."

"Joose like da old carrot and onions?"

"Just like Buck's, that's what she said. On her sixth margarita she dragged me into the ladies'. And bingo—right between her titties just like this. We bust a gut when she squeezed them together and it looked like Buck himself was rooting around in there."

Engstrom's narrow shoulders shook like a marionette on strings.

Satisfied now, Maggie threw a tarp over her three month's hard work. At least it was a job for pay: half a thou down, four and a half to come. Serious money. And like a serious artist, she was ready to deliver as promised. To Luann Buckworthy, her patron, whose mythical likeness was a birthday surprise for her husband.

Luann was a former Southern sorority princess, and now was the sun-speckled queen of the most gaudacious estate on the fashionable Hillclimber "Banana Belt" above the center of town. She doused herself in so much cologne not even Maggie could catch her true scent. Husband H.L. "Buck" Buckworthy, crew cut and stout, was twenty-five years her senior.

The Buckworthys were recently arrived from Loredo, and we couldn't figure out why. They were not your garden variety of Hillclimber, no wilting gardenias but thorny succulents with a single gorgeous blossom, namely Luann. Wily and irascible Buck Buckworthy, true to his name, had recently amassed a goodly fortune. From a barn full of Mexicans in Ciudad Juarez who mass-produced untold numbers of his patented Bible Belt®, advertised exclusively on religious radio. By simply depressing a tiny button on the Texas-sized buckle, a "shadow miracle" was cast onto the nearest wall, automobile dashboard, or large household appliance. The Virgin of Guadeloupe model was extremely popular in the Buckworthy's south Texas, and the vast market south of the Rio Grande hadn't even been tapped yet.

Maggie caught whiff of Buck right away: unmistakably, bacon grease with undertones of doused charcoal. She met them both soon after their arrival in town, when they chartered Captain Roy's DOUBLE DARE to fish for king salmon at the Duxbury Reef off Bolinas. The swells ran to fifteen feet that day, but Buck would not be deterred. His complexion got even greener when Luann hooked the prize catch, and he grumbled she was "some kinda sea creature" herself to outshine her sugar daddy.

To which Luann burbled right back, "Why, Buck honey, I thought you knew. Before I fell for you and the Lone Star State, Mama was one of them half-human, half-fish things. Don't tell me you ain't seen the scales on my precious butt!"

Luann Buckworthy, mistaking her husband's snort for approval and having no bounds to her own vanity, decided something then and there. This fetching young woman who was baiting their hooks said she was a painter and sculptor, so why not let Maggie immortalize her? A man-mesmerizing mermaid likeness of herself, in weighty bronze no less, would be the perfect gift for her all-mighty Buck, and the crowning touch for their splendiferous home.

And that unique birthmark? Call it a touch of whimsy, a note of realism, an irresistible anatomical imperative. Call it whatever you want—it was the artist and not the model who decided she must render Buck's unremarkable boner every inch as *faithfully* as Luann's beauty queen figure.

This very special *mama d'leau*, Maggie decided, would not be complete without it. And when Maggie decided on something, that's the way it would be.

13.
The Earth Moves

I CAN FEEL IT—IT IS COMING.

Aye. Being freed from the human corpus does it, I'll wager.

Spirits are closer to the source of all things.

If you say so. I'm still waiting for this source to show His so-called self.

He is asleep.

Who, the Creator?

The human. The one who makes his cooking fire in your shack. Should we warn him?

Let him be. The shack'll hold, I'm sure of that as of my name.

IT FELT AS if someone had grabbed hold of the earth's crust and was snapping it. Like it was some sandy beach towel.

At eleven past noon, Pacific Time, a "moderate" earth-quake measuring five point nine on the Richter Scale sent tremblers in concentric waves from an epicenter ninety-odd miles northeast of Sausalito. The Earthquake Shack rolling lightly, a small boat at anchor. One-Eyed George rocketing off the Boardwalk in alarm.

Up on the Hill, where Bel and Jake were in the act of lib-erating the ancient Farnsworth from the rectory of Star of the

Sea, Bel's eyes went white as coconut cream. Onto the pavement went the heavy walnut console, smashing its vacuum tubes and twelve-inch screen. Later, this would provoke Mephisto to inform Bel his brain was "puny as a neutrino," as if he had any idea what that was. As punishment, Bel was made to swallow several of the Army's little pink pills. But the experiment proved a bust. To Mephisto's dismay, instead of turning Bel *verrückt*, the big guy only yawned. Then he pulled off most of his clothes and circled like a cat curling into sleep.

At Juanita's, a frightened cook spilled a steaming pot of tamales, scalding his legs and ankles, as stacks of dishes slid off shelves and all manner of ingredients tumbled from the kitchen larder. In Galilee Harbor, houseboats whipsawed in their moorings, rocking and colliding with their floating neighbors and tied-off dinghies, dories, and work rafts.

All around town we were shocked into silence and stopped whatever we were doing. Wax figures who melted with relief when the waves passed by, grateful for only a messy clean-up and not a catastrophe.

Damage may have been light, but it was not without serious consequence. A few boats away from Maggie, old Bunda, a gnomish sail maker who was recovering from a broken hip, fell victim to a violent slosh of a neighboring roof-top bath tub. Strange as it sounds, the spill setting off a tragic chain reaction that resulted in a cast-iron pig being catapulted across six feet of bay.

The forty-pound porker, a scavenged relic that moments earlier had been in peaceful repose on a two-by-six supported on sawhorses, managed, by the precise hydrodynamic impact of the tub overflow, to fly in a high arc and crash through the window by the convalescent's bed. The blow rendered Bunda unconscious, and a shower of glass daggers left him bleeding. No one thought to check on him for hours afterwards.

Instead, Officer Mack responded to a call for assistance

from a panicky woman in the Banana Belt, her pet rhesus monkey having fled a balcony to a large persimmon tree. There it screamed and pelted neighbors with rock-hard orangy missiles.

Will, waking at half past two, wondered why his picture frames were listing to starboard and in a tiny tide pool next to his fish tank there was a lifeless yellow tang.

14.
Varda the Greek

"**T**AKE ME WITH YOU."

"Where?"

"On a dive."

"You mean a rescue? A search?"

"Why not?

"Don't think so."

"And why not?"

"It's not like that."

"Like what?"

"Like tourists diving to see pretty fish."

They were dining by candlelight, just the two of them, looking out to the indigo bay. Pinpricks of illumination silhouetted the Bay Bridge and San Francisco.

"The switch for the city lights is over there," Will told her when they first sat down. "Sometimes I leave them on all night."

Maggie laughed despite, maybe because of, his hokeyness. She liked that he was showing off. In fact, she liked everything about him tonight. His seducer's supper of Dungeness, wild asparagus and watercress with a chilled Sonoma white. The papery bougainvillea of a lurid magenta and the ivory of angel's trumpet blossoms from just outside the shack, the melt-in-your-mouth jazz trio softly circling the turntable. She read female significance into it all, and it was adding up to a sum far greater than a stopover to grab him for a hike on Mt. Tam or to drop off his Bulova left behind at her place. Something much more than *her* cooking for *him* while Fifa pointedly shunned the male intruder.

As the aromas swirled around her, Maggie luxuriated in the attentions of a man who had apparently figured out the way to her heart was through her nose.

"Not every guy knows his way around a saucepan," she had said, honestly curious. A baker at age eight, he told her matter-of-factly—since his first lumpy jelly roll oozed his grandma's berry preserves. And by ten the one who fixed dinner for his younger brother and sis after his mom had to get a job.

An opening, she thought with pleasure. He's letting me in. "And why what that?"

"Dad was sick."

"Oh."

"Head case."

"Oh, my."

"Yeah, watch out. Runs in the family."

"Should I be scared?"

"Sure," he said with a tight grin, in a way she read as reluctance to say much more.

"Okay, so I'll go on more practice dives with you first."

He was staring out at the night now.

Maggie shivered a little. The Toasted Cheese Man was a challenge. A mystery ship come to port. The scope of his rode greater than most and set for riding out a storm, not calm anchorage. But even more than before, she wanted permission to come aboard.

She looked around, taking in what he chose to live with. Everywhere there was the sea. An antique diver's helmet, brass boaty things, conchs and chambered nautili, a brain coral big enough to fill the skull of a baby whale, salvaged bits encrusted with barnacles and rust. But most impressively, the hundred gallon saltwater tank—lit like a drive-in movie to showcase Technicolor hues not native to these dark northern waters. Will, returning his glance to his dinner partner and seeing her interest, recited their names: queen angelfish, bluehead wrasse, honey damselfish, spotted drum, scrawled filefish, trunkfish.... Loners. Hiders. Darters. Pairs in perfect unison staring at who knew what through glassy eyes, self-absorbed. A world apart.

Maggie asking him the obvious: why this fascination below sea level? The right question, as it turned out.

"The pure wonder of it," he told her, pouring wine into her glass and then refilling his own. "The completely different feel of it—the light diffuse and layered, like you're sliding down the evolutionary ladder into a lost world with different rules, creatures and plants living by different instincts."

Sipping the wine, all at once she felt intoxicated.

"Starting as a kid I loved the water. We lived by Lake Erie, and in the summers—hot, muggy like a steam bath—I lived in the lake. It sucked me in and kept me there, day after day." His words began to spill out in a rush. "It's big. That surprises people who've never seen the Great Lakes before. Nothing on the horizon but water. Usually it's not wild or dangerous like in saltwater, but there's lots more than just pan fish in it. Ancient-looking things, gar and Northern pike. It can sure fire up a kid's imagination, I learned that. You can dream of real adventures on that lake. I'd find things other swimmers lost and pretend they were pirate treasure. Beer bottles were pirate grog. I had this cheap mask and flippers, and even when the water was so murky after a summer storm, I practiced holding my breath and feeling my way along. I got so I could stay down a full five minutes. I'd totally forget there was any other reality except underwater."

He noticed Maggie's unfocused gaze, taking her wooziness for lack of interest. "I felt more at home in the water, that's all," he concluded too brusquely. "I still do."

Hearing the change in his voice, she struggled for a coherent question, but before she could say anything, he rose from his chair and extended a hand in her direction. She was startled, not sure what was coming next. "Valhalla for dessert?"

Nodding dumbly, she took his hand and managed a smile. Into a night turned cool and gusty, they made the short stroll along the boardwalk arm in arm, their world seemingly restored to balance and harmony.

Just inside the Valhalla, Will nodded to Sally Stanford perched on her antique dental chair at the end of the long bar. They settled into high-backed bar chairs. Will ordering a Tom Collins, Maggie asking for the dessert tray, craving something sweetly aromatic and gooey. She was feeling better after the night air but not up to another drink.

"So why not take me on a real dive soon," she started in again. She was stubborn, but it was the alcohol talking, betraying her desire to show him she was capable of holding her own in his world.

"Come on, Mag," he protested again. "I trained for this and have years of experience. In these waters—"

"*Bon sôir, cheris!* How's my favorite neighbor!" At the unmistakable voice, they turned like seagulls to the sun. Her radiance was refracted through cut crystals that dangled from her piled-up hair, her earlobes, her chins and swollen bodice—a magnificent human chandelier. A cigarette jutted from a mother of pearl holder clasped in stained teeth. Tucked behind one ear was a delicate yellow hyacinth.

"Hi, Sal." It was "Miss Stanford" to most. Will was one of few granted use of her first name, even though it was only one of many aliases over a long life begun as plain vanilla Marcia Owen.

"Hello, Miss Stanford," said Maggie.

"Such wonderful hair." Sally reached out to run a manicured hand through Maggie's tangles. Maggie smelled violets and sour milk. "When you gonna come work for me, honey?"

"I'm plenty busy, Miss Stanford. Thanks, though."

Sally Stanford gave the professional smile. Her eyes were dark coals. Will watched with amusement, guessing not even this famously steely lady would bend Maggie to her way. Sally returned her gaze to him. "Had your friends from up the hill in tonight, Will."

He grinned. "Buy them a round on me?"

"Didn't have to. They were being romanced by a big shot I never seen before. Cleaned me out of Chateau Margaux and went through a whole bottle of Louie the Thirteenth—what they poured down their throats could feed a family of four, bless their pickled gizzards." Crystallized light sparked off her like fireworks.

"Then the big shot tried swiping my ashtray, said he collected them from the best dinner houses in the world. He wanted to put mine next to Galatoire's from down in New Aw-leans."

"Big mistake," said Will. "What did it cost him?"

"Ten bucks, on principle. I told him the check's the only thing you get at no extra charge with Valhalla written on it." She cackled, a smug brood hen. "I *love* this business, don't you know."

"And them. What's their business, if you could tell?" asked Maggie.

"Tell? These eyes and ears don't miss much, my dear. Those boys were trying to be hush-hush, but they were so full of themselves a deaf mute would've caught the drift. They were carrying on about some project they're planning."

"Here in town?" Will wanted to know.

"Near as I could tell. Has to do with a pier. A big one."

"A pier?" said Maggie, puzzled. "We've got plenty of those already. What kind of pier?"

Sally Stanford sent her painted eyebrows skyward and slid her cigarette holder between her ruby painted lips. She took a deep puff from the glowing Galloise and exhaled as if the answer would win her a prize.

WILL WAS STILL pecking at Sally's crumbs but finding the platter littered with the indigestible stones of memory.

He and Maggie walked together on Bridgeway, chilled by the rush of air streaming from the Headlands. Saying little but holding hands. Maggie stealing glances toward him, trying to sniff out his mood. Will's eyes were downcast, his thoughts obviously elsewhere.

His past was welling to the surface like a frogman's bubbles: *Pickle as he loved her in the beginning ... that sweet feeling of having escaped the old man's grasp ... his mother, wan and stricken, still loving the bastard at the funeral ... Pickle, collapsed at his feet ... Ariel ... Ariel.*

Another drink. Another drink, he thought. *I need another damn drink.*

Knowing what he really wanted was to feel the strong gravitational pull of the woman beside him now—the one who was beginning to hope for more, much more, than last call at the No Name.

The gusts quieted past the Trident. They crossed at Princess by Purity Market, passing the bank, the city hall. "Hey," said Maggie, breaking the silence. "It's Bunny night."

Just ahead, Bunny's floppy pink ears and sallow face were bathed in a flickering glow. As he did every Saturday night, he was stationed in front of the Sylvanias and RCAs in the window of Borden's, the appliance store. When they neared, Will saw the words *Playboy's Penthouse* across the multiple screens as if through a fly's eye. A skittery saxophone and trumpet played tag through a small speaker under the eaves. They joined Bunny in watching the fuzzy images in black and white until Maggie finally said in a loud stage whisper, "Have you met our new neighbor? This is Will Du—"

Bunny flapped an arm to silence her. At that moment Hef was clutching pipe and martini glass, telling Belafonte, Lenny Bruce, and some author or other about the sign on the door to his Chicago mansion. "The Latin reads '*si non oscillas, noli tintinnare.*' I translate that to 'if you don't swing, don't ring.'" The author smirked and Belafonte showed avaricious white teeth.

"Bunny ..." Maggie persisted to no avail. He was entranced.

"We enjoy putting a little mood music on the phonograph," Hef was saying, "and inviting in a female acquaintance for a quiet discussion on Picasso, Nietzsche, jazz ... sex."

"Wow. Nietzche," murmured Bunny.

"What a phony," said Maggie.

Bunny hissed at her. "If you can't dig it," he said without taking his eyes from the broadcast, "do me the courtesy of *amscraying*. Pronto."

RAUCOUS CHATTER AND the clinking of glass spilled onto the street even before they reached the No Name, and Will's faraway look began to dissolve. Maggie watched his expression lighten, his shoulders square. As they passed through the open doors, barroom bedlam wrapped around them like sweaty flesh. The slam and shouts of liar's dice. Chairs scraping the plank floors, empty bottles being tossed aside by the bartender, who was busily pulling good steam beer and pouring indifferent tequila and vinegary jug wine. Will overheard snatches of impassioned declamations on the affairs of the day, politics, sexual prowess and preferences ... yes, even art and philosophy too. Beats the hell out of a pseudo-intellectual in a bathrobe, he thought to himself and grinned.

"Can we go after one?" Maggie asked. It was a statement more than a question. Her nasal sensors were on the edge of meltdown, and her stomach was doing somersaults.

The shout rang clearly over the clamor. "The goddess Artemis reincarnate! Your presence required over here, O mighty huntress!"

Without looking, they both knew the cry's originator. Jean Varda. Artist of renown and lightning rod for everything and everybody the Hillclimbers decried. And a famed attractant of women, many of them daughters of the Hill. Maggie, who thought his secret must be his powerful blend of billy goat musk and dark chocolate, was one of the few local beauties not lured by his sticky charms—making her, of course, all the more desirable in his eyes. The rest were flies to his flypaper. But Varda was more than just a lady killer. He was a charmer of universal dimensions, and also infamous for the free-for-alls he called revelries and hosted on his salvaged ferry VALLEJO, which he shared with our resident Zen philosopher Alan Watts and his wife.

Varda sat at a table against a wood-paneled wall playing the part of the flamboyant peasant, his dark compact figure in pure white except for a Greek fisherman's cap and a chartreuse scarf looped around his neck. At his side was a bleary-eyed fly of about nineteen, her arms draped loosely about his shoulders and thick neck. Maggie and Will recognized his other companion, a hulking man with a full beard, as the actor Sterling Hayden, star of *The Asphalt Jungle* and *Johnny Guitar*, who lived aboard his schooner off the Johnson Street pier.

Hayden stared moodily into his Scotch as they approached, but Varda jumped to his feet, slipping the young woman's grasp, his arms outstretched.

"*Yassou! Kalispera!* Welcome to my humble orgy! Soon we will be sacrificing a virgin, if any can be found!"

Will noticed the look of adoration on the girl's face. Seeing his glance, Varda continued, "Will ... darling Maggie ... meet the delightful Kiki, who aspires to immortality upon the Mt.

Olympus of art. Alas, she has not tested positive for virginity, which is why I find her most irresistible."

A slack hand was extended. "Hi, y'all. Kiki Buckworthy."

"Related to Buck and Luann?" Maggie asked.

"Yup. Buck's mah uncle. I'm the daughter of big brother Earl."

"And what brings you to Sausalito, Miss Buckworthy?" Will's tone was decidedly riverboat gamblerish, but the girl didn't seem to notice.

"Shhhhh…." She motioned them closer. "Uncle Buck thinks I'm here just so Luann and me can ride those dumb little cable cars and shop at Gump's. But it's for his surprise party next week." She looked pleased to be revealing her secret.

"Then back home to lasso steer and ride wild broncs?"

"I might just stay a spell. Study under Mr. Varda here." She gave Varda's cheek a wet kiss. "You seen his work? Why, course you have!"

Hayden snorted in appreciation and began flicking a forefinger in time as he hummed Beethoven's "Ode to Joy."

"Why is that man doing that?" Kiki Buckworthy, who obviously did not recognize that there was a genuine celebrity at her table, wanted to know.

"Never mind him, dear one," said Varda. "He is a spoiled Hollywood ham who thinks the world must revolve around him. Your young brilliance outshines his fading light."

Hayden looked up. His eyes were glassy. "The only light emanating from you, Varda," intoned the trained voice, "is the flame shooting straight out your ass." He lifted his glass. "Nevertheless, I salute you as a great master of your art, the sculpting of bullshit."

Kiki Buckworthy, looking to Varda with alarm as if expecting a Western shoot-out, was startled to hear his loud hoot of approval and see him throw his arms in a bear hug around Hayden. "I am in love with this man!" Varda cried out. Then, seeing the girl's uncertain glance, he reassured her, "In my country, my resplendent rose, men embrace each other freely and express their mutual love without stigma. We Greeks invented brotherly love ... not to mention bisexuality."

Kiki Buckworthy smiled uneasily, feeling she was missing the joke and vaguely suspicious it was at her expense. "Time to get back to Uncle Buck's, I guess," she said. She stood up, a pout on her scarlet lips.

Removing his cap, Varda bowed low. "Excellent. You are a most promising student and will need a clear mind as we create together. Arrive at my studio tomorrow no earlier than noon. Wear few clothes." He winked at her, and she burst into a toothy smile, pleased to be the center of his universe again. Kiki Buckworthy wobbled off on her Western boots, turning to give him a little wave. Varda waved back.

"A tasty Texas squab, no?" he said when she was gone. "Tomorrow I will have her for lunch. With red wine."

He turned to Maggie. "Unless you are available, dear one. I still dream of mounting the summit of the gods." He glanced over at Will and winked. "Forgive my Greek boldness."

Maggie replied before Will could. "He doesn't decide my availability, Varda, I do. But I have my own project tomorrow. I'm learning to geld Greeks."

Varda grabbed his crotch and groaned in mock horror, as Hayden howled and said, "I always knew you'd make a damn fine castrato, Varda!"

"No, my friend. A Roman perversion, not Greek. We love our balls more than our music."

To Maggie he said, "Do me the great favor of falling asleep in that class."

Will was enjoying the verbal sparring yet wondered whether he should feel more protective toward her. Varda was harmless but ... this evening was not turning out how he imagined, even if he was not really sure what he wanted exactly. Sensing it was time to do more now than play bystander, he ventured, "I'd be careful with that Buckworthy girl, Varda. You know about prairie oysters? Texans eat them."

"Thoroughly disgusting," Varda declared.

"Happens in Hollywood every day," said Hayden. "They've got man-eating agents and ball-busting studio bosses. Not to mention ex-wives—"

Suddenly all conversation was eclipsed by a roar, followed by an engine noisily sputtering out. Blue exhaust rose toward the tin ceiling. Heads turned to see Mephisto climbing slowly from his Indian Chief, which had come to rest at the end of the bar. He extended a leather-clad arm, and Marilyn Macaw hopped from the handlebar to make her way to his shoulder. Scanning the barroom, he seemed about to head in the direction of Varda's table when he wheeled abruptly and settled onto a bar stool instead, turning his back to the tables. Will watched as the bartender scolded him for his entrance.

Hayden glanced briefly at Mephisto's dark form at the bar and then returned his gaze to the tiny ice floe in his drink. "Cheap Brando," he muttered.

Varda looked at Hayden but said nothing. But a few minutes later when Hayden growled, "Time to walk my lizard," and rose to make his way through the maze of tables, Varda nodded toward the bar and leaned in. "Bad blood, if you cannot tell," he told Will and Maggie. "Sterling and Mephisto, they are like brothers who end up hating each other." Maggie reacted as if this was old news, but it was the first Will had heard of it.

"Mephisto won't forgive him for testifying to that creep McCarthy," she told Will.

"No, not quite, my sweet," Varda corrected her. "It was Senator McCarthy who cost Mephisto his job, so I have heard, when Eisenhower ran Columbia University and he knuckled under to the evil drunkard from Wisconsin who saw a pinko grading every math exam. Both our friends, like most of us, thought bolshevism was about social justice then, but what Mephisto can't forgive is that Hayden panicked. During the witch hunt. He fingered others in Hollywood to save himself."

"You mean to the Un-American Activities Committee?" asked Will. "I remember Ronald Reagan and Orson Welles testifying, but not anything—"

"Shush, he comes." Varda sprang to his feet again, holding out his coat as if he was a matador awaiting the bull.

"Your skinny ass ain't worth goring," snarled Hayden upon his return.

Maggie felt sober now, and suddenly very tired.

"Hey," she interrupted, "Will fixed me a great dinner, and I think he needs to tuck me into bed." Looks passed between the men, which irritated her somewhat, so she said to Will, "Are we going, or should I sleep with my cat?"

Will turned to Varda and Hayden and shrugged. "Duty calls, I guess," he said. "Sorry, guys." Knowing it was not the right thing to do or right thing to say. Hearing his words as if some stranger was delivering them.

Maggie reacted without thinking. She leaned toward him and slapped him. Hard. Then she got up from the table and began to walk out, not looking back.

Will sat motionless and watched her go. He was angry but not at her. Why had he said what he did? Why had he let her disappear into the night like a squandered fortune? *What's wrong with me? She's what I want, isn't she? But I push her away. Why? Because—because I can't—*

Trying to figure it out made him feel no better.

Varda stared at him as if he was crazy. "I will see you at Bunda's funeral tomorrow, will I not?" he asked quietly.

15.
The Morning After

HEEDLESS OF ALL HUMAN FOLLY PERPETRATED DURing the previous planetary spin, dawn showed up right on cue. In her houseboat Maggie was hidden under blankets, oblivious to Fifa curled by her head. In the Earthquake Shack Will was finally in deep sleep after waking in a sweat, cruelly sober, thinking he heard noises—thumps, maybe shouts—and then being unable to sleep again while the previous evening replayed in his head.

In his tiny New Town apartment Bunny had not slept at all. He was wide awake and pining. He had written love letters before, but this one he planned to mail in an envelope marked PERSONAL AND CONFIDENTIAL....

Dear Hef,

You are very busy at the mansion, I know, being hip and generaling your empire. But if you could just get to know me, I am sure you would like me as much as I like you. At risk of seeming stuck up, some people say I'm adorable!

I know what you look like, I see you on TV all the time! Ha ha!

On my recent trip to your Chicago, I so badly wanted to introduce myself to you. Obviously, my hopes were ix-nayed. I won't even BEGIN to recount the uncouth behavior exhibited towards me by a few of your employees. I'm

*not the kind to get anyone in trouble, but you would be
very ashamed of them, take it from me.*

*Hef, I have a very important question just for you. You
love bunnies and rabbits, but could you ever love a man
whose name is Bunny and who always, always wears bunny
ears like the ones in your Playboy clubs? I hope so!*

Cause guess what? It's me!

*Don't ever change, and on your chain of life, please
consider me a link! Write back!*

Love, Bunny

*P.S., I can't wait to share my thoughts on Picasso and other
important subjects! And when you see Sammy Davis Jr.,
tell him for me—he's tops!*

BEL, AS USUAL, was up with first light. Showering, like always
when his momma turned him out and he bunked with Jake on
THE SQUIRTLE, at the foot of the Napa Street pier in Galilee
Harbor. This open-air facility—a rust-speckled water heater
and salvaged plumbing running on pirated water and electricity—was shared by houseboat dwellers, drifters, and the
anchor outs. Its illegality, not to mention the public nudity, was
a perennial cause for outcry from the Hill, yet even the most
priggish of the hillside social set admitted this arrangement
was preferable to the spectacle of Bel and the others splashing
in the Spanish-style fountain at the center of town.

Which he still did with regularity anyhow.

The sun on this early morning was unusually hot and
brilliant, and it bathed Bel's ebony form in a white glow, the
trickle of water from the showerhead throwing off a slice of
misty rainbow. He cranked off the water. The rainbow vanished. Slowly and deliberately he dried himself with a tea towel
borrowed from someone's clothesline. He looked like a hip-
popotamus with a hanky.

Singing softly to himself, he filled gaps with lyrics of his own invention. "Someplace ova the rainbow, way up high, I know dere is a … hmmm … waitin' in the sky…. Someplace ova the rainbow, who knows why—"

"Right here is perfect."

"Careful, Buckworthy, we don't want word out yet."

"Don't worry. Them dopers ain't up, Mr. Bogart. Not these Commie artsy types. Not till past noon, when they get up to pee in the bay and before goin' back to their fornications. 'Scuse mah French."

Bel instinctively ducking for cover at the sound of voices not resident to the harbor. Trying to make sense of the words, failing miserably, thinking they must be important somehow, telling himself to ask someone with a brain bigger than a neutrino what they meant.

Not Bunny. Not Jake.

Someone like Mephisto. He would know.

16.
Duty Does Call

FORTUNATE, YOU HAVING LOVED ONES TO MOURN YOUR passing.

You also were missed, Malachy. You have said so.

'Tis true. Yet nearly, it was not. Have you forgotten?

You forget, Malachy. I am a spirit like you, but I am a young girl's spirit. Tell me again. Even our shaman's stories did not cast your spell.

Mi-Wash, upon occasion I do thank whatever Higher Power may be responsible for our cohabitation.

Even trickster Coyote?

Even him, aye. So … I had just escaped the brigands and drunken whores at the Mint.

Yes, begin there.

Me and the piano, we came at last to Mrs. Billingham's, the boardinghouse at Fourth and Mission where I lodged, and it were a total shambles. The fires raged in nearly every direction. And I were exhausted already—uphill in any direction was out of the question. I decided to follow Mission in a westward direction, cross Market to the flats, and head for the Golden Gate Park.

You would not let go of your music box.

Not till my life depended on it. And soon it did on that day, as you should recall, but I'll remind you I also survived crazed steers charging in panic, corpses littering the streets—human and animal—and the wounded pleading for rescue but buried so deep under timber and stone a crew of ten stout men would take hours to free them. One poor devil beseeched me, Finish it! For God's sake, kill me! I couldn't do it, but he wouldn't have been the first snuffed out from pity. There was hundreds chloroformed and shot at Mechanic's Hall when the flames came knocking. They was all too hurt to be moved. I nearly got caught myself by the Ham and Eggs Fire.

Wait, Malachy ... what?

'Twas started, they say, by a mother cooking breakfast for her family. They was giving thanks for their home being unscathed. But there were an unseen breach in the chimney, lurking like Lucifer, and when it caught the timbers of this house, soon the whole of Hayes Valley were done for.

So you pushed your music box faster, as fast as a deer?

More like a much belabored ox ... till I heard the shout. You there! Halt or you're dead!

Aiiiiee!

Picture it, lass. On the first day a hundred thousand was reduced to the clothes on their backs and whatever pitiful possessions they could drag or carry. Mister Mayor Eugene Schmitz, the filthy scoundrel and baton waver, ordered looters shot on sight. But the militiamen sent by Governor Pardee, they was the worst of the looters, drunk on pilfered booze and killing for sport. General Funston's regular soldiers was little better. Anyone, man or woman, found with a necklace or earring in his pocket was assumed guilty. Bodies lay everywhere placarded "shot for stealing." Others was gunned down for not clearing rubble from the street or refusing to carry a hose. So there was I, facing this farm lout with a flattened nose who stood no more than twenty paces away with the barrel of his carbine leveled at my head. Well, you can imagine my heart were in my stomach—

He did not shoot you?

I could see his trigger finger twitching. I quick blurted out, 'Tis mine, the piano! I'll prove it. His eyes got big. I could see he was terrified as me. Be quick about it, he said. Or I'll nail ya good.

The music box did belong to another.

Course it did—to damned Bassity! But this was my mortality on the line, so what was I to do? I'll tell you what. I threw myself at the keyboard and into a double-time rendition of "Wait Till the Sun Shines, Nellie." And when the lout didn't lower his cannon, I pounded out "It's a Hot Time in the Old Town Tonight." I flashed him my pearly whites, like he were Caruso or Charley Crocker. I could almost see the gears working in his hayseed head, and finally … slowly … he lets the carbine droop. I say, Am I free to go, soldier? And he looks me square in the eye and snarls, What's the serial number of that there pie-ano! My heart stopped in its tracks. Tears welled into my eyes. I must have been babbling. Then the dunderhead lets out a jackass bray and stumbles off.

THE TELEPHONE JANGLED a very long time. Will's head feeling roughly the size of the Farallons when finally he answered.

The grim voice at the other end was to the point. Lake Tahoe, fishing party struck by lightning, vessel burned and sank, a dozen missing, plane waiting in Novato.

Will checked his Timex. Seven-thirty.

On his way out of town at quarter to eight, he passed Galilee Harbor and saw a flash of someone under the communal shower. Then he remembered again the mess he had made with Maggie and vowed to make things right when he got back. There was still time to clear his head while he sped past Mill Valley, Larkspur, then San Rafael and hillsides dotted with cattle already grazing the dry grasses and horses in dusty corrals and ranch buildings sheltered behind sprawling oaks. More time as the small aircraft nimbly eased off the ribbon of macadam and gained altitude to cross the Sierra on a course almost due east.

What better vantage point to seek perspective than this, high above a cottony archipelago of white?

Memories, as usual, came with a mind of their own. He was eight years old again, when Leo the brawler taught him to fight. His father on his knees, lacing up boxing gloves and showing him the crouch, how to feint with his left, sneak in with a right cross.

"Go for just right of my nose, boy," he dared his elder son. "Like you're punching right through my head, at someone in back of me." Leo pulled in his hands and elbows, as if to protect himself. "Go on, hit me hard—if you can."

Will felt hollowness in his stomach. He felt a fear of failure and of success.

When he landed the blow, he watched in amazement the thin trickle of red onto Leo's white undershirt. Watched as his father rose unsteadily to his feet. Had he been fast and lucky or did he deliberately let him in? Will dropped his gloved hands and stood frozen, staring up at the man who up until that moment had been as invincible as Kong. And he saw something new in those eyes—what? Astonishment, anger ... doubt?

Leo cocked a glove, and for a moment Will was sure his father would hit back. He braced for the blow.

It never came.

That was the first time Will realized he might win.

After that he stood up to him. Not with fists. On his own terms. In that respect, as in most everything else, he was a disappointment to his father. But by then he had perfected the knack of closing a door inside his head and insulating himself from the pain—his mother's, his brother's, his sister's, and his own. His father got worse by the year, sinking more deeply into his Stroh's and his mental sinkhole. But Will knew now what to do when attacked. He took it and fought back with stony silences. The attacks became less frequent and then stopped. All the same, he pleaded with his mother to leave her miserable excuse for a husband and father. Tearfully, she would promise and then relent.

Now he saw his mother's plight more clearly, at least. She bore the burden of a Catholic upbringing, and women don't leave marriages easily. She thought what she was doing, or not doing, best for her soul and her children. And after all, she still loved him. The high school sweethearts were riding it out no matter what. Looking back, Will saw again how he had distanced himself. Distanced himself, to be honest, from all conflicts, even when confronting them was the right course for putting a stop to them before they escalated and aggregated to that point where there were no winners, only losers.

What am I but a loser, he said to himself. *I lost you, Ariel.* And Maggie? *Will I lose you too?* This time it was no easier to view things from a safe distance, as he did now, ten thousand feet above it all.

When the plane touched down at Truckee with a gust of blue smoke from the tires, it was nearly nine-thirty. Will piled his gear into the waiting pickup and made the driver stop at the nearest phone booth. He arranged for an outlandish bouquet to be sent to Maggie's houseboat with a card.

> DUTY REALLY DID CALL. AM IN TAHOE.
> FORGIVE ME. WILL.

WHEN THE DELIVERY came later that morning, Maggie found the jumble of scents so overwhelming they made her woozy all over again, just like the night before. Gathering up the flowers, she went straight to the French doors open at the stern, where she and Fifa watched the stems and loose petals drift aimlessly away on gently rippled water. She re-read the card and swiped at a hot tear.

THE MEMORIAL SERVICE and burial was conducted at Daphne Fernwood Cemetery on the apron of the Headlands. Maggie was late. Nodding and murmuring apologies as she worked her way toward the front. Tears escaping for the second time that day when she peered into the casket.

The undertaker had outfitted Bunda's shrunken body in a brocaded vest of old-fashioned Hungarian design, white silk shirt, and pleated striped trousers; at the center of his chest, above the sinewy hands of a sail maker, rested his best naval cap. Strewn about the body were offerings of affection and *bon voyage*. Stunted wildflowers from a coastal bluff. Kaleidoscopic bits of burnished beach glass. A tiny boat of carved driftwood with a linen triangle of sail.

But what got to her was the framed photo—a Bunda years younger, gesticulating wildly while umpiring a close play. It was a role he relished annually at the Labor Day picnic. It brought him such obvious joy despite his limited understanding of the great American pastime. "Oh," she gasped, recognizing herself as the adolescent standing awkwardly to the side, a bat slung over one shoulder. She had known the Bundas since childhood, and Magda Bunda, a tireless engine whom her husband would now join in the stony soil, was her baby-sitter.

A sudden writhe of wind worked loose a lock of Bunda's colorless hair. Leaning closer, Maggie rearranged it and lightly touched his shoulder. He smelled of radish even in death. She stepped back and shivered. Drawing her woolen shawl more tightly to her, reproaching herself for not anticipating the chill of Tennessee Valley in November.

Now she gasped and murmured "Oh!" again. Next to the dead man, in a rough wooden box painted a shocking fuchsia, lay the perpetrator. Atop a bed of straw, there was the iron pig. Someone had tied a black ribbon around its neck and placed a purple blossom between its hams. She frowned, speechless.

"Fitting, *nicht war?*" Mephisto had appeared noiselessly at her side. For the occasion he wore a Harris Tweed with weathered elbow patches that might have been swiped from the cloakroom of the Bodleian. "Completely *richtig* that this exemplar of Newton's Third Law of Motion be interred alongside the unlucky target."

"I—"

"I view it as dialectical, in the Hegelian sense of the realization of a concept being fulfilled by its opposite. That is to say, motion begetting the absolute repose of the grave."

"Um," she managed.

"It was my idea but Alan who insisted. He imbues it with spiritual significance. To which I reply, the square root of the square of a number always equals twice its absolute value. *Lächerlichen.* Poppycock. In case you were wondering."

Maggie turned to face him. Before she could come up with any sort of reply, there was a hand on her arm. "Varda," she said with relief.

"You are late. Come. I have saved you a place."

Alan Watts stood between the two caskets and faced those assembled to see off their neighbor and the killer pig made of pig iron. It was a big turnout. The Bundas emigrated as newlyweds from a tiny village on Lake Balaton and had lived and worked on the waterfront since before the Depression. Dr. Watts lifted an open palm above his head for attention as a cherry-scented smoke signal swirled up from his briar. "Dear friends," he began, in the modulated voice of the Anglican minister he was until turning to the pursuit of Zen. "I see you standing there in sorrow over the loss of this good man. That is to be expected. Times such as these call into question the very nature of things. In fact, today we ask about the nature of

Nature herself. Her seemingly random act, an earthquake, setting in motion events doing fatal harm to a man already infirm from age and injury. To add insult to this fate, the engine of his destruction is a pig. A pig! Or the likeness of a pig, at any rate, which likeness had heretofore exhibited the essence of pigness—stubbornness, inertia, resistance to movement and change. And yet move it did. Change it did. This pig soared! This pig flew! This pig became, in its essence, more bird than pig. Then, crashing to earth, it became a missile, an asteroid fallen from its orbit as if old Bunda were the last dinosaur and his extinction was necessary to advance the Age."

Varda leaned closer to Maggie and whispered, "Where is Will? Why is he not here?"

"Ask him." The words rang more loudly and sharply than she intended.

"I cannot. He is not here."

"Shhhh!" came a voice from behind. Maggie turned to see a reproving look from an elderly Chinese woman she recognized from a laundry in New Town. She mimed an apology.

"So you see," Dr. Watts was saying now, "everything changes and yet everything stays the same. Change and connection. Change and connection is where it's at. We all change and we are all connected with everything else that is. Bunda … the pig … all of us. We are, each one of us, a separate planet—yet we are also at one with all the other planets, all the other galaxies, to the Milky Way and beyond. Our orbits may change. We may change. But still we are part of the whole. And in knowing this, we never die. We are the eternal thing that comes and goes … that appears now as Bunda, now as the pig, now as Alan Watts. And so it goes, forever."

A child's voice asked from the back of the chapel, "Mommy, do I have to be a pig?" A wave of titters rolled through the mourners, and Dr. Watts grinned widest of all.

"Have faith, young lady," he said. "You know what faith

is, don't you?"

She did not answer and neither did anyone else.

"Faith is not hanging on at all cost to whoever you are or whatever you have, like a drowning man. It's being open to whatever happens. Relax. Be in the moment. Maybe the life of a pig can be a gas. Think of all the mud you can play in!"

Dr. Watts outstretched his arms. "Now let us return these two souls to the dirt so they can have some fun together."

Relax, thought Maggie as she was furiously pedaling her bicycle back home.

17.
Luann Unveiled

SEVEN MORE DAYS LAPSED. A WEEK IN WHICH WEIGHTY matters transpired: births, deaths, milestones of athletic, scholarly, and scientific pursuits, disasters of man and the natural world, heroic and unspeakable acts in the name of God, glory, and tribe. And in Sausalito, our Hillclimbers nibbled at canapés, sipped their martinis and brandy alexanders, and gave Maggie the back of their hand.

Will knocked timidly on DHARMA's door. He had heard the whole sordid story from Hayden, who had been a glittery extra at the Buckworthy soiree. How a *Who's Who* of the Hill surrounded the shrouded surprise. How they gasped and whispered exclamations at the unveiling, then turned to watch the birthday boy go from tinkled pink to *el toro* red as he zeroed in on what was so faithfully revealed for all the world to see.

The swollen bronze titties were scandalous enough, but Luann's most distinctive birthmark! As clear and unmistakable as one of Buck's Bible Belt® miracles!

The wounded beast roared, and Luann dissolved into tears, followed by her pitiable protests of not having laid eyes on the foul and satanic obscenity until the very moment of the unveiling. She certainly hadn't intended *this* repulsive thing, and damn to hell those godless lowlifes who call themselves artists in our wonderful town. "The whole pack of 'em deserve to be stomped like filthy *cucarachas*," she had declared.

Will knocked again, louder. He called to her.

"In here," came a small voice from inside.

"Mag, it's me."

"I smelled you."

"Can I come in?" She said nothing, and he was unsure what to do next.

"Okay."

He found her sitting on the pull-down bunk, hugging the bedcovers. Dishes piled high in the wash basin, but he saw she had been working on a new canvas. It sat on an easel near the French doors and its mood was decidedly gloomy. He guessed it was some kind of self-portrait. Clothing was strewn over the plank floor and dangled tenuously from lamp shades and a small sky-hopping humpback on a shelf of her beachcombing finds—driftwood oddities, feathers and sea-sculpted stones, a leopard shark's jaw. Fifa leaped from the bed as he approached. Carefully, he sat on a corner near her feet.

"I just heard."

She looked away. "Good news travels fast."

"Maggie, I—"

"Got your flowers."

"I wondered."

"Threw them in the bay. One at a time."

"Oh." He stared at his shoes.

She turned to face him again, and he could see her eyes were wet. "I'm not mad anymore. At you anyways. I—I liked the card."

Will steeled himself to say what he had practiced so many times in Tahoe. "When I wrote I was sorry, I … oh, shit." His canned speech vanished as if into a fog bank. Now he had to feel his way along. "Plain and simple, I was an ass. Not the being sorry part. I mean, I behaved like one. It's so hard for me to explain because I don't get it myself." He looked at her hard. "Listen to me. You're the best thing in my life in a long,

long time, hands down." Something new came into his eyes
then, and she saw it. A plea. "But this is the best I can untan-
gle it. I feel you getting close and I want that. But there's a
switch in me wants to power down, a door that wants to slam
shut. Sweetheart, I swear—"

Maggie cut him off. "I don't want any promises, not now,"
she said. "And I don't feel like anybody's sweetheart. I'm too
pissed. And too sick and tired of being rejected. I'm a serious
artist, damn it! What did they expect, some piece of crap? I
don't do cutesy stuff that looks good next to the toilet paper
cozy."

He was feeling uneasy about how his apology had gone
down and he didn't know if it was a good thing her anger was
aimed away from him or not. "They're idiots," was all he could
think to say.

"And now she won't even pay me! Do you have any idea
how much time that thing took? How much the materials cost,
even if it's mostly scrap?"

"The hell with the Buckworthys," he said. "Two shit kick-
ers with money. Don't give them another thought."

"I want my sculpture back."

He straightened and tried to regain surer footing. "The last
thing they want is to keep it. They hate it."

"Yeah," she repeated miserably, "they hate it."

"Cheer up. They hate being the town joke even more, specially up on the Hill. I can't believe she let you get away with
showing her knockers."

At that she lunged, wrapping her arms in a vice grip around
his shoulders. He moved with her heaving sobs. He kissed her
wet cheeks, and then their mouths met and soon the sounds
of despair were replaced by small moans.

"I want to feel your cock inside me," she gasped then.

The intensity of her desire startled him, and he felt himself struggling against the magnitude of her pull. He fought

against this reluctance of his. Let go, he told himself. *Let go.* He wanted to unfold to her, to give her more than just what she dared ask for.

They made love recklessly at first, until she slowed them down. "Easy, go easy this time," she whispered to him. She asked him to look at her and not to close his eyes, and he watched her as she climbed to a glorious summit. Then he took his turn. Afterwards, believing they had ventured closer together than ever before, he fell effortlessly into a deep and sweet sleep.

Later, he woke wondering why. Why flee from this? Why not give in completely? He felt her warmth next to him, heard her light breathing. Outside, water slapped against the gentle sway of the houseboat. He exhaled slowly and fully. She had given him another chance—even if, for them both, lovemaking had also been a way to shut out the world, to soar above themselves and their unhappiness. Another promising beginning, that's all this counted as. He knew that. But when would he be ready to give himself to her for good?

Not yet, not nearly. His journey to where she called to him was not over. This he knew too.

"Where am I?" She sat up and the bedcovers slid from her. He found himself staring at the gentle curve of her spine, the smoothness of her back, the ripeness of her buttocks.

"Kidnapped to an undersea world."

She fell back and turned on her side to face him. Her breasts tumbled toward him and trembled with her heart beats. "And who are you?" she played along.

"Guess."

"A clue."

"We have sex for fun, like humans."

She bit lightly at his reawakening penis. "Too easy. But tell me, dolphin, do you ever have sex for love?"

"We are very loyal to our mate. You need more?"

Maggie shrugged and threw off the bedcovers. Padding to her refrigerator, she returned with Chablis. Then she rummaged through her jewelry box until finding a half-finished joint. As she did, Will was reminded that there existed no finer sight, at sea level or below, than a woman at ease with her nakedness.

A flick of a Zippo, a flash of yellow blue flame. Maggie leaned into it.

Before filling his lungs with the pot, Will chugged a mouthful of the wine and held it, then enjoyed the chill as it splashed down his throat. The combination renewing some of the delicious euphoria of before.

He passed the joint back to Maggie, who took another hit but did not inhale as deeply as him or hold it as long. Her wine glass rested on a window ledge, still half full. Her eyes were calmly on him as if gauging what had passed between them.

"Nice down here in the deep, isn't it?" he said.

Maggie nodded, not taking her eyes from him. She shivered slightly and reached for the blanket to cover her shoulders.

"What came down in Tahoe?" she asked.

18.
The Great White Ride

AND SO HOW DID IT COME TO PASS THAT LUANN THE mermaid became the newest resident of Galilee Harbor and a watchful presence near the communal shower? How was it that, once resident there, she showed herself, like her mythical inspiration, to be an irresistible lure to passing sailors and other wayfarers to our town (her fame due in equal measure to her undeniable beauty and to those uncannily lifelike—if by then verdigris green—genitalia nestled between her pendulous breasts)?

Buck Buckworthy had definitely had it in mind to rid the town forever of Maggie's rendition of his manhood. But here Sally Stanford came to the rescue. By grabbing certain local powers-that-be by the short hairs, so to speak, and "convincing" them the statue was still the property of the artist—who, she reminded them, had not been paid the balance of her commission. So you would be right in guessing that Buck's disposition was not improved one fine morning by the arrival at his door of the mermaid rescue squad, ready to load the bronze Luann onto Arvie Engstrom's pickup. Will tried keeping things calm. First he handed over a refund of Luann's down payment (a loan from Sally), then he heard out Buck's demand that the statue stay completely shrouded.

Of course, *mama d'leau* was laid bare as soon as she left the Hill, and she was paraded through town with the truck's horn sounding, Bel dancing a lumbering jig at the foot of Luann's likeness and Bunny waving to all like a Rose Bowl queen. Will was not inclined to stop them.

Luann herself, apparently chastened by her husband's reaction to her patronage of the arts, was seen on a few occasions creeping into Galilee to affix a halter-top over the metal mammaries and their offending cleavage. These cover-ups unfailingly disappeared within the hour. And it soon became clear Luann's modesty was mostly for show, and to appease Buck. After all, what Southern siren who would not revel in such frank admiration? Would not love turning so many heads and being the object of such fuss? Certainly she was as susceptible as ever to Varda's flirtatious effusions, and, with or without her young niece Kiki in tow, was spied boarding the VALLEJO.

Don't think Buck Buckworthy didn't get reports on this too. And if there lingered any doubt we Rats were on that man's shit list, these were erased only a few weeks later, once and for all.

IT HAPPENED LIKE this. Varda was browsing the Marin Hardware. In walked Buck Buckworthy. And by sheer happenstance, so did Will. As you would expect, Buck Buckworthy ignored them both. "Hah, Will!" declared Varda in his trombone voice. "I come to buy mineral spirits for my brushes, but also a stronger line for fishing. Can you believe something so powerful came last night to my dinghy dock? My bait and hook, and all the line tied to the dock. Gone, all of it! Now I fix this sea monster. Let's see what he can do with this...." He held up a coil of wire meant for hanging painted canvases or mending chicken coops.

Will asking, "What bait?"

"Another oddity! On the hook, for fun, I use leftover hunk of roast lamb, Greek style. What fish likes *arni sto fourno*?" Varda found the mineral spirits in their hiding place on a high shelf at the back of the store. "A pirate map is needed to locate treasure in this establishment," he groused to himself.

Will was still ruminating on Varda's story. "Was the lamb bloody rare?"

"Of course! Overcooked lamb is an abomination and affront to the sacrificed beast."

Will was poking through a maze of marine gear. "A Great White then," he said matter-of-factly.

"A shark—in the bay—*skata!*"

One aisle over, behind a stack of zinc wash tubs, the little big man from Loredo was able to contain himself no longer. "Shark mah ass," he said.

Not itching for a fight, Will tried being diplomatic. "Your skepticism is understandable, Buckworthy. But why not a big predator? They're ancient in these waters. Great Whites feed off the Farallons, and they go after the seal weaners by Año Nuevo. Ask any surfer if you don't believe me—one gets hit every so often at Stinson or down the peninsula. By mistake most likely. In wet suits they look like seafood."

By this time Buck Buckworthy had invaded Will's aisle and was eyeballing him with disdain. "But not in the bay, bubba."

Varda watched the two of them closely while Will put down the brass geegaw he was examining and gave Buck a goofy grin. Like a mosquito in the dead of night, a crazy thought had just alighted on his mind. He was trying to ignore it. Not a chance. So now he said in an off-handed way, "You may be right."

Buck Buckworthy acknowledged Will's concession with a grunt.

Will pretended to be interested in another boaty gadget until Buck turned to leave. Then he called after him. "Only one way to know for sure."

Slowly, Buck Buckworthy wheeled to face Will. His eyes narrowed. "That so? Ah s'pose you want me to strap on that air tank of yours and go huntin' for one."

"No, nothing like that," Will replied. "I just thought, you being from Texas, you might get a kick out of shark riding."

Varda's imitation of a bronco rider's *eee-haw!* caused old lady Copple behind the cash register to start and pull herself away from her latest *True Confessions*. Seeing it was only Varda, she scowled and returned to a story about some semi-literate trailer trash in New Mexico who swore they had learned instant French, including many colorful colloquialisms not fit to print, onboard a flying saucer shaped like what one abductee described as "one of them *crow-sants*."

"Shark ridin'?" Buck asked.

Will nodded. "Come by the fishing pier tonight. At dusk. I'll show you."

Of course, this made Buck Buckworthy more than a little suspicious. He hadn't made himself into the *jefe* of the Bible Belt® by being anybody's damn fool. "Now wait just a dang minute here," he sputtered. "If ah decide to oblige you—ah ain't sayin' yet ah am—and there ain't no sign of a shark nowheres, how's about something in return ... for yours truly here?"

"Oh, and what exactly would that be?" Will wanted to know. Varda was frowning. His Greek wariness didn't like where this was headed.

"The mermaid. Ah want the mermaid back," Buck Buckworthy declared. "So ah can heave her straight to the bottom of the ocean where she belongs."

This caught Will by surprise. He stole a glance at Varda, who emphatically shook his head.

Buck set his jaw. "Take it or leave it, bubba."

Will thought for a moment. "And if I'm right?" he asked finally.

"Shoot."

"You pay Maggie full price for the mermaid and let her keep it."

Now Buck Buckworthy beamed. "You got yorself a deal," he said with a fearsome smile.

WILL HAULED THE Mercury outboard from his dory as dusk approached and rowed from the Earthquake Shack to the fishing pier. One-Eyed George followed, until he veered off toward Tiburon. The tide had nearly crested. The bay was quieting. The moon would be full tonight, revealing itself above Angel Island not as Dean Martin's pizza pie but as the genuine harvest variety, a leering, bright-eyed jack o' lantern. In the dying light, terns and cormorants dove for their bedtime snacks, and a seal barked before disappearing with a graceful plunge.

And as happens each day at this time, pelagic predators began arriving from the deep. It was prime time for feeding.

Tying up to the end of the pier, where the depth measured six fathoms or more, Will laid the oars alongside a package wrapped in butcher paper—beef kidney, raw and bloody. The dory was stripped bare except for a flotation cushion and a knife. At the bow several yards of stout fishing line was tied securely, with a weight and a number ten hook fastened to the other end.

Varda was already waiting, and he had invited Hayden and Arvie Engstrom along for the spectacle. But no sign of Buck Buckworthy. If he didn't show, that was just fine with Will. Too much was riding on this dare, pardon the pun, and his heart boomed in his chest. He was pretty sure he had this figured right, based on what he knew of *Carcharodon carcharias* behavior and what some kind of sea monster had already done to Varda. He was trying not to think what would happen if it didn't. Most of all, he hoped some happenstance did not bring Maggie by. She knew nothing of this winner-take-all bet.

After half an hour passed, they decided to give Buck Buckworthy ten minutes more. At two minutes to go, Will was starting to breath easier—until through the gathering darkness he recognized a portly shape topped by a Stetson ambling in their direction. No doubt about who that was. Someone was with him, also in a hat. It was Officer Mack.

"Glad you could make it, Buckworthy ... evening, Mack."

"And why wouldn't ah come?" Buck Buckworthy shot back, a little out of breath. "This officer of the law here is to make sure everybody's on the up and up. Remember our little wager? Officer, you be witness. No shark, the mermaid's mine." He glanced over at the waiting dory. "Now what's this tomfoolery all about?"

Will proceeded to explain the simple rules for "regulation shark riding." (He had made them up since the idea came to him that afternoon.) As directed, Buck Buckworthy took a seat in the dory while Will baited the hook and tossed out the line. Hayden took his position on the pier, standing ready to release the stern line from its cleat at the first sign of "something so big it could eat you" taking the bait.

"Wait a damn minute," objected Buck Buckworthy. "So something does snatch the bait, how we know it's a damn shark?" He gave a meaningful look to Officer Mack.

With as much awful portent in his voice as he could muster, Will assured them all, "Believe me, gentlemen ... you'll know."

"Pure horsepucky," snorted Buck Buckworthy. "Well, let's get this done with. How long we gotta wait?"

"Thirty minutes."

"Fifteen."

"Twenty."

"All raht, all raht. Officer, mark the time!"

Will nodded toward Mack, who checked his watch. "Oh, one more thing, Buckworthy," Will said. "See that knife?"

Buck Buckworthy grabbed up the fishing knife and brandished it. "Yeah? Mah s'posed to stab the shark too?" As he cackled, his soft belly jiggled. Will faked a grin. "Stab it if you want," he replied evenly. "But you might feel more like cutting the line if some sea bronc takes you too fast ... or too far."

Buck Buckworthy spit into the bay and regarded the Water Rats with disgust.

The sun had already scooted behind Mt. Tam. Darkness was not far off.

So they waited. And waited. And waited. The dory sat all but motionless, the fishing line stretched taut into the murky depths. Buck Buckworthy killing time by making use of the knife to tidy his fingernails. Will scanning the bay, not expecting to spot a big dorsal fin but for any sign of smaller fish in terrified flight from bigger ones.

A dozen minutes into it, Buck Buckworthy lifted his head and called up to the pier, "Ain't we done yet?" Mack shook his head no, but Varda could contain himself no longer. He edged closer to the dory and announced for all to hear, "Enough! It was I who started this. I cannot bear to see my very good friend and his vengeful goddess Artemis"—Will winced—"as sole parties to this wager. My gold Rolex says a *karcharias* takes the bait!"

Officer Mack looked blankly at Varda. "What the Sam Hill's that?"

"A Rolex or a *karcharias*?"

"He mean da shark," said Arvie Engstrom. Hayden snorted.

"Shoot, I know what a Rolex is," huffed Mack. "Could be yours ain't the real deal, though." He held out a hand. "Lemme see that."

Varda looked stricken. "Is genuine twenty-four karats! A present from an admirer ... also of the family of Buckworthy!"

Buck Buckworthy abruptly abandoned his mission of personal hygiene. "What the hell you talking about? What admirer do you mean?"

Varda smiled serenely. "The Buckworthys' *only* true patron of the arts, it would seem. The very generous Miss Kiki."

"That does it!" Buck shouted. He promptly jumped up, rocking the dory from side to side, and began making noisily toward the stern. "I'm done with you people!"

As in most matters, timing is everything.

At that very moment the dory rocketed forward as Hayden nimbly freed the line. With a wrenching lurch, speeding off into the twilight. As if a whole school of giant fish had lifted it onto their shining backs and were shanghaiing it out to sea. The initial jolt causing Buck Buckworthy to let out a yell, and he nearly tumbled overboard. Ending up flat on on his back, clutching desperately at the gunwales, boots swung high into the air.

Varda howled in triumph. Hayden loosed a belly laugh.

"Ride 'em, cowboy!" shouted Will.

And Buck Buckworthy was off. Hollering and whooping the whole way.

As his cowboy cries receded into the distance, it became clear his "mount" had set a course straight and true. The little dory was slicing out bow waves that rocked tugs and schooners moored on far distant shores.

Will and the others stood transfixed and watched him go. And go. And go. Within minutes Buck Buckworthy was but a dark smudge on the horizon. Then only his Stetson remained in sight, as it bobbed gently in the bay a few yards off the pier.

That Texan may have been having the ride of his life, but he was headed for the Gate and parts unknown.

They all wondered if he had lost the knife.

19.
The Perfect Crab Cake

HOW MANY THE SEA CREATURES WERE.
Eh?
How easy our life was. Before the barbarians....

You naughty girl, don't be getting my bellows wheezing again.

The small silvery ones, so easy to net in the shallows. The big salmon, as many as the stars. Clams, mussels, abalone, oysters. We gathered these like ripe berries. Aiii, and the crabs, the sweet crabs!

I could die for a sweet Dungeness with a frothy pint.

We dug onions and potatoes and cut the root of the feathery fennel and pulled watercress from the streams. Our baskets were heavy with acorns to boil for soup and pound for flour. Our men hunted so many creatures. Elk. Squirrel. Wild pig and bear, quail. So many, Malachy, so many.

THAT WEEK'S MAIL brought a surprise. Will stared at it for a full minute before opening it, though he knew who it was from. His mother. The faintly scented envelope was addressed in her familiar hand. She wrote infrequently now that she was remarried and living in Shaker Heights.

Deciphering her cramped cursive, he read bland news of brother Ben and no news of sister Grace, for whom the phrase "struggling New York actress" was invented, and Will wondered, not for the first time, how it was that some never leave while others flee the first chance they get. Why it was, among brothers and sisters who spring from the same source and share everything growing up, some take root, others turn restless as Bedouins. Grace and Will were the nomads. Ben was different. He strayed only three miles from where the Uselma box house had stood before it killed their father.

Near the end of the relentlessly cheery letter Will found what he was expecting, the pitch after Nadine's warm-up. She had been talking to Pickle again. She had listened as his ex-wife complained what a bastard he was and told her again how everything wrong between them was his fault. "This time I so wanted to tell her it didn't sound anything like my Will," she wrote. Oh oh, he thought. Here it comes. "But you know how much your step-father and I adore your little darling. Ariel is growing so fast! You wouldn't believe how big she is! Can't you please try patching things up a little? We hate having to walk on eggshells every time just to be close to our *only* granddaughter."

He thought about that. He thought about Ariel, just turned five, rushing up to his mother's new husband, a medical equipment salesman, and begging to be spun in circles the way Will used to do it, until she shrieked with laughter and was wobbly on her feet and bumped into the furniture before finally collapsing to the floor. He thought about the other things Ariel and he did together, daughter and father. Her special ticklish spots and favorite hiding places and the unimaginably good feeling of those two small arms hugging his neck.

For the millionth time he asked himself: how did I let Pickle win? *How did I let her win so completely and absolutely?*

He had thought he knew better than to fall into any more of that woman's traps, but he had also counted on the courts to keep the scales of justice balanced. He put his faith in telling exactly what had happened. He didn't deny striking the blow, he only tried to explain it. But "why" didn't matter. The judge, he discovered, was more than ready to believe a cleverly convincing wife who wanted his scalp.

So she got what she wanted and more. Alimony. Child support. And the worst: an order against any physical contact with Pickle or "visitation" with Ariel without his ex-wife's consent.

He remembered how, afterwards, Pickle's words cut him like barbed wire. *You'll see your daughter again over my dead body, even if you beg ... even if you're dying.* She would burn the girl in her sleep first, cook Ariel's delicate flesh with her cigarette and say he did it. *They always believe the mother, everyone knows that.*

That was how it would be. Until his daughter was sixteen, he might as well be invisible. He might as well leave town. Leave the state. He did.

He saw the terrible irony of his mother's plea. All that pleading he had done to her—to leave their battered household and escape the rages and being slapped around. He had even been hopeful once. There had, after all, been that one time Will saw her fight back. It began when his father hit her with the leather strap he usually used to whip his kids. She came back at Leo with the pot of oil she was using to brown his chuck roast. Throwing it over him, searing his neck and arms.

And that had also been the only time since his boyhood boxing lesson he ever dared to hit back. He was barely fourteen at the time.

He had grabbed the strap from his father's hand, and he began to beat him with the doubled-up leather. Over and over. Again and again. Leo, cowering in a corner, trying to protect his burned flesh.

Finally Will's mother pulled her son away, screaming, "Stop it, stop it! He's your father!" After that Leo never strapped any of them again. But his mother never thanked him either. What happened was never spoken of.

He reread the letter. *It didn't sound anything like my Will....* "My Will," she used to tell him, "should never ever get a B in math." "My Will should be first in the spelling bee." "My Will can grow up to be President!" In her way, not intentionally perhaps, helping to create and then widen the gulf between father and first-born son. *You know how your step-father and I ... can't you please try ... so we don't have to walk on eggshells just to...."*

Sure, Mom," he said, sliding the letter into its envelope and pushing it to the back of a bottom drawer.

THAT AFTERNOON MAGGIE peeked her head into the Earthquake Shack and called Will's name through the top half of the Dutch door. Coming to her, he was startled. Framed in that door open to the salt breezes, smiling, eyes sparkling, she had a kind of light radiating from her. A bright beacon from beneath that glorious penumbra of hair. He had seen such light before, once upon a time even from Pickle. He called it the love light.

Breezily, she said to him, "On my way to Mrs. Legasse's on South Street. She's laid up with rheumatism now, but she used to baby-sit me." She held up a cookie tin. "I take her snickerdoodles, my mom's recipe."

He could not deny the warmth he felt in her reflected glow. But it also seemed obvious to him that she was firming up her expectations. She had begun sculpting him in her head, and before long he would be an ideal, a type of perfection. Why did women falling in love always do that? Was he ready yet, or able, to fit into the image she was creating of him? He thought again of his mother's letter and wished it had not reminded him of how such creations seldom wear well. How they crumble and sometimes can never be patched.

"Here," Maggie said. She had reached into her Greek peasant bag and was handing him a small wooden box. "I want you to have this."

Startled again, Will could only murmur, "What is it?"

"Open it, silly."

Prying off the lid, he found inside a small golden key. He picked it up and then looked back at her. The light from her eyes nearly forced him to look away.

"I'll show you," she said, taking the key from his hand. Tugging at a delicate gold chain around her neck, she pulled out from beneath her blouse a golden oval etched in filigree. "My mother's," she said. "She got it from my dad. She gave it to me when I turned twenty-one. I was waiting for the right time to start wearing it." She inserted the key into a tiny keyhole in the oval and it fell open.

"Where'd you get that!" Will stared at the tiny locket photo.

"Don't worry. It's only a copy," she laughed. She reached into her bag again. "Here's the original."

"But…"

"Don't be a blockhead. I stole it. I saw it lying on a stack of things and I slipped it in my pocket. You were so cute, I had to have it. Are you mad?"

Will was not sure what to say.

"Do you think I'm being too sappy, like a bobby-soxer or something?"

He looked down at the locket and shook his head and then took another peek at himself as Hopalong Cassidy on the hobbyhorse.

"I want you to have the key," she said. "That's all."

Afterwards, tucking the key into his shirt pocket, he wondered how long it would be before Maggie finished shaping him into the perfect crab cake.

20.
Adventure Afloat

WE WERE ABUZZ WITH TALK OF THE MISSING man. The *Chronicle* was covering it on its front page, and we eagerly tuned in for updates on the radio and the six o'clock news on TV. Soon the story attracted national and even world interest. We stopped each other along Bridgeway and Caledonia, the sloping streets of Old Town, at Juanita's and the No Name, to share whatever we heard. Will, who refused to buy a television and preferred his LPs to the radio, depended on the rest of us and the newspapers to keep him informed. Understandably, though, he took a keen personal interest.

Although Hayden had been talking about it for months, few of us thought he would actually go through with it—even after he had spent a small fortune refitting WANDERER, that old wooden schooner of his, and had provisioned her with boxes of Cuban cigars, cases of beer, his favorite single-malts and French Bordeaux, the complete Shakespeare and the major Russian novelists. Still, in hindsight, most of us agreed the ad in the newspapers and *The Saturday Review* was a blunder.

IOO-TON EX-PILOT SCHOONER SAILING FROM SAN FRAN-
CISCO. NEED SIX ACTIVE INTELLIGENT YOUNG MEN AND
WOMEN. SEND DETAILS TO STERLING HAYDEN, BOX 655,
SAUSALITO, CALIFORNIA.

Will said Hayden knew exactly what he was doing, which was firing a broadside across the enemy's bow. It got the attention of the former Mrs. Hayden, that's for sure. When she saw the ad in L.A., she ran straight for her lawyer. Her children, who were staying with Hayden in Sausalito, were not about to be parties to any dangerous adventure. Absolutely not. She would never stand idly by.

Naturally, the court gave her what she wanted, an order forbidding the children to be taken out of the state without court approval and a stern warning from the bench to the man who played pirates and cowboys in the movies. "You are not in a swashbuckler now, Mr. Hayden. Do not attempt to cross swords with this court."

But *this* actor had been practicing for *this* maritime role long before he ever romanced Joan Crawford on screen. One morning Hayden silently gathered his kids and crew, and they just crept under the Golden Gate like the fugitives they were. "A born salt-water sailor," crowed one of the old sea dogs who whiled away afternoons at the No Name drinking white rum and spinning tales of his own voyages. "Went to sea at fifteen, worked a cod schooner on the Grand Banks the winter of '34. Ask him yourself when he gets back … if he comes back."

We noted Will's elation about Hayden's outlaw adventure but were unaware he was an aggrieved father himself. Ariel was still a private wound, unknown even to Maggie. The four kids were what hooked him, of course—that and the way Hayden was thumbing his nose at both the court and his ex-wife. "What father," he asked anyone who would listen, "doesn't dream of showing his kids the world?"

The former Mrs. Hayden was "placed under sedation" on hearing the news, according to the United Press International. Her lawyer spat out the word "kidnap" and demanded that the Coast Guard be sent in pursuit. "All members of the crew," he avowed, "will be subject to a charge of murder or manslaughter in the event of the death of any one of these children."

By then WANDERER was plying the high seas well beyond American waters. Hayden manned the helm, dead reckoning by sun and starry nights, without so much as a radio transmitter in case of trouble. Forty-one days passed. A French report first brought word of WANDERER, in Papeete, Tahiti, French Oceania. The gendarmes who clambered aboard found all hands alive and bursting with good health. "I had the time of my life," Hayden told them in his rudimentary French.

A double Scotch and a pint of beer was set at Hayden's customary bar stool as Will read his press statement to a packed barroom. "At last, you know who I am," it read. "Not Hayden the cowboy, tall in the rented saddle, king of the non-frontier. But the guy with the boat and the kids who told ex-wife and lawyers and judges and courts: you can all go to hell."

Maggie, behind the bar that day, bought a round for the house. And she offered the toast. "To WANDERER and her crew!" To which Varda added, "May their happiness be deep as the sea, their troubles light as foam. And may she under fair skies and favorable winds return."

"Hear, hear!" cried Will as we cheered and whistled and downed our drinks in honor of our far-away hometown hero.

OH. YOU MIGHT be wondering about the fate of that other "missing" man. Well, Buck Buckworthy's voyage hadn't turned out quite so triumphantly. But it could have been a lot worse.

Yes, he was rescued. It's worth mentioning, however, that on that very same day an unlucky swimmer near a San Luis Obispo seal rookery was mistaken for a tasty treat by a huge fish with a brain the size of a stewed prune. The swimmer bled to death from the Great White's bite. Our own shark rider was returned home safe—and as unscathed as anyone could be after being towed out to sea, where heavy swells boiled over into the dory until she sank. Then the boat was literally yanked from beneath its terrified passenger.

We'll never know if it really was a shark. It's possible some other Jules Verne horror could have grabbed the bait. All we do know is, Buck Buckworthy was abandoned in the dark of night with only the kapok-filled cushion to keep him afloat; finally rid of the beast but paralyzed by the fear it might come back for him, for sheer spite. Not until four o'clock the next morning was he rescued by a fishing trawler that nearly ran him down. His considerable girth insulated and saved him from severe hypothermia, said the doctor who examined and admitted him to a hospital down the Peninsula.

For quite some time after that we didn't see Buck Buckworthy around town, although one day the mailman brought Maggie a welcome surprise. A check for the full agreed-upon price for Luann the Mermaid.

A portion of it went to buy Will a replacement dory.

21.
Dig It, Man

MY FATHER WARNED ME CURIOSITY KILLS. HE WAS right. But I must ask. Why here? Why to my Miwok beach?

A superb choice, was it not?

But your own village, your own people …

Them? Them I left behind long ago, in the Auld Sod. But that's not what you're asking. To satisfy your deadly curiosity, I need to take you back to when I lost everything—the whole kit and caboodle but my piano and the clothes on my back. Got time to spare?

Malachy! My people would sit you by our lodge fire. It is the place we save for those who make us laugh.

Truly? You make a dead man blush. For sure, 'twas my silvery tongue as much as my musical fingers that kept me fed in the old days. That gets to the very nut of it, in fact. If not for the Big Shake, I would've gone on just the same. The Barbary Coast bawdy houses was the world I knew, dependable as the Ferry Building clock. And then … gone, all of it gone. And everywhere around me, others in similar straits: a few measly possessions saved, just grateful to be alive. Exactly twenty-four hours after the end of our world, a Thursday morning a few minutes past five, I remember resting on a lovely patch of green at the edge of the Golden Gate Park. With me sat the flotsam of the city—Japs, Eye-talians, Chinks, even a couple niggers. 'Twas like we was meeting to figure out why, if this were hell, we still shivered in the damn morning fog. A man comes along. Only the day before, this man would not give us the time of day. He were a nabob pioneer from Forty-nine, one of San Francisco's most respectable gents, but he sits right down with us. There, in the faint light of dawn. Nodding toward my piano, which were parked nearby, he heaves a big sigh. Mine's gone, he says to me. I nod back. He looks me straight in the eye, and, as if commenting on the weather, says, "Yesterday morning I was worth two million dollars."

Your hearts were heavy.

Some, yes. But with me it weren't so, that's my point exactly! Where others saw darkness and ruin, I saw the new day beckoning. A fresh life was at hand, and it quickened my pulse like a flash in a miner's pan. All of a sudden I was overcome with thirst, the most powerful thirst I ever knew—to be away from Bassity, who survived too, by the way. With this revelation I began surveying the human tide swept into the park with genuine wonder. We was all the same, except for the heathen Chinks, who was made to go off to squat in their own camp. We all made our nests together as best we could, none of us wanting to return to city streets and be crushed by the collapse of another building or caught in another shake. Relief supplies and tents began arriving quick enough, and though cooking fires was banned, we made do. We helped each other freely—the usual walls between the differing classes lying in ruin like everything else. I was liberated! The blinders fell from my eyes, the bit from my gob.

You found your love then?

Patience, lass. I'm still circling your first question. So ... my piano made me a very popular fella in this new society. On clear nights, me and a few hands would roll out my beauty onto the open meadow, where hundreds would gather to sing and dance and raise a ruckus for being alive. Usually I were joined by some roosters who'd played a dime vaudeville on Market—mandolin and banjo men mostly, and one fiddler. So well I remember a white-haired old lady in her fancy evening gloves and hat who always appeared at this celebrations. She had a baby pig on a leash, and the two of them was cozy as lovers on a scavenged sofa under a tree. But the pig bawled so, the fiddler finally threatened to eat it for dinner, and the lady and her pig hightailed it and never came back. Hah! I also recall on one particular night in the meadow, while we was catching our breath, there were a rumpled man with dark hair and eyes bright as torches who sidled up to me. Right off, he started making conversation. After a while he got around to telling me he were writing for *Collier's* about us survivors.

You talked and talked until the sun came home?

Hey, now. Be glad for this Jabberwocky! Who else would fill your eternity!

Jabber—?

Anyhow, this writer, he impressed me. He were very well informed as to the state of things. San Francisco, he tells me, was like the crater of a volcano, ringed by thousands of refugees like me. At the Presidio alone was twenty thousand. We could travel free on the railroads anywhere we wanted. A hundred thousand or more was gone already. 'Twas then it hit me. I asked the *Collier's* man, where would you go? Where would you start a new life, if you was me?

On our sand!

Bull's eye. He says to me he lives in Sonoma, that it's sensational country. I tell him I favor the sea over cows and sheep. He replies, why then, there's only one place for you. Take it from an old oysterman, he says. Go to Sausalito! I'd never set foot in Sausalito. Never been across the bay on the North Shore ferry, not even to catch the Gold Spike Special for Eureka. Never had a saltwater bath in the Miramar or a downed a pint at the Arbordale, never woke to the whistles calling for the railroad and ferry workers, or strolled Water Street as the boat waves was drowned out by the huffing of the steam locomotives impatient to depart.

Your path was found.

Nearly so. I thanked the man, and he went on his way. 'Twas only afterward a fellow Irisher, Billy O'Rourke, sidled up to ask, Know who that feller was, don't you? Sure, a magazine writer, I say. Righto, Billy says. And Teddy Roosevelt's just another Rough Rider. Now what would you be jaw-boning with Jack London about?

PAST LIVES OF Water Rats. Sometimes they demand our attention unexpectedly, like the thumpings of a séance.

That late October afternoon it was not one of Mephisto's usual fellow travelers grinning wildly from the sidecar of the Indian Chief. Together they thundered into the No Name, lurching to a halt near the piano. Mephisto gunned the throttle, the machine belched smoke and died. Marilyn Macaw hopped onto a gloved hand as Mephisto rose from the seat. And his other passenger, darkly handsome but paunchy in a tight pullover shirt and dungarees with rolled-up cuffs, rose unsteadily. Gimpy in one leg, he made tentative steps toward the bar.

Mephisto spotted Will and signaled to his companion. "*Mein freund*," he said to Will. "Here's the coolest cat I—"

"Kerouac," the stranger interrupted. He had a weak handshake and his breath reeked of alcohol. His eyes scanned the barroom uneasily, as if looking for a place to hide.

"Will's a professional frogman," Mephisto said.

"No shit."

"No weirder than head beatnik," Will replied with a trace of the awe he felt in suddenly facing the world's most famous beat. The lyric rant *On the Road*, famously typed on one long continuous scroll, was a best-seller now that it had finally found a publisher. But Herb Caen had just coined the term "beatnik." Will regretted repeating it as soon as he saw the uneasy glances exchanged between Kerouac and Mephisto, who, as Will was about to learn, had shared the celebrity beatnik's early orbit at Columbia. Along with others whose names were now linked in *Time* and *Life*. Ginsberg, Carr, Corso, Burroughs, John Clellon Holmes, Cassady. Apparently, it wasn't making Kerouac happy. "No affront intended," Will apologized.

"It's all right, Jack." Mephisto tried consoling his friend.

Kerouac seesawed but waved a dismissive hand. "Hate the word," he muttered. "Try to make something f-furtive and incisive and to see it trivialized ... on that level ... the level of the commonplace, it burns me. It's over, we're lost, man, pray to St. Theresa—they got Jack Daniels in this place?"

Before long Kerouac sat at the far end of the bar tugging at the bottle set in front of him. At a table, Mephisto moved closer to Will and in a voice low enough not to be overheard said, "The fame's been hard on Jack. Losing something you love, this changes you." Will's bewilderment was evident. "They wrote for kicks before, *ja*? He was free. They were all free. Now Ginsberg's off with Ferlinghetti in Chile, Cassady's in San Quentin for those two joints but Jack won't visit him. So when he calls to say he's in town, could I refuse?"

Mephisto eased back in his chair, lost in his thoughts. His bird rearranged herself. Then he leaned in again. "Light years from last time I saw him, let me tell you. That was the zenith ... and the beginning of the end." With a wistful smile he added, "I see it like yesterday."

Will looked over at Kerouac, who seemed to be in a reverie of his own as he chewed at a hang nail.

"It was Jack who told me about Ginsberg," said Mephisto. "'He's all poet meat, man, you ought to come,' he said. That's how I found out about the reading." Again Will looked at him blankly. "You know, the Gallery Six? Union at Fillmore. Kind of a proletarian space, maybe because it was an auto repair before. But that afternoon the place jumped with *fantastische leute.*"

Will still wasn't following. Mephisto put on a show of exasperation but continued with his story. "Amazing characters. Excuse the *Deutsch.* I fall into it without warning. Jack used to call me the math *führer.*" Mephisto flashed a sardonic smile at Kerouac when he noticed he was finally paying attention. Kerouac winked back like he was flirting. He tipped back his bottle and took another big swig.

"Believe me when I say Jack was a magnet among iron filings. He knew everybody there. Phil Whalen, the poet. *Zehr zaftig.* Gary Snyder and McClure. But where's Ginsberg we all wanted to know." He bent closer. "First time I ever met him, Jack said to me, 'Look for this spindly Jewish kid with horn-rimmed glasses over burning black eyes.'"

He arched his brow. "When Ginsberg finally appeared out of nowhere—you know, at the Gallery Six?—he hadn't changed a bit." At that, Mephisto reached inside his vest and pulled out a skinny cheroot and lit it with a match scratched across the table. He sucked in the smoke. It smelled of cheap tobacco and something sweet. "Know where he's been? The *schmuck* took the wrong bus."

He chuckled and took another puff. "This was just before Ferlinghetti published *Howl.*" Smoke swirled out the corners of his mouth. "Man, that night. Did Ginsberg ever cast a spell."

Suddenly Mephisto jumped to his feet. Gesturing to Kerouac, he began to recite with a pirate's swagger the famous first stanza.

> *I saw the best minds of my generation*
> *destroyed by madness*
> *starving, mystical, naked,*

Kerouac grabbed up the bottle of Jack and flourished it to

Mephisto's exaggerated cadence. He drummed in time on the bar top with his other hand.

who dragged themselves thru the angry streets at dawn looking for a negro fix....

Mephisto cried to Kerouac, "Still got the juice, Jack, *nicht wahr?*" Kerouac raised his bottle again, and Mephisto seemed pleased with himself as he settled back into his chair and retrieved his cheroot.

"All night he and Cassady gulped alley juice and played Greek chorus, shouting out 'go, go, go!' We were high as Telegraph Hill, and not from beat tea. Afterwards we all went to Vesuvio's, and Jack told Ginsberg his poem would make him famous in San Francisco. But I said, no, the fascists would hear this howl coast to coast. A G-bomb, I called it."

He stubbed out the cigar and tucked it into his vest pocket. "I was always more political than them."

Now Kerouac looked lost somewhere again.

"Funny thing," Mephisto mused on. "Jack says he despises Jews. Ginsberg doesn't believe it, neither do I. Me, I hate the Nazis *and* I hate my Jewishness. I agree with Jack about one thing. To be a Jew is to wear the stigma of the schlemiel. Instead of fighting back, the Jews damned themselves. We didn't believe it could happen. We didn't think Hitler would dare."

It struck Will that he had never heard Mephisto talk so freely about himself before. Apparently Kerouac's visit had put him in this uncharacteristically reflective frame of mind. "You lost family during the war?" Will ventured to ask.

Mephisto nodded. "Father. Sister. Many aunts, uncles, cousins. *Mutti* and I came to America when I was fifteen. I won a scholarship at Brandeis. My father was a rabbi, he stayed in Hamburg with my sister. While Hitler reared up, a Valkyrie's stallion, *Vati* kept writing to us. Be patient, be patient, this cannot last. We pleaded with him as the news got worse, until finally he promised to flee." Mephisto's mood was quickly darkening. He was glaring at the tabletop, and his gloved hands were clenched. "Too late. Much too late."

Slowly, he lifted his head and his eyes were hard. "What's the expression in English? He who falters is … lost?"

"Sometimes," said Will. "But it's tough to see what's coming. I mean, when you're in the middle of it."

"Bullshit. Consequences of actions are typically predictable," Mephisto shot back. "The consequences of inaction—that is hard to know."

Will found himself wanting a less consequential subject. He took a flier. "And what about your mother?"

"I buried her. Right after they took away my job." Mephisto reached into his vest, retrieved the foul cheroot, and relit it. He scattered the smoke with one hand. "I warned her. IBM moved her plant to Poughkeepsie and it killed her. 'They're such good people,' she would say. She thought the Krupps were good people too, before they chained the Jews to the machines. It made her angry when I reminded her of that. But she loved her *wunderbar* corporation."

Abandoning all attempts at conversation steering, Will took a resigned swallow of his steam beer.

Mephisto began fidgeting with his empty glass. Marilyn Macaw nuzzled at his ear. He seemed not to notice. "You are one hundred percent American," he said. "Enlighten me. I do not understand the so-called separation of church and state in this country."

Will sighed inwardly and girded himself for another oration from *herr professor* with the adoring bird. "Okay, I'll bite," he said finally. "What do you mean?"

"*Zehr leicht.* The corporation is all-powerful, it runs the state. The holy corporation is the church. Both tell us how to live, how to dress, how to act, how to think. What separation

is this? The only way is separation from *them*. Being totally
free." Mephisto did not wait for any rebuttal Will might have
to offer. "All enemies of this freedom the people must destroy,"
he declared.

"What about Jack and Ginsberg and the other beats?" Will
asked. "What enemies of freedom are they destroying with
their poetry and speed freak stories?"

At this Mephisto shrugged. "So far they destroy only
themselves and their own brain cells," he answered quietly.
"But we march on."

Kerouac stood to test his balance. Draining the last of the
bottle, he shambled uncertainly toward their table. Will tried
reading his expression. He thought he saw anger and pain
mixed in with the booze. That unsettled him, it hit too close
to his fire-brewed daddy, to himself.

Heavily, Kerouac sat down across from Will. There was
intelligence in those haunted eyes. "Don't believe what you hear
from this d-d-dark Nazi buccaneer. I knew him when, before
he slapped on this new label." Will glanced over at Mephisto,
who pretended to be watching Bridgeway traffic beyond the
bar's open doors. "I sketched him, man," Kerouac continued,
"just after he crawled out of the primordial ooze." Then he closed
his eyes, slid his arms across the tabletop and gently lowered
his head onto them. In moments he was nodded out.

Mephisto looked down at the dozing Kerouac with apparent unconcern.

"How long's Jack in town for?" Will inquired.

22.
A Pilgrim's (Lack of) Progress

BEEN THINKING, MI-WASH. AN INCORRIGIBLE HABIT that I've acquired, I'm afraid. Do you realize? All this time and we've still seen neither hide nor hair of Him. The way I'm sizing it up, God's very existence is called into serious question.

Your Spirit Father is too busy with the living?

If that be so, what Almighty would orchestrate such terrible events as the Big Shake, no matter how wicked we was?

Coyote loves to laugh at us.

'Twas no joke! So many was snuffed out like candles in a blow. Yet …

I know. You learned a great lesson. Our spirits survive.

Aye. 'Twas a spirit led me into the arms of my beloved.

I never grow tired of this story. Tell me again.

I see him in my mind even now, though it were near nightfall—a small bearded gentleman attired in a woman's frock, it were quite lively, as a matter of fact, as were his sequined skull cap. By my stars, I thought myself back on the Barbary Coast till he strolled straight through a giant redwood in the park. Then I should have been quaking in my boots, but I stood stock still, calm as you please, calm as the silent waters of the ocean deep.

Your heart was at peace.

That's it exactly, peace. I trailed after him till he vanished as suddenly as he came. It were then I seen her, hidden in the tall grass—my dark-haired beauty. At her sweet tit she held a wee one. She took no notice of me, and so stunned were I at seeing the ghostly gentleman and then this beautiful appari- tion, I stared at her, struck dumb. Finally she chanced to look up. She screamed. I knew then she weren't no spirit! Retreat- ing quickly till she'd rearranged herself, I called out to her. I begged for her forgiveness. She sensed I meant no harm and inquired as to my name. And she told me hers was—

Delphine … like a bird song.

Aye, Delphine Gomes. And her son were called Artur. Portugees, they was, and all alone in this world. Their board- ing house had been sucked two stories below ground, and her man run through by a bedpost. They found the infant cuddled in his father's arms with nary a scratch, a miracle.

You loved them.

We soon fell in love, yes. A fortnight later, we was wed. And I begun rearing that boy as my own. That's how we landed the shack.

The spirit led you to my sand.

No, no. In the months after the quake they commenced building these shacks—hundreds of them—to relieve the primi- tive conditions of the camps. They was sought-after prizes, I'll tell you. Families got first dibs, and I were lucky to know the man in charge. One of the regulars at the Rooster.

Malachy …

Eh?

You found love. You found a family. And a strong new lodge. Do you not see?

Aach, you're barking up the wrong tree now. It were not the doings of any Creator! 'Twas the ghost I will thank if ever we meet up again! But here's another puzzler—how was it I could see him plain as day but you are just a voice in my head?

———————

KEROUAC CHOSE THE shack to sack out. Or that's at least where Will found him toward mid-morning after he slipped quietly out of bed so as not to disturb the sliver of bare shoulder and sprawl of kelp hair next to him.

The details were fuzzy in the extreme. He dimly remembered an unsteady amble from the No Name, Kerouac declaiming loudly on the silvery constellations that canopied the sky. Now, through window panes radiating the morning sun, Will saw him on his deck. Hidden in the sleeping bag as if gulped whole by some fearsome reptile. One-Eyed George eyeing him warily from a safe distance.

Will heaped Maxwell House into the percolator and tried to recover more shards of the evening. His head hurt, his heartbeat felt labored. He remembered Mephisto roaring off to an unspecified assignation, promising to return but leaving Kerouac passed out at the bar. He remembered intending to make his way to the Glad Hand for some nourishment. But then Maggie relieved the day bartender and Kerouac, waking with a start and lifting his head to reveal those penetrating eyes, called for another round.

Leading, inevitably, to another and then another.

The bar filled, and blue smoke and noise gathered at the tin ceiling. Guitars materialized. Soon someone was killing Woody Guthrie, the early Buddy Holly, and almost everyone joined in on a truly terrible rendition of "The Purple People Eater." Kerouac sat off to one side, anonymous and free, a crooked grin on his face.

Something else. Something more. Will had this unmistakable feeling more had transpired, if only he could make out the shadows in his memory. Slowly and deliberately he began tending to his tropical fish, with a sensation of being underwater himself, when suddenly there it was: a dark glimmering at first, then the full big-footed stomp of morning terror itself.

That very afternoon. Three o'clock sharp. He had summoned all of Sausalito.

"A Dumont thanksgiving!" he had shouted through the din of the No Name. "Everybody come!"

Though the real Thanksgiving was weeks away, it had seemed to him, in the gauzy embrace of those many steam beers, the perfect time to host his own *personal* thanksgiving. To show his gratitude. To offer his thanks for the fertile shores to which his leaky ship of fortune had delivered him, a battered pilgrim welcomed by a strange new land. Or some such.

What the hell, he thought now. He was drunk and so was everybody else, and it seemed like a good idea at the time. Then he groaned.

"Mag, quick, wake up," he urged into her ear. "I need some help. I need some help real bad...."

BELMONT LEANED IN close. His thieving eyes following the beautiful choreography of Will's many-colored pets.

"Swiping from your host is *not* sophisticated!" warned Bunny as he slipped the latest Ella vinyl onto Will's turntable. Crestfallen but obedient, Bel abandoned the fish tank to pad after one of Sally Stanford's girls offering canapés in a Moulin Rouge bustier and fishnet stockings. These were compliments of the Valhalla, where the kitchen help was still piping yolky custard into cream puffs for later on. Sally herself was stationed near Will's desk, ladling out her famous punch from a crystal bowl. "Don't be shy," she hailed anyone in earshot. "Drink like a fish, it'll make you fly!"

FLYING FISH PUNCH
JUICE OF A DOZEN LEMONS
1 LB. SUGAR
1 PINT BRANDY

½ PINT PEACH SCHNAPPS
½ PINT JAMAICA RUM
3 QUARTS SPARKLING WATER
IN A PUNCH BOWL, MIX IT UP
REAL GOOD. ADD A BIG CHUNK OF ICE.

Outside on the deck, Will tended to the king salmon, a pair of beauties that had come courtesy of Arvie Engstrom. Maggie, in the shack's galley, was bent to the chore of scrubbing a bucketful of Black Sand Beach mussels and ripping away the pubic thatches between their shiny bivalve lips. Princess, the platinum blonde from next door, was nearby at the porcelain sink, and she caught Maggie's eye.

"Be sure to wash those twice," Maggie told her. "They're from Mrs. Tate's garden and looked real dirty." Princess's expression registered no response as she scooped a handful of lettuces from a peck basket. But she had heard.

"Mrs. Tate?"

Maggie stopped scrubbing to regard the young woman more closely. Barely past her teens and shapely to the point of excess, beautiful, she concluded, but for ears that jutted out like street signs. Maggie smelled a musky pungency on her and saw post-coital zombiness in those ovoid eyes.

"Bel's mother."

"Oh."

"In New Town."

"Oh."

Princess plunged the frilly mass into cold water and swirled the leaves without inspiration. "What kind is this anyway?"

Maggie almost dropped the dripping mollusk in her hand. "Leaf lettuce."

"Leaf lettuce," Princess repeated slowly, shaking her head. "I only like iceberg. With tons of thousand island."

Child, Maggie thought, try living at sea level more often.

WHAT HAD BEGUN as a flurry of panicky phone calls only hours before was now a celebration of comradeship in the Water Rat kingdom.

We sat under the warming sun around a jerry-built table on folding chairs lent by the I.D.E.S.S.T. hall. Or in the back yard at a smaller improvisation of sawhorses and plywood. Or inside the shack alongside Will's fish tank at the varnished wooden table where he usually ate alone. Or on the rumpled bed in the room with many doors, where a foursome happily picnicked. Or at any other spot that could be commandeered. Seventy-some Rats tucking into the bronzed salmon, the *moussaka* from Varda—"only Greeks understand the enigma of the eggplant!"—and Maggie's aromatic mussel stew. Sides and salads passing eagerly from hand to hand. The instant anyone found the bottom of a glass, it was replenished by one of Sally's well-schooled girls.

Whaler's Cove on this afternoon was glinting filtered sunlight, and the milky blue-green bay was decorated in spinnakers and mainsails glowing a pulsating white. Along the boardwalk there passed an unending parade of young mothers strolling infants, gum-shoed ferrymen on their way to work, weekend anglers and plein air artists making the most of the waning day.

Will sat at the head of the long table on the deck and surveyed the marvel of it all. It astonished him. His boozy inspiration, the frenzy to make it happen, but *just look at this*. The old shack so alive, it *overflowed* with life. This is why I love it, he thought, why I love this place. For the first time in the longest while, he knew feelings of contentment. He felt intimations of something close to peace.

Turning toward Maggie—she was in animated conversation with Kerouac—he felt ... what exactly? He pondered this and he wondered. In the dark of the morning he and Maggie had made love. Fumbling, half-drunken, hurried. But was it anything more than that?

Maggie saw his eyes on her, and when Kerouac noticed her glance over his shoulder, he swiveled in Will's direction. A cigarette hung from his lips and his eyes telegraphed the news that he was loaded again. "I've always d-d-dug this town," he announced loudly. "It's kept its big toe in the water. *La tranquility qui complete.* But your lady here's been putting the scare on me."

Will, wanting to hold onto his inner monologue, had no clue what Kerouac was talking about. Kerouac dragged deeply on his cigarette. "The d-damned threat, man!" His words worked their way into a space between all the others being spoken around the table, and heads turned.

"What threat, *cherie?*" asked Sally Stanford.

"You know, the pier thing," Maggie said. "I was telling Jack how it could ruin everything."

Then the questions started flying, and Sally was made to repeat the sketchy details she had overheard several weeks past at her table of "liquored-up big shots." Kerouac expelled smoke rings with a sour expression. There being no more Jack Daniels, he got up to pour himself a tumbler of wine.

"Who were they?" Mephisto wanted to know.

"The *moussaka*, is it not beautiful?" Varda interjected to no one in particular. "Always when I eat it, I give thanks to the gods of simple farmers and gentle shepherds."

Will, grateful, nodded toward him. "Varda, as usual, you understand what matters."

"Tell us the names," Mephisto insisted.

Sally Stanford glanced over at Will, who sighed and motioned his assent. "Go ahead, tell the man the names. I guess I'm the only one wallowing in this fine moment."

She had barely begun when suddenly Hayden erupted. "Buckworthy!"

Murmurs and guffaws from around the table.

"A cowboy rodeo clown," scoffed Varda.

"*Ja*, he is dumb bell," agreed Arvie Engstrom. "No one seen him since he steals Will's dory."

Mephisto stared stonily at his plate. Stabbing at a forkful of something, he muttered to no one in particular, "McCarthy was a buffoon too, so we thought."

Someone else said, "Whatever the Hillclimbers are up to, one thing's sure—it's no damn good for us!" Several others quickly seconded.

Maybe Will's mind, shadowed by his hangover and weary from the mad race that had brought them all there, just couldn't bend itself around this particular topic. Why let a new worry begin circling when he had plenty of old buzzards already hanging around to see if he was dead meat? He looked from face to face around the table, and his eyes appealed for a cease-fire. "Why get so worked up?" he asked. "We don't even know the real story...."

"Oh, come on!" It was Maggie. Will looked sheepish, and Sally Stanford tried coming to his rescue. "Hon," she said to Maggie, "they can only rape you if you open your legs."

"You can't be serious!" Mephisto interrupted now, his voice in crescendo. "A pier sticking out in our bay like an industrial erection?" He had that mathematician's need to extrapolate to the nth power, to follow the string of logic like a trail of bread crumbs. "Big ships spewing their shit into our water? And all the trucks and machines loading and unloading these monstrosities? Are you going to ask them, *bitte*, be quiet when they rumble past like Rommel's tanks in the middle of the night?"

"Precisely," said Dr. Alan Watts, who had been sucking on his briar pipe in Zen contemplation. Sandwiched between Maggie and his pretty wife Dorothy, he leaned forward now to rest his elbows on the tabletop. In that mellow KPFA voice of his, he said, "Man's inability to accept the basic unity of organism and environment leads to alienation between man and nature, to the using of technology in a spirit of aggressive hostility." A pause for the pipe. "We feel this compulsion to bend Mother Earth to our will instead of intelligently co-operating with her."

"Thitt!" said Jake the Anchor Out.

Jake, as he burst out of the shack clutching a tumbler of punch, had tripped while avoiding collision with the Turban Woman. The drink splattered onto his threadbare corduroys and made sticky puddles on the rough-hewn timbers of the deck. Reversing himself sharply and cursing a blue streak at the doe-eyed dear whose hair was wrapped in a blue bath towel as usual, he retreated back inside.

"My sentiments exactly," said Will under his breath. *Look, everyone! The sun is shining! The bay is beautiful! We are together!*

"Any more crappo alley juice round here?" It was Kerouac this time, and his tone indicated the booze had flipped a cranial switch. He swept cold eyes around the table. "Whatsa matter? You a bunch of dingledodies?"

Before anyone else could reply, Will stood and raised his glass. "Everybody! I ... I'm glad you're my friends, that's all." He sat down just as abruptly, and the table fell silent.

Maggie bit her lower lip and stared at him as if his toasted cheese had gone moldy.

23.
Barbarians at the Gate

QUEER, THE HUMAN SPIRIT.
You speak of those across the Great Divide.
Aye. From adversity can flower the loveliest blossoms.
I seen them with my own eyes. But this is fragile beauty, Mi-Wash. Too soon after our terrible disaster, it falls away like so many rose petals.

It is sad. I knew much kindness in my people when the barbarians first came. All quarrels were put away....

Truly, 'tis never long before we humans uncage our base natures again. Then the social classes all retreat to their own and shun the rest, and pettifoggery and odium are reborn. Oh, there was some that changed. Them that climbed into the bottle and never found the way out, them that was freed from all constraints with their wives or families wiped out or gone and who indulged in the licentiousness their previous station would not allow. It were fertile ground for prophets of revolution and doomsday, that's certain sure. As usual, the women-folk held things together.

You came here.

We was luckier than many. We loved our shack, simple as it were. Except for a roughneck or two, our neighbors was a fine lot. We looked out for each other, and looked the other way when privacy or decency required. Little Artur had his regular gang of pals to brawl and feed the woodland critters with,

Delphine made a few greenbacks with sewing and nursemaid-ing, and I pulled strings to receive a stipend as superintendent of our patch of refugee shacks. It weren't a bad life, though it did get wearisome hauling water and not having a privy of our own. But we was all being pressured to move on. We'd been more than a year in the park. Delphine and I agreed. 'Twas time for a new start. Take the shack with you or lose it, they said. So I did what nearly broke my heart.

The music box ...

Sold it. I never seen Mr. Jack London again, but I never forgot what he said. Delphine, she knew a distant cousin on her mother's side, and he lived somewhere north of the Golden Gate. My first ferry to Sausalito was to meet up with this rela-tion of Delphine's, a man with walrus mustaches named José Sousa. Together we walked straight to a solicitor's office, where I handed over the proceeds from my beloved piano to a Hill-climber man willing to part with the closest thing to heaven I've seen yet ... this little piece of your beach.

THEY CAME BY land and by sea—on a moody morning when fog mist hung in the air and the horizon was nowhere to be seen. Barely past dawn they gripped clipboards and pens and were armed with official forms requiring completion in triplicate. Rushing past Luann the Mermaid, they paused to red tag the communal shower. They swarmed over the mothballed vessels and the rigged-together flotsam that served as our Water Rat homes. From motor launches and accompanied by uniformed men, they boarded the anchor-outs like plunderers.

Giving no quarter, entertaining no plea that pipes had oozed like that forever or wires had always hung in imitation of jungle vines, they issued citations for malodorous sanitation and plumbing gone awry, ludicrous construction and electri-cal circuits frighteningly haywire, hazards of fire and flood and pestilence. Even the very legality of human habitation. It amounted to the first blizzard on record for our waterfront, a bureaucratic white-out of Donner Pass proportions.

Too many tempers flared, so perhaps it was best Jake was absent, happily unaware while abalone hunting near Ft. Bragg. And so he did not witness Officer Mack and one of the sheriff's crew-cut bulls insert the carbon copy into his pawnshop choppers—official notice that THE SQUIRTLE, Jake's leaky haven, would soon be towed and sunk.

When it was finally over, physical injuries, miraculously, were limited to one sprained ankle and a minor bump on the head—a Water Rat disposing of an illicit substance took a dramatic pratfall on an algae-slick deck, and a jittery inspector tumbled backwards on discovering a fifteen-foot boa constrictor coiled lazily in a covered hatch.

But all of us were left in a daze, and no one comprehended at first what a serious threat to our way of life this was. We just resumed going about our business. In her DHARMA Maggie reached for Fifa behind some canvases propped against the bulwarks, where the cat had been in hiding since an inspector's gruff knock. Sleepily, she scratched her cat's ears. Several of us casually balled up our citations and tossed them into the bay. Most of us just went back to bed. We were used to being hassled by the Hill and their flunkies in Sausalito's officialdom. We knew how much they enjoyed poking their sticks into our nests to watch us buzz and squirm.

Yet some of the old-timers realized there was a difference this time. Crusades of the past mounted against the Water Rat kingdom were never this big ... this organized ... ham-handed. Or so thorough.

It was Varda, whose VALLEJO took the prize for most violations—a total of sixty-two—who was first to grasp the dark portent behind it all. He closely examined the documents, noting they required all cited problems to be remedied within thirty days. He closed his eyes and mentally calculated the cost of fixing only the most serious insufficiencies on his converted car ferry, then began to guess at the enormous sum repairs would require for all concerned. "The barbarians," he announced to us in solemn tones at a hastily convened gathering a few hours after the assault, "breached our moats and stormed our gates. They meant to burn and pillage our easy existence. And they took no prisoners."

At that same instant a shiver ran across a still-sleeping Will, as if a tremor had shimmied across the earth's crust beneath the Earthquake Shack. It roused him. He sat up with a start, but heard only the soft gurgle of his fish tank pump. Still, somehow, he knew.

Buck Buckworthy was back.

Will's premonition and Varda's xenophobia were both dead on. Buck was indeed on a revenge bender. Under the flag of civic duty and the betterment of our town, he had rounded up a Hill posse of "concerned citizens" who wanted, no, *demanded* that we be gotten rid of. Not only were we artsy-fartsy scoff-laws and unconscionably messy, we were a godless and prob-ably Communist element that deserved eviction once and for all. Their traps were set out while we paid no attention, and now they had been sprung in unison. We Rats were caught, and caught good.

As you might imagine, in the days that followed talk around town was reduced to this single subject. Water Rats huddled at our usual haunts, in Old Town and along the harbor jetties, piers, and docks; Hillclimbers did the same at dinner parties and over mahjong boards in their *House Beautiful* homes or at the Sausalito Club, the yacht club bar, on the commuter fer-ries to San Francisco. The sole common grounds, more or less, were Juanita's and the Valhalla, though Sally Stanford was quick to make her loyalties clear enough.

"Get out of my sight," she told Buck Buckworthy when he

tried showing up for dinner soon thereafter. "Your money ain't good here no more."

Luann, her bouffant already in shambles from Hurricane Gulch's gales, dissolved into tears on the spot and ruined her makeup too. A waitress escorted her out while her husband called Sally every name in his big-as-the-Lonestar State book. The old gal never flinched, and when Buck Buckworthy had finally sputtered out, she said in her caustic rumble, "Running a whorehouse, I seen lots of little pricks, Buck. Yours don't scare me."

Well, Juanita, hearing what Sally Stanford had said, was not about to be outdone. When her laughter finally subsided—she threw back her head and shook like a giant Jell-O mold—she sauntered over to Officer Mack, who happened to be nursing his third cup of coffee. Grabbing him up by the nape of his neck, she lugged him the length of her Galley, then unceremoniously dump him in the dirt outside her front door.

THEN, LATER THE same week, the other shoe dropped. Mayor J.R. Archey called a press conference. Like all town elected officials, J.R. was a part-timer and pliable as a rubber knife. And though he was also publisher of a chain of small weeklies in the county, it was his wife who had the money, and Luann Buckworthy was her new best friend. Being a newspaper man at least assured that the press swarmed around this sheep in wolf's clothing, his visage framed by ringlets of hair, his eyes small and nose bulbous, lips liver-like, as he announced the big news about Sausalito's "waterfront redevelopment."

NEW PIER FOR PASSENGER SHIPS HAILED!

So, afterwards, gushed the Archey broadsheets. *The Marin Scoop*, *The Mt. Tam Peak*, *The Novato Tattler*, and *The Fairfax*

Ferret. Not surprisingly, the story also received wide play all around the bay. The mayor-publisher was quoted extensively even if the details he offered were sketchy.

A "major ship line," he said, sought a new port and Sausalito "intends to be first on board."

Where would this pier be located? "We have two or three potential sites."

Someone was smart enough to ask if the timing of the crackdown at Galilee Harbor and this momentous announcement were pure coincidence.

"Yes, of course. No connection whatsoever," assured Mr. Mayor.

Meaning anyone dumb enough to believe that should buy an ice sculpture business in Death Valley or the beach umbrella concession in Fresno.

24.
Father to Daughter

NTS, HE TYPED. ANNNNNTTTS. O TO BE AN ANT!
Heavy seasonal rains hit us early that year—right after Buck Buckworthy did. They began when a high Pacific wind shouldered the first large front landward, an armada of gunmetal gray and lamp black, at an astounding speed. Meteorological bomb bays yawned and the air turned liquid. It poured sixteen hours without pause. Afterwards, clusters of soot-bottomed cumuli conducted rear-guard sorties, soak-and-runs, for another ten hours. Then, at last, the sky cleared, scrubbed clean and speckled with starlight. A high lunar tide lifted the bay, and it crashed against the low seawall protecting the underbelly of the Earthquake Shack.

Shortly after the rains finally stopped, Will stood peering out a window clouded by the moist warmth inside. The shack had the presence of a ship's cabin even more than usual, and he could feel the sea's power as it exploded into froth and dark rivers under his feet. Just behind him there was a *plink plink* as a leak from the sodden roof fell to the chowder pot positioned to catch it. He turned to walk slowly back toward the galley and was rinsing his coffee mug when he first noticed them.

Ant season was underway too.

This was a phenomenon Will had not known growing up in Ohio. Tiny black refugees on the march, hundreds and maybe thousands of them, fleeing their flooded underground nests.

Escaping upward and into the shack through unseen cracks and crevices. Single-file caravans as if on creepy-crawly spice trade routes, startling in their sudden commerce across countertops and floors, up and down walls and plumbing fixtures. An endless procession—follow the leader, keep moving.

Fortunately they were harmless. They had no bite or sting, though on discovering a crumb or, heaven forbid, the sugar bowl, they gathered and swarmed. Will had lingered, empty coffee mug in hand, like a young boy mesmerized at the amazing bug world. But also marveling from a grown-up perspective at how they had fled their destroyed domestic lives.

Such control, precision, orderliness! There was no room for remorse or regret in the emotional life of an ant. They did not look back, they simply carried on. Impulsively, he swept a hand in a swath across one parade line, scattering the tiny creatures. At the newly made break the lead ant reared on its hind legs and pawed the air like a miniature stallion, head feelers waggling; others, refusing to be halted, passed on either side but then fell into wild confusion in the gap. They circled back or veered off the path, in search of missing comrades or simply for the lost way. But confusion was brief. Quickly the chain was restored and unbroken again. The refugees resumed their disciplined retreat to—where? Anywhere until the rains ended, that was all.

Leaving the galley to the nighttime visitors, Will returned to his desk. He could avoid no longer what he vowed to do. The sheet he had inserted waited in his Royal portable, and he began anew. ANTS he typed another time in the clack-clacking of two fingers. O TO BE AN ANT!! Ripping the paper from the carriage, he fed in another. He expelled a deep breath and squared his shoulders. "Okay," he said.

Dearest Ariel, he wrote to a daughter who would soon be old enough to read Dick and Jane.

EXCERPT FROM *A letter (never mailed) from Will Dumont to Ariel Dumont*: Your father sees himself on a bright yellow school bus. If I think hard and close my eyes, I am looking through finger smudges at the trees and houses of my neighborhood, the parked cars, the lazy dogs and the little children playing. I am maybe twelve. On the bus it is noisy and hot, and the ride is bumpy, but outside all is quiet and peaceful as I watch it go by.

Appearances can fool, I know that, but this is the first time I wonder how the world gets to be the way it is—and whether there is anything we can do to change that.

I think about my family, my neighborhood and town, and then, who knows why, our whole country and what it says it stands for. And then our whole giant, confusing planet. From nowhere, the question comes to me: how come my dad—your grandpa you don't even remember—was supposed to kill as many Japs and Germans as he could, but now they are on our side against the Russians, who used to be on our side but now want to kill us? I don't suppose many kids that age wonder about such things. Maybe you won't. I was probably too serious for my own good.

Yet what was I, a boy riding the bus from school that day, to make of this? I couldn't shake it. So I sat there and thought about it, thought about it hard while the familiar sights of my childhood passed by. I didn't solve it then. It took a long time before I could come up with an answer that stuck with me.

Now I want you to try thinking hard, like me on the bus, and remember what I tell you. I don't expect you to understand yet either—but maybe someday before I'm laid out like salt cod, you will.

No one can claim the world is, or should be, only one way, all black or all white, when any fool can see it has more colors than can be imagined. Truth is not simple, even in mathematics and science, where what's "true" today was a heretic's theory yesterday and will probably be obsolete and forgotten tomorrow. Yet we all crave certainty. Why? Your dad is no philosopher, but I know enough to understand how wandering off the well-worn path is pretty damn tough, even dangerous.

And I know "thou shalt not" is a lot easier than "thou shalt not except maybe...."

I once met a man who claimed to have traveled around the world thirty-one times. And what great lesson did he take from this? Everything, he discovered, is illegal. Somewhere. Imagine that!

As long as we humans walk on two feet, there will be a parent or teacher or priest or an entire government that insists one way is the only way—but we don't have to believe them.

That is my first lesson to you.

My darling girl, so much time together has been lost. When you read this—I won't write "if"—there still may be time to give you more than your biological first step. I want to give you my eyes, so you can walk where I stumbled and jump the big potholes where I fell. Is there a father anywhere who does not want this? Or who doesn't deserve the chance to offer as much?

Someday I hope you will find it in your heart to forgive me these missing years.

HE PUNCHED AT the keys until the thumping broke though his concentration, and he stopped to peer up at the ceiling of the shack. The roof, he thought. The 'coons are early tonight. He couldn't hear any of their chattering, and the windows were too steamed-up to see if they were already nosing around on the deck.

He stared back at the Royal, dissatisfied.

Too preachy.

Instead of starting over, he lowered his head. Slowly, he

traced circles on his forehead with his fingertips and then began to massage his temples. The exertions of trying to capture on paper his "lesson" had made him more tired than he realized. His mind flashed to Maggie, and he thought about her and Varda and the others at Galilee and his silly advice about waiting to see if anything would really happen. About not taking Buck Buckworthy and whatever he might be scheming seriously. Suddenly Ariel felt very far away, and not for the first time. He was having trouble remembering exactly how she looked, the details of her face and her expression when she said goodbye to him the last time. Of course she would be different by now. So it really didn't matter, did it?

His eyes still shut, he took himself away from all the lives he had led, the places where he lived. Away from the yellow bus and Uselma box house, his ivy-covered college, the rundown colonial he shared with an ex-Navy Seal when he first met Pickle. Away from the elm-shaded nineteen-thirties neighborhood where he and Pickle made their home and where she and Ariel still did. Away even from the Earthquake Shack and the life he was trying to make for himself now.

He lost himself to a fantasy. His favorite fantasy. Not the arousing kind or the usual dreams of power or wealth, but one that transported him to his twilight, when a man finally sheds the yoke of his labors. Some men dream of the emerald golf course with the sprawling split-level just off the ninth tee, of going eighteen in the morning and swapping lies and reliving memories over clubhouse cocktails in the afternoon. Others, of endless happy days carving duck decoys or hammering driftwood furniture; or watching sports on television, playing grandpa and keeping up the best manicured lawn and biggest Christmas light extravaganza on the block.

In Will's fantasy, he was forever the nomad.

Like a tumbleweed, he blew into each new town with everything he owned, wandered into the nearest saloon or mom's diner and made the bartender's acquaintance, or the waitress's. He would sweep a glance around the place and offer up a toothsome smile to all the locals who were roosting. They all lived there. Their lives were there. There and only there. He paid close attention to what was on their minds that day. The weather. The high school football hero. Town politics. The latest local gossip or scandal. Their hometown soap opera. If someone happened to be singing or picking a guitar, he listened for truths that spoke to these people's lives and loves and losses. He would remember the best of their stories and songs. He put them in his journal afterwards. They were like road signs on his memories.

Then someone always asked him. What about you, mister? What's your story? And so he would begin unfolding his own tales—and they could hardly believe their ears. He was like a tropical orchid that had strolled right into their unassuming garden. Hell, he might as well be from another galaxy. Some of them would think he was putting them on, or trying to make their own lives seem small or insignificant. They might get angry. He sensed their heat and had to talk them down, reassure them he wasn't the kind of stranger who gets his kicks from peeing on lives that were rooted and had tidy, secure boundaries.

It was *his* fantasy, so Will never got the bejeezus kicked out of him. And he got taken home by the sweetest, prettiest woman in the place, who thought she was bedding as close to a movie star—Elvis, even!—as she'd ever get. So what if he was a little stringy, his joints kind of creaky from being so many miles on the road? So what if he was old enough to be....

Next morning, of course, he was gone. *Hasta la vista*. An old man, still roaming. The wanderer, like Hayden's schooner reaching into the wind. And the long string of girls he had seduced? He liked to think some of them would never again see their two blocks of Main Street the same, that their whiff of an interesting stranger's scent had awakened them to the world's limitless possibilities just a bus fare beyond.

Will smiled. It was a rueful smile. Just a fantasy, he reminded himself, sort of like diving for treasure inside my head. Then he remembered a poet he read in college, an unpronounceable Polack name. The guy was practically the poet laureate of going nowhere. In his verse he praised what he called the courage of an ordinary life. Who would want such a life? That's what he had wondered then.

The courage of an ordinary life ... now he understood too well.

He had come here, to this life in the Earthquake Shack, because the courage of an ordinary life had failed him, and he needed to heal and grow strong to face up to being ordinary again. But now this new life threatened to become something else ... another test of who he was ... of what he could find within himself. In order to win with the hand he had been dealt and had played. In order to make a stand, to stay. He felt like a crab whose rock was being overturned. He was in danger of being flushed right out of his hiding place.

There was one thing more about Will's fantasy. When he was not telling his stories or listening to new ones in whatever place he happened to be, he tucked long accounts of his wanderings—minus the seductions, of course—into an envelope. These he sealed with care and, licking another four-cent stamp, sent them on their way to Ariel, day after day.

25.
The Ice Pick Cometh

THE BAD STUFF, AS EVERYONE KNOWS, COMES IN threes—so there we were, reeling from the week's bureaucratic and meteorological deluge, when all at once we realized our world was one Water Rat short. Bel and Bunny were first to notice. The Turban Woman was gone. The poor dear was nowhere to be found. Not in the town's parks. Not wandering along the waterfront, where she would usually be spotted muttering to herself and shaking her towel-enshrouded head as if debating an invisible foe. Nowhere. A few of us speculated she might have skipped town, but that seemed unlikely. Where would she go? And why?

We were organizing a search party when Dr. Alan Watts, seated in the lotus position on a grassy patch near the VALLEJO, motioned at Will, who was happening by on some errand that morning, and told him in a meditative tone of voice, "I have an old friend at Marin General. Dolores Swain is currently resident there."

Will stopped to loom over Dr. Watts. "Dolores who?"

"That's her real name. The Turban Woman." Our Zen philosopher's face was an ocean of serenity with a surf line or two that revealed an as yet untamed churn beneath the surface.

Will whistled lowly and crouched down so as not to mistake what he was hearing. "What happened? We've all been worried sick about her. Was she hurt?"

"Not at first!"

Will searched the Zen doctor's expression for clues to his meaning. He found not a one. "So …?"

"She was sent to the psychiatric ward."

This hardly explained things. "Why?" Will asked.

"A complaint was lodged."

"What, her turban on crooked?"

"No, brother," Dr. Watts said with an enigmatic glance. "It was her undiminished libido." Closing his eyes, he tilted his face skyward to bask in the sunshine that had just broken through the cloud cover.

Will waited him out as long as he could, until finally his frustration could not be contained. "Alan? Could you possibly share a little more of what happened?"

Dr. Watts said nothing.

"Alan!"

Dr. Watts's eyelashes fluttered open, and he looked at Will dreamily. "Took a try at humping the Reverend Nash, that's all."

"But he's close to ninety."

"On Litho Street," Dr. Watts continued. "At half past two in the afternoon."

"Fuck …"

"Precisely!" Dr. Watts rocked back and forth on his haunches. "The old girl broke his hip. An ambulance conveyed them both to hospital."

"I see," was all Will could manage. He wasn't sure whether to laugh or cry. There was obviously more yarn to unravel in this tale. "And …?" he asked.

"The Reverend is fine."

"The Reverend?"

Dr. Watts closed his eyes again. "How to explain it …," he wondered aloud.

"Try."

"Right. Brace yourself. Here it is. My good friend, the physician, asked me, 'Alan, are you aware that a classic symptom of female hysteria is an inappropriate sexual advance?' Mrs. Swain's history, it seems, indicates previous instances of anti-social behavior, and in such cases he said a special procedure is often employed."

"Jesus. Please get to the point."

"Patience. As a white lotus blossom is not stained by water, so we must not be stained by the world. The Buddha tells us that." He exhaled gravely. "It's a struggle sometimes, nonetheless."

"C'mon, Alan. What did they do?"

"A hundred years ago they might have performed a clitoridectomy ... to expunge her sexual pleasure."

By then Will was struggling for calm. "But what about today? What do they do *now*?"

"I've been reading up on the subject, as a matter of fact. An American neurosurgeon—"

"Christ, no ..."

"—With the unfortunate name of Watts, no relation whatsoever, has legitimized a surgical technique to relieve symptoms of anxiety for psychiatric patients. He severs the *leukos*, the white fibers connecting the frontal lobes to the rest of the brain. It's since been promoted as a remedy for *all* human sadness, especially among females." Will rose from his crouch and stared blankly toward the bay—the things humans do to each other could make anyone feel like hiding his head in a casing of cotton. Dr. Watts continued, "This Watts has a colleague, a man named Freeman, who once remarked, 'Lobotomized patients make good citizens.'"

"Lobotomized ..." Will repeated the terrifying word.

"Indeed."

"How ... what did they ..."

"She was fully conscious. The organ of human intelligence

is incapable of feeling pain—philosophers and poets always have fun with that." Dr. Watts looked up at Will and saw he did not appreciate the irony. "Holes were no doubt drilled on either side of her skull and a steel instrument rather like a butter knife was inserted. The whole while, they conversed with her, because the patient's responses determine how much has yet to be destroyed. Transcripts can often pinpoint the precise moment at which an aspect of personality vanishes forever."

"This is so wrong...." Will shuddered and felt his stomach going queasy.

"Keep your pecker up, dear boy. You won't believe this next part. Watts tells his patients to sing 'God Bless America' and then merrily joins in. And this Dr. Freeman once asked one of his, 'What's going through your mind?' To which came the beautifully lucid reply, 'A knife.'"

"Please. Enough."

"Just go with it!" said Dr. Watts "Reality is illusion anyway." He paused to breathe in and out deeply again. "Shall we talk of the other technique ...?"

Who knows why, but Will nodded dumbly.

"First, the patient's eyelids are lifted. Then, to a depth of precisely two and one-half inches, a sharp instrument is hammered through the orbital bone of each eye socket. The device looks much like an ice pick. It takes about ten minutes."

Will's nausea was now too real to ignore.

"My doctor friend wasn't certain which procedure was employed on our Mrs. Swain. He did, however, overhear a surgical nurse laughing about how they had to promise not to remove her turban. After the operation, of course, she no longer cared."

26.
Waterloo

I-WASH?

Here. Is it not funny how we remember? I was by our lodge house, with my family. Our village was full of our people—the men smoking and gambling, the women preparing the midday meal and caring for the small ones. The children running and playing, the older ones like me helping our parents, pretending to be grown up.

Truly.

I was a girl who thought my happy life would go on without end.

Delphine and me, we thought so too, when we arrived here with young Artur. We loved this village from the first.

But you were strangers. These barbarians, they greeted you warmly?

Some was barbarians dressed in London fashion, cold as ice if you chanced upon them. They was the high and mighty who lived upwind, in the hills. But most folk were welcoming to us and our shack. They brought us covered dishes and fresh-made berry pies while we settled in. We felt at home.

Like the first of your people, the great waters carried you here.

Aye. Delphine's cousin, José Sousa, got his Portugee cronies together to sledge the shack from the barge what brought us over, up past the tide line and onto her resting place. We gave her a grounding of rocks and pilings and laid a low sea wall across her front. Then we was here for good. Delphine, especially, wanted to leave the old life far behind. I did too. But it were not so simple. "Wanting" and "doing" being two quite different beasts....

EACH MORNING NOW, the Water Rats woke with a collective hangover. The gruesome news about the Turban Woman merely gave a new turn to the thumbscrews that dug into our temples as we faced the stark reality. *The Hill ... meant ... to get rid of us.* Our position was more precarious than ever before, that we knew, and *some* action had to be taken—but what? No one had the ready answer or cash to fix the violations, and even if we did, new ways would only be thought up to force us out. Most of us were sure of that.

Once again it was Varda who put voice to our dread. "First," he said, "they chase away as many as possible, *all* of us if they can. They build their pier. Then camera-toting tourists descend on Sausalito and they begin to chant, 'There's nothing to buy! There's nothing to buy!' So we must offer them trinkets and beads and quaint carvings of polished redwood burl. And soon our idyllic waterfront becomes a tawdry bazaar. It fills with souvenir sellers and saltwater taffy stands. Gone will be the fresh vegetables and earthy breads of the Purity Market, the gadget for our every whim and the hobbyhorse out front for the kiddies at Marin Hardware, and then we say goodbye to Duke Eno's plumbing and Willie Yee's, and our treasured, homespun hangouts like Juanita's. All gone, pushed out by the invading hordes. But that's still not the worst of it. Then these uninvited guests will say, 'Oh, just look at the way these people on the waterfront live. So untidy! So dirty! We hate the sight of them!' And before we can draw another breath, Archey and his henchmen will condemn what's left of our dwellings, and

the wrecking crews will sweep over us like wildfire chasing
every woodland creature with legs to flee. The Sausalito we
love ... lost forever ... dead. *Nekros*."

OUR FIRST MEETING to decide on a course of action was at Juanita's. But the gatherings soon moved up to Arvie Engstrom's
to give us the added privacy of the abandoned shipyards of
Marinship. Those waning October evenings were nothing if
not memorable, and as usual we did things our own way, even
when faced with possible extinction. As six o'clock neared, we
began arriving one by one or in pairs, to avoid attention. Boat
builders, fishermen, shipyard hands, plumbers, electricians,
and carpenters still in coveralls and knitted caps, their wives
in housedresses with scarves to protect their perms. Artists in
paint-spattered clothing, beats and bohemians in their military surplus and faded denim. As for the order of business,
eating and drinking, naturally, came first. It was a potluck for
the revolution. Mama-san, the tiny and fierce empress of our
only Japanese restaurant, regularly brought steaming sukiyaki,
and there was almost always a homemade chowder or a gamey
raccoon chili with sourdough, a salad of miner's lettuce and
purslane plucked from the Headlands. Someone brought home
brew and there were jugs of cheap wine. One time a Water Rat
we knew as Orphan Annie passed around a tray of her famous
brownies, but the noticeable lack of concentration that followed
forced us, most reluctantly, to ask her not to bring them again.
There were limits to what even we were able to ingest and still
maintain a semblance of decorum.

After the chow, musical instruments came out next, mouth
harps, fiddles, banjos, and guitars, and after an interlude of
playing and plucking and often singing, occasionally a verse
or impromptu doggerel was offered up by droopy-eyed Hilda,
a long-time Rat who gleaned her living as "a muse for hire."

Those on the Hill,
they may have great views.
But in sum their numbers are few.
So from high in their nests,
they began to insist
there should be a Water Rat quota.

But they forgot the thing that's easy to do
when you're down with the low of the low
is reach up high, squeeze real tight,
and grab 'em fast and hard by the scrota.

At eight-thirty or maybe nine or even ten o'clock, when finally we got down to business, it became immediately clear why we were best at ignoring our predicament. In democratic fashion, we gave each Water Rat a chance to complain about the state of affairs, past, present, and future. Democracy, as we all know, can be a terribly messy business. Ours degenerated quickly. Half-drunk Rats were too quick to lob catcalls of "oh, yeah?" and "that ain't nothing compared to ..." and "you think that's bad, why...." Someone was needed to keep the lid on this boiling pot, and Will was our overwhelming choice.

And so he tried, he really did.

Will's Waterloo was the third meeting at Arvie Engstrom's. More reluctantly than we knew, he climbed atop the scaffolding encircling the pale skeleton of a trawler and called the meeting to order. We sat on the workshop floor below, a crazy-quilt jumble.

Will asked us to pipe down and called the meeting to order. "Mephisto, you wanted to go first tonight. Go ahead, just keep it civil, okay?"

Mephisto, dressed in black as usual and with Marilyn Macaw perched on his head, stood and faced us. His eyes gave off a glow some might call messianic. "Fellow Rats," he began, thumbs jammed into his leather vest pockets, "I've been listening to you carp and complain and blame this one or that. But I'm here to say, we ignore the true threat. Don't be misled. Our enemy is not the tourists or that *trotel* Archey. What will it take for us to get the true picture? Ask yourselves, who intends to use this new pier—who plots to steal our peace in the name of profit and greed? I mean, who is this corporate sea monster? The only words understood in boardrooms are *gelt* and *krieg...*." He got no further before the first taunt came flying from the back of the workshop.

"Talk American!"

Which prompted swift retaliation from over near the tool rack.

"*Chutdafuckup!*"

Will jumped in, intent on heading off another free-for-all. "Keep it clean, Jake," he admonished before pointing a finger at the source of the original outburst, a tinkerer of note from New Town. "Orville, you take it easy too. Mephisto's only saying they respect money and power."

"*War*, Will. I said war, not just power," Mephisto corrected him. "Our only hope is to fight to our last cent and last breath."

"I ain't got any cents but I'll breathe all you want!"

"Thanks for that, Hal," Will shouted back over hoots and an outburst of applause. "You still growing garlic in those old nail kegs? Your breath could be our secret weapon." That got more laughter going, and he thought things might be back under control. After he thanked Mephisto, he scrutinized our faces for someone unlikely to provoke a new outburst. Maggie raised her hand and waved it at him. Relieved, he nodded. "Go ahead, Mag."

She stood, her back to him, her hands resting on flared hips. "Everybody," she pleaded, "force is *not* the answer. It never is. Look what Gandhi did—one man stared down the whole damn British Empire. Peaceful, that's the only way. First we get public opinion on our side—"

"Hell's bells on that!" came a loud voice. "They're driving us out like we was worse than rats!"

"How about we shove a few of their fancy mansions over the edge!" shouted another. "A good Cat diesel would do 'er!"

Maggie seemed about to take on her hecklers when Will jumped in. "Hey, hold on, hold on," he pleaded above the agitated murmurings. "*Please*, let's keep an even keel. I second Maggie's peaceful tack." A look from Will convinced her, with obvious reluctance, to sit down. "Raise your hand to speak next, okay? That's right. Yes. Mrs. Emerson? You must have something reasonable to say."

The town librarian, a septuagenarian in sensible shoes, rose to her feet. "You're a sweet boy, Will," she said. Her hair was neatly tucked into a wispy bun, and wire-rimmed bifocals sat halfway down her nose. But Will lost any sense of relief when he saw her jaw muscles had started working. "I say finish the job we started," she barked out. "Feed that Buckworthy to the sharks—starting with his itty-bitty, teensy-weensy nubbin of a dick...."

"That would get his attention, all right!"

"Sharks'd spit it out!"

A few of us noticed Will's face redden as old Mrs. Emerson delivered her payload. His resolve seemed to flee like a flock of panicked seagulls—all shit, flapping wings, and a rubble field of empty mussel shells. His arms slumped to his sides, pinned and held motionless by an invisible force, and he looked out at us in distress. *How could I do this to these good people? How could I be so stupid, taking on a mad bull like Buckworthy?* Of course, his inner turmoil had nothing to do with that, not really, and his fight was not even with the Hill. As was revealed in his next wave of inner anguish: *I can't do this anymore ... I came here to get away from this ... I just can't.*

Finally Mephisto's voice rose above the continuing chaos to deliver the knock-out punch. "What are you?" he shouted at Will. "A man or a fog bank? *Ein geist*? Show some backbone!"

Will awoke to the present. The burden he had carried to this moment was too heavy, suddenly, and he could pretend no longer. "I ... sorry ...," he said. No one heard him. "*Sorry!*" he yelled over the din.

A hush fell over Arvie Engstrom's workshop, and when all eyes turned toward Will then, we saw a face the color of raw tuna. "We're getting nowhere," he gasped, as if out of breath. "I ..." With that, he leapt from the scaffolding and landed on his feet with a heavy exhalation of breath. His hurried sweep of a glance over us did not focus. He started toward the door, forcing those in his path to part like the Red Sea. Saying not another word and disappearing from our sight.

Maggie alone trailed after him into the night air. "Will ... wait."

He kept walking.

When she caught up finally and demanded to know why he had fled, he brushed away the question. "This is crazy," is all he said. She smelled beer on his breath.

"It's not that bad," she tried to calm him. "Heck, if we all walked in lock step, we might as well live someplace else. In Russia or something. We may be a little disorderly, but we just want to figure out what to do."

Abruptly, he stopped, and he had a disoriented look she had never seen on him before. His features seemed out of kilter, and there was something different behind his eyes. He was like a total stranger. At first she didn't know what to call what she saw. Then it came to her. He looked *hunted*. "Will, this isn't like you. What's wrong with you? Talk to me. Please."

He started walking again, faster than before. "I'm gone, gone, out of here," he dismissed her over his shoulder. "This isn't my fight. It's your fight."

"Will …," she called after him. "Don't just leave like this." But he kept walking and did not look back.

MAGGIE WENT LOOKING for him later that evening, leaning into the chill. Bridgeway was quiet. The black dome of sky was pierced with faraway pin holes of light. They were too distant and too cold to inspire anything but a shiver.

He was nowhere to be seen at the Glad Hand, the No Name or Trident. Nearing Old Town, she stayed alert for any whiff of him in the shifting winds. At the Valhalla Sally told her, no, he hadn't been in all night. Finally she found herself by the Earthquake Shack, where she noted that One-Eyed George was absent from the decayed piling at one end of the shack's beachfront, his usual roost. On the boardwalk directly in front of the cottage, she turned her back to the show of lights from San Francisco and the sentry glare of Alcatraz but could barely make out the shack's low roofline in the dark. Across the narrow beach, inside, the only visible light was the fish tank's ghostly glow.

After steadying herself, she started slowly up the gangplank. She knocked, tentatively, and the Dutch door rattled on its hinges. A faint scent of him escaped, though she knew this was not absolute assurance he was at home. She knocked again, loudly this time. She had to know why he ran out on them. What was eating at him so.

And there was news to tell him.

Varda had arrived shortly after Will left, to pull a folded yellow paper from his Greek cap. He read aloud the telegram from Tahiti relayed by ship short wave to the mainland.

HEARD ABOUT TROUBLE STOP WIRED MY ATTY
TO ASSIST STOP CONTACT M MUSSELMAN ESQ
LOS ANGELES STOP HAYDEN.

Finally it seemed we had a way to fight back. A big-time
L.A. lawyer could be expensive, but how wouldn't it be worth
it? Sharp legal maneuvering might at least delay the pier and
stop the harassment of Galilee's residents and the anchor outs,
wouldn't it? But how much *would* this cost, we wanted to know.
And how would we pay for it? "Five thousand for starters" was
Varda's guess. That monstrous sum put a pall over our celebra-
tory mood, but still … for the first time in weeks there was
genuine hope. And without hope, we were only marking time
in a march to our own funeral.

Maggie was buoyed by Varda's news, but she had another
reason for wanting to find Will. Something much more personal. Their bleary fumblings before Will's thanksgiving
seemed so long ago, yet they had not rekindled their passion
since. Nobody's fault. He had been called away again for several days, and she had been pushing herself on a series of new
paintings. The work had left her feeling exhausted. In truth,
she woke up queasy these days too, and noticed a soreness to
her breasts. Her period was late.

All this she wrote off to worry. She fretted over how to
save her DHARMA and refused to take the signals for what they
could be. But she could not deny the powerful need she felt
now. She needed both to reassure him and to seek reassurance
of her own. And thus she craved connection to him. Her body
longed to be with his, alongside his warmth, and she longed to
hear his soft sputterings as he slipped into the silent deep.

There was no response from inside the shack. She peered
into the nearest window. Saw only the penumbra of fish tank
light. Turning to leave, she noticed for the first time that his
dory was gone.

I should have known, she said to herself and smiled know-
ingly. Refuge on the water.

27.
Return of the Turban Woman

WILL DID NOT SHOW AT ARVIE ENGSTROM'S THE next time or any time after that—though his disappearing act came just when we could have used him most. That's because it was only a matter of days before Maggie awoke in her DHARMA feeling like puking but also smelling a rat. Or worse, smelling pig—a whole herd of them.

We might have figured Buck Buckworthy wouldn't dawdle while we dithered. And, looking back, why should we have been surprised when, on one of those GREETINGS FROM SAUSALITO mornings, Officer Mack and his boys positioned themselves to guard the bulldozers? These steel predators rolled off their flatbed trucks and began by devouring the dozen weathered sheds and lean-tos huddled at the edge of Galilee Harbor, used for years as shelters for stores of maritime tools and gear, studios for waterfront artists and even a pee-wee Buddhist shrine. What the machines missed, goons with crowbars quickly finished off.

Then the bulldozers shoved aside the mountain of debris. They were clearing the way for the fencing crew. At first Maggie and her neighbors watched from their waterborne homes, disbelieving and in shock, as if a dear friend had died a sudden and terrible death. Finally, somberly, they dressed and gathered on the shoreline, where they huddled together to witness what they still did not fully comprehend. Maggie's impulse was to jump on her Schwinn and pedal fast as the wind to the boardwalk. *Will would know what to do!* But she did not. His recent odd behavior had exposed a fault line of doubt in her mind, narrow but ominous. Could scents be misleading—even false—after all? For how much did she really know about this man called Will Dumont? What was he trying to hide?

Besides, he would hear about all this soon enough. A convoy of flatbed trucks bearing these monsters of construction could not resound through town without word flooding like a high tide onto Gate Five Road.

Already the scooping and digging and unloading of timbers resembled the workings of a mutated insect colony. In the mayhem one cast-iron mammoth had already rear-ended Luann the Mermaid, pitching her forward, and Maggie's famous creation now rested face down near the communal shower. Buck's shame was burrowed deeply into the mud.

Sausalito's "waterfront redevelopment" was absolutely, *most definitely* underway.

As you can imagine, sleep that day was cut short. Once we had no doubt this nightmare was for real, there was someone besides ourselves to get mad at. The mood turned ugly. Jeers and taunts began to be hurled toward the construction crew, who returned the favor with a rich vocabulary of their own. Then a police boat arrived to clear a path through the anchor outs, making way for a construction barge and the incessant pounding of the pile driver mounted atop it. This towering beast rent the air and sent seabirds fleeing. In the houseboats glassware flew from shelves.

Overall, the panoply of this day was like a re-enacted D-Day or an entertainment for fierce Norse gods. Amazingly, that first morning only a single arrest was made. This was occasioned by the remarkable accuracy of a welcome present catapulted into the bobbing police craft—a human turd, still warm.

THAT NIGHT'S GATHERING at Arvie Engstrom's took on singular urgency. The usual foreplay of food and music was forgotten, and without Will as ringmaster the animals ran amok through the circus. Their shouts, their snarling, their cries of panic—all were wild and unchecked. Worse even than before, we completely forgot again that *we* were not the enemy—that *those* generals and their aides-de-camp were up on the Hill, that their foot soldiers below wore hard hats, not bandanas and berets.

In what passed for debate the most radical stance was assumed, of course, by Mephisto. He cried out for immediate counterattack. He demanded guerilla raids on the fledgling pier, and sabotage for the bulldozers, and these calls for destruction (and maybe worse) were predictably echoed by Jake the Anchor Out and several others. Again, Maggie pleaded for nonviolence, but she was joined this time by a handful of her own supporters, including Dr. Watts with his opaque Zen-isms. The rest scattered into the spectrum between these extremes.

More than a few Rats muttered that we might as well face the awful truth—that we were just mosquitoes to be slapped in the rich man's back yard.

Off in a corner the Turban Woman mouthed sentiments only she could decipher. Yes, here was another of the startling developments of those unforgettable days. The Turban Woman was back. And of all her possible knights in barnacled armor, Jake was the one who rode to her rescue. Managing somehow to override his aversion to womankind with an even greater outrage over the theft of an IQ. Since taking her under his wing, he was sharing his cramped quarters on THE SQUIRTLE, and watched over her like she was a helpless newborn. Which, in a manner of speaking, she was. He even shoplifted her a fluffy brand-new towel—white anchors resplendent on a field of navy—to cover her surgical scars.

It was Mephisto who related the tale of her rescue.

Only the afternoon before, he and Jake had thundered up to the state home in Glen Ellen where Dolores Swain had been taken after her lobotomy. Mephisto himself lurked behind an oleander hedge while Jake crept onto the expansive grounds. At first Jake watched the comings and goings of staff and pajama-clad inmates while crouched behind a parked ambulance. Then he found his way to a laundry room, where he slipped into an orderly's rumpled whites, stuffing his pony tail into a beanie-like cap. In this disguise he strode back into the sunshine, and fortunately the grizzled cheeks of a four-day growth went unnoticed when a nurse began to bark at him, ordering that he guide the wheelchair of some wilted soul to a spot in the shade.

Jake did as instructed, using the cover of an ancient live oak to continue his surveillance for the turban-less Dolores. But patience was not his forte. He'd never seen the woman without a towel around her head, and these gentle hills were *alive* with lumpy ladies with vacant stares.

"Thitt," he swore under his breath.

Finally, in desperation, he settled on a plan. Swinging the wheelchair around and making sure he wasn't being watched, he set his course for the parked ambulance. The driver's door was unlocked. He opened it and grunted as he lifted his charge's dead weight and deposited her onto the seat. Arranging the woman's arms on the wheel, the head rolled back and the mouth gaped to reveal yellowed teeth.

As gently as he could, Jake eased shut the ambulance door and pushed the empty wheelchair back toward the other zombie women. Hoping to avoid the butch nurse, he began wheeling from woman to woman, almost deciding on a ginger-haired resident with a dazed Mona Lisa smile before realizing it was hopeless. He also worried *he* might be pounced on by some suspicious goon: the last thing he needed was a surgeon's ice pick in his own noggin. Meantime, Mephisto was getting ever more antsy too. He decided if Jake didn't return soon, he had to be squirming inside a straight jacket, hissing sibilants.

Then all at once Jake saw something—something familiar in a way he could not place. A few feet ahead, gleaming with sweat from the Sonoma sun, there stood a doughy woman with wispy hair like a wind-blown bird's nest. *Think, Jake, think. Bingo ... the bracelet!* "

Root Dicktee Dik ...," he exclaimed.

This was indeed Dolores Swain, our own Turban Woman, because on her knobby wrist glinted a golden last link to her loved ones—a bracelet and a pair of charms engraved with the names and birth dates of her stolen kids. Years earlier, they had been sipping cherry Cokes with their mother at a drive-in on Route Sixty-Six, near Needles, when state cops snatched them away, acting on information from the FBI in Little Rock. Though Mrs. Swain was acquitted of the kidnap charges, and the trial brought to light the sexual predations of the kids' father, a good-looking blackjack dealer from Hot Springs, the state of Arkansas took custody, nonetheless; it placed the children in a public orphanage, then in separate foster homes. Jake, like many of us, had heard this sad story after the Turban Woman's son, who was then fifteen, ran over the Catholic priest. Afterwards he smashed the parish Lincoln into a telephone pole with Little Rock police in pursuit, still dressed in altar boy's vestments from the eleven o'clock mass. The Turban Woman's former in-laws, according to Marin sheriff's deputies, were looking for her to foot the funeral bill.

Edging closer now, Jake circled behind the woman and rushed toward her. He never slowed, and he hit her running. Her knees buckled, and she fell backward into the wheelchair with a whoosh of air. Her mouth moving but no sounds coming out. He continued wheeling her fast as he dared, peering around furtively to see if anyone was after them. But he saw only empty stares, indifferent glances, until suddenly there came a loud and continuous blast of horn.

Nurses snapped to, scanning for the source of the alarm. Then burly orderlies raced in the direction of the ambulance. There they were startled to discover a drooling inmate, head pressed against the steering wheel horn. It was the perfect diversion.

With a final rearward glance, Jake guided the Turban Woman through a gap in the oleander hedge and over to Mephisto's Indian Chief, which was roaring to life. He struggled to lift her from the chair and onto the sidecar seat. Then he hopped on behind Mephisto and peeled off the orderly's tunic and cap as they sped away. The Turban Woman's bare head was thrown back, her jaws still moving, foamy saliva at the corners of her mouth.

EVEN THE TURBAN Woman turned and looked up as Varda shouted, "Friends!"

He was scaling the same scaffolding where Will had presided, and he announced over our continued squabbling, "We must fight money with money. And I know how!"

A devilish smile crossed Varda's face, and we saw his eyes were wild. Arvie Engstrom's place became eerily quiet.

"A celebration!"

We stared back in silence.

"Yes, good friends, a celebration ... of us." His voice boomed through the workshop like the bullfrog at the bottom of the well. "We are not like them. Each morning we don't wake up to scheme. 'How do I make money? And more money and more money?' We live! We enjoy life. We create. With our hands, our minds ... and with our loins." At our howls of approval he winked. "That is what makes us special. Why we live here in dear Sausalito, so favored by the gods, a place of beauty and celebration. Friends, we must use what we have, what we know, to defeat these money grubbers ... these turkey vultures who look down their bloody beaks at us. If we unite, we cannot lose! And why is that? Because, deep down, *they want what we have!* We are free. They are not. And so they are drawn to us like grunions to the beach, flies to shit. So what do we do? I tell you what. We give them shit that is the sweetest smelling they have ever seen. We throw the biggest, the craziest, the most amazing shindig in the history of Sausalito!"

Varda stood before us, a hoary-headed Neptune hauling in his nets. "This I say to you: here, on our beloved waterfront, we will rival the court of the Sun King ... the legendary Caligula ... even the revelries of Mt. Olympus itself. A work of art, that's what we will unveil! A fatted cash cow, for the preservation and perpetuation of the Water Rat kingdom. And ... we ... will ... make them ... pay!"

No amount of wriggling could free us from *this* net. We were caught. Spilling out of Arvie Engstrom's that night, we were the Horsemen of the Apocalypse after a Knute Rockne pep talk. We were the good people of Bedford Falls after Jimmy Stewart convinced us into not giving up on his beleaguered savings and loan. We were Spanky and Our Gang scheming how to beat Butch and his bullies by putting on a show. Varda had us, and from that moment forward, we knew our best common defense against this enemy was ...

... A party.

28.
What's Good for Gandhi...

EVER STOP TO CONSIDER WHY WE'RE THE WAY WE are?

We replace what has gone—that is our teaching.

Come again.

Have you not seen how, in every village and family, only so many are the shy ones, the strong or weak ones, or the brave? We are taught our spirits come from the Great Spirit—from Coyote, who decides how many of the people are grasses and how many flowers.

Injun hokum … yet try as I might, there was no changing who I was. Like a moth, I were drawn to the flame.

So was I. The music box …

Ah. Yes. In my case I felt the pope's own hot breath on my neck, but what was I to do? Delphine, precious girl, she wanted to raise a big brood and me to have respectable work, day work. But I weren't no shopkeep. I couldn't stomach it as a ferryman. 'Twas not in my blood, not like the rhythms from my kind of music box.

Good! You made people dance and sing!

Good? Aye, at first. I got that day job—at the Miramar, a posh joint on pilings off the foot of Johnson Street, playing for the ladies and gents come to tea or to splash in the saltwater tubs. The Miramar were billed as "catering to the trade of the better element." We got locals from up the hill, a heap of well-heeled San Franciscans ferried across the Gate. Delphine was happy. I brought home a decent wage, and was even making the acquaintance of Sausalito's upper crust. From time to time my old Red Rooster ways still come in handy, though, as when I did the wee favor for Mr. Hearst, who owned the *Examiner* newspaper and a big estate in town. Sea Point. He were one of our big chiefs, and he had a new bride and a New York architect in tow. Word was he was planning to build her a fairy tale castle above Water Street. Mr. Hearst was tall but he had a high voice. It took me aback the first time he squeaked a request for his wife's favorite rag—a nigger song called "Possum and Taters." Some of the British colony snobs was shocked, it being too low-down for them, but I put my all into it. I liked Mr. Hearst and his pretty wife. He didn't give a hoot what anybody thought and thanked me with a swell tip. Then, a week or two later, he was back by himself ... so I thought. He were nervous, I could see that by his eyes. Walked up to me and whispered, "Friend, I need a favor." An old paramour were waiting for him in a private booth, he said. This lady friend was threatening to raise bloody hell. Hearst said he needed me to keep a sharp lookout for his wife, who was due to pop in at any minute. When she did come in, I told him, I'd start banging out "Possum and Taters" to beat the band. Well, it weren't but ten minutes and there she was. I threw myself into the rag, never played louder nor faster in my life—I was nervous now too. But there were a grand smile on Hearst's face when he re-emerged. And later, he saw to it a fat envelope got dropped off. A thick wad of General Grants inside! An augury, Delphine called it. A sign of good fortune. I thought so too, though not long thereafter the Miramar burned to the water line. The owner rebuilt, that was in 1912, and then it burned again. A pity Hearst gave up his plan to build that castle ... having him in my corner might've headed off what was to come.

THE VANDALISM BEGAN almost immediately, dory-borne, hit-and-run raids in the predawn. But an overnight guard and new fencing at water's edge put a crimp into that game and thereafter work on the new pier proceeded without interruption. As Maggie would say later, "I *had* to do something." Something other, that is, than spending her days—more than a week, in fact—brooding in her DHARMA. Watching, dispirited, as her creative muse was hounded farther away with each new belch of bulldozer exhaust and every thunderclap from a timber being slammed into the mud; suffering the skin-crawling guilt that comes from observing horror at a safe distance—like staring, trance-like, at the mangled remains of a head-on car crash, at grisly photos from a crime scene, or a cobra swaying in a basket only inches from the fakir's flute.

Next thing we knew, there she was.

Our Maggie, past the security somehow, and revealed by the yellow sunburst of morning. Twenty yards offshore, chained and securely locked to the very top of the looming pile driver, she towered over the embryonic pier as she unfurled her bedsheet banner against a cloudless sky.

S.O.S.

SAVE OUR SAUSALITO

STOP THE PIER!

In those days, when citizens of a town like ours wanted to halt "progress," it was news. Newspaper photos and television footage of our Gandhi girl, magnificent in the breezes atop the giant obelisk, were seen coast to coast and even beyond. So were those Rats who paraded placards (courtesy of Miss Mortimer's third-graders) with the new S.O.S. slogan; especially Varda, who became chief spokesman for our cause in Will's continued and unexplained absence. As editorialists weighed in with their yeas, nays, or who-can-says, hundreds of letters found their way to Varda's postal box—crudely lettered and icily typed condemnations but also exclamations of support and donations from kindred spirits; many were addressed simply S.O.S., SAUSALITO, CALIF.

Buck Buckworthy, naturally, was hotter than Juanita's five-alarm chili. Even in front of the sizable crowd of gapers and the assembled reporters and photographers, it was all he could do to keep from grabbing at the bullhorn as Officer Mack affected an Old Testament tone: "MAGGIE! COME DOWN RIGHT NOW OR WE'LL COME UP AND GET YOU! I MEAN IT! YOU'RE IN SOME SERIOUS TROUBLE, YOUNG WOMAN!"

Maggie shook her head in defiance and gave us a jaunty wave. Buck glared at his boots. Mack scowled and lowered his bullhorn. His threat rang hollow anyhow. Could you imagine Mack—or one of his spry and gung-ho brothers of the badge, more likely—on page one and the six o'clock news trying to wrestle Maggie down from her perch? This was too awful for Mayor Archey, a publisher who hated negative news of any sort, to contemplate.

Just in case, we instituted a round-the-clock vigil from the houseboats. We would alert the media should the authorities be foolhardy enough to try something in the middle of the night. But what if they did clamber up and accost our wild-haired scourge of civic betterment and good order? What then? Would they take a bolt cutter to the heavy link chain and force her fingers from the rusty girders? Cuff her up there in the clouds, so some dumb cop could toss Maggie caveman-style over one shoulder and carry her back down, screaming and kicking?

They reasoned that she might come down on her own after she'd had enough of being tired, dirty, and hungry. If not, a crane would do the trick. This would offer more dignified access for what Mack would call her "apprehension and incarceration." And no awkward climbing up and back down again would be required. This option presented yet another challenge, however. An onshore crane wouldn't reach. A barge-mounted crane was needed, and it would have to be floated in. The one nearest, as luck would have it, was more than a hundred miles away, near Sacramento—four or more days across bays and inland waterways.

Thus it became a waiting game for our side and theirs. At least the pier was at a standstill in the meantime. And our little town stayed in the spotlight, with money and encouragement arriving with each morning's mail. Days dissolved into nights and became dawns again, and we told each other it was a brilliant thing our Maggie had done all by her beautiful self.

THEN THE WINDS shifted. It was the beginning of Maggie's third day aloft. Gusts came at twenty-five knots from the east, and they kicked up moguls of froth and spray. The sky darkened. The mercury began falling. Houseboats in Galilee rocked and swayed and strained against their moorings; halyards jangled crazily against masts in the marinas, and on land leaves fled the oaks and the scaly eucalyptus.

We didn't know it, but she had already begun to flag. Her protest had been meant as symbolic, a way to win attention for our cause, and she did not anticipate this delay. The wait perplexed and worried her. What could be holding things up? By far the hardest were the nights, when heavy fog swooped down on the waterfront and temperatures dipped. This time of year was mood-altering enough on a drafty houseboat, let alone when you were fifty feet in the air protected only by foul-weather gear on loan from Captain Roy's party boat. Her bones ached and her muscles complained of being wrapped around cold hard metal; the noxious combination of industrial lubricants and oxidizing iron filled her nostrils and made her head ache. Her stomach was still giving her small fits too, but whose wouldn't? Salmon jerky would never look the same again. And she was thirsty. Careful rationing of her canteen (sun tea to keep her alert) had made it stretch, but the salty fish left her tongue and throat raw and swollen. She longed for a huge glass of cool tap water.

In truth, she was afraid to eat or drink much. That was the one thing she hadn't been able to figure out in advance—in plain view of the whole world, how could a gal relieve herself? She'd just have to hold it. So the days wore on, and she tried ignoring the dull ache in her bowels. But, heavens to Betsy, did she ever have to pee! At night, as she was enveloped by darkness and cold, the urge was nearly irresistible. Just ... let it ... *happen*. Let it go, let it gush, let it stream into her pink cotton panties, bloom across the seat of her dungarees and down her legs, into her socks, her shoes. Sure, it would be wet ... but oh so warm.

Oooh, then it would turn cold, icy cold—and stinky.

Her *nase*, her very Swissness, could never tolerate that.

Maggie's spirits might have lifted some had she known how much attention her solo act of civil disobedience was attracting. She saw the crowds, though with several days gone by and the weather taking a turn, they were more like clumps of the curious: passersby lingering a minute or two before hurrying on with their lives. Periodically, to feel better, she glanced over toward the Galilee houseboats, where her neighbors had draped canvas, cloth, and beaverboard with hand-lettered slogans that gave her succor and made her smile.

MORALITY, LIKE ART, MEANS DRAWING A LINE
SOMEPLACE—*OSCAR WILDE*

WATER RATS SURE CAN CLIMB!

WHAT DOES NOT DESTROY ME, MAKES ME

STRONGER—*NIETZSCHE*

STAY HIGH, MAG!

ONLY TWO THINGS ARE INFINITE, THE UNI-
VERSE AND HUMAN STUPIDITY, AND I'M NOT
SURE ABOUT THE FORMER—*EINSTEIN*

A WOMAN IS LIKE A TEA BAG, YOU NEVER KNOW
HOW STRONG SHE IS UNTIL YOU PUT HER IN
HOT WATER—*MAE WEST*

DON'T WORRY, WE'RE FEEDING FIFA!

Good thing we thought of those signs. The glory of that
first brilliant dawn was definitely over. The adrenaline rush—
for pulling it off, for the Water Rats cheering her on, the TV
crews jostling for the best angles, Mayor Archey and the other
big shots huddled and trying to figure out what to do, for all
the amazed, curious, angry, and confused faces—was long
past. Now she felt only the cold, the ache in her temples, her
cramped muscles. She longed for her soft bed, for the warmth
of Fifa's body when she crept to her pillow and snuggled in.
Her mind raced far ahead, out of control. She was alone. She
was abandoned. She was afraid. Finally she caught up and
calmed herself. The pier and Buck Buckworthy and all that
she was fighting for emptied from her. She thought of nothing, and was a blank canvas.

MAGGIE STARED AT the empty expanse, wondering how her
mind could fill it. Wondered which stray asteroids of thought
might flash across the inner space; what aspects of herself would
rush forward, demanding attention, spoiled children yelling

hey, look at me! watch this! look, over here! Oh-oh. Here they come. Her parents, Derek and Carola. Looking just like they did when she was in first grade and old enough to notice. Most of her classmates got bused from Fort Baker in the Headlands. They were Army brats. Their dads and moms talked Wyoming or Kentucky and put their kids in pressed chinos and pleated skirts; they gave them no-nonsense haircuts and took them to a Jesus church on Sundays. They taught them All-American things like football, gave them steaming mugs of Ovaltine before school.

Maggie's dad Derek was a part-time nudist, part-time woodworker, part-time clarinet player; Carola baked Swiss-formula muesli and sold it at art fairs and health food stores. They were both disciples of Rudolf Steiner, the Austrian guru, educator, clairvoyant, and expert on medicinal plants and peasant agriculture. Little Maggie, her hair becoming less domesticated by the day, wore flea market hand-me-downs and refashioned—though immaculately clean—rice sacks to school; she was dragged to Berkeley lectures for Steiner followers or to the Unitarian-Humanistic Judaism-Quaker-Pagan Full Moon free-form weekend service, got parental warnings about "American Caesars" and "bread and circuses," and started her day with a frothy glass of juiced carrots. Derek and Carola were hippies before there were hippies. Maggie just wanted to be "normal," which, to her young mind, meant fitting in with the military kids. She dreamed of standardized housing, not a rotting old ferryboat. She begged her mom for Betty Crocker and told her dad to put his clothes back on—the ready-made kind from Monkey Ward.

Then, around the time her dad renounced his alternative lifestyle to split for southern California and begin a twenty-year gig as a Champagne Melody Maker on the *Lawrence Welk Show*, she had a change of heart. It had to do with a boy.

His name was Max. He was a head taller than Maggie,

broad shouldered and narrow hipped; his good looks were the wholesome, clear-eyed kind. He was a natural-born halfback; he talked Tennessee. His father, a supply sergeant, oozed regular Army from every pore. Max and his twin brother Cleve went to Maggie's school; they were seniors when she was only a freshman. Nevertheless, Max took a keen interest in Maggie, drawn by the age-old attraction of opposites: she was an exotic tropical in his regimented world of starched khakis. Maggie's mom did not bless her daughter's infatuation—at that time she was somewhat pissed at all males and her runaway husband in particular. Plus she had the Swiss aversion to anything relating to warfare. Of course Carola's disapproval made not the slightest difference to Maggie, who adored the cat-like way Max moved, his well-scrubbed looks; how he smelled of licorice and shoe leather. She thought she was in love with him.

The day Max and Cleve turned eighteen they both enlisted. No surprise—a foregone conclusion. They had been bred to it. Within two months the brothers were in Korea. Max's letters to Maggie were cheerful but vague; they yearned for the things they would do together again after he got back, the places they would go. They were sweet in a boyish way. Then the letters stopped.

When his brother came home to San Francisco for Max's burial, Cleve wrapped strong arms around Maggie's shoulders and took her aside.

"Me and Max," he said in a quiet voice that was an eerie echo of her lost love's, "we was stupid." She scrutinized Cleve's face for his meaning and noticed he looked different. "We listened to our old man. He gives out canteens and clipboards and closest he ever gets to seeing action is when he takes target practice." Cleve was in dress uniform, and the midday sun glinted off his metal buttons as he leaned closer. "Wasn't just him, though. It's the whole damn govermint. They're feeding us a load of crap, Mag. You Water Rats got the right idea.

Don't follow blind like everybody else."

After that she saw her own life with new eyes. Saw how those who shared their ferryboat home had rallied to her mother and her since her dad left. Saw how the whole waterfront had closed ranks around them, made sure Maggie and her mom were all right, reminded them they were wanted and loved. The Water Rats were like a very big and very weird family. From then on she embraced this weirdness, the proud refusal to fit in. For the first time she understood *that* was worth fighting for. The feeling grew stronger over time. Now when she thought about her indestructible bond to the Water Rat life, she also remembered it was forged on her first love, and a boy named Max.

WHERE WAS HE? Why has he deserted me? Is he okay?

New thoughts wormed their way in. This time the name was Will. She missed him, and it hurt more than she admitted to herself. Why hadn't he united behind her along with all the others? In fact, why hadn't he shown the least indication he might be worried about her up here in the sky, facing jail or worse?

What's his problem anyhow? Why has the guy folded like a lawn chair?

Her questions hung in the air. She tried pushing them out. They circled like dark birds.

LATE IN THE morning of Maggie's fourth day, rain began to fall. Lightly at first. Then harder. A gentle mist becoming a downpour. The wind gusted again. The sky turned ugly as a bruised knee.

Maggie wrapped her arms more tightly around the hard wet metal and was thankful to be chained. She hunched her shoulders and sank into her oilskin; her amazing kelp hair fell limp in the sheeting rain, and she could feel rivulets of water working their way down her neck and back. She shivered hard, and her hair pelted her in needles of cold water like a dog shaking himself after a swim. The construction zone below was all brown mud and massive puddles. Idle bulldozers and backhoes were great sodden beasts enduring nature's cruel whims. Beyond, the streets were emptied except for the occasional car or truck feeling its way along Bridgeway, headlights on, wipers thrashing. The high-spirited signs of her houseboat neighbors—she envied the warm yellow light in their windows—were now soggy and sad, and her DHARMA sat moodily black. More than ever, Maggie was miserable.

But there was nothing to do but hang on, wait it out.

About then her mind hit on its own means to broom away depressing thoughts: a sudden and much more urgent preoccupation.

All around me! All this water!

It filled the air, soaked the land, deepened the seas.

I have to pee. Jesus, Jesus, Jesus, I have to pee so—oh.

Oh, no.

The pleasure, the relief, so warm, an orgasm, an orgasm of the bladder.

I can't believe this....

From inside her head came her mother's voice.

Ach du lieber droscht!

She groaned and opened her oilskin to let in the driving rain: a frigid rinse for her Levi's and skin already soaked and dripping. She breathed in deeply, flaring her nostrils, and tried to detect what she had done. Her extraordinary olfactory sense, even in the downpour, reported back the tangy stew you would expect of a woman in the same—and now pissed-on—clothing for these many days and nights. Hastily, she buttoned up again, revolted. And with another violent shiver recognized that a new sensation had replaced the clarion call of nature. She couldn't believe how very, very cold she was.

This was the exact moment when dark wings flew into her consciousness. Despair, she thought—those big wings of despair again: indistinct but foreboding. Then, watching blurred movement through the leaden gloom, she realized these wings were real. Wings beating against a water-filled sky.

Birds don't fly in the rain, she said to herself, not in rain like this.

This bird flew alone. Maggie craned her neck forward to make out the approaching shape. Closer and closer it came, until she recognized the beak and body, the enormous wingspan. A pelican. *Why would a pelican*, she wondered, *fly straight at me at a time like this?*

"George," she whispered.

With noisome fluttering, One-Eyed George alighted on a metal strut not three feet from Maggie's face. He cocked his head and fixed her in the gaze of his liquid brown eye.

"Why, George," said Maggie. "Come to keep a drowned rat company? I could sure use a friend." She reached out to offer his head a scratch.

George's beak yawned open. In his pouch, just below his pink tongue, Maggie saw a shiny something that froze her arm in mid-reach; her heart missed a beat. As if in a dream, her fingers extended to grasp for the object, which was attached to a length of frayed cord. She retrieved it, then stared at it dumbly in her palm. George continued to observe her until, letting out a shrill cry, he rose in a fusillade of flapping. Maggie kept her eyes fixed on the pelican until he disappeared into the gray distance.

Only then did she look into her hand again to inspect what she had recognized immediately, yet failed quite to believe. She touched her mother's locket at her throat. In her palm was its golden key: her gift to Will, her gift of love. Returned by a half-blind bird in the middle of a rainstorm at one of the most dismal moments of her life. She shivered anew and could not stop. The tremors wracked her shoulders and made her hands quake. Was it the cold and wet, or did they originate from a place much deeper? The answer came in the form of hot, bitter tears that melted into raindrops on her cheeks. She hung her head and tried to block the pain out, to block out everything.

ROTTEN WEATHER PROLONGED Maggie's suffering two days more, while the long-awaited crane barge hid behind the safety of a breakwater near Vallejo. At last, however, the dark clouds fled and the sky was blue, the sun visible, and Maggie was brought down. It was on the afternoon of the seventh day. Another round of press images showed her being led to Officer Mack's squad car, handcuffed and bedraggled. Her face was drained of color but her eyes glowed. As we would learn, these were signs of her pneumonia, as were the panting for breath and the nasty cough. Her week in the air had left her badly dehydrated, painfully constipated. Worst of all, she was heartsick. For the next two weeks home for Maggie was a bed at the county jail infirmary.

TOUGHER SECURITY MEASURES were in place even before the end to Maggie's brave and lonely protest. There would be no more work stoppages. Another guard was added, doubling night surveillance. Klieg lights glared after dark, giving the pier site and the nearby houseboats the unearthly glow of a used car lot. At the end of each long day that was making up for lost time, construction crews herded their machines into a separate corral.

Day by day the pier grew and the pilings extended, a string of exclamation points across the bay.

29.
When It Rains, It...

THE STORM WITHIN US WAS TRUMPED BY THE REAL McCoy. We had not stopped the pier, but the worst weather since *el Niño* was named the devil spawn of meteorology succeeded where we had failed. With Maggie safely under the infirmary roof, the sky blackened to cinders again. On one of the worst nights of high winds and high tides, the same barge on which Maggie had mounted her protest rammed and battered the still-skeletal structure, rendering higgledy-piggledy a section of planks and timbers roughly the length of an ocean-going tug. For good measure, another stack of timbers was hoisted on the surge and sent like battering rams through the new fencing. Unsecured pallets of other construction materials hurled themselves into the bay.

The abominable winds and pelting rain made us prisoners of our homes except for curt encounters on flooded streets, where delivery trucks draped curtains of water onto those foolhardy enough to venture out. Trees lost grip of their hillsides, and, followed by avalanches of mud, toppled onto parked autos and blocked roads. The angry bay turned the ferry commute into an amusement park ride, and our postman in Old Town was forced to live up to his credo of "neither snow nor rain nor gloom of night" by deftly timing his dash down the boardwalk or risk being swept off his feet by the monstrous breakers that cascaded over it. Even Putty and Princess were awakened by gnarly tentacles of salt spray loudly drumming at their bedroom window.

The easy life of the houseboaters became a fight for survival. Everything was slick, treacherous, a moving target. The gusts of wind and rollicking bay turned the waters around the houseboat jumble into a junkyard afloat, as if a sinking ship had released its flotsam of oars and paddles, scraps of wood, flotation cushions, tarpaulins and deck furniture, bottles and plastic pots, snakes of rope and archipelagoes of trailing flora. Worst of all was the unceasing storm's impact on those anchored out. In the midst of one harrowing night a nearby neighbor of THE SQUIRTLE paid an unexpected call on Jake and the Turban Woman; the man's trawler, a trashed affair that ordinarily listed to port, had righted itself—taking on water until it rested at the bottom. Jake, in no mood to do the decent thing, ordered this unlucky visitor back into his dory and told him to start rowing or risk holes in this hull too.

In Maggie's absence Fifa disappeared. On a dreary Tuesday a neighbor who was called Little Hope to distinguish her from a mother of the same name noticed when she came by to pry open a can of Puss 'n Boots that the cat was gone. She guessed Fifa was on the prowl. Returning to poke her head inside DHARMA's door on an equally bleak Thursday, she was greeted by the overpowering stink of fish. The cat's bowl was untouched. Little Hope, in oil slicker and rubber boots, searched for Fifa in the sea of mud edging Galilee Harbor and called for her up and down the waterfront, checking everywhere an animal might seek shelter. To no avail. If the tide had carried her into the gloaming, a bobbing ball of fur might return in a week, a month, or not at all. Little Hope continued to pray to St. Jude, but, true to her name, figured Fifa was gone for good. No one had the heart to tell Maggie.

Certainly not Will. His absence from her life—from all our lives—continued.

Varda was among the few to brave the elements to visit Maggie during her infirmary stay. He told her of the considerable attention she had won for our cause, the money raised, the imminent arrival of Hayden's lawyer as a result. "Because of you," he said, "we will now rout the enemy. You were our Trojan horse."

"I was a horse?" she asked, slowed by her medication. "Have you seen Will?"

Varda's face clouded over. "You have looked out the window? The world is under water. I have been much too busy growing gills." Seeing the hurt in her eyes, his expression softened. "Your frogman is in his element," he continued more gently. "No doubt he is off to the rescue somewhere."

"I don't think he's my frogman anymore."

"Ay hyessou, darling girl," he said. "In the first place, even he would not be so stupid. You are the flag on the highest tower of his life. And in the second place, the rest of the male species hopes that he is."

She did not mention she was positively, definitely, without question pregnant. She had confided in no one, not even her mother. No doctor had to tell her. She was a ripening seed pod. A gestating mammal. The latest member of the secret society of womanhood to know life within life. Her awakened body told her loud and clear: there was someone other than herself to consider from now on.

MAGGIE WAS BROUGHT into a courtroom to hear a prosecutor describe her as a danger to society so great she ought to remain a guest of the county. The prosecutor wanted bail set at twenty thousand dollars. We gasped. Excepting Will, we were all there, ignoring the continuing bad weather to pack the seats not pre-empted by the press. When the judge, a stoop-shouldered Solomon with a papery face and scanty white beard, asked, "Young woman, the prosecutor thinks you may try to climb up that thing again—will you?" and she replied, "Your honor, I just might...," we erupted into a bedlam of whistles and guffaws. The judge pounded his gavel, threatened us with expulsion, but never lost sight that he was up for re-election in the spring. He let Maggie go home with a stern admonition to be more "ladylike."

As a matter of fact, our Maggie had no intention of trying it again. Not only because of her condition. Convalescing in her infirmary bed had given her plenty of time to think. She reflected on what she did. She came to regard her time in the sky as something more than a way to win sympathy for our cause and her homage to Gandhi, noble as that was. The means she chose, she decided, had *drama*. It showed *creative* flair. Scampering up a pile driver and chaining yourself to it, unprecedented so far as she knew, was a *statement* that had as much chance, maybe more, of getting inside people's heads as any painting, any sculpture, any object she ever created. Over the summer, at a rent party in Fairfax, she had met a young woman named Meredith Monk, who rhapsodized over what she called "performance art." Maggie liked the sound of that; it elevated what she had done, no pun intended. And if the miracle in her womb was not enough to persuade her to forget sneaking up the pile driver again, calling it art did it. The thing she hated most in her art was repeating herself.

BUT HOW DID she manage it? How had she gotten past the guard? When Maggie returned to Galilee Harbor, she smiled mysteriously and said, "The *nase* knows." Then she told us the whole story.

From her DHARMA, she had watched night after night as a stubble-headed man in a rent-a-cop uniform left the guard shed around nine o'clock and, walking with a slight roll, made his rounds; twenty minutes later he returned, sat heavily on a stool, and warmed himself by a fire in a blackened oil drum. Then she watched the man rise again and disappear into his shed, returning with lumpy packages wrapped in tin foil. As he hunched over the barrel, the flames made his round face glow. The unmistakable smells began dancing in Maggie's direction. Singed brats, pork with boiled potatoes, the vinegary snap of warmed-over sauerbraten. "And you wouldn't believe the *fortzes* that followed," she said. "Whoo, what a symphony that man let fly!"

She knew what to do. First it was off to Purity Market for flour, sugar, cocoa powder, buttermilk, vanilla, whipping cream, chocolate, pitted cherries. Hardest to find for black forest cake was the cherry liqueur known as *kirschwasser*. When the batter was mixed and ready to pour into round pans, she added the secret ingredient: a pink powder from half-a-dozen crushed pills. These had cost her five bucks apiece, but Jake swore they were "great thiit," enough to knock out a Visigoth. (It was only a matter of time before this particular pharmaceutical found its way from the experimental military lab to the local pharmacy, where it was abused on a continual basis as the brand name Valium.) The rest was easy. The irresistible confection, frosted in whipped cream and decorated with curls of chocolate, sat on the stool when the guard returned from his evening rounds.

He was snoring heavily within the hour.

As Arvie Angstrom put it, "Dat dumb Kraut never knew what hit 'im."

30.
Court Costs

LIKE SOME CHEAP MIRACLE, THE SKY EMPTIED OF clouds but for a single lost lamb, pure, white, and so fluffy you wanted to reach out and pet it. It was a Monday, the third week of November.

The return of fair weather brought the pier work crew back but also someone new. Overnight, in a cream and mint Eldorado Biarritz styled for interplanetary travel, Hayden's lawyer drove up from Los Angeles. Myron Musselman, Esq., emerging from his rocket ship by Cadillac, showed himself to be a wire terrier of a man who looked like he might bite. He wore an expensive glen plaid suit and elevator shoes of reptile skin. He lost no time informing us he made a handsome living from Hollywood stars, that he was all business with no time for small talk. As Water Rats we were accustomed to the bottom rungs of life, and we had the native intelligence to avoid getting stepped on too often, but most of us had little firsthand knowledge of the actual workings of lawyers and judges. We shared the citizenry's basic faith in the legal system. We thought a fair-minded judiciary would see the virtue of our cause. What we didn't know yet was, justice was neither blind nor cheap.

"He's from Beverly Hills," Mephisto did argue, suspicious mainly because Musselman came via Hayden. "What does he know about us?" He called for a vote on our hired terrier:

should we call him off or let him loose? To give us the lowdown, a delegation was formed consisting of Mephisto, Varda, and Ethel Edelman, a Water Rat who owned Ethel's Live Bait & Brew and therefore had a good head for business. They would grill our would-be legal counsel and report back to the rest of us. Musselman bristled but finally agreed. They met in a back room of the Valhalla.

Mephisto went on the attack even before Sally Stanford brought in the first round. "That *feigling* Hayden had to run like a fugitive after you lost *his* case on your home turf. Why should we believe you will win here?"

"Ever see *Island of Desire*?" Musselman asked in a perfectly calm voice.

"I did!" exclaimed Ethel Edelman. "Tab Hunter, he was this shipwrecked marine, and Linda Darnell—"

"Who cares?" Mephisto barked at her. Ethel Edelman blanched, but Mephisto did not seem to notice. "Answer my question, Musselman."

Musselman smiled and the gold in his mouth glinted. He turned to address Ethel Edelman. "Absolutely right, madam. That film made Arthur Gelien a star."

The three Water Rats stared at him.

"And what about *I Was a Shoplifter*?" Musselman asked then.

They stared at him.

"Roy Scherer played a store detective," Musselman said.

"*Dummkopf!*" shouted Mephisto. "Completely not relevant. So what?"

Musselman *tsk-tsk*ed and shook his head with feigned pity. He ignored Mephisto and again spoke to Ethel Edelman. "I'll tell *you* so what, dear lady. Those pictures could've been *sayonara* for the both of them. Their movie careers could have been washed up, finished. Hollywood made Gelien into Tab Hunter and Scherer into Rock Hudson but who kept the maggots at

Confidential from *un*-making them? No guesses?"

"Why would they want to do that?" It was the first time Varda had said a word.

"Quite simple. They're both pansies."

"No!" protested Ethel Edelman. "Not Rock Hudson!"

"Halt, hold it," Mephisto jumped in again. "That's got nothing to do with us. You still haven't said how you will stop the pier and get the Hillclimbers off our backs."

"Yes, answer this," agreed Varda.

Musselman took his time sipping at his whiskey sour. Then, his lips curling into a sneer, he replied, "If I can silence the Hollywood gossip mill and take on that tinhorn fascist Disney and Hoover's FBI when they say some dumbshit actor is a threat to our way of life … why, I'll eat your little pier for lunch."

Said Varda afterwards, "It was like watching two Godzillas do battle."

BY COMPARISON THE meeting at Arvie Engstrom's to take the vote was anticlimactic. Mephisto harangued us to muzzle Musselman, and Varda and Ethel Edelman said he was our best shot. Only four hands went up for firing him. Mephisto's, Belmont's, Jake the Anchor Out's. And Jake voted the Turban Woman's proxy with his other hand.

And so we sent our dog on the hunt.

Oops. Wrong dog.

Despite much furious tail chasing, Musselman came back whipped. True, he had barked, barked, and barked some more—in court, to the press, and behind closed doors. And none had been spared his lawyerly bite, not Mayor Archey, Buck Buckworthy and his fellow pier investors, not even Officer Mack, whom he accused of "deliberately and maliciously" backing into Mephisto's motorcycle near Galilee Harbor on Maggie's first morning aloft. But against the arrayed might of City Hall, the Hill, and some steely three-piece suits from San Francisco who showed up on behalf of the shadowy ship line said to be interested in using the pier, Musselman could not win even a cursory pet on the head. Not even a temporary stop of construction. "Your honor," he pleaded, "allowing work to continue while this matter is before the court would be like firing more bullets into a grievously wounded man. We ask that no more damage be done while we gather the requisite experts to substantiate the highly deleterious impact of this pier and resultant ocean-going vessel traffic not only on marine flora and fauna, but also on the many upstanding Sausalitans contiguous to said site." Blah blah blah. Motions denied, suits dismissed.

Unsuccessful in building his edifice of unassailable argument, Lawyer Musselman did what he actually did best.

He presented his bill.

And he declared as he was leaving town, "Not to worry, it's only intermission!" All we needed for more of this legal beagle-ing, he said, was Hayden's personal guarantee that he would be paid in full. "Then, as God is my witness, I'll be in Sacramento with appeals so fast they'll mistake me for Superman." He struck a thoughtful pose and scratched his chin. "Strike that. George Reeves just shot himself." Slamming shut the Eldorado's door, he was gone.

Musselman spent all we had, and still we owed hundreds for his fees and expenses. His brief stay had not been at the Sausalito Hotel nor had he sampled the wondrous meatloaf of The Glad Hand. Our retainer barely covered his bar and supper tabs at Tadich's, room service on Knob Hill. The pier, meanwhile, now jutted nearly seventy-five feet into the bay ... and counting.

We tried cabling Hayden. Back from Tahiti came an unwelcome reply.

WANDERER SAILED TUESDAY LAST POSSIBLY BOUND

FOR MARQUESAS.

In no mood to quit, we found new ways to raise cash. Juanita sprang S.O.S. pancake breakfasts on her unwitting clientele. "You heard me right," she informed all her customers excepting the Turban Woman, whom she fed for free as always. "A ten spot for breakfast or don't bother coming back again *ever* ... if you get out alive." Not to be outdone, Sally Stanford sent over two weeks of proceeds from a nightly raffle for the favors of her latest attraction, a muskmelon-haired demimonde from Quebec City. Several Rats put heirloom jewelry in hock or shoplifted clothing and other goods for resale at the weekend flea market in Marin City. We were closer to settling our debt with Musselman but not to shutting down the pier. Our best remaining hope was still the party. If that raised enough, maybe Musselman or some other hired gun *could* do something in Sacramento.

So we all hoped and some even prayed.

31.
Lights Out

JUST LOOK AT HIM. LOWER THAN A SERPENT'S BELLY he is ... get out of the shack, young fella, fill your lungs with the sea air and your nostrils with the smell of life!

He does not hear you ... you know that.

Aaach, what I wouldn't give to be in his shoes. Hey, you— you'll be a stiff before you know it. Wake up, horse's ass!

Malachy, it does no good to howl at the moon.

Don't I know it. But I feel like the lad's pap at times, you know. If only I could grab hold of him and give him a good what-for....

WHERE *WAS* WILL, you might be wondering. Truth of the matter is, we wondered the same thing. What at first we brushed off as a lover's spat between him and Maggie had grown now in our minds to something more. He was avoiding all of us. Those who chanced to see him around town, at the Purity Market or Marin Hardware, found him to be, well, changed. Polite, of course. Friendly enough. But changed. As if, like you see in the movies, an alien had taken over his body. We reacted to his changed self the way humans will do. Instead of moving in for a closer look, to find out if maybe we could help our friend, we pulled back too. We let him alone. He must have his reasons, we figured, and when he was ready, he would come back to us.

MALACHY, LOOK.
About time, by Christ.

THAT IS, ALL but Maggie.

Back on her feet and none the worse for her travail, she found excuses to walk the boardwalk day or night. Most of these times she would pause in front of the Earthquake Shack at the point where the boardwalk met his long gangplank over the beach. She would stand there, peer in. Too angry to walk right up, knock, listen to any weaseling excuses; too stubborn to swallow the hurt; too much in love, still, to face that it was over between them. As for her Big News: wanting to tell him, *not* wanting to tell him. Her inclination depended on the day, the weather, signals she decoded from the womb. Standing there on the boardwalk she might be able to see into the shack or she might not. Sunlight ricocheting off the window glass was blinding until mid-afternoon; on fogged-over days, the inside of the shack was darker still, so she could never be sure if he was holed up in there or not. Nights were easiest. Will had no curtains, so she could see right in if there was a light on. The lights were out a lot, she noticed; he seemed to be gone more than usual. Newspapers piled up on his deck. A package wrapped in brown paper sat by the door for days, until she could contain her curiosity no longer. Creeping up to it on a moonless night when the shack was dark and silent as a tomb, she blinked on her flashlight and saw it was addressed in his hard-to-decipher hand to a Miss Ariel Dumont at an Ohio address. The name meant nothing to Maggie, who had never seen or heard it before. She saw that written in a large, spidery cursive were also the words: RETURN TO SENDER.

Then one day after the newspapers and package were gone, and the only light she saw besides the fish tank glow was what escaped between the plantation shutters to his bedroom, she realized he was wise to her vigil. He must even eat in there now. And probably nothing healthy at all, she thought, trying to muster up her disgust.

Another time, certain he was not there, she left him a note. She tucked the envelope under a corner of a rusted, barnacle-pocked sextant on display by the door.

DEAR STUPID, DO I HAVE TO SPELL IT OUT FOR YOU? CAN'T YOU SEE I NEED TO KNOW WHAT'S UP? YOUR (FORMER?) BEDMATE, JAYNE MANSFIELD.

The note went unanswered.

Finally, when she was fairly certain he was at home, she screwed up her courage. She knocked. No reply. She knocked again.

After a chilling silence she heard footsteps. There was a clatter of hardware and the top of the Dutch door opened about a foot. His face appeared. He looked haggard. His hair a mess, cheeks and jowls unshaven. His smell was sour.

She had rehearsed what she wanted to say, but now words would not come. They stared at one another. At length, she said all she could manage. "You look like death eating a cracker."

"Mag."

"Surprised you know me." She had promised herself, no matter what, she would not cry.

"I—I heard about it."

"You did?" She was taken aback. How could he know?

"What you did. Glad you're okay."

Shaking off the other thought, she refocused. "You are? It still matters to you? Why are you making yourself ridiculous by hiding in there anyway?"

Too many questions, apparently. He ignored what she had come to find out and answered only, "I'm a coward."

"A coward," she repeated. Thinking, *I'm the damn coward.* "What in the world are you talking about?"

"I don't have fight in me anymore. I can't rescue anybody. Not you. Not my—not me. Especially not me."

"So that's it then. You're done. We're done."

Their eyes met, then he looked away. His lips curled into what struck her as a childish pout, but it might as easily have been his way of keeping a grip.

"You know what I think?" She tried not to sound as angry as she felt.

He made no reply.

"Pitiful," Maggie said. "I think it's just pitiful."

32.
To Happen or Not to Happen

THE "MEXICAN FATS DOMINO" FROM THE MISSION District was on board, and so were two rock bands from San Rafael, some bluesmen from Oakland and a couple of folkies from Mill Valley. Chimerical posters, Varda originals, were tacked to utility poles and storefronts as far north as Ft. Bragg, east to Truckee and south to Carmel. The S.O.S. Happening—as Maggie persuaded us to call it—would go on, rain or shine, the week before Christmas, on a Saturday night. The place was long settled: the ferryboat VALLEJO, which Dr. Watts estimated could handle a thousand crazed partiers and Varda said twice that many, no problem.

Varda insisted we should have music all over the boat, non-stop, so the call went out for still more players. The sole proviso was, everyone performed gratis. Singing chicken ranchers from Petaluma signed on; so did four girls from Mills College who sang madrigals in Elizabethan gowns and a young bluegrass plucker named Jerry Garcia. Talent from Sausalito came from the New Town brothers who did Portuguese Fado and our own Water Rat Ramblers, a scruffy assemblage of fiddlers, banjo pluckers, a wash-tub bassist. Not yet content, Varda also began angling for what he called "our atom bomb": three locals named Shane, Reynolds, and Guard.

Ever since their "Tom Dooley" went platinum, the Kingston Trio was as big as it got on the pop scene. Their latest, "MTA," was being played to death on the radio that fall. Like many of us, Varda had hung with the Trio at their Trident, but the boys were so famous now, we figured our chances of getting them to our Happening were slim. Still, as Varda boasted, "I am like *adelphos*, a brother, to that Werba"—Frank Werba, the group's manager —"and if he can arrange even *one* song, even if they just wiggle their cute asses and wave, our success is assured."

Maybe even if they did not. A rumor about their surprise appearance swept through town on the fog wind. After Herb Caen got hold of it, tickets started moving like a North Beach burlesque diva. Varda, of course, professed total innocence.

The Decorations Committee, headed up by Maggie and Varda's protégé Kiki Buckworthy, had been equally busy. Deciding against seasonal twinkles and garlands, they wanted instead what they dubbed a "dotdotist" motif: a whole boatload of dots and spots. Hundreds—*thousands*—of polka dots. Very small to very large, everywhere you looked on the big old ferryboat, a job that could take every spare drop of paint in the entire Water Rat kingdom. Leftover boat paint, artists' stores, anything that could be slapped on with a brush. At the center of each of these many dots they wanted a letter **S**. Like this:

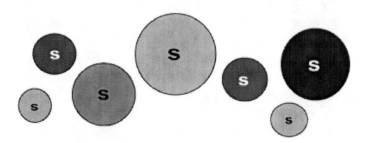

"Plain as the nose on your face, ain't it?" enthused Kiki Buckworthy. "Dots are O's, and y'all can read the S's and O's as S.O.S. ... or just plain SO ... as in, '*Soooo* ... how we gonna stop this hellacious dock deal?'"

Varda adored this notion, proclaiming that his home would thereafter be rechristened the SUISON CHEESE. Dorothy Watts, not as enthusiastic, resisted until her husband exhaled his own streaming pageant of ghostly O's in pipe tobacco smoke and pronounced with eyes bright, "Feels very *wabi-sabi*." In fact, the dot décor was early indication our party would truly be something more than a run-of-the-mill holiday affair. Much more. For weeks Varda himself had been relentless on that subject. "An artistic Armageddon, that is what we need," he hectored us. "A collision of creativity such as the world has not seen since Aeschylus tangoed with Sophocles in the Agora!" As the day approached we realized his seeds of inspiration were germinating up and down the waterfront. "What you got going for the Happening?" became as common a greeting around town as the sly rejoinder: "Oh ... you'll see."

Up on the Hill there began a flurry of "disappearances." A martini shaker, cocktail glasses, a seltzer dispenser ... a sterling candelabrum and its bee's wax tapers ... a silk dressing robe with velvet lapels and some patent leather slippers ... an Oleg Cassini intended for the New Year's gala at the Sausalito Club. Most puzzling of all, Mrs. Trouette's rhesus monkey was missing. Officer Mack interrogated the hired help of all the victims and asked anxious neighbors if they had seen anything suspicious, yet no one was able (or willing) to finger the culprit (or culprits). Mack's professional hackles went to full alert, nonetheless; his instincts shouted this all had something to do with our Happening. He began staking out the VALLEJO, and watched from his patrol car as the flow of visitors and goods increased day by day.

"Looking like a damn tramp steamer, Arch," he reported to the mayor.

"*Mr.* Mayor ..."

"Sure. We gonna do something about it?"

A day or two later, when Mack and two other officers crept

up the ferry's gangplank just after daybreak armed with a search warrant, they found Varda's quarters fragrant with cheap wine and mineral spirits, and Varda himself, snoring heavily, sprawled across Kiki Buckworthy, who was wide-eyed but equally naked. Mack poked Varda with his Billy club. Varda opened a heavy eye lid, then narrowed his gaze like an angry hawk. "Get out! Get out! No Gestapo in my studio!" He jumped up from his bed, his tangle of chest hair white and damp against olive skin, swatting at the air as if these intruders were swarming yellow jackets. He began pulling on voluminous canvas trousers that resembled an upside down, collapsed umbrella, fumbling to tie the drawstring.

"Where's Watts?" Mack wanted to know, unaware that Dr. Watts and Dorothy had gone to Ojai the night before. He pawed noisily through a battered pine wardrobe and a jumble of chests and boxes that contained the artist's worldly possessions. No monkey. No sign of the other missing goods.

"Nowhere in this room, as you plainly see," said Varda in a calmer but icy tone. "Leave immediately so the lady may dress."

"Kiss my beautiful bee-hind," said Mack. He chortled. "We already searched the rest." He motioned to the other officers and they moved toward the entryway. "I guess you know this party has got the whole town talking. Personally, I'll be glad when we settle down to Christmas shoppers with sticky fingers."

Not everyone shared Mack's eagerness for the big day to arrive. Buck Buckworthy, or his cronies, had torn down almost as many Happening posters as we had plastered around town, and through Kiki we heard he practically ordered his brother Earl in El Paso to haul his daughter back home pronto, away from "them fairies and pinko agitators." Around the dining tables of the Hill—and within earshot of the servants who were our lowland neighbors—adolescent black sheep were being warned not to even *think* of squandering their allowances on

Happening tickets. These ran a cool twenty bucks apiece, a lot of money in those days, but even if they were half or a tenth as much, the same thing would have happened next.

Just seventy-two hours from blast off, Officer Mack exited slowly from his sedan, slammed the door and again made his way up the gangplank to the VALLEJO, head down. The morning was crisp and the sky a topaz blue, a fresh breeze romped in the treetops and sent ripples over the bay as if Jerry Lee Lewis was running a hand across a liquid keyboard. The polka dot painters and set-up crews were working at full tilt. Varda, who had been alerted, was waiting on deck, his face a wary mask.

"Ought to get this ramp replaced," huffed Mack, short of breath. "Rickety damn thing."

"Keeps smart people away," Varda said. "Welcome aboard."

Mack straightened and pulled off his policeman's hat. His bald head was smooth as an egg. From inside the hat he retrieved a nearly transparent sheet of printed paper that Varda could see had scribblings added to it.

"Not a speeding ticket, I hope. Can't you tell we're beached?"

"This is serious," said Mack with gravity. "Varda, you appear to be the one behind this foolishness, so here's your citation." He held out the paper, and it fluttered in the breeze.

Varda stared at the document but did not take it.

"May's well read it. It's all spelled out. Citation for violating the local ordinance requiring all entertainment venues be licensed. Here, all yours."

Varda accepted it with a look of disdain. "Entertainment venue? Are you and our esteemed mayor denser even than Greek marble? This is not a nightclub. This is where I eat, sleep, make love, and shit. Am I not permitted to have a party for friends in my own home?"

"Not when you sell tickets." Mack's smile was smug.

"*Skata*," Varda muttered. He crumpled the paper in his fist, barely glancing at Mack, and tossed it into a breath of wind; it sailed into the bay.

From a hip pocket Mack pulled out a rumpled hanky to wipe his brow. "Your funeral," he said. Then he replaced his hat and tugged on the stiff black bill. "Just don't you be stupid and go ahead with this thing. Me and the boys'll be here in case, with a bunch of sheriff's deputies and maybe the National Guard too. You know, when all them kids come to see the Kingston Trio start demanding their money back, a riot could break out." He let out an acid laugh and turned to wobble his way down the gangplank, which bridged the mudflats at low tide.

"This—ramp's—a—menace" were his parting words.

33.
Musselman Redux

H E'D SKIN AUNT LUANN ALIVE FOR TELLING, BUT UNCLE Buck practically pistol-whipped the mayor into shutting us down. She says he ain't been so worked up since Truman fired MacArthur." Kiki Buckworthy leaned across the table to reach for the cigarette that peeked from the pack Mephisto held out to her, and Varda did not miss yet another opportunity to leer down her blouse. He sighed theatrically and announced, "No one has yet invented two forms more perfect than a violin or a woman."

"Pul-*ease*," Maggie admonished him.

"I am very serious."

"*Ja*," said Arvie Engstrom. "We must tink."

"How much we collect from selling tickets?" Kiki Buckworthy was now lost to Varda's admiration by a nimbus of blue smoke.

"Four thousand something. Almost two hundred tickets," Varda said.

"That all?" Maggie was hoping for at least twice that.

"Most will wait to pay at the door."

"Hell, that's not near enough to call back the fancy pants lawyer, even if—" Kiki Buckworthy did not finish because Mephisto, uncharacteristically silent until then, had slammed the table with his open hand. A nearly empty tumbler of red wine danced crazily; Marilyn Macaw flapped her wings in fright. "That *schwein*," he growled. All eyes were on him now. Savoring this attention, he sat back and limbered his lips into a satisfied smirk. Gingerly, his bird hopped back onto his arm. "You'll remember," he said at last, "I was against hiring him in the first place."

"You'd be against Clarence Darrow," Maggie shot back, "if he was Sterling's lawyer."

"Correct. Any friend of our resident B-movie actor is no friend of mine."

"We can't afford him anyway."

"Not so fast," came Mephisto's retort. "Since his recent ineffectual visit in his obscene Caddy, I have made it my business to find out more about this Lawyer Musselman."

"Arrrrwk," said Marilyn Macaw, showing a tongue like a plump slug.

Mephisto smiled. "Hear that? My *mädchen* says this time Musselman will eagerly agree to slave for our cause for not a *pfennig* more." We stared at him in amazement, but he lifted his palms to forestall our questions. "Leave it to me," he said, tickling his bird just under her pearlescent beak.

And so it was that in the pre-dawn two days after that, Myron Musselman and his Eldorado returned to Sausalito. The S.O.S. Happening was only forty-eight hours away. But this time our Hollywood lawyer had a case he knew something about: show biz. And instead of facing big guns hired by the backers of the pier and the cruise ship line, this time his opponent was our inept town attorney, chiefly known for his repeated attempts at shuttering our one homosexual hangout (which ended, finally, when its prominent patrons pointed out what the loss of their "immoral" support would mean for numerous pet civic and cultural events around town). When he stood in front of the magistrate to argue that we were charging admission for entertainment without "proper permit and licensing," Musselman exuded confidence and called Mayor

Archey to the stand.

"Mr. Mayor," Musselman began, "did you or your supporters raise money for your most recent re-election campaign?"

"Naturally, I—"

"Objection!" cried the town attorney. "Irrelevant to the facts of this case, your honor."

"Overruled. Answer the question, Mr. Archey."

"Yes. Money must always be raised. But you aren't trying to compare—"

"I'll ask the questions," Musselman interrupted. "And, Mr. Mayor, as a money-raising tactic, do you or your supporters ever throw a party?" J.R. was justly proud of his annual crab cioppino bash at his Banana Belt hacienda; it had kept him in office for years.

"Objection!"

"Overruled."

"A political fund-raiser … yes."

"You supply food and entertainment?"

"Of course."

"Your supporters buy tickets to this event?"

"Um, they make political donations. But—"

"And do you or your supporters possess a license to serve food and provide entertainment?"

The town attorney's shoulders slumped as he sank into his chair. It was over. The judge ruled the S.O.S. Happening could go on as planned. Afterwards, Buck Buckworthy, who had watched with an expression that went from "lynch mob" to "lynch victim," shoved his way past the throng of courtroom spectators. He paused momentarily to glare at his niece, who, in beads and dangling earrings, flowing skirt and a low-cut, filmy blouse that seemed to be a serving suggestion, was doing her imitation of a gypsy princess. Afterwards, Lawyer Musselman loosened his bow tie and accepted our congratulations with none of the swagger we had seen previously; then he quietly excused himself, saying he was driving straight to Sacramento to files appeals to our cases against the pier. We looked at each other and shrugged. Mephisto merely nodded in satisfaction.

NOT UNTIL THE following year, when Maggie visited him at San Quentin, did Mephisto finally reveal how he had gotten Musselman to save our party (if not, due to ensuing events, our cause). Simple, really. He had tapped into his old lefty connections. Long before Myron Musselman could even afford the high-test for his fancy automobile, he had been another young idealist on Hollywood's back lots, just like Sterling Hayden. Then came the dark period: the studio black list, the witch-hunt for anyone even faintly tinged by radicalism. No one knew for sure why Hayden, when he renounced his Party membership to the FBI, hadn't named his pal Myron along with the others, but Mephisto knew Musselman would want to keep it that way.

"Even as a quisling, Hayden's the *pappnase*," Mephisto declared to Maggie before asking, "Marilyn Macaw? She is *gesund*?"

34.
S-O-S

MI-WASH, EVER NOTICE WHAT WE SORELY lack? Hands. And feet.

Aside from that, princess. I mean, 'tis all cut and dried now, you see. No risk, no surprise, no heights nor depths. Pleasant, mind you, but still ...

Among my people you would have been a hunter of bear.

Me? Heavens, no. Just show me a night full of promise! That I could never resist.

Resist?

The excitement! Don't you see? Me, Delphine and Artur, we was basically happy as three peas in a pod. But over time, 'specially seeing as how no more kids arrived in our household, I began to feel the tug for my old ways. For the night life. It became irresistible.

You again played your music box?

Course I did. But that's not the half of it. By then what we called Prohibition was racing at full tilt. The law of the land said no more booze could be sold anywhere, anytime.

Ah, blackberries with honey ...

I mean *real* booze ... hooch ... the white man's firewater, I do believe you injuns call it. 'Tis mother's milk to most Irishmen, myself included. After the Miramar burned I had tried my hand at Mason's Distillery, in Whiskey Springs at the north end of town. The Mason's owners were big shots, so instead of being out of business like the breweries and other spirits makers, they kept right on distilling through the whole of that era. For *medicinal* use, wink wink. The local chemist sold enough Mason's elixir to cure the whole damn state.

You made this firewater?

I soaked up the technique, so to speak. Them was wild days, lass. The gangster Baby Face Nelson were hiding out in town at the time, working incognito at the Valhalla ... which called itself Soft Drink Parlor Valhalla even after its proprietress got hauled off kicking and screaming. The Prohis found near five hundred quart of home-brew and jackass brandy on her premises and a trap door leading from the bar to the beach, so small boats could make a quick booze run. Oh, the very fact it was illegal made folks downright crazy for their booze. Rumrunners was rendezvousing off Tamales Bay almost nightly with ships from Vancouver. But the Canadian hootch still didn't meet the demand. It didn't take no genius to figure out how to make a good living. So I dug up the backyard behind the shack, laid in copper tubing, and in no time at all, I was bottling my own genuine twelve-year-old Scotch. I just needed a place to peddle it. And it were Delphine's cousin, José Sousa, who came to the rescue again. He had a friend, another Portugee, with a sweet little shed on a secluded spot at the edge of New Town. Perfect. Practically overnight it become Malachy's, the best speakeasy in Sausalito—with yours truly seated at his piano. What a party! 'Twas the Barbary Coast all over again....

THE VIGIL BEGAN in the pink dawn of that famous day. Below the imposing presence of the VALLEJO those who waited in the early morning had eyes filled with sleep but faces flushed with expectation, like the excited children who would gather round their yuletide trees in another week's time. They had been drawn by what the deejays and underground press from here to Nevada were touting as the biggest, wildest, craziest party of the year. The publicity juggernaut, good, bad, but never indifferent, had been unstoppable. In his many interviews Varda had elevated to mythic status his own hedonistic revels of the past, as well as our town's uninhibited history and its creative citizenry. The predictable thin-lipped editorials and Sunday pulpit bombast that he inspired served to whet appetites even more. All who stood in that dawn's ragtag line, it was fair to say, had followed the on-again, off-again saga of the event, the bizarre rumors and exaggerations of what might happen and whom they might see: not only the Kingston Trio, but also Ricky Nelson, Marty Robbins, the Impalas, the Weavers, and heaven only knew who else.

By midday a multitude of more than a thousand, some of them even old enough to vote, snaked in the shadow of the polka-dotted ferryboat, from which hung a massive twin of Maggie's plea from on high: s.o.s.—SAVE OUR SAUSALITO— STOP THE PIER. Officer Mack had already radioed for more help in crowd control, but the waiting throng stayed in a festive mood, and with each load of last-minute supplies or equipment carted aboard, good-natured shouts followed. Even the weather had showed up in fine spirits. Spooky tendrils of mist rising from the bay in the half-light had, by early afternoon, turned into sparkling waters and clear skies, and a high sun chased off the last reminders of damp and chill.

For the Water Rat kingdom, the day was promising something close to perfection. Pure exuberance, unbridled and spirit-levitating, swelled in our bosoms as we counted down the final hours. And yet, to those who chose to hear them, somber notes also sounded from the distance. Rhythmic pounding and steady clanging. This was our provocation for this day. The pier was now fully two-thirds completed.

At three o'clock, Varda, silhouetted in sunlight, appeared

at the top of the gangplank. His chest was bare. He wore loose canvas pants and had unshod feet. His hair was a pure white cloud. Surveying the realm, he scratched a stubbly cheek and smiled broadly. He proclaimed to no one in particular, "Today we make a legend!"

Minutes thereafter came a crash of cymbal and the sounding of horns. Thus was heralded the procession of Water Rats. Across the ferryboat's lower deck and down the gangplank to the beach we began to wend our way. We wore white, the women with blossoms tucked into their hair. Several of us were minstrels, wanderers with guitar and mouth harp, and many carried baskets laden with refreshments and sundries—sun tea, home-brewed ginger beer, sweets and savories, beaded necklaces and amulets, fanciful headgear, tiny replicas of the VALLEJO covered in measles spots. Others passed out leaflets promoting the S.O.S. cause. But the greatest stir, without doubt, was made by the appearance of the lamb bearers. Five pink carcasses, adorned with herb garlands and studded with toes of garlic, were stretched on lengths of pipe shouldered at each end by a sturdy Rat. With care, these bearers made their way down the gangplank and to a broad fire pit, where blazing driftwood that had warmed the morning now glowed red. Each yearling lamb was hung above the coals, and the bearers began to rotate them slowly. As the lamb flesh colored and sizzled, it was basted with rosemary brushes tied to broom handles, and before long, the sweet smell of the roasting meat perfumed the air in every direction.

As the afternoon wore on, more and more people kept arriving, until all semblance of orderly assembly was lost, and the entire beachfront was packed with humanity. Mack and his crew lost all hope of supervision, and the party got prematurely underway wherever alcohol or doobies had been smuggled under jackets or hidden inside purses. Fits of impromptu dancing broke out at the edges and in other pockets of space.

Girls weaved like sea grasses on the shoulders of their boys.

At five o'clock, the sun a glowing yolk above the western hills, Varda reappeared at the head of the gangplank. This time he wore a flowing white caftan; his hair was pulled back and tied with grapevine. Across his forehead was an olive wreath. In one hand he held a drinking vessel, in the other a long fennel stalk wrapped with more olive twigs, and this he lifted as signal for quiet.

"Friends!" he shouted out.

"Hey, daddy-o, let's party!" cried a voice from the crowd.

Varda made a mock attempt to look stern. "In due time, young reveler," he said. "First, for all my fellow rodents of the waterfront, I welcome you. I welcome you to our S.O.S. Happening. This is a terrible reason to host such a gathering. But we must not allow this to diminish our spirits. You will find us ready to entertain, enlighten … amaze you even. And that is why, in keeping with a tradition renewed every third winter in my native land and the storied cradle of Western civilization, I dedicate this day to the immortal you now see before you. I am Dionysius, god of the glorious grape, intoxication, and creative ecstasy."

Cheers and whistles at this.

"And I am father, by the goddess Aphrodite, of Priapos, whose prodigious sexual organ is the object of awe and honor throughout the ages...."

"Go, old man!" someone yelled above more cheers.

This time Varda smiled. He raised up his drinking vessel. Then, putting the cup to his lips, he drained it.

"Let the festivities begin!" he declared.

It was Little Hope of Galilee Harbor who, climbing atop the second deck railing to peer over the side at that moment when the crowd began surging forward and up the gangplank, murmured with genuine alarm, "Holy shit."

EVERYWHERE YOU LOOKED, a primal tempo was building. Music blared from every angle, performers appeared at every turn. Dogs in lamé and silver bells danced giddily on hind legs. Stilt walkers dipped and weaved in gauze and silk. There were clowns carrying slapsticks, jugglers, and twirlers of fire. A pair of burly bald men, naked to their waists, wheeled about a huge Trojan horse festooned with polka-dotted garlands and mounted by an Oriental lady who fired Ping-Pong balls from between her thighs.

Only later did we learn that, at the last minute, Varda had lured these acts from a circus troupe wintering in Santa Rosa, yet the evening's extravaganza only began there.

All the many hundreds who had plunked down their double sawbucks to see the Kingston Trio or Marty Robbins found themselves instead in a Dadaist fun house. As they fanned out over the VALLEJO, they encountered more and more odd angles and distorted reflections of ourselves. Looking back, it was clear the Happening became a sort of dream fulfillment for many of us, even those who lived usually quiet lives on the waterfront. That explained the many forms we took, the multiple species within the genera, subspecies within the species. We had done exactly as Varda urged: set free our innermost selves and made the party our own. To wit: Water Rat artists attacking canvases in a helter-skelter of styles … Water Rat musicians playing with uninhibited zeal everything they knew and then what they did not … Water Rat beats, far aft under a haze of hemp, sounding their bongos into the gathering darkness for miles over the bay, *thunka thunka thunka*, and hanging out their angst to dry.

> *We heard our own screams …*
> *… but did not scream them.*

They pierced us, penetrated us ...
... with a loathing of things...

Said to be normal but not normal ...
... said to be civilized but not civilized.

But only sick to death ...
... of the normalizers and civilizers.

The screamers of sameness ...
... the merchants of insanity ...
... posing as sane.

AND MORE ...

"Smile, you big oaf," Bunny hissed toward Bel. "Remember what I told you. You're *welcoming* them to the hippest pad in the whole galaxy." He smoothed the flowing organdy silk of his gown and tugged at its beaded bodice. Patting his rabbit ears, he asked, "Are they perfectly, perfectly straight?"

"Pretty," managed Bel. He was rattling ice in the martini shaker.

"Stop stop stop! I need to look at you."

Bunny gave his partner in swinging sophistication a final once-over. The collar of Bel's shirt showed threadbare under the luxurious silken dressing robe with velvet lapels. His puffy dark feet looked like overstuffed squash mashed into the patent leather slippers.

"Perfect," Bunny pronounced. "Jeepers, isn't this just something?"

"Yeah."

"Don't forget to pop your fingers to 'Something's Gotta Give.' Like Sammy does."

"Yeah."

"Quick, be cool, here they come." He straightened and smiled dazzlingly. "People, welcome to the Playmate Party of the Century...." Next to Bunny was a chrome and glass cocktail trolley and a portable phonograph tethered to a long electrical cord. Other furnishings with spare modern lines were littered artfully with volumes of Nietzsche and Keats (stamped PROPERTY OF SAUSALITO PUBLIC LIBRARY), yellowed issues of *The New Yorker*, a sterling candelabrum with pale waxen fingers tipped in yellow flame.

The first guests to arrive stared with wary eyes, not unlike prey sensing danger at the watering hole. They skittered quickly past.

"Enjoy!" Bunny called after them.

"Yeah," said Bel.

AND MORE ...

The furry thing scampered underfoot like a fleeting shadow.

"My purse! It's got my purse!"

The tiny monkey disappeared in a bramble of legs, and beyond a bulkhead below deck leapt into waiting arms. The primate traded the stolen handbag for a grape. "Only free bucks," groused Jake the Anchor Out, pawing through makeup cases and crumpled tissues in search for more.

"Three more for the cause," said Mephisto with a shrug, restraining an impulse to pet the grinning animal. Only Jake, who had trained Mrs. Trouette's monkey to be the best pickpocket and purse-snatcher in the county, could get away with that; besides, the monkey and Marilyn Macaw despised each other, and bird jealousy was not a pretty sight. Mephisto motioned toward a growing pile of leather goods. "Heave these over the side before your *affe* goes out again."

AND MORE ...

"Gather round!" cried Varda. He stood like a colossus on the overhang above the first deck, brandishing his drinking cup. "Welcome to the fabled agora, from which debates and declamations ring forth in the golden light of ancient Athens!"

"When's the Trio on, pops?"

Varda glowered down at a crew-cut youth who sported a letter sweater from Stanford. "Young man, only Socrates may question Dionysius. And then only if I have consumed enough of the grape. Which I have not." The college boy flushed and turned to go, but his raven-haired girlfriend grabbed onto his arm. "Hey, wait," she begged. "This could be a gas." By this time a sizeable crowd had been drawn to the sight of our own Greek god: they were the idle curious, no different from those who heed carnival barkers, gawk at street performers, or watch demonstrations of revolutionary vegetable peelers. The night was young, and they were in a mood to be entertained. "Friends," Varda addressed them again. "You come from far and wide, your lives are as varied as pebbles on my beach, yet you share one thing. Tonight you have the rare opportunity to see as we do." He swept his cup across the horizon. "*This* is our way. We create. We invent. We celebrate the senses. We bow to nature's beauty and try to be worthy of her."

At this he frowned. "But we do not celebrate possessions, nor so-called progress. Lest we regress to pitiable lives in a sterile nursery where all is fed to us: all sustenance, all experience, empty of what is real and vital and, yes, even dangerous. As citizens of this realm, we are enemies of the packaged life, the pre-measured dosage, the premeditated replacement of chance, the raw and unfiltered, the pure and unadulterated, the messy, the impromptu, the excessive...."

"Huh?"

"What the hell *are* you jabbering, mister?"

Varda paused and glanced down to determine whether this latest interruption signaled sarcasm or incomprehension. He saw that the first interjection had come from a comely young woman he would ordinarily love to bed. At this moment he regarded her as sexless as a doorknob. The other was from her male companion, whom he took for a junior manager of an industrial fasteners company or maybe a certified public accountant. But before Varda could muster a reply, a Doris Day look-alike came to his defense. "Let him finish," she scolded the couple. When she returned her gaze to him, Varda recognized his own heroic reflection.

"I am far from finished," he said, locking his eyes onto his Doris Day. "*We* are far from finished. You ask my destination in this ramble? It is to sing the praises of an old and venerable race: small in number and perhaps diminishing, but the torchbearers, if you will, of life on the razor-thin edges. They live a life of refusal to be herded … they live life as *art*." Varda had the Greek gift. His words, sensual as a canvas, molded clay, or a sonnet, gripped them tight and then tighter still. As another voluble tribe, the Irish, liked to say, writers are merely failed talkers.

He raised a cautionary finger. The fading light cast amber across Varda's face and made the folds in his caftan velvety and mysterious, like the soft creases of a coastal cliff. "The bohemians to which I refer have existed in all climes and ages. In my land of antiquity, to go back no further, there were many. They ate the bread of charity in fertile Ionia and halted in the evening to strum their lyres and sing of the loves of Helen and the fall of Troy." At this cue, we began lighting fat chimney candles in paint tins and Oriental lanterns suspended from the railings and overheads all over the VALLEJO; these lights flickered and swayed in the breezes, casting fantastic shadows onto the polka-dotted surfaces, and reinforcing Varda's widening web of drama and unreality.

"Are you at one with me?" he asked now. Few heads nodded. "Good. Ascending the steps of time, bohemia finds ancestors at every artistic and literary epoch. In the Middle Ages they were the minstrels and ballad makers. In the grand century of the Renaissance, when art was the rival of God and the equal of kings, bohemia finally found, in Balzac's words, a bone and a kennel.

"Michelangelo scaled the Sistine Chapel and watched with anxiety young Raphael with his sketch of the Loggia under an arm, even as Cellini meditated his Persius and Ghiberti carved the Baptistery doors and Donatello affixed his marbles on the bridges of the Arno." There was no stopping him now. "Marching on in time, the literary rivalry that fueled transition between the sixteenth and eighteenth centuries was waged by those two illustrious bohemians Molière and Shakespeare. And the most celebrated names of eighteenth and nineteenth century also filled bohemia's rolls—Jean-Jacques Rousseau was only the most glorious."

Sounds of the party from every compass point on the VALLEJO washed over Varda and his onlookers, who numbered now at least a hundred. He lifted his hoary head toward the swiftly purpling sky. "And what of our own times? Today, as of old, every man or woman who enters an artistic career without means of livelihood other than art is forced to walk these same paths of bohemia: we are as determined as those of centuries past to make something out of nothing." Varda began to radiate an unaccountable, wild light, as if he was possessed by some boho ghost. Whatever trick it was, it worked. The crowd gasped and took a backwards step. He grinned and declared: "At the heart of every bohemian is the child who refuses to play by the rules. We artists make our *own* rules. And the making of it—why, that is art itself!"

He concluded with a flourish of arms, "It is, for us, the only life!"

At this, Varda bowed deeply. He straightened and reached out to a rope that hung within reach; and, grabbing hold, gave a mighty outward thrust with his legs. Arcing above his slack-mouthed onlookers, he swung to an apex beyond the starboard railing. With a fierce and bloodcurdling cry, he let loose of the line. He plunged out of sight. The crowd, stunned, went completely silent.

Finally, a pert young thing murmured to her date, "Crazy old coot."

"Yeah," came the reply. "This whole shindig is nutso. I bet the Trio don't even show."

AND, YES, STILL more ...

"Omigod. Look."

On a platform suspended from davits, in a circle of votive lights, lay Maggie ... in repose. Her hair, true to itself for once, was the sea-dark color of kelp; as was the little sister bramble of her pubis; as was, in fact, her entire naked form. Caked head to foot in smooth greenish clay, her peaks and valleys, slopes and drop-offs, gentle curves and sharp ridges seemed frozen. There was not even the tiniest flutter or movement. On her notice-ably globular belly rested a ship. It was a sleek white ship with China-red smokestacks and a swimming pool on the afterdeck of azure blue. The ship appeared to be empty, its promenades deserted, its gangplank lowered to her navel.

"Gosh, what's all over her?"

"Looks like people."

"Little people!"

Indeed, she was overrun: everywhere on her reclining form these Lilliputians clambered in loud Bermudas and his-and-her leisure outfits. Many had tiny cameras slung round their necks. They snapped souvenir photos of their fellow passengers posed at a nose or nipple or big toe. They swarmed to tacky tourist shops that sat on her forehead and collarbone; they sipped lurid drinks through straws and chowed on pizza and corn chips and cheeseburgers. Their food wrappers and paper cups and lost sunglasses and golfing caps were strewn willy-nilly over Maggie's limbs, in her hair, in the gully between her breasts. Nearby, a Philips reel-to-reel intoned a classical dirge punctuated with incomprehensible Nepalese chants from a recording on loan from Dr. Watts.

"Well, shit for Shineola."

"You can say that again."

35.
Mack Attack

HE PHALANX OF POLICE VEHICLES CREPT INTO A SEMI-
circle on the sand. It included black-and-whites from
across the county and a pair of paddy wagons. Their
headlights out in the early evening darkness, radios muted.

Officer Mack waved them into position and held up both
hands when he was satisfied with their array. Then, silently, their
doors opened and out slid the uniformed army. Gathered in the
shadow of the candlelit VALLEJO, the men glared up at her. The
sounds of the party were everywhere on the breezes. Shouts.
Wild laughter. Music of so many types and tonalities.

They gathered in a tight bunch. "Boys, you know why we're
here," said Mack in a loud whisper. "Can't you smell it? They've
been handing out Mary Jane like trick or treat candy. Right
now the sons and daughters of our law-abiding citizens are up
there smoking that shit. There's our probable cause. They're
drinking underage too, count on it. And who knows what
other depravities are being perpetrated. Listen to 'em hollering and squealing like stuck pigs."

Gimlet-eyed officers nodded. A few tugged on their uniform caps. They fingered their nightsticks.

"Let's move out," said Mack.

He led the way. They quick-marched the few remaining
steps across the beach and up onto the gangplank. Single-file,
they headed up. The gangplank bowed and swayed under their

double-time rhythm and weight. The invasion was about to begin.

And it was about to met. Mack's head was nearly in view from the ferry's entryway when Varda—the old bohemian was changed into dry trousers and a leather vest—gave the signal. A greased pin was pulled. Cries of alarm went up. The gangplank and the flailing officers were sent crashing downward. Half of them thudded back onto the sand, the others found themselves splashing in the shallows. Mack himself managed a brief fingerhold on the VALLEJO's cold hard steel, but it did not last. He tumbled down like the rest.

Varda let out a cry of triumph. The cheer was taken up by the rest of the Rat defenders. Thank our lucky stars we had anticipated a moment like this, and that Little Hope, bless her soured soul, had been vigilant in watching for a signal from our sentries on the beach. The VALLEJO was safe. Secure as a castle with its drawbridge drawn high and its ramparts impregnable. The party could rage on.

But this skirmish was not quite over. Below, officers who had been awaiting their turn for the gangplank were assisting their fallen comrades when the second prong of our counterattack began. Gallons of pastels—paints left over from the dot dotist decorating and thinned with sea water—now rained over the side. The cops milled about in total confusion, a rainbow of hues from head to toe, thoroughly routed. They began a helter-skelter retreat. We were not through yet. Our sentries had lashed together the rear axles of their vehicles with anchor line. When the first car wheeled and spun out across the sand, the chain reaction was truly a sight to behold. Smoke and the stench of ruined transmissions filled the air.

Mack staggered from his disabled sedan, a cop in clown colors illuminated in the glare of his headlights, and he turned to look up at us. He shook his fist. "We'll be back!" he shouted. "With the Coast Guard!"

AFTER THAT, IN truth, the party did get somewhat out of hand. But we didn't care. We knew only that it was a glorious night, and one that even "naughty" Sausalito had never seen the likes of before.

The energy fueling us seemed to infuse every soul on the VALLEJO, not only the Rats, as if the entire partying throng had been waiting for just this moment to have the kind of time about which, afterwards, you could only say, "Hell, I can't explain it. You just had to be there."

Of course, the ready availability of numerous and varied stimulants didn't slow things down any. It was almost as if Juanita and Sally Stanford were in a contest to see whose crew could dispense more kegs of steam beer and gallons of jug wine. Bottles of the hard stuff materialized everywhere. And Mack was right: mood-altering substances were passing freely from hand to hand.

The result? Spectacular, and more than a little debauched. Along about midnight, a well lubricated contingent from the Tamalpais High marching band and baton twirling team converged in uniform at the center of the upper deck. There they blared out their fight song as comely majorettes threw their batons with such abandon many were lost to the night sky. Then, abruptly, they switched to a less traditional halftime routine, one that apparently had begun as a dare from one majorette to another. The band launched into a raunchy rag, and one baton twirler started a striptease. Soon the entire squad joined in, and so did more than a few girls from the crowd. The approval was thunderous. When the bras went flying, the trombone section responded by baying at the moon through their instruments and then dropping their pants in unison.

The air was cold. No one cared.

Soon partyers of both sexes were disrobing right and left, and some even flung their shirts or skirts or shoes over the side. When one band member refused to join in this display of hedonism, his fellows lifted the protesting percussionist above their heads. We did try to stop them. But it was too late. The unfortunate young man was left to paddle himself and his bass drum back to shore.

It was Bunny who first noticed an epidemic of heavy petting by half-naked couples in nooks and crannies throughout the boat. Fistfights broke out when others tried to cut in and jealousies flared. "Not cool, not cool," he admonished repeatedly. "At least discuss the arts or philosophy first!"

Even Maggie had to interrupt her "performance" to threaten a pair of leering youths. One of them had tried jabbing at her with an unsteady fingertip, while the other, grinning like a maniac, egged him on. These fellows were deciding their next move when they noticed a glowering presence.

"Go!" barked Bel.

The young men's eyes went white at sight of a tar baby giant, and they fled.

"Thanks, Bel. I could have handled it, though," Maggie declared, as unfazed as the Lilliputians still arrayed across her. "Did you notice the one smelled like cat pee?"

UP ON THE second deck, the band, almost all of them nearly naked, blared on. Nearby, a trio of gymnasts from the circus troupe was describing perfect arcs and flips and other gravity-defying aerial maneuvers as they were thrown repeatedly aloft from a canvas tarp manned by a dozen or so burly Point Reyes 4-H-ers stripped to their underwear. Hundreds of Chinese firecrackers and dozens of Roman candles began exploding at the stern. The racket and flashes of light were awe-inspiring, but it was even more amazing no one lost an eye or was struck down by a whistling orb of color. The finale to this act came when another circus performer, a hairless man in canary yellow tights who called himself The Human Ricochet, was propelled through the curtain of blue smoke above the fireworks. He caught neatly hold of a flagpole off the stern and spun around full circle to sail back through the smoke and into a net rushed into place by his assistants.

The crowd went nuts. Even the frolicking band stopped to join in the applause.

But soon it became clear these latest feats weren't all that was being cheered. For as the smoke fell away the decibel level suddenly spiked to new highs. Hoots and whistles were now directed at none other than a beaming Arvie Engstrom—or rather, at the candle-lit pontoon he was towing behind his workboat.

This, finally, was the topper of toppers. The cherry on the ice cream sundae. The ace of the royal flush.

To the harmonic strains of "The Tijuana Jail," there they were: the much-anticipated Trio.

Varda had pulled it off. And, immodestly, bare-chested and arms upraised, he stood at the rear of the floating stage, accepting kudos from all.

The S.O.S. Happening was now an unqualified success.

36.
The Ungrand Finale

OR SO WE THOUGHT.

Maggie smelled it first, after the Trio had been on stage the better part of an hour.

"It can't be," she cried out, lurching upright, tumbling the props of her performance in every direction. Grabbing up the flannel shirt she had stashed—Will's, left behind long ago in the DHARMA—she raced toward the stairs connecting the decks.

Unmistakable to her, this acrid smell. The VALLEJO was burning.

Bunny and Bel, intending to refresh their martinis, found flames dancing through their impromptu pad on the upper deck. "My sacred vinyls!" moaned Bunny at sight of his stack of albums already melted beyond recognition. Bel threw the contents of an ice bucket at them as Bunny kicked off his high heels. "I'll find an extinguisher!" he yelled. He hiked up his skirt and raced off. But none was to be found, so next he sprinted toward the stern to shout the alarm.

"Fire! Fire on the boat!"

Maggie was halfway up the stairs when she heard the screams and was met by the downward stampede. "Hey, take it—" She was nearly trampled, and with all her strength managed to flattened herself against the stairwell and hold fast to a hand railing, bracing as best she could for the panicked rush of pushing and shoving. A roly-poly Golden Gate toll taker that Maggie knew from the No Name was first to lose footing, and his bulk brought down others; past her they tumbled like collapsing dominoes. Still the mob would not be stopped: sensing a closing window of escape, it pushed harder. Crazed, uncaring bodies climbed over the fallen, those unfortunates who had succumbed to the unchecked momentum. In this terrible madness, Maggie felt her grip weakening.

The fire was spreading with terrifying speed. Varda and dozens of other Rats were attempting valiantly to fight back, but the deadly combination of old, sun-bleached timbers, combustible art materials, and, in the Watts' quarters, thousands of volumes of print, proved more than anyone could hope to battle. With increasing ferocity, the blaze was eating its way from bow to stern, deck to deck. Bulkhead doors yawning open beckoned the firestorm below decks, where it was propelled by deadly winds of its own creation.

Soon the night sky all around the VALLEJO was alight in the brilliant colors of dawn and dusk, hues that bespoke of violent and hellish consummation. Against this vivid backdrop the silhouetted figures of hundreds of terrified people could be seen fleeing every corner of the ferryboat. The gangplank being gone since the aborted police raid, jumping was the only way off.

Numerous reports, speculations, and rumors later claimed to know how the disaster began. Many said Buck Buckworthy was behind it, though if Kiki had not managed to pull Luann from the path of the fleeing throng, she might have been trampled along with the many others. Surely the most trustworthy witness was a guileless young nurse from Greenbrae, a Miss Laurel Beckett, who was also widely praised for her first-aid provided at the scene. Nurse Beckett swore she saw a small dark animal clutching a pair of gabardine trousers—"a hairy little thing, like a monkey," implausible as that sounded to investigators—upend a candelabrum while fleeing pursuers and then overturn a can of soaking paint brushes.

"Pfoof!" she said.

Our town had suffered catastrophic fires before. Earthquakes and brush fires ignited by nature or heedless humans were typically to blame. As a result we were justifiably proud that our firefighters were trained to meet every emergency—with one exception. Fire over water. In San Francisco they have fireboats capable of sucking up massive quantities of seawater and spewing it back upon a burning vessel. We had none such. Consequently, our houseboats were quaint firetraps, our anchor outs disasters waiting to happen. The VALLEJO, luckily, sat on an isolated strand of beach, yet this isolation also sealed its fate. A safe and stable conveyance for more than a generation over the moody waters of our bays, she began collapsing into herself and casting her glowing raiment aside.

Maggie, with the danger intensifying by the second, clung stubbornly to the idea she must reach the upper deck—that, despite the thick unctuous smoke and intense heat, the scent of escape was also to be found there, that there she would know what to do. Somehow then, after the initial push of the fleeing mob, she managed to struggle her way up, battered, shaken, but able finally to wipe her shirtsleeve across the streak of red where an elbow had caught her nose.

She peered around. The hiss and crackle of the fire filled the night; embers floated off crazily on the breezes. The smoke stank. She felt hotness in her throat, and it made her cough. Those she could see through the haze were all in motion—but they were just shapes, not recognizable. Some were crawling; some running; others climbing over the side. Those who had chosen to fight beat with blankets, jackets, whatever could be found, at the thousand tongues of flame. She heard names being yelled out, in tones of shock and desperation. At the railing, she leaned over and looked below: scores of heads bobbed in the bay, as if a jumble of net floats, and she saw dozens of swimmers stroking toward shore. Pandemonium reigned on the lower deck too, but there she spotted a man who looked all too familiar.

Could it be? Will? Here?

The man was feverishly hauling up a rope with a bucket of water tied to it. He grabbed hold of the bucket, spilling half of its contents before handing it to another man. Craning out as far as she could, Maggie shouted down to him. The man didn't hear her, apparently, because he made no acknowledgement of her cry. Then finally he turned to give another bucketful to the man next to him, and she could see it was someone she had never met.

Her heart sank.

A lightning crack sounded from above.

It was the last thing she heard.

A falling timber, striking at the base of her skull, toppled her like a tin duck in a shooting gallery, spinning her over the railing and down, straight down.

Thirty feet into the dark and frigid bay.

37.
You Can Go Home Again

E NEEDS HIS PEOPLE, MALACHY.
Like a hole in his noggin he does.
They will remind him of the old ways and show him the path.

Aach, returning to a yellow jacket's nest gets you stung again....

HE LEFT BEFORE dawn, it was Thanksgiving day and raining again, in his Chevy Nomad which still had the Ohio plates. He pointed the station wagon south to pick up the same highway, Route Sixty-Six, at Barstow. Then, driving twelve hours at a stretch, he progressed eastward under late autumn skies through Flagstaff to Albuquerque to Amarillo, then on to Oklahoma City, where the blacktop suddenly caromed in a northerly vector toward Tulsa and St. Louis. Farmlands were barren, towns and cities drab in grays and browns, their streets outlined in blowing leaves and trash. No snow to speak of, thank goodness, though flurries danced the windshield off and on. Mostly he took his chances at roadside diners that promised home cooking, but these were homes to which he would not welcome another invitation. A single night, on the outskirts of Indianapolis, he splurged on a Bonnie and Clyde motel for the steamy comfort of a half-hour shower; otherwise he spent his nights cocooned in a sleeping bag in the back of the Nomad, and washed up in cold water at the greasy sinks of filling station rest rooms. Talking to nearly no one except the hitchhikers he collected along the way, college kids thumbing back to campus laden with c.a.r.e. packages from home, and sheep-dipped servicemen bound to or from their bases. With nothing to do but think, stare at flat countryside, or listen to the radio, he fiddled incessantly with the dial. Quickly he tired of the Jesus stations. Growling and lunging for the tuner when ambushed by twangy deejays—broadcasting "direct" from the local feed-and-seed—who recited ad copy for the "$12.99 miracle Bible Belt®." But on one clear and starry evening barely across the Mississippi and into Illinois, he nearly swerved off the macadam. Through the Nomad's tinny speaker came a lugubrious voice all the way from Sausalito. He had lucked onto an telephone interview with our one-and-only Zen master, Dr. Alan Watts, on WJR, the mighty "Goodwill Station" from Detroit. The interviewer was Jimmy Launce. Will cranked up the volume and listened in total astonishment.

> LAUNCE: Tell us, Dr. Watts, what exactly is Zen Buddhism?
> WATTS: Hah! Why, Jimmy, it is the mystical transformation of consciousness. Dig it?
> LAUNCE: Um, that's kind of way out for the Motor City. Could you put it in words we can all understand? I mean, what are you really all about?
> WATTS: Trying to define yourself, Jimmy, is like trying to bite your own teeth.
> LAUNCE: Give it a try. Please, Dr. Watts.
> WATTS: All right. Let me put it this way: Zen Buddhism teaches us that nothingness is absolutely everything.
> LAUNCE: Uh—
> WATTS: For example, take us. You and me, Jimmy. We

exist at this moment on a radio wave. The radio wave is
invisible. We are nothing, yet we exist. Do we not?

LAUNCE: Ah ha. But you and I, we aren't exactly nothing, Dr. Watts.

WATTS: Those who say don't know, Jimmy. And those
who know, don't say.

LAUNCE: I see ... sort of. Let's move on. I hear you are
involved in some kind of a protest. Something about
a shipping pier out where you live in California. Tell
me, Dr. Watts. Is that nothing too?

WATTS: Yes and no! You see, life is a game, the first
rule of which is that it is not a game!

So it was, rolling through the frostbitten countryside on
that cloudless night, that Will heard about the S.O.S. Happening for the first time.

"I'll be damned," he said to the dozing Oberlin sophomore
next to him.

Crossing over the Indiana-Ohio line, he found U.S. Twenty
near Toledo. He knew it could take him the rest of the way, but
he veered onto a new freeway instead, suddenly impatient to
be in the places he had avoided thinking about the entire way.
In truth, his only plan was this journey. It had called to him,
and he had heeded that call. He sensed that whatever needed
to be done began back where he'd begun. Back where, in his
haste to flee, he had apparently jettisoned pieces of himself:
his heart, his backbone, also his balls, evidently. If he did not
know why, exactly, he had traveled all this distance, he wanted
to find out, and soon.

A few hours more and there they were: the familiar land-
marks of his alien youth, as removed from Sausalito as two
places on the same continent could ever be. He passed by the
SOHIO filling station run by identical twins he could tell apart
because one oil-spattered brother was absent a thumb; and

just down the street, there was Koppel's Sporting Goods with its ship model kits so wondrous to him as a boy. Next came Bondy's E-Z SHOPPE, where bug-eyed Bondy cheated neighborhood kids on change when they bought their Zagnut bars, and, finally, the gargantuan presence that was the Bargain Barn, surrounded by asphalt that could accommodate a hundred cars or more. He kept going. Until, in a fading afternoon in early December, he nudged the Nomad into an empty parking space. A sign warned:

RESERVED FOR FISH'S CUSTOMERS *ONLY*!
ALL OTHERS SPLATTERED WITH PAINT & TOWED!!

"Ben," he said to the man inside in a handyman's apron who had their mother's pale blue eyes and fair complexion.

"Will!" Ben exclaimed. "Why didn't you say you was coming? Jeez, you just missed Thanksgiving. How's California? Everything okay?"

"Sure. Just thought I'd check in on things. How's Mom?"

"Same as always. Fine. You're going to see her while you're here, aren't you? Hey, 'scuse me a minute. I've got to wait on a customer. Don't go!"

Ben hurried over to the cash register and a lady with two kids on the verge of spontaneous combustion; the young mother, with an *I am damned* look, slapped several paintbrushes onto the counter. Ben rang up the sale. He was now assistant manager of Fish's, a family-owned paint and wallpaper store where he had worked since dropping out of college and marrying a local girl. Both his job and his wife had been a source of disappointment to their mother ever since. To make matters worse in her eyes, Ben was happy with his life. Will watched and wondered how his brother had managed to escape their childhood. Or maybe, like him, just how to bury it. Still, it was Ben and not him or Grace who had stuck around. When, in the past, Will had asked Ben if he remembered certain things, he said no or only vaguely, and his eyes were so clear and his expression so unguarded that Will had finally decided to believe him.

"Will, you've gotta come for supper," Ben said on his return. "Abby will be tickled to see you." Abby was Abigail, Ben's wife of eight years. More customers arrived, three in a row, bringing the first trace of anxiety to Ben's face. He followed them over Will's shoulder. "Hey, look's like I'm getting kinda busy, and Mr. Fish'll cream me if I don't get back to work. How about it? Around six-thirty?"

"Thanks but I'm bushed," said Will as gently as he could. "Later in the week maybe."

"Sure, sure, stay with us then," Ben persisted. "I'll call Abby to set up the spare room. Go straight to bed if you want."

"Ben, you know how I am."

Now Ben looked crestfallen.

A thought came to Will. "Can I ask one thing?" he said to his brother now.

Ben noticed a customer staring at him from the Sherwin Williams display. "Hey, I really gotta go. Think about it. Abby won't mind a bit. You'd be no problem." He turned to wave a hand at the customer. "Be right there!" he called out.

"Ben," Will said. "Do you know where Ariel goes during the day?"

His brother, who had moved off a few steps, stopped.

"When Pickle's at work," Will added. He saw his brother's expression tighten.

"Will."

"C'mon. Help me out here."

"What for? I mean, why do you want to know?" Ben searched Will's face for clues, then shrugged and cast a glance over at the waiting customer. "Hell's bells, okay. Mrs. Mole-dina's. On Seminole. She's a customer." He started off again but stopped once more to turn and face Will. "Be careful, big brother," he whispered loudly. Will recognized the tone of voice from when they were kids and Ben was afraid.

"She's a happy little girl," Ben said.

"Thanks, Toad."

Will slid back into his Nomad and backed it out onto the street. Though he felt like a zombie and craved another hot shower, he could not avoid taking the detour. And in no time at all there it was, the very spot. He had been back only once since it happened, at Pickle's insistence. He had broken his silence about his childhood to her then; he told her what it had been really like. She had kissed his wet cheeks, a sweet moment of emotion and tenderness between newlyweds who wanted no secrets. Later on, whenever they fought, she detonated "just like your father!" as her personal A-bomb: it was the ever-present mushroom cloud over their marriage and subsequent divorce. Coming to a stop on the short street punctuated by red maples, he saw a cyclone fence guarding a gaping hole on a weedy lot cleared of debris but never rebuilt. Nadine Truax (*née* Dumont) still held title to the property, unable to part with it. The neighbors must love her for it, Will thought. An eyesore then, an even bigger one now.

He had been away, it was his first year of college, when the Uselma box house imploded. The perimeter foundation, weakened by the excavation that became the cellar, was less able to bear the burden with each passing year, until, after unremitting April rain and on a night of fierce storms inside the house as well as out, it finally gave way. Nadine, badly shaken but otherwise unhurt, found eleven-year-old Grace, her slender arms clinging to the upstairs toilet, sobbing, "Daddy ... Daddy ... no." Ben and his entire bed fell through the ceiling to the first floor below, where he was saved from an avalanche of plaster, lath, and splintered flooring by a closet door their father, Mr. Fix-it, had removed it from its hinges weeks earlier. Mr. Fix-it, intending to replace it, had only leaned it against a hallway wall. In the collapse, the sturdy castaway toppled across Ben's headboard, sheltering the terrified teenager.

Leo Dumont, down in his cave brooding, was crushed.

Will still marveled at the cliché of fate: his old man, rooting in the cellar of his own creation and no doubt cursing the memories piled everywhere, had been interred along with everything else his wife could not bring herself to give up.

For a long time Will stared at the cyclone fence. It was nearly five o'clock. Afternoon light all but gone, harsh, elongated shadows crept over the wire enclosure. He could see that someone, neighborhood kids most likely, had pried an opening at one corner. Steeling himself, he pushed open the Nomad's door. Brittle grass crunched under his boots as he walked slowly toward where his childhood home had been. The cold air forced a slight shiver, and he pulled at the collar of his pea coat. Lifting the torn fence, he crouched and eased his way through. This was it. He was now peering straight into the Dumont crypt. It was dark and empty: the black hole of the family psyche. He watched his frozen breath writhe over the chasm.

A new thought: *Could I also be witnessing the source of our salvation?* His mother was safely in Shaker Heights. His sister in New York. His brother snug in his own house blocks away. And he, too, had escaped, hadn't he?

The spell was broken, wasn't it?

We all made it. Didn't we?

HE FOUND MOLEDINA on Seminole in the phone book. In a light rain the next morning he drove past the address: a suburban ranch of white clapboard with wainscoting of local sandstone. A string of colored lights, forlorn in the rain, drooped from the eaves; in the yard a plaster statue of the Virgin Mother prayed near low evergreens festooned with more colored lights. The curtains in the house were drawn. Nowhere was there any sign of a five-year-old girl. No abandoned doll's carriage or bicycle with training wheels, no smudged chalk drawings or hopscotch grid on the walkway leading to the front door. He kept on driving.

The radio warned of real snow, and the temperature was dropping further; it was already near freezing when he left the motel, he guessed. The Nomad's heater pumped warmth at his feet, but his fingers were stiff on the wheel. He had forgotten gloves. The thought of this caused his mind to wander back to Sausalito, where it never got this cold, and he let it flood over him. He hoped his fish were not being overfed, and he pictured One-Eyed George puzzling over his absence. He wondered about the pier. He hated to think what it would look like when he got back, jutting into the bay as another dividing line between the Hill and the Water Rats. Maggie. He thought about Maggie. The way she looked at him when he saw her last, at his door, her wild hair framing her lovely face that held an expression that was a plea. He had wanted to hold her, tell her none of this was her fault.

"So why do I feel like her body is quicksand and her heart a trap door?" he said aloud. He laughed—too much hillbilly radio.

Heavy snowflakes began to melt against the windshield, but he barely noticed.

The drive to his mother's should have taken thirty minutes at most, but an hour and forty-five minutes later he was nearly there. He had watched two cars fishtail off the road. Wet snow and frozen rain would bedevil traffic until the salt trucks reclaimed the pavement. Even after years of living with the so-called "lake effect"—which basically meant the homicidally drunk Canadian winter staggered across Lake Erie to upchuck all over northern Ohio—he never got used to it. Now, every time the Nomad began to lose grip, he clenched harder to the wheel and felt his stomach knot.

Finally came the turn onto Malvern. Her street, Will thought with a sardonic smile, was a Hollywood back lot— Louie the Fourteenth's France next door to Henry the Eighth's England. Why didn't they require residents to wear corresponding period costume? A Tudor bodice would be no more out of character on Nadine Truax than the high-brow lady's apparel from Halle Brothers she could afford now.

"Hel-*lo*, dear," his mother greeted him after he trudged up her neatly shoveled driveway. "When you phoned, I almost said come tomorrow. This weather's wretched."

"Hi, Mom," said Will, mentally cataloging *wretched*, a word never heard on Uselma. Could he ever forget the time he stammered on their telephone about an available summer *position*? From behind a thunderhead of cigarette smoke came, "Kiss it goodbye, buddy boy! You want a fucking *job*." In this Leo Dumont was right. The *job* went to another kid. Now his mother affected an English melodrama vocabulary for the same reason her neighbor in the junior Versailles had slipped into something more comfortable by changing his surname from Stankiewicz to Gorsham. We can restyle our exteriors like the latest Studebaker, Will thought, but under the hood, Mom, you're the same old Dumont. *And so am I.*

Even after stamping his shoes to leave winter at the threshold, Will trailed footprints on the parquet as he headed toward the kitchen. He knew better than to sully his mother's lavish living room, where little living was done.

"Will, really," she called after him. "Can't you take off your shoes?"

He chuckled guiltily. "Too late now, Mom."

She brought them coffee, and they sat facing each other in the breakfast nook in a bay window that looked to the white expanse of back lawn. They talked like stones skimming the surface of dark waters. She asked how he liked California now. He said he did not miss Ohio winter. He asked if she had heard from his sister Grace lately. She said not for several weeks and wondered if he would find time to visit his father's grave. Enough of Leo had been retrieved to fill a casket, now interred beneath a flat bronze marker that memorialized his USMC service. Will said nothing in reply to this question, and so she asked another. "Did you have a good bowel movement today, dear? You look pinched." Glancing out the window, he was startled to notice in a far corner of the yard a smaller twin of his mother's grandiose house, even to its diamond lattice windows and a slender chimney of crosshatched brick ringed in Christmas lights.

"What's that?" He nodded toward the tiny Tudor.

"Isn't it precious? Your stepfather built it for Ariel. He's absolutely fallen for her. You should see the two of them together, it's—"

"Mom, he's not my father. He's your husband."

She sighed lightly. "Well," she sniffed, "he's been wonderful to me. I wish you would just let Newt into your heart."

"No room in my heart for another father."

She frowned. "You should see how he dotes on your Ariel. It's *so* touching."

Carefully, he set his bone china cup onto its delicate saucer. Their skipping stones of conversation were now plunging and sinking. "How is she?" he asked, fighting to keep a steady voice. "How's Ariel?"

She sipped from her cup without her eyes leaving his. "She's fine. Is that why you're here?" She had the look of a mother appraising an unreliable thirteen-year-old. "You aren't planning anything … *crazy*. Are you?"

He felt his face color. "Mom …"

"She's such a happy child, Will." Her eyes had still not left his. "Ask your brother if you want more than just an old grandmother's opinion. Ask Ben."

"You're not old, and he already told me the same thing."

"You see?" She brightened and smiled. "This may seem hard, but I think when both mother and father, for whatever reason, no longer reside under the same roof, it's almost better if the missing parent is, well, dead. I mean, so long as the child is loved and feels secure, it's *so* much easier." She settled back into her chair. "There, I've said it."

Will, unable to respond, could only stare at his mother. He felt a sudden compulsion to occupy his hands and wished he smoked; he did not dare try picking up his coffee cup again. He seized upon a loose thread on one of his shirt cuff buttons.

"You left. That was the best thing," she said now with motherly finality, rising to take their cups and saucers to the kitchen sink. "Stay for lunch. Newt will be home, he'd love to see you."

At the moment Will could not imagine small talk with Newt Truax over the Indians' prospects against the Yankees or the incomprehensible arcana of medical equipment. "No … I've … I've got someone to meet downtown," he managed to say. "Don Bean, remember him? He worked with me at the paper." His chair made a loud scraping sound and nearly tumbled backwards as he came too quickly to his feet.

"But the roads," Nadine protested. "Wait a while until they've got them properly salted. I'm sure your friend will understand."

He glanced out the bay window again. Snow tumbled downward in mounting accumulation. The steeply pitched roof of his daughter's playhouse already lay under a thick cushion of marshmallow. "Gotta go, Mom." His voice was strangled, submerged under water, struggling for air. "Tell Newt hi for me." Quickly retracing his steps to the front door, Will heard his mother following behind on the parquet landscape spattered with tiny lakes of melted snow. At the last possible moment he turned, and they gave each other perfunctory hugs.

"Nice seeing you, Mom."

"How long will you be here?" she asked with a flintiness that could not be concealed.

"Don't know, a couple more days. Got to get back. Winter's my busy season, you know ... all the storms at sea."

Nadine Truax shivered but not from the gusts that rustled her skirt as Will manhandled open the heavy oak door. "How you do it I'll never understand." She had never bothered learning to swim and water frightened her to death.

"Bye, Mom."

Picking his way gingerly down her steps and onto the walkway toward the snow-mounded Nomad, he gave her a wave. She gathered her sweater to her neck and called after him, "Where are your gloves?"

And then he was alone again, the Nomad moving stolidly, like an igloo on wheels. The wipers slapped at the wet snow and the tires crunched through blowing drifts, every so often spinning out over the frozen patches. The truth was, there was no plan to see anyone: he still had no plan, period. He merely inched back the way he came, over the same treacherous roads. He flicked on the radio: Bob Neal droning his sports show, Dorothy Fuldheim and her cranky questioning of visiting politicos and celebrities, the usual used car carneys, and Cleveland's Christmas elf—Mr. Jingaling—luring kids and their parents to the gossamer wonder of Halle's seventh floor—but he barely heard a word of it. Just as the raging snowstorm outside the Nomad's frosted windows was lost to a vision of Newt Truax playing merry old Tudor house with Ariel while Pickle, legs primly crossed, again reminded Nadine what a shit of a firstborn she had delivered into this world. Banishment in his own mother's eyes had not been bargained for. Being the invisible father, that was painful enough: but to be a liability to his own child ... to be better off *dead*. That he did not deserve. Taillights ahead glowed red through their snowy overcoats. Will hit the brakes too hard. The Nomad began to skid and slide.

The impact traveling up the steering column and through his clenched fists and arms and shoulders, tossing his head back and then forward again.

38.
Twig Tea For Three

THAT NIGHT HE WAS EXPECTED AT BEN'S. HIS BROTHER and his wife Abby had a small colonial on a corner lot close enough for Ben to walk to work, yet he always drove. When they met, Abby was doing piecework at a small factory, and after their marriage she quit to keep house for Ben and their two overweight cats; they had no kids, even after Nadine's many unsubtle urgings. (For that matter, neither did Grace, who showed no inclination toward a husband either.) Ben loyally defended his wife's contention that she was "too nervous" to be a mother. He gravitated toward women who, as household pets, would be the least likely adoptees at the S.P.C.A.

Over dinner of stewed vegetables and a roasted twig tea they called *kukicha*—the only visible trace of Ben's derailed higher education was his conversion to macrobiotics—Will recounted the horrors of his afternoon (omitting Nadine's death sentence): how he and an irritating man named Fogel who turned out to be a urologist in a hurry to a hospital had spent the better part of an hour waiting for a cop to show up to document the busted taillight and dented fender on the doctor's splendid new T-bird and to issue Will a ticket. The Nomad's bumper had absorbed the impact without so much as a dimple, though Will had found himself spitting blood into the snow after his face bounced off the steering wheel and cut the inside of his mouth. Now his neck and shoulders ached miserably and his lower lip was swollen and sore. For once he minded neither the overcooked mush on his plate nor Ben's admonishments to chew each mouthful with meditative care.

"Youse shouldn't be driving in weather like this," declared Abby as she refilled Will's cup with the bitter twig brew without asking. "I told Ben he should stay home." She spotted one of their cats, a black longhair, rubbing against Will's trouser leg with unbridled passion. "Satchmo, no!" She nudged the cat away with her foot. "You know better than to beg. Go on, leave our guest alone."

Ben grabbed the cat up and began petting him. Will had never heard a cat purr like gargling mouthwash before. Turning to his wife, Ben said, "Baby, how would it look to Mr. Fish if I stayed home when we live ten blocks from work?" With his free hand he reached under her long and straight chestnut hair to rub the back of her neck. She did not purr in response and would not be dissuaded. Instead, she pouted, "Most car accidents happen close to home." Will repressed a grin. Abby was notoriously reclusive, reluctant to leave home or yard except in dire urgency. "I read it in *Reader's Digest*."

Giving up, Ben reached now for the brown rice.

"Ben, you having *more*? Save room for baked apple."

When he first arrived Will noticed both of them had managed to put on weight eating their fill of starches, fruits, and vegetables. Ben, prone to adding pounds, was more jowly, but Abby's features were filling out as well. How much they had really changed was difficult to tell as they sat at their kitchen table, hidden under Abby's pilled cardigan with a Nordic reindeer pattern and Ben's bulky flannel shirt.

Ignoring Abby, Ben piled a fresh rice mound onto his plate. "Mr. Fish was on my case all day," he said. "It was storming but we were busy. Bad weather makes people feel like tidying their nests." Now he reached for more stew. A smile crept across his face. "Say," he said to Will, "remember how on a day like this we'd have the whole neighborhood in our back yard, sledding on our hill? All the little kids, they'd be pushing and shoving and screaming to be next, and you'd get it all organized and make them take turns." He chuckled as he forked up some rice to begin chewing carefully. "Just like little angels," he said at length. "Those were good times." He picked a morsel from his plate and fed it to the black cat. Like its cream-and-caramel companion fast asleep on the davenport, it had wandered into the yard one day and never left.

"Ben," reproached Abby. "Not at the table."

"Yesterday I went by the old place," said Will.

"How come?" Ben snuffled. Same old allergies.

"I don't know why really."

"Is that why you've come?" Abby seized the chance to ask the question.

"Hey now, baby," Ben scolded. "Don't be so nosy."

"I'm not," she replied, sounding wounded. Then, as if Will had left the room: "He drives across the country without letting anyone know, shows up at the store like he lives round the corner—"

"Baby ..."

She acknowledged her brother-in-law with a faint smile. "We're happy you're here, Will. Curious, is all." From the table she pinched up an imaginary crumb.

Ben went thin-lipped and reddened visibly. Staring at his plate, he edged his fork into the stew. At moments like these Will always wondered whether his brother regretted happening upon this stray. God knows that was a question he had asked himself often enough about Pickle. Ben, though, seemed free of regret.

"I want to see Ariel," Will announced.

"See her?" said Abby with unconcealed surprise.

Ben fixed his brother in a stare. "Pickle won't let you."

"She doesn't know I'm here."

"Then what? You go peek in a window?" Abby's tone struck Will as the unfortunate result of too many episodes of *As the World Turns*. He'd seen enough of the soaps and quiz shows to know he did not want a television, though he did get a kick out of the swagger of David Brinkley in his quips to Chet Huntley. "Something like that, I guess," he replied quietly. A silence settled over Ben and Abby's kitchen.

Finally, Abby arched her eyebrows and asked for Will's plate.

BEN INSISTED ON walking Will to his car. The sky had finally cleared. Moonlight reflected off tree boughs weighed down with snow and the neighborhood glistened. Clouds of their breath shimmered and disappeared. "It's pretty," Will conceded. He slid behind the wheel as Ben stood in his rutted driveway, hands jammed into his pockets, stamping his feet against the cold.

"Will," Ben said, "I want to tell you something in private. But you gotta promise not to do anything—off the wall, I mean. Abby's right, in a way. It *is* sorta weird, you coming all this way on a whim. It isn't like you."

Will looked up at his younger brother's pellucid face. His light brown hair was moving gently in the chill breeze. Will nodded, nearly imperceptibly.

"Well. I told you Mrs. Moledina, the lady who baby-sits Ariel, she's a customer."

Will waited.

"Well. The other day she comes in to look at paper patterns, and of course she knows me and knows I'm Ariel's uncle...." Ben hesitated.

"It's freezing, Toad. You want to get inside the car? I'll get the heater going."

"No—that's okay. I just wanted to tell you … Mrs. Moledina, she took me aside before she left. She's a nice lady but kind of a busybody, Will. And she says to me, 'Can you imagine, Pickle's been telling people your brother isn't Ariel's real dad!'"

"She said what?"

"It's ridiculous, I know—every day Ariel looks more like you—and it's just the sort of stunt Pickle would pull, even if it makes her look bad. She needs keeping us all off balance, to make sure she's in control. You shoulda seen her at Thanksgiving, that's another story. What I'm getting at is, then Mom heard about it somehow. Who knows how. Maybe at the beauty parlor. You know, she still comes all the way back here to Miss Josey's, same as she has for thirty years, to get her hair done. Well, hearing about this spooked her. Spooked her big time. More even than when Pickle said you had wanted Ariel aborted— she's still on us about more grandkids, you know? So Mom can't stand the thought of the only one she's got getting away from her. Ever since then, every chance she gets, she's buttering Pickle up. Anyways, that's it. I had to get it out. Sorry."

In the ride back to the motel the Nomad's heater struggled to cut through the cold. But at least now Will knew what he was going to do.

39.
Ariel

BLINDING WHITE LIGHT THROUGH A GAP IN THE DRAPES of the motel window made Will wince. For an instant or two he was disoriented, that fleeting panic of not knowing where he was; there were no water sounds, no smells of the sea. *What the hell?* Then he remembered.

He threw off the bed covers and bolted to his feet.

On the toilet he amused himself with the juvenile notion he was taking a dump onto Pickle's face. Mephisto, in a voice in his head, was saying she was a prime candidate for natural *de*-selection. Will flushed, watching as if her visage was aswirl in the bowl, gasping for breath. "Like it? People deserve exactly what they get. Sometimes."

Stupid, but he felt better after that.

Showering hurriedly, he didn't bother shaving. He pulled on the same clothes he'd worn the day before—brown corduroys and a navy wool turtleneck—and packed up. Still sore from yesterday's collision, he saw that the swelling on his lip was down when he checked himself in the bathroom mirror. He practiced a grin to see if he looked scary. No, just retarded, he said to himself. Not too bad. By tonight they would be where no one knew him. They would be in another state.

Seminole was a street where autos sat in driveways or were safely stowed in garages, and so Will brought the Nomad slowly to a stop near the top of the commercial cross-street nearest to the Moledina's and switched off the ignition. An idling car might draw more notice, he reasoned. There was a clear line of sight to the house, and it was an intersection Pickle was unlikely to cross to or from the baby-sitter's. Roads had been snowplowed throughout the night, and with the sun quickly drying the pavement, reaching this juncture after a stop at a Kenny King's for a dishwatery coffee in a paper cup proved a simple matter. Now there was nothing to do but wait. He sipped at the steaming coffee and swiped at the condensation that clouded the Nomad's windows.

Only minutes later his vigil was rewarded. Pickle's red Fury appeared at the far end of Seminole, two blocks away and closing fast. Still the lead foot, Will thought with a grim chuckle. One of his oldest memories of her was that morning in traffic court when she shook like a frightened animal as the judge warned that one more moving violation would introduce her to the overnight accommodations of the county. Even then he had wondered why she had begged her new boyfriend to witness her humiliation. Instead of seeing this as a warning of his own, of course, he had encircled her in his arms. The Fury swerved into the Moledina driveway and came to an abrupt stop. He saw the passenger door open a crack, and then there were Pickle's long legs making their way around the rear. She was wearing a patterned scarf over her head and only a light car coat, despite the cold. Flinging wide the passenger door, she extended an arm inside to tug on the hand that reached for her. Out slid a tiny figure. The parka coat and matching snow pants were a pure white, and from Will's far-off vantage point the little girl all but disappeared against the snow. Shuffling up the sidewalk to the front door of the house, she appeared to be a pair of magically animated red boots.

Will watched his daughter and ex-wife disappear into the Moledina's. Then Pickle reemerged, backed the Fury onto the street in jerky movements, and gunned the accelerator to retrace her route. He did not take his eyes from her until she was a distant haze of blue exhaust. Pickle would be the Bargain Barn's problem the remainder of the workday. Heaven help them.

Will's coffee, what was left, had gone bitter and cold. Opening his door just enough to pour it out, he created a perfect brown crater in the snow, then quickly slammed the door shut to ward off the frigid air. Luckily the sun streaming into the Nomad was warming, even though his feet were twin blocks of ice. Now he must wait again. He wished he had thought to buy a newspaper: at least he could have hunted for bylines he knew, check up on what his old boss, the comics editor, thought was comical these days. Did anyone, he mused, still think Mary Worth was worth it? Perhaps it was unfortunate he had only his own thoughts to keep him company, for that meant risking exposure of his newly hatched plan. It was too young, too tender to ward off potential attackers. As a diversion, he tried basking again in the thrill of seeing her. *He had seen Ariel!* He had witnessed his own daughter—he harbored absolutely no doubts about whether she was really his—waddle all the way from car to house. Definitely more grown up since I left, but don't all kids grow up too fast? Doesn't everyone say so? Then it occurred to him: really, how did he know? With that snowsuit she might has well have been slathered in meringue. He sighed deeply and let his mind drain itself of thought.

And before he could even try stopping them, the predators of newly hatched plans, snarling Second Guesses, rushed in to begin circling their prey. It was no contest. What had represented itself only the night before as the *best*, the *only*, the *rock-solid* plan of action—for him, for Ariel—suddenly began to lose its substance. The Second Guesses snapped at flesh and sinew. Soon the defenseless plan might disappear altogether. He disliked this sensation even more intensely than the absolute numbness of his toes.

Just as his resolve was becoming as alien to him as his feet, the door to the Moledina's garage shot up. He rubbed desperately at the Nomad's clouded-over window, and saw a short, stoutish woman who had to be Mrs. Moledina standing with arms upraised at the trunk lid of her car, which he could see was a pale green. In the next instant he lost sight of her, and so he craned his neck forward until his forehead pressed to the cold glass. He muttered oaths but relaxed when she returned into view with a child's snow sled under one arm; it looked to be the same Flexible Flyer he had found for Ariel at Koppel's when she was three. The woman deposited the sled into the car's trunk, yanked the lid shut, and soon was driving slowly away. Ariel was nowhere to be seen, but could there be any doubt she was riding beside her?

He did not think about it further. Bringing the Nomad to life, he was off in pursuit. Stepping hard on the gas, shooting forward much too obviously fast for the quiet residential street. That might be Pickle's style, but hardly the thing for someone bent on abducting his own child. With an eye to the speedometer, he slowed and prayed he would not lose the car far ahead. At the end of Seminole the green car turned left. Mrs. Moledina was a careful driver. He was following at a safe distance by then and saw her turn left again.

All at once, he knew. It was obvious. Passing the street sign with a quick sideward glance, he was reassured by the sight of Mrs. Moledina's brake lights. This was all the confirmation he needed.

Ariel was bound for the best sledding hill for miles around.

He parked on Satin, the next street over from Uselma, in front of the house where Freddy Gibson grew up. The last he heard, the Gibsons had gone back to Maine. He had no idea who had their ramshackle Victorian now. What mattered was, no one seemed at home and the backyard was catty-corner to Mount Dumont. The squeals of the young sledders, quite a few evidently, nearly drowned out the Nomad's V-8 as he coasted to a stop. If the historic rules still applied—his inventions, all of them—the kids trudged with their sleds to the top, single-file, on the Uselma side, then flew down on the Satin, the longer slope. There was an extremely good chance no adult would be in sight for the moments it took each sledder to crunch across the snow from the bottom of the run back to the starting point, where the parents gathered to gossip. When Will was younger, the neighborhood looked to him as chief cop for sled traffic. Now it was left to the parents to mediate disputes over whose turn was next.

Nonchalantly as he could, he trudged through the crusted snow, hands stuffed inside his coat pockets. He was wearing short engineer boots, and snow from the deeper drifts melted down his ankles and into his boots; he could feel the wetness even with numbed feet. He noticed his pounding heart; he could hear its rhythmic beating in his ears. At least no one seemed to have spotted him so far.

A small shed, the kind used to store garden tools, stood at the back of the old Gibson property. That was where he headed. The bright sun was throwing a deep shadow on the shed's far side. A man could conceal himself there. Only his ragged trail of footprints through the snow would betray his presence.

Will flattened himself against the shed and pulled his head back until it rested on the cold corrugated wall. He waited for his pulse to slow and took deep breaths. Finally, he dared to peer out from his shadowy hiding place at the spectacle of Mount Dumont. The magnificent sledding hill was operating just as he remembered. He watched in hiding as sledder after sledder appeared at the top to take on the steep glistening run. Is anything more joyous than children barreling downhill on fast fresh snow?

And then he saw her.

A white snow bunny with a rosy face tottered into view at

the summit. She seemed to be looking straight at him. *She's spotted me*, he thought in a panic. Reflexively, he backed himself into deeper shadow, then carefully edged forward for another look. She had not moved. She was hesitating. Another child came into view, an older boy; he urged her onto her sled, and when she had taken a mittenhold on each shiny wooden steering arm of the Flexible Flyer, he gave her a mighty push. Down, down she shot, a scream of delight in her wake. Her aim was true. The Flyer was fast. At the bottom she narrowly missed another sledder on one knee adjusting a boot, sliding right past and on and on and on, continuing into virgin snow, stopping not twenty feet from where Will was waiting. A huge smile was all he could see inside the parka hood.

He wanted to shout his congratulations. He wanted to yell out how proud he was of his little girl. Her wondrous feat had brought back the umpteen thousands of times he himself had sailed down Mount Dumont, the cold in his face, the wind in his ears. How good that felt. How free and powerful. As if nothing else existed, not in the whole world. Nothing but the snow and the sled and the hill. He had basked in the glories of Mount Dumont until that day when he suddenly outgrew it; when the thrill was gone, and he felt cheated. From then on it was just a little hill for little kids. Like *this* little kid right in front of him—his little girl. In a frozen moment she lay sprawled on her sled just steps away. Her nose and cheeks were rosy, and he could see the frozen clouds of her breath. He knew this hill. One run in a winter's sledding carried you this far. There would be no better time. If he was going to do it....

But he did nothing.

He shrank back into the shadows. He heart raced and he felt sweaty even in the cold. But he did nothing.

Why? Was it fear? No. Indecision? No. It was not even a swift kill by the Second Guesses.

Like the hill itself, he had simply outgrown the idea.

Let her be, he told himself. Let her be.

Only then did he notice Pickle racing across the snow toward Ariel, calling out her name. Only then did he notice the siren growing louder.

Flattened against the shed wall, he did not see Ariel's mother scoop her up, look around with a face dark with anger and alarm, and carry the girl in her arms back toward Uselma. When he dared to peek out again, they were gone. With the siren very close, he ran. As fast as he could he sped back across the yard where he and Freddy Gibson used to play kick-the-can and red rover, red rover, let Willy come over....

The Nomad was waiting. He fumbled with the key but in five minutes he was beyond the town limits. In fifteen he was heading west.

West was where home was now.

AT HIS FIRST STOP to gas up and stretch his legs, he dialed a number he asked the information operator for. A familiar voice answered, "Hello, Fish's."

"Ben," he said into the pay telephone.

"Will!" The voice assumed an excited hush. "Where are you?"

"On my way."

"Oh. Good. Alone?"

"Of course alone. What else?"

Silence on the line except for the long distance crackle. At last, Ben said, "Oh my, I don't know what to say. Will, it wasn't me, I swear."

Will listened, saying nothing.

"Will ..."

"Damn it, Ben."

"Mom," Ben blurted. "It was Mom."

"Christ," Will swore.

"I talked to her this morning. She called Pickle, Will. She called Pickle and told her you were in town. I told you she's all hung up on staying close, to keep the door open to Ariel."

Will felt his chest tighten. "Okay, fine. She told Pickle," he heard himself say with exaggerated calm. "But I was almost arrested at our sledding hill."

"I know. The cop stopped here wanting to know if you was still in town. He said Mrs. Moledina called in. She must have seen you."

"Toad?"

"Yeah?"

"You were right."

"She's a real busybody like I said."

"No, not that."

"What?"

"She's a very happy kid."

40.
Thump in the Night

EARLY EVENING, EIGHTEENTH OF DECEMBER. WILL was back in the shack. If the events chronicled here were fictional inventions, then the happenstance of this also being the very day of the S.O.S. Happening might over-stretch the girdle of believability. But there you have it. Life is like that, or else comets could never collide. Of far greater importance in Will's mind was the long yet liberating drive home. Whereas on the eastward slog he had assiduously avoided peering into the rearview mirror of his own psyche, fearful the demons would blind him in their glare, this time he had wallowed in backward glances. He slalomed without heed through the receding mindscape that was peopled with friend, foe, and versions of himself. There were byways flooded in high tides of regret and shame. There were signposts promising roads to majesty and new purpose (some of these being barely passable during construction). But with each passing mile marker, his look backward took on sharper focus. He began to sense he might have made it through the worst, the hardest going. He felt cleansed, healthier than in years.

Looking forward, then, he thought he spotted a chrysalis of pure white ahead: acceptance, it was called. For he had seen Ariel. She was well. And he had stared into the Uselma pit. It had not sucked him in. He even saw how a mother could value ties to a granddaughter more than to her firstborn. Nadine

Truax, in her reconstituted life in the Shaker Tudor, needed a child's unformed soul and unconditional love, and Ariel was this new chance. All right, so be it. We all need new chances. Some never get them or never take them. Had his father lived, he wondered, could there have even been reconciliation within the Dumont clan? A bridge rebuilt between a father and his son? Comets do occasionally collide, don't they?

For the first time Will had grudging pity for Pickle. For the first time he was stronger than her need to pull him down. It was provisional, he knew: not enough to go ten rounds. But with nourishment, if he did not squander this newfound strength, it was a start. Such intimations, fragile as new-grown tissue after a burn, gave Will hope. It was a good feeling. Many bandoleers of weights had been stripped off, and he was now free to rise to the light.

As he left the desert scrub of Arizona for the desert scrub of California, his thoughts turned to his new home, his new life. To Maggie, darling Maggie. He tapped his chest, imagining the presence of the small golden key to her locket. Damn. How had he managed to lose it? The woman, he hoped, was not lost as well. He, too, wanted another chance.

Those final long hours the asphalt turned to molasses. What, only Bakersfield? Just Fresno? He tired of the Central Valley and its monotony. He was sick of Burma-Shave.

> *Doesn't*
> *Kiss you*
> *Like she useter?*
> *Perhaps she's seen*
> *A smoother rooster!!*
> *Burma-Shave*

More promising:
> *She will*

Flood your face
With kisses
'Cause you smell
So darn delicious
Burma-Shave Lotion

When the Nomad's tires finally sang in the high register of the Golden Gate, Will let out a shout and craned to spot the Farallons and the ocean-going freighters fanning out on routes to all the major ports of the Pacific. He reveled in the white sails fluttering on the bay, the craggy solitude of Alcatraz, Fort Point guarding the southern flank of the Gate, Fort Baker to the north. The magnificent Marin Headlands lay ahead. Almost Sausalito! Almost home!

Monterey pine needles the color of rust littered the gangplank and the shack's deck, and there were also whorls of sand, bits of blowing scrap from the boat works. No shingles had blown loose from the shack's front, as sometimes happened, and the sole missing fixture appeared to be One-Eyed George, nowhere to be seen. The beach showed evidence of storm—a washed-up spar with grayed-out varnish, a gnarled tree root, half buried. He was glad to see his dory still secure between the stanchions below the deck.

Inside, the shack was cold and dank. He relit the pilot on the small gas heater but kept his pea coat on; he knew it would not take long to warm up. In his gently gurgling fish tank, his beloved pets looked well fed, their aquatic world in order, and his houseplants were leafy and green. Princess hadn't zombied out on him, and he made mental note to thank her for her care while he was away. He riffled through mail heaped on his desk, all solicitations and bills except for one envelope addressed in Maggie's loopy hand. This he set aside, too weary suddenly to deal with its freight. It was nearly five-thirty, and already dark outside.

The ringing of the phone startled him. He had been home no more than twenty minutes. Pawing through his gear in search of a turquoise amulet he bought from a Navajo woman for Maggie, he thought about not answering. But when the ringing did not cease, he reached for the receiver.

"You wife-beating bastard."

"Hello, Pickle." She was silent. "Let me guess. My mother gave you the number."

"Or should I say," Pickle continued now, "you wife-beating, *kidnapping* bastard."

"I'm hanging up." He said it calmly, evenly.

"Don't you *dare* hang up on me. Do it and kiss any chance of seeing your daugh—"

Gently he returned the receiver to its cradle. Then, thinking better of it, lifted it again and laid it next to the phone. He knew she must be furiously redialing. "Bye, Pickle. Take care of yourself ... and Ariel." He felt strangely unfazed by her assault. *Jeez, a good sign.* All he felt was the weariness, the aches in his limbs from all the hours in the Nomad, and a mental exhaustion that was the inevitable counterweight to his euphoria a short while before. What he needed most, he decided, was sleep. He crossed the hall and entered his bedroom. The shack still felt cold. Pea coat, boots, and all, he fell heavily onto his bed. In moments his breathing slowed and deepened. As the hours passed, the dreams were vivid.

Thump athump athump ...

Pickle's balled fists were beating on his chest, and she was hurling names at him.

Thump thump athump ...

Pickle, clutching a bouquet of Bargain Barn balloons, was being swept aloft, through a tornado-like vortex, and her head was banging against a twirling Tudor playhouse.

Thump thump ...

He opened his eyes, bewildered. Where was Pickle? Where

was he? What was *that*?

Thump athump.

The roof, he thought, coming from the roof ... not raccoons ...

Rolling off the bed and moving in one motion to the plantation shutters that closed off the bedroom from the front room, he threw them open wide.

The room filled with lurid orange-magenta sky. It seemed to pulsate and swirl, like the devil's own fog bank or eerie northern lights.

He stared, open-mouthed. What was it?

Then he knew.

If ever he pulled down his dory, dragged it to water's edge, scrambled aboard, yanked the outboard's rope starter, and throttled up any faster, he could not have told you when.

The stench of fire was already overpowering the smells of the sea, and the cool air whistled in his ears as the dory raced forward. Along Bridgeway he saw the flashing lights of emergency vehicles. With a quick backwards glance at the shack—was that One-Eyed George's quizzically cocked head on his roof?—he steered for the boat channel, then swung left in a tight arc toward the circus sky.

Not until Will rounded the sand spit near downtown did it dawn on him it was the VALLEJO—that Varda's and the Watts's grand old ferryboat was on fire. He could see the flames licking at the sky now, against the plume of thick black and colored smoke. The thought hit him like a bellyful of bad oysters. Raising himself up from his seat and leaning forward to try for a clearer look, he was nearly pitched overboard when a stray boat wave slammed the starboard bow. Heavily, he sat again, fearful and impatient, until, closer, he could finally make out the terrible dimensions of the tragedy.

All around the ferry was a penumbra of firelight. He pointed the dory straight for it.

From thirty yards he was blistered by the heat.

He was nearest the bow, which was completely engulfed by flames. They shot from the upper deck the height of three men. In disbelief he saw what looked like hundreds of dots, singed measles spots, on the ferry's hull and cabins, amid burning tatters of colored fabric and ruins of trampled party decor. There seemed to be a throng crowding the stern, their cries muffled against the overwhelming roar.

There were other boats, including Coast Guard, already fishing out the jumpers. He slowed to avoid floating debris and swimmers flailing. Once before had he witnessed such a harrowing conflagration: back in Ohio, when the threadbare cliché of the dangers of smoking in bed came too terribly true one night at a decrepit Cleveland hotel. Memories of that fire were as indelible as what, in his journalist's role, he witnessed afterward. Fifteen dead from a visiting thespian troupe, laid out at the morgue, men, women, and children, their smoke-dark bodies naked and still for eternity. He shuddered at the thought of his neighbors and friends of the waterfront ... of Maggie most of all.

He was rounding the burning ferryboat, searching for those most in need of aid, when he heard the thunderous crack. Looking up, he watched the timber go, trailing smoke and embers like a rocket's tail.

He saw it strike someone at the rail—a woman, face darkened in soot. He watched her topple headlong over the side.

He did not hesitate. Tearing away his coat and stripping off his boots, Will plunged, following the woman into the bay. Even with the shock of cold, he was in his element now. Several strong strokes took him to the spot where she had hit. Treading water, he spun in a furious circle, searching for a sign of her. He guessed the depth at this point to be about three fathoms—eighteen feet. Visibility below he knew would be zero.

Gulping breath, he upended himself and kicked hard to

propel himself downward, wishing for his wet suit instead of these sodden street clothes. With his arms he described wide arcs, as if making snow angels, knowing his only hope of finding her before the currents did was to actually come upon her, to brush against her body. Thrashing like this as long as he could, he finally returned to the surface to seize more breath, looked hurriedly around, reversed himself again for another try.

And another. With each time moving a few feet further out, in the direction he guessed the bay would want to take her.

The water temperature was beginning to affect him, despite his pounding heart and aching lungs. On his fifth attempt, about to head up for more air, he felt something lightly tap his left wrist. It was fleeting, a second's sensation.

It was enough.

Lungs are amazing organs: when called upon in emergencies, they can yield reserves of life force ordinarily never tapped. Instead of returning to the surface, as his mind insisted, Will made three titanic kicks in the direction of the momentary touch. His hands groped wildly in the inky darkness. Had it been a trick, an underwater illusion? Where was she? How could she not be there?

His arm became ensnared. It was as if the bay had reached out to him. He was now entangled in a thick web, yet still floating free. Wrapping his arms around the mass, he searched for a center. He felt a solid. He had become snared in a kelp forest. A kelp forest of hair. It was a head.

By now his lungs were on fire. He wanted to gulp the sea, become a manfish, breathe as he had in the womb. He saw himself diving from a high cliff, weightless, falling. His body screamed at him.

Just breathe! Just breathe!

Instinctively, his legs kicked. It was lucky he had not twisted or turned to lose his orientation. In this watery void he could have just as easily spent himself in one last misdirected motion, propelling himself sideways or into the dark depths. He broke the surface in an explosion of gasps and coughs, swallowing water but reclaiming his place among the living. In the next instant realizing he still had hold of another human.

They were thirty yards from shore. The fire lit their way. The last few feet strangers dragged their bodies across the soft muck.

As Will lay in the ambulance on the ride to Marin General, he did not remember ever having felt so exhausted. He looked over at the woman on the gurney next to his. The mud had been washed from her, but there were still traces, in her creases and hair, of the green clay from her performance art. Her jaw was slack and mouth open, her eyes closed, hair damp and lank. He saw a dark stain above her right temple.

Shutting his eyes, he appealed to a God he did not believe in. He prayed that, this once, he had been able to rescue and not just recover.

The remainder of that December night he spent in the war zone of the emergency room, wrapped in a wool blanket, waiting while cases more serious than his mild hypothermia were attended to. Dozens suffered from more serious exposure. More than a hundred in all had been carried from the scene, and were four hurt critically. Two were D.O.A., trampled in the panic. Maggie, admitted immediately and wheeled to intensive care, was still unconscious, in grave danger but hanging on.

IN THE SOLEMN days following, a Water Rat fisherman found Will's dory on its way out the Gate to the Pacific. Seabirds had made a mess of the pea coat. And charred remains of the VALLEJO washed up everywhere.

41.
Nice Try, Suckah!

I ENDED WITH A BANG, I EVER TELL YOU THAT?

Malachy, not now. My heart is heavy.

Lass, lass—can't let the living get you down! Hear my tale ... 'twill be far more entertaining!

Malachy....

So I was saying, my own departure from this mortal coil came far too early, but came at least in a fashion befitting the likes of myself. Which must be why I hang round this old shackful of memories—apart from the view, of course.

Malachy, please ...

There was I, the big success. My speakeasy booming. Packed to the rafters night after night. Delphine, none too keen on the late hours nor the occupation, but enjoying the fruits of my labors, let me tell you. That year she sent all the way to Lisbon for a bolt of taffeta for her gay Chamarita dress.

Chama—?

Festival of the Holy Ghost, my dear—Pentecostal Sunday, the fiftieth day after the Christian Easter. Local Portugees do it up in grand fashion. For weeks, nothing but feasting, music, dancing. By the hundreds they flock from the countryside into Sausalito, and they drape their cattle in flowers and drive them through the streets. My strapping boy-o Artur had acquired my own eye for the ladies by his teenaged years, and he could hardly wait to see the pretty lasses parade by, 'specially the one chosen as queen in a crown topped by a white dove.

From this you died, Malachy?

No, no, from the supplications of José Sousa, our old bene-factor! The *sopa, carne,* and *vinho* served up after Mass at Star of the Sea not being enough for him. He were insisting on Malachy's special blend for all his cronies! I was low on it and should have said no, tired as I was. But I lust for greenbacks dangled right before my eyes, so here I was, back of the shack, hurrying my way through a brand new batch. Luckily, Artur were up at Bolinas eel jigging, and Delphine were sitting with a sick friend, when ... *kaboom!* Up she goes, me with it.

How, Malachy?

But a single stray spark is all she takes.

A ghost doctor might have saved you, if you were dead but taking in breath.

Dead but ... pshaw!

Like her ... the one with hair like the blackberry bush who has been many times to your shack. The living death means a ghost like you or me is stealing her as a companion in the spirit world.

You mean I didn't have to be alone till you came along?

It is good we have each other.

"SWEETIE, MR. BOGART'LL see you now," said the secretary whose matchstick limbs, corona of yellow hair, and bent posture made Will think of a droopy sunflower. He followed her down a narrow fairway laid in thick emerald carpet, its mahogany walls hung with heroic portraits of ocean-going ships. Will had made his way to these Lower Market offices after many a day divided between Maggie's bedside and equally long hours at the library and town hall bent over plat maps, yellowing newspapers, legal documents. Christmas came and went barely noticed. His vigil for any indication of Maggie's awakening had so far been in vain, but he had managed to dissect the pier project and put it back together again. Now it was abundantly clear why Galilee Harbor had been targeted: not only did it offer a deep-water anchorage, it also had the most untapped potential for commercial development once the houseboats were driven off. They meant to rename the town *El Rancho de las Turistas*.

He had also read up on the man he was about to meet. This was not hard to do, but the careful eye noted the chameleon in Kyle Bogart. At times his ties were said to be in the East, at others in the Midwest; his family was in auto parts or insurance, his education impressive or barely alluded to. If changes in his coloration were called into question, as they occasionally were, he laughed them off with a paraphrase of Ralph Waldo Emerson, "Consistency, that's the hobgoblin of small thinkers!"

Yet in one detail his story never wavered. Yes, he would freely admit, Humphrey Bogart *was* his distant cousin. Will saw a likeness from the photos: a lean and wiry frame, thinning dark hair, ears like tree mushrooms, a vulpine smile.

This Bogart, through much apparent cunning and charm, had managed to build up the largest fleet of passenger ships on the West Coast. Now, at a time when the new jet aircraft were swiftly consigning passenger ocean travel to the same dustheap of history as the chariot, and his competitors were mothballing their luxury liners, Bogart saw only opportunity.

He was buying up seafaring hotels at sheriff's-sale prices. And he was building brand-new pleasure palaces to suit his own specifications.

But his ships would *cruise* rather than transport. He was betting heavily that travelers would pay for the experience of going nowhere necessary while being overfed and entertained every minute of the way. (His bet, of course, was right on the money: thus was the cruise-ship industry launched.) But this gamble had also left him with an immediate and pressing need:

seaside attractions, for a few hours or a few days. To secure his passengers pleasurable ports of call, Bogart had been promising a bountiful harvest of vacationing cardiologists and free-spending honeymooners from Vancouver to Acapulco. It was working. His ships now ranged the Pacific coasts of North and South America and sailed weekly to Honolulu.

But why Sausalito? Why not San Francisco, already a full-fledged tourist trap? Here was where Will thought it got interesting. He'd happened upon one of Herb Caen's three-dot squibs which had reported a falling-out between San Francisco's port commissioner and "a certain throwback to privateers who once plied these waters in search of booty." It was Caen's kicker that iced it: "Here's looking at you, Capt. Kidd." Maybe this gambler named Bogart was not all that serious about Sausalito after all; maybe he was just calling San Francisco's bluff. At least there was a chance, and Will was pinning his hopes on it. For Maggie's sake, he reminded himself as he trailed Miss Sunflower to the end of the long hall. Remember how they schooled us cubs in the newspaper city room, he also told himself again. Kowtow at first, get him off-guard, then go for the jugular.

He tried to think about what he would say first. Instead, he could not help but think back to the night before.

Visiting hours were ending at the hospital, and quietly he had told her, "Mag, listen to me. Tomorrow I'm going to see that bastard that wants to dock his ships here. I'm going to beat him at his own game. Thank me when you get better." He had leaned closer to her, alert for any sign she had heard. Accidentally he brushed against smooth skin. The sensation caught him by surprise. It encompassed all possibilities of her: more deep-seated than desire alone, released from a place he once thought boarded up and closed for good. He wanted simultaneously to run away and shout for joy. Instead he kissed her lips, tentatively, and found them wonderfully warm.

Not enough. Looking around, seeing no one, he tugged shut the curtain around her bed. He avoided the tube that fed her, the wire linked to her heartbeat, and was careful not to brush against the bandages where surgeons had opened her skull to relieve the pressure of blood pooled on her brain. Slipping next to her under the thin hospital blanket and sheet, for a minute or two he just lay still. Feeling the heat of her body and the rhythm of her breath.

Then he screwed up his courage. He slid a hand under her gown. To the soft swelling of her breasts. The prickly heat of her sex. He felt that somehow she was urging him on.

His hand still resting gently atop her mysterious crevice and folds, he made quick, furtive movements with the other. In moments it was over.

He wiped himself with the bedsheet, carefully got out of bed, rearranged the bed covers, zipped himself. Maggie had not moved a muscle. The steady beep of the heart monitor was unchanged. Yet as he stood over her, he could have sworn there was the slightest flutter beneath her eyelids.

"I love you," he told her.

HIS OFFICE WAS predictably enormous and had sweeping views. Alcatraz. Coit Tower. The Bay Bridge. Sunlight cast the man seated at the far end in harsh grays and whites, as if a lousy signal made the TV picture fuzzy and washed out. "Sit please, Mr. Dumont." The grainy image gestured toward a leather arm-chair across the giant desk. Will sank into the seat and tried to project confidence. Seeing the face from the news stories clearly then, though the features were more furrowed and reminded him vaguely of someone he could not place.

"Mr. Bogart," Will began.

"Please. Kyle."

Half-smiling, Kyle Bogart stood. He wore a dark suit and

white shirt, and his patterned tie spilled onto the broad desk-
top as he extended his hand. The grasp was soft. As the man
settled back again into his chair, Will noticed the silver-framed
photographs on the wall behind: champagne christenings of
sleek ships, poses with politicos and the instantly recognizable—including one of the famous cousin. Kyle Bogart grinned
toothily beside the dour movie star, who was dragging on a
cigarette at what appeared to be a glitzy nightclub.

"My wall of fame ... or shame," Kyle Bogart said, noting
Will's gaze. "Bought and paid for, every man and boat." He
flashed the same smile as in the nightclub photo.

"Even your cousin?"

"You'd be surprised." Bogart sat back now and pursed his
lips. "Let's get down to business. You told my secretary you
represent a citizens' group in Sausalito. What group would
that be?"

"That why you agreed to see me?" Will regretted saying
something so stupid sounding even as the words escaped his
mouth. Where had his plan gone to butter him up first? Why
did he feel this knot in his stomach? "I represent those on the
waterfront who love Sausalito the way it's always been," he
answered in a voice he hardly knew. "I'm here because we're
dead set against what you're doing."

He found it hard to keep up a determined stare into Kyle
Bogart's eyes, which he saw were a ghostly pale blue, and he
berated himself once again. Why so nervous? He steeled himself and plunged forward. "And I'm here to inform you we'll
go on opposing you even if your dock gets built. Even if your
passengers start taking over our streets. I can't imagine you'll
want them finding the natives unfriendly. It might ruin their
expensive fun. They might talk Aunt Betty and Uncle Bud
right out of booking your next cruise. And the press could tar
you with bad publicity. Your ships could end up with a lot of
empty cabins ... Kyle."

Kyle Bogart studied Will like some lab specimen. Finally, he said flatly, "First of all, it's not even my pier. Your own neighbors are building it."

"Yes, but …"

"Second, just give it time." Kyle Bogart had not taken his gaze from Will. "Opposition will fade away. It always does."

"No, I don't think so."

"And third, do you take me for a fool? You're here on your own, representing no one, and you don't even live by the pier. Am I right … Will?"

Will struggled for a semblance of calm. What was it about this man? All at once, he again felt lost in the dark caverns of his boyhood, as if back on the receiving end from his father. He could not let it conclude like this. He needed a draw, at least. He searched for the means and the will to go the final round even as his composure was disintegrating like an ancient buried thing exposed to new air.

"It's wrong," he blurted, knowing he was flailing. "Your godawful stink boats don't belong in a little seaside town like ours. You'll ruin it. You'll foul our harbor. Turn our bay into a total dead zone. I'm a professional diver. I know what giant ships do. Go park your floating Ho-Jos someplace else … in the city.…" It was the speech he had rehearsed but it had been delivered without heart.

Bogart's mouth fell open as if to answer but for some reason he stopped.

"I know that's where you want to be anyway," Will continued. "In San Francisco, I mean. Don't think I haven't done my homework.…"

Kyle Bogart leaned back into his big chair. "Where I want to be, you have no idea." His tone was one of vague disappointment, and there was a momentary softening of his expression. Quickly that was replaced by the public persona of his framed gallery. "How could you, Mr. Dumont? You can't even decide where you belong. Is it your quaint Sausalito, slumming it with the low-lifes? Or is it back in Ohio, with your only daughter? Maybe there you could protect the poor girl when she realizes how crazy her mom really is."

Kyle Bogart's eyes bored holes into Will's. "Ariel, isn't it? I think you both know all about growing up with a wacked-out parent, don't you? You see, I've done my homework too."

At this, Will's remaining resolve buckled completely and he felt as if he was crashing to the canvas. He went limp. This prize fight was over. There was no sense even waiting around for the ring announcer to make it official.

ONE-EYED GEORGE saw Will's return to the shack, though none of us did.

When a person on the mend takes a chance and falls short, it can be worse than not trying at all. Think of tender spring growth caught hard by a late freeze. At worst it can kill you. At the very least you feel spent, ridiculous. Stupid for even sticking your neck out. Worth less than nothing.

It can make someone say when no one can hear but an uncomprehending pelican, "A coward can't save shit."

42.
Belated Christmas Cheer

ANOTHER LONG AND RELENTLESSLY CHEERY LETTER arrived from Will's mother. Nadine packed it with Christmas Day spent at Pickle's, with Ariel, in excruciating detail. Of her many, many presents, Ariel most "adored" a socialite Barbie with spare outfits and accessories for both entertaining and leisure that packed neatly into a vinyl-covered, leopard print travel case. Boy, did Grandpa Newt get a kick out of his granddaughter! The two of them sprawled on Pickle's living room rug and played Ariel's new Candyland game. It was all anyone could do to get them to the table for baked ham with pineapple rings, candied sweet potatoes, buttered beets, and Nadine's famous Christmas salad (green Jell-O in the shape of an evergreen, decorated with miniature marshmallows and ornaments of preserved pear). Dear little Ariel, so tuckered out from all the excitement, fell asleep on Grandpa's lap during Mitch Miller's sing-along special. Grandma and Pickle had a sweet little rag doll on their hands as they shrugged her into peejays and tucked her in for the night.

Ben and Grace also wrote. Ben and Abby had not been invited to Pickle's for Christmas but probably would have stayed home if they had. Abby was uneasy around Newt and his monogrammed shirts, and Ben had his fill at Thanksgiving of hints from Nadine about another grandchild. Grace thanked Will for the autographed copy of *On the Road*. She hoped Kerouac was as Benzedrine wild as he made himself out to be. Her new "best friend" was an aspiring stage actress like herself, name of Mandy, who just begun cohabiting Grace's East Village cold-water flat.

The big news around town: Hayden was back. The WAN-DERER bounded through the Gate three days after Christmas, tacked toward Richardson Bay and dropped anchor off the sand spit. The following morning Officer Mack pulled aside in the police launch and boarded the sloop to arrest Hayden for transporting his children, all of them bursting with good health, in violation of court order. Within hours Lawyer Musselman had him sprung on bail, after which Hayden repaired to the No Name to regale all those present—absent Will—with grandiose tales of his South Seas adventures.

Maggie's condition was unchanged. The pier was now completed. Will could not remember a new year he looked forward to less.

His glimmering of hope after the trip back to Ohio had been all but extinguished. First and foremost by Maggie's unaltered tragic state, and then by his "pathetic" try at swaying Kyle Bogart. Again he had sequestered himself within the shack's walls, negligent even in his routine of daily visits to Marin General, wondering anew how to make a habitable construction of his life. As usual, the shack offered up its solace. There was comfort in its familiar groans of age, the way the light played through it on those January days of no fog and unblemished skies. The rains had gone on hiatus, it seemed. Long hours he spent gazing toward the bay and its unending traffic: ferryboats knifing back and forth, tugs and pilots on escort missions to and from the Gate, sailboats in regattas, their billowed spinnakers all colors of the rainbow. No sign, thankfully, of the first cruise ship of the Kyle Bogart fleet steaming towards the new pier.

Not that Will was altogether free to tramp through the

ruins of his life. Periodic calls for his professional services came
with the season: winter storms that capsized fishing trawlers and
sailing sloops and dared foolhardy surfers to take crazy chances
on skyscraper waves above Half Moon Bay. An entire day of
the new year's first week he spent diving off the Headlands,
near Point Bonita, after a young couple made the mistake of
parking at a popular sunset spot. The two lovers had huddled
together in their Rambler to watch seabirds against the dying
light and the orange ball of sun turn pear-shaped before it
melted beneath the horizon; then they let passion take over and,
catastrophically, failed to notice they had jostled the gearshift.
Their car crept lazily toward the precipice. It was two hundred
feet straight down. Will and another diver located the bodies
with forty feet of water resting on their car's roof. They had
a hell of time wresting out the deceased. "That boy's jaw was
locked," marveled Will's partner when finally they stripped off
tanks and wet suits. The coroner's report mentioned "puncture
wounds consistent with teeth marks" on the girl's inner thighs.
Hearing of this gruesome fate, Putty and Princess vowed they
would always, always double-check the hand brake.

ONE AFTERNOON WILL sat at his desk and fed a sheet into the
Royal.
  Dearest Ariel, he began in a two-fingered burst. *It's been
weeks since I wrote, though I remind myself you haven't read any of
my earlier efforts. If you ever do, they will come as one giant gulp, I
suppose. Oh, well. I write for myself as much as for you.* His mind
went to the stack of typewritten pages tucked into a small
wooden chest in the shack's storage reef. He saw them as a
beating heart, as in a Poe short story. Pulling back his thoughts,
he focused again on the enameled keys of the portable.

———————

EXCERPT FROM *A letter (never mailed) from Will Dumont to Ariel Dumont:* Dear girl, I actually saw you. A few weeks before your fifth Christmas, bundled up in a cute white snowsuit, there you were on top of Mount Dumont—do kids still call it that?—on Uselma, where your Uncle Ben, Aunt Grace, and I grew up. And where Grandma Nadine lived too, before she married "Grandpa" Newt. We all lived there with your *real* grandfather on my side of the family. His name, if nobody's told you, was Leo Dumont.

   I'd like to tell you about him, not only because he was your grandfather, and my father, but because he helps to explain me. I need you to know who I am: especially why I'm not there with you and you aren't here with me (and, by the way, you would love my little house on the beach in California).

   Leo Dumont was a xxxxxxxxxx wife beater, a child beater, and xxxxxxxxxxxx I loved him.

YANKING THE PAGE from the Royal's carriage, he balled it up and tossed it to the floor. With a fresh sheet, he began anew. *Dearest Ariel, Your grandfather, Leo Dumont, lived in the dark shadow of his failure as a man.*

EXCERPT FROM *A letter (never mailed) from Will Dumont to Ariel Dumont:* He lived in fear of it taking him down. And so he was a bully to his own wife and kids.

   When I married your mother, I vowed I would not be like that, no matter what. Please try to understand this. I loved your mother but did not know her. We rushed things. I'm not going to sugarcoat this. I did not want a child with her. It wasn't *you* I didn't want, Ariel. I can't imagine a world without you. But when your mother got pregnant, I was already doubting the two of us should be man and wife, let alone mother and father.

But I was not a bully, not yet.

Before you were born, we fought about you. Your mother said you would bring us closer. I said you would suffer for it. Well, you were born and your mother and I grew apart even more. She blamed me. She accused me of wanting to rescue everyone in the world but us. She decided not to let me get away with it. When we argued after that, there were no limits, nothing was too close to the bone.

She knew what I feared most.

One night, a Friday as I recall, I came home after eight o'clock. I hadn't called. There had been a going-away party for a guy on my diving crew who landed a cushy job with a salvage outfit in Florida, and I envied him. We met at a tavern near the East Ninth Street Pier. I drank too much—a family tradition—and that night I dreaded facing your mother.

The moment I walked in, she started in on me: I was this, and I was that, and most of all, she said, running away from you and her made me "an even bigger coward than your father." She knew what she was doing.

I slapped her. She fell back as if I had thrown a punch. She crumpled to the floor, clasped a hand to her face, and slowly she looked up. Something new was in her eyes. Pure triumph.

The rest you know. I tried to stay in your life from a distance. I mailed you reminders of a father who loves you.

Returned to sender. All of them.

So I did just what your mother accused me of: I ran. Like a coward. I hoped that by starting over—a new place, a new life—I could find peace, maybe even a little happiness.

I miss you so

HE LOOKED UP and thought for a moment. Then he rubbed his palms over his brow, and he was surprised when they came away damp. Rereading, the words floated on the page and he couldn't follow them. He pawed clumsily at his eyes with his shirtsleeve but could type no more.

43.
Fifa Found

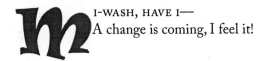I-WASH, HAVE I—
A change is coming, I feel it!

FIRST HAYDEN, NOW Fifa. Ten days into the new year, healthy and none the worse for it, Maggie's cat miraculously reappeared, and only she knew the adventures she had survived. We took it as a hopeful omen and guessed she might have stowed away on a coastal sail, but whose? Maybe she had fled the racket of pier construction, then simply decided to return, or someone had grabbed her and kept her locked up till now. With a cat, you never knew. Varda, encamped in the rear of Arvie Engstrom's workshop until his leg cast came off, took her in because Maggie, clearly, couldn't.

Hayden stopped by the shack the afternoon of Fifa's homecoming. He found Will looking rough, unshaven, with red rimming his eyes. He was invited in, nonetheless. Hayden said afterwards the shack smelled stale; there were piled-up dishes and half-filled drinking glasses abandoned here and there. Over by Will's desk he saw wadded-up sheets of paper and sheaves of typescript. These were commingled with snapshots—someone's baby pictures, he said, from the looks of them.

"Your memoirs?" Hayden kidded. Will, who had slumped

in a chair after closing the door behind his visitor, glanced at Hayden and insinuated a smile. "Something like that," he said.

"Hear about Maggie's cat? Damnedest thing."

Will shook his head.

"Just showed up after being gone for months. Skittish as ever. She wouldn't let anyone but Little Hope get close to her."

An uncomfortable silence fell between them. Hayden scanned the flotsam of Will's surroundings. "Got anything to drink around here?" he asked. Will returned with two bottles of steam beer and a church key. Prying open the longnecks, he handed one to Hayden, and they settled in at the dining table.

"They miss you at the No Name," Hayden said then.

"Um."

"So I thought I'd come by."

Will said nothing.

"Say hello."

"Yeah."

"You should see the WANDERER. I'm outfitting her for another run."

A flash of interest passed over Will's face. "Where to?"

Hayden winked broadly. "Dunno yet," he said. Draining his bottle, he swiped at his lips. He saw that Will's beer was untouched. "Terrible about Maggie."

Will stared at the floor and both men were silent again until Will looked up and fixed his eyes directly at Hayden. "I'm curious about something," he said.

Hayden breathed easier, as if they had made it to the top of a difficult hill. "Name it."

"Would you do it over again?"

"Do what?"

Will continued to search Hayden's expression. "Kidnap your kids."

Hayden laughed at that. A hearty, incredulous laugh, as if starring in the role of some outlandish Caribbean pirate. "Are you kidding? Course I would!" he said. "Greatest time those kids ever had, once they got the hang of life at sea. The rest of their lives they'll remember it. Even their lame-brained mother admits that now." He laughed again, then stopped himself and his manner became suddenly guarded. "Why do you ask?"

"Don't you think it's better, when two parents split up, that one of them just butts out? You know, disappears. So the kids can live regular lives."

"Hell, no!" Hayden roared. "Don't tell me you do."

THAT SAME NIGHT, near ten o'clock, Will was at the Royal again, reading over the words he had just typed.

EXCERPT FROM A letter (never mailed) from Will Dumont to Ariel Dumont: I'm not sure what will come of my life, darling girl, but there is someone I want you to know. I have met a wonderful woman. Maggie is her name. The two of you would be fast friends, I am sure of it. Maggie is smart and strong and a talented artist, and she's told me she loves me. I love her too, I can say that now, though it may be too late. You see, she is badly hurt and has been in the hospital for weeks now. When the accident happened, I tried saving her—*wanted* to save her more than anything (except having you with me again).

Even if she's paralyzed for good or if there's damage that won't ever heal, I don't care. This time I've promised myself I won't run.

Someday, I hope you'll know—and love—your father too.

HE WAS STARTLED by the thumping overhead. "F'crissakes, George, cut it out," he muttered, but there followed a sharp knock at the door. Evening fog wind hurtling down Hurricane Gulch had apparently snatched away the approaching footsteps and stolen them out into the bay. No matter. He decided this intruder would be ignored: whoever it was at this hour had no business at his door. Pretend not to be home, he thought. There came a second, more insistent knock.

"Damn it to hell," said Will.

Opening the door barely more than a crack, he saw a face he did not recognize. The face was stony.

"Mr. Will Dumont?"

Will nodded.

The man shoved a small envelope at him. "For you." As noiselessly as he had come, the stranger disappeared back into darkness.

Dumbfounded, Will turned the envelope over in his hand and he retreated to his desk to examine it under the glare of a crookneck lamp. The crisp pale vellum was addressed in a precise hand. But otherwise it gave away nothing. Tearing angrily at the envelope, he drew out a folded note card and saw that it was embossed in a formal typeface. He read: KYLE BOGART. Inside, in the same careful script as the envelope's, he found an even bigger surprise.

> *Will,*
>
> *I have news regarding plans for the Sausalito pier and myself. If this interests you, meet me at precisely quarter past midnight on the Golden Gate Bridge. Come alone.*
>
> *K.B.*

44.
Ship Ahoy

PARKING THE NOMAD JUST OFF THE BRIDGE'S northern terminus, Will turned up the collar of his pea coat and forged through the chill along the pedestrian walkway. At that hour there was no one else in sight on foot, and only the occasional auto or delivery truck on a late-night run rumbled past. He came to the first tower and kept walking until he was nearly to the span's midpoint.

He still wasn't sure why he'd come. Hadn't he had enough of this Kyle Bogart? But who knew, he told himself. Maybe this time he would make up for the last time. Maybe this time he would figure out a way to best this unaccountably daunting stranger who seemed to know more about him than anyone else who was not thousands of miles away and part of a life he was desperately trying to leave behind.

Finding him proved relatively simple. Even in blowing fog and dim lamplight, how difficult is it after midnight to spot a lone figure in a lumpy green jumpsuit on the Golden Gate Bridge? Will found Kyle Bogart in just such a fashion seemingly surveying the traceries of the city through the fog. But any thought Will had of taking charge of this second encounter was derailed even before he could get out a word. As he neared, and was about to demand to know what the hell he was doing there, Kyle Bogart glanced at his watch and held up a hand in a signal for silence.

He pointed a finger in the direction of their feet.

Will looked down and saw nothing. Only the hazy chop below. It was then he also realized how cold he was. Still needing to know why this man—and a bizarrely dressed man at that—had presumed to lure him from his warm cottage in the middle of the night, he was again about to blurt out that very question, when suddenly he felt himself drowning. Drowning in noise. Encased, weighted down, in danger of being crushed ... by sound. It was a lowing that jarred him to the bone and reverberated through every pore and left him gasping for breath.

Reflexively, he peered downward again. There, gliding directly beneath, shimmering like a mirage, was the largest ship Will had ever seen. Glowing, brilliant, alight like a carnival ride, this mighty vessel slid without effort to the accompaniment of its own horn under the bridge and entered the bay; she was a passenger ship but not a soul was visible on her promenades or in her staterooms. Her swimming pools were asparkle but devoid of swimmers, lounging chairs in neat formation yet deserted. Heading on a course directly toward the city, she began sounding her horn in burst after burst. The decibels sang to the steel and sinew of the bridge, and set its cables pulsating. Finally her stern slipped silently into a low fog bank. Disappearing into it completely, as if by magic.

As if Will had only imagined her. In frank astonishment he searched for some sign of her.

Kyle Bogart, hair stirred by the wind, remarked as if to no one in particular, "I named her the s.s. LAUREN."

"The LAUREN?" was all Will could say.

"For Bogey's Bacall."

Still stunned by the spectacle, Will asked, "She sure can whistle. You do know how to whistle, don't you?" He immediately felt like a fool for parroting the famous line.

Kyle Bogart, lost in his own thoughts, took no notice. "I

hope you got a good look," he said. "She's eight hundred feet long, her beam is ninety-five, and she weighs thirty-nine thousand, eighty-three gross tons. Her turbines can do a service speed of twenty-four knots, and she's got the latest stabilizers to minimize *mal de mer*. She's divided into watertight compartments, any three of which can flood without endangering the ship, and her lifeboats can be lowered in a list of twenty-two degrees. Except for the bridge and crew quarters, she's all conditioned air, stem to stern. Every cabin has hot and cold running water, and those without portholes have circular lights that glow in the morning to ape the dawn. There's a library and writing room, three restaurants, a swell nightclub and a first-rate movie theater that doubles as concert stage. She'll carry one thousand, nine hundred and twenty-one passengers and a crew of two hundred thirty-three. Very comfortably."

Will, though still staggered by the sheer preposterousness of it all, finally began to find his voice. "You brought me out here," he managed to say, "to gloat over your she-monster?"

"That's right."

"I see. I'm supposed to be impressed, is that right? Well, why not? You'll dump off more people at one moorage than live in all of Sausalito. Terrific! And while they're waiting to disembark, all their filth will go straight into the bay. From your sinks and showers and laundry rooms and galleys … the oily bilge and those nasty chemicals from dry cleaning and processing their souvenir photos … and how about the piss and shit of all these fat-cat customers, even? That's *very* impressive, Kyle." He was no longer cold, he realized, but his body felt like it did at the onset of the bends. "And what's with the grease monkey get-up anyhow?"

Kyle Bogart gave him a wry smile. "Don't remember?"

"Remember what?"

"You answered the door. You were just a snot-nosed boy."

An awful sensation now stirred in the pit of his stomach,

but Will was nowhere near ready to give in to it. "Hell's bells, Bogart," he lashed back. "I'm losing sleep over this, I'm angry, and I have no frigging idea what you're talking about."

Kyle Bogart regarded Will coolly. His eyes were calm and self-possessed. "Think harder, kid. The outfit, recognize it? It's property of the state of Ohio. I wore it when I walked away from the headshrinkers at the Lima funny farm."

"You can't mean—"

"My name then was Lyle."

The wind whipped at Will's pant legs, and a shiver that was not from the cold shot through him. He turned to grip the railing as if to protect himself from being swept away. "But you and Humphrey Bogart?" he struggled to say.

Uncle Lyle let out a sympathetic sound and put a bony hand on Will's shoulder. "I am that man's biggest fan," he said. "A weak little guy who wanted to be hard-boiled and strong like him, that's all. Of course I knew *you* from my first report about the waterfront bunch lining up against me in Sausalito. Then you walked into my office, and there was Leo written all over you."

"So why didn't you—"

"I haven't been a Dumont for a long, long time. That life was buried for good."

"Why now? Why now then?"

"Simple. I needed to see you again."

"Here. In the middle of the bridge."

"The LAUREN'll be in China Basin for a few days. Final checks and outfitting. Then her first passengers will board in Sausalito."

Will glared miserably at his uncle. "How the hell could you?"

"If I didn't, someone else will."

"Sure, some other escaped psycho."

As if jolted by electricity, Uncle Lyle jerked his hand from

Will's shoulder and stepped back. Just as quickly he recovered and said to his nephew, "There's more I want to say."

Will waited, wondering what else there could possibly be.

"We're a messed-up family," Uncle Lyle said in a voice less cocksure than before. "I suspect you know a lot of it. Your Uncle Ellis shrugged it off, but Leo and me, we had big problems with our dad—your grandfather. We hated being lugged around so he could knock on strangers' doors to tell them Judgment Day was just around the corner. We blamed him for mom dying in that crummy Alabama hospital. As far as we were concerned, his judgment was rendered. He was damned to hellfire forever. Your father, he got the angriest. I just fell apart. I avoided most people except Leo and your mother. Then Leo went off to war. I tried to help out while he was gone and ended up ..." He hesitated. "I got in a situation," he said so softly Will could barely hear over the wind. "I got in a situation no one should get in." Glancing over at Will, he added, "Not with your own brother's wife."

When Will did not respond, Uncle Lyle blinked back gathering emotion. Completely gone now was the tough guy stance of moments before. He continued, "Leo, he came back a wounded animal, shivering with malaria and a big chip on his shoulder, and saw right away something wasn't right. He could always read me pretty good. After that I stayed away more. But I missed your mother."

Will did not feel anything but numb. He did not hear the wind. He tasted something bitter and metallic in his mouth and he spat and watched the wind steal the spittle away. Even though he had guessed, long ago, there might have been something between Uncle Lyle and his mother, he never expected to hear that it was so. Not this way, not here. Breaking his silence, he said, "I remember the day we took you to the bus. Dad had tears in his eyes on the way home."

"Tears? Leo?"

"Yeah. Go figure." Will shoved his hands deep into his pea coat and looked away. "I don't care about you and Mom, if that matters," he said, not completely sure that he meant it. "She put up with so much. I hope you made each other happy."

Again Uncle Lyle looked at Will with surprise. "Thanks, Will," he murmured. "I wasn't sure you'd feel that way. The main thing is, I want you to believe I knew it couldn't be. It was Nadine who said again and again she didn't care, that she would tell the Pope himself to go straight to hell rather than live with Leo the way he was."

"She said that?" Will looked at his uncle in genuine amazement. "I'll be damned."

"Then he put me away. It was Leo signed the papers committing me to the hospital," Uncle Lyle said. "At Lima I tried getting over her. I couldn't. That's why I ran. I figured if I came out here and made a new life, I could forget what I'd left behind, know what I mean?"

"Don't I though," Will said but it was lost to the wind.

It was then that Will decided to tell his own reasons for running, for shedding the weight of his own past. He took his time, starting back in the Uselma box house, working his way to Leo's death and his marriage to Pickle, and finally to the birth of Ariel. How he had fled the mirror image of his father he saw in himself. How he had fallen for the Earthquake Shack and the crazy-quilt life of his adopted town; fallen for Maggie but had not found the means to accept her love and give it back. He told of his need to rescue others as a way to shut out his own cries for help. Uncle Lyle listened, and when Will had finished, they both fell silent again.

For what seemed a long time the only sounds that rose above the wind came from the odd car or truck feeling its way across the bridge, the moaning foghorn and clang of bell buoy. At length Uncle Lyle straightened and turned to Will. "I talked to her a few weeks ago, you must've figured that out by now. Her voice sounded the same, only different. She seemed glad to hear from me but that's all. Our time together is gone. Both of us know that. We didn't talk long."

Will nodded. "You might not recognize her. That Shaker Heights stuff isn't her but she loves it."

"We all do what we need to do. She told me you were home to see your daughter."

"I was there to kidnap her."

Either Uncle Lyle wasn't listening or now his mind was full of what he had to say next. For he told Will then, "All these years I said to myself: be tough as Bogart, be a big shot in your new life. I gambled I could outrun her. I thought I had won."

"So did I when I came back from Ohio," said Will. "Then the shit really hit the fan."

"That's rough, kid. I guess I had a part in that. I'm sorry. But we're all damaged goods, and at least a little crazy. Running doesn't change things. Shelters are temporary, get it? Your demons will always find you: they're inside the whole while. There's only one way and that's to get them out."

"Easy to say," Will protested.

"Okay," said Uncle Lyle. "Listen to me. I brought you out here to make it easier. You won't be able to sit on the sidelines anymore."

"What are you talking about?"

"Until now I wasn't sure. Now I am."

"About what? What the hell are you saying?"

"Hear me, Will, and hear me good. I'm saying I didn't just want you to see my newest toy. This may be my last chance, don't you see? I'm going to expel my demons once for all, and, who knows, maybe yours too."

"I still don't follow."

Uncle Lyle looked at Will and said, "Welcome to Bogart Cruise Lines, nephew."

Then he vaulted onto the low railing with the ease of an acrobat. At the sight of him teetering on the edge, Will's every nerve ending went on highest alert and alarm bells began screaming from every joint and muscle.

What happened next seemed to unreel in slow motion but in reality all happened in just an eyeblink or two.

"Uncle, don't …!"

Will lunged.

"Be stronger than me!" Uncle Lyle cried out.

Will's his encircling arms came up empty and all he could do was watch, helpless, as jumpsuited Uncle Lyle flew into the wind.

Then Will watched him plummet. He dropped as fast and straight as a freighter's anchor. Even in darkness he saw his impact with the bay, feet first, become a crater of splash and foam. His long lost uncle disappeared and was admitted to the depths.

There was, Will knew, not the slightest possibility of rescue.

THE SUN BARELY above the hills of East Bay, Will did make the recovery. You may remember him finding balled-up Uncle Lyle that fateful morning in the wet brown sand under the Valhalla—and how that was about all he could take of his newly inherited, and as yet unrealized, life. The shack stood in silent witness to his anger's upsurge, his despair and pent-up pain, Will's own little earthquake.

45.
The Porthole

BUT AS IT TURNED OUT, WILL WAS NOT ALONE IN recoiling at the sight of Kyle Bogart's dream ship. Following the ill-fated S.O.S. Happening and the completion of the pier, most of us, sad to say, had conceded defeat. On the other hand, a few along the waterfront grew more ... emboldened.

We were, after all, Water Rats. And rats persevere when the less cunning do not.

And so it was that two nights after Will's midnight rendez-vous—Uncle Lyle's body still lying unidentified in the county morgue—that Mephisto guided the Indian Chief to a shabby wooden affair lit by the glow of neon reflecting from a round window in an ironclad door. Jake huddled in the sidecar, Bel was draped over the Softtail; Marilyn Macaw occupied the usual forward position, on the handlebar. As we've noted, Mephisto saw himself as a man of action, odd as that may seem for a defrocked mathematician. But he saw no contradiction in his chosen dialectic. Every combatant in mathematics, he would say, knows nothing *but* action. For what is mathematics but the constant battling against the odds, a never-ending contest with digits and calculations, the resolute aim of which is an outcome, a change, total conquest.

Mephisto—and Marilyn Macaw, of course—were already well known in the grungy haunts of seafarers along the San

Francisco waterfront. This, too, we were soon to learn. Here, among navy seamen, the merchant marine, and, yes, passenger ship officers and crew, the spirit of the Barbary Coast lived on. Cheap drinks, cheap company, watch your ass. Hayden, another sometime *habitué* of those dives, knew the brawls there were not fake movie fights. He slid out the back whenever Mephisto bellied up to the bar like a surly deck hand and demanded a boilermaker at two bits a round and a shot glass of steam beer for his "fine feathered friend"—into which he plopped a plump purple grape.

Word traveled fast in this netherworld. The bartender, if you were not a cop, a reporter, or a process server, was the town crier. The Hedda Hopper of shipping news. Mephisto already knew the LAUREN was on her way from the Seattle shipyard where she was built. He knew this a full week before she slid through the Gate.

This afforded ample time to calculate a plan. Mephisto's solution to the pier problem became this elegant equation: *ship divided by ramming speed divided by pier inertia = destruction²*.

The place was named, aptly, The Porthole. "*Wie bist* the finest mixologist in paradise?" Mephisto inquired as they settled onto bar stools. On his shoulder Marilyn Macaw hopped from foot to foot in anticipation of her beer-dipped grape.

"Wouldn't know, don't care," replied the giant who was idly polishing highball glasses behind the bar. He stood six-seven if he stood an inch and pushed the scales at least three hundred pounds. His piggish eyes were crafty and surmounted by bottlebrush eyebrows. Completely bald, the name of course was Cowlick. "Brung fresh meat, I see."

Jake grunted and Bel smiled. A silky Dinah Washington tune swirled in the air, barely audible above a roomful of maritime leaves loosed upon land.

"My storm troopers," said Mephisto. Nodding toward Jake, he continued, "This one's a gross ignoramus—that's a hundred forty-four times worse than an ordinary ignoramus. And the other one, if he was any dumber, would have to be watered twice a week."

"Thiit," muttered Jake as Cowlick roared and slammed his ham of a hand to the bar.

Mephisto swiveled to sweep an eye across the dim barroom. No fights brewing yet, he noted with satisfaction. Assorted characters of motley description occupied the other bar stools, and at most tables grizzled patrons hunched in various states of alcoholic oblivion. He noted one table in particular: a party of revelers that did not share the Alabama chain gang mien of the others. Less worn but more polished, they looked like slumming naval academy. Mephisto leaned in toward the barman, forcing his bird to scramble to the small of his back. "The table by the jukebox," he said in a low voice. "The LAUREN?"

Cowlick worked his tongue as if searching for something wedged between his molars. "Maybe," he said at length. His eyes following Jake's hand as a twenty slid across the bar. He looked up at Mephisto and nodded.

"Send a round on us," Mephisto ordered.

Cowlick set up a line of longneck beers and mixed drinks, put two fingers to his fleshy lips and flung a piercing whistle toward the table. Laughter and conversation died as heads turned. Through the mirror on the back bar, Mephisto saw the men of the LAUREN notice Cowlick motioning them to their waiting round. They exchanged looks of surprise until the most junior of the group finally stood and made for the bar. Gathering the longnecks into one fist, highball glasses in the other hand, he said something to the bartender. Cowlick jerked a thumb toward Mephisto, who gave a small nod of acknowledgement. Back at the table the drinks were greeted with good cheer, and glasses and bottles raised in Mephisto's direction. It was evident they were well on their way to drinking the evening away.

A few minutes more, and Mephisto winked to his compatriots. He stood and strode over to the LAUREN table with his boilermaker in hand. Faces flushed by alcohol looked up at him as he announced, "Gentlemen, allow an introduction. I am the world's greatest admirer of luxury passenger liners … cruise ships, as we have lately begun to call them. I understand you are fortunate to be in the service of the Bogart fleet, on the new queen who made her regal entry through the Golden Gate just the other day. My friends and I wish to salute you. Which of you is *herr kapitan?*"

"That'd be me, mate" replied a ruddy man with hair and moustaches the color of straw. "Captain Roland Harrington." He rose and extended a hand. "Call me Rolly!"

Mephisto clasped the captain's hand, a watermelon slice spreading across his face. "Mind if I join you?" he asked.

AT TWO A.M., after last call, Mephisto still presided at the LAUREN's table. By then he had long since been joined by Jake and Bel.

After Cowlick locked everyone out, they all—ship's officers and Water Rats—stumbled arm-in-arm through the wharves and quays of China Basin, shouting out a loosely recognizable "Tom Dooley." The hours before dawn had brought a fresh miasma of fog. Lights were yellowed and barely visible until a few feet away. Finally, after a wrong turn or two, they found themselves all at once athwart a massive presence.

The LAUREN had seemingly materialized out of nowhere. Resting silently, her heavy mooring lines slack to the pier, gangplank lowered and ready for boarding. Mephisto threw back his head and stared up at her. A shot of electricity traced his spine. So big—so amazingly big. Later he would say he was as sober then as ever before in his life.

Inevitably, the press drew comparisons to the ANDREA

DORIA. Only a few years before, after all, the flagship of the Italian luxury fleet, outfitted with the latest radar and communications gear, had collided with the Swedish American liner STOCKHOLM, off New England. STOCKHOLM survived; ANDREA DORIA sank. Forty-six people died. Piero Calamai, her skilled captain, at first refused to abandon ship, and then spent the rest of his days in mourning. On his death bed, his final words were, "Is everything all right? Are the passengers safe?"

Of course these comparisons came before the truth was known: that the pride of the Bogart line had been shanghaied, that a former math professor, brilliant but mentally unstable, had taken the giant vessel for a joy ride.

In the official investigation, the captain's journal and radio logs proved useless, for no entries were recorded on that harrowing cruise. And so, interrogations of those involved became paramount. Captain Rolly Harrington, like his colleague Calamai, was a very good captain, and he testified he had not meant to leave port that morning, but only to show off the electronics of the LAUREN's bridge to his newfound friends. How was it, then, that he and his fellow officers had ended up hostages on their own vessel? "The damn booze ..." was all the answer he gave.

First Officer Riester and Chief Purser Pellagrini echoed their captain's account. And they corroborated the others by testifying that their captors' leader, the one with the bird, held a pistol to Captain Harrington and ordered him to back the ship from her berth and make way toward Sausalito. After the other two, the large Negro and the smaller man with the ponytail, freed the mooring lines, the abducted crew had been ordered to raise the gangplank and rouse the engine room.

Questioned why no one alerted shore authorities, Communications Officer Parsons told how the large Negro demonstrated frightening efficiency with a fire ax as he hacked away at their ship-to-shore.

The ultimate mystery, of course, and most eerie parallel to the fate of the ANDREA DORIA, was how radar could show the Sausalito pier off their port bow—attested to by both First Officer Riester and Third Officer Wayne Jones—when in fact it lay starboard and more distant than anyone realized. The ship's course-recorder put their forty-five degree turn hard to port in Richardson Bay more than half-a-mile off course, leading investigators to conclude that only two explanations were plausible. A failure of radar—or of the frightened, drunken men who were reading it.

Captain Harrington was never again master of a great passenger ship, another parallel to the ANDREA DORIA's Calamai. This was in some measure due to two troublesome admissions under official questioning. He stated he never actually saw a gun, but only felt the prod of a solid object concealed in Mephisto's jacket. And secondly, he conceded responsibility for the collision because, after all, he was in command, even under duress, of a ship that sailed in heavy fog at practically full speed.

46.
Will to Live?

ALACHY?
... Um?

WILL FLOPPED AGAIN onto his back. He groaned. The bed sheets were corrugated, the bed unwelcoming as stone. Half awake, clammy with sweat, he threw off his blankets and wormed to a new position. Sleep inhabited by such dreams was worse than no sleep at all. In exasperation he lifted his eyelids and surveyed the darkness, traced the quick sweep of light from Alcatraz across his ceiling.

MALACHY, WHY AM I afraid?

A SMALL CRY ESCAPED his lips and his eyelids fluttered. In deep sleep at last, he found her there and she spoke with a voice of scorn.

AFRAID? THE DEAD have no fears.

HER REBUKE WOULD not be denied. That angry female mouth, those angry female eyes. He heard the angry female voice. She called him the worst: the worst of sons ... the worst of husbands ... the worst of fathers. The mouth and eyes and voice that hurled these charges kept changing, bending, contorting, as if reflections in a fun house mirror. Just when he thought he knew, whenever he was nearly certain, the image shifted once more, her identity eluding him again, taunting him again. And then ...

FOR HIM—I am afraid for him.

THERE HE IS ... he comes. It's dark, cold, but I know what I'm doing down here. Plenty of air for two! I'll catch you, okay? Hey, no problem, I've got you! Uncle Lyle? Is that—I've got you. Maggie! I've got ... how ...?

AACH, WE CAN'T be interfering. Don't meddle, lass!

THAT SOUND. WHY won't it stop? Not female. Not Maggie. Not Uncle Lyle. What? Is it angry? What ...

WILL STRUGGLED AGAINST it. He fought returning to the surface. Unwilling to abandon even troubled sleep, he clung to the murkiness. But it was no use. And he rose slowly, slowly, abandoning the dream world. In its place, his dawning consciousness tried to make sense of it: the sound. It was a thumping, a heavy, insistent thumping. He knew it now. *That damn George.*

Slapping at his pillow, he was determined to ignore it. Then he paled. There was a sudden and terrible flash of light, and a stench filled his nostrils. His bedroom reeked, and it made him gag and weep. What the hell was this? This putrid smell … of something … someone … dead?

THUMP, ATHUMP, ATHUMP…!

THE DAMN SOUND, that execrable stench, they would not go away. They only grew. They billowed like thunderheads. Will, scowling and not yet fully alert, covered his head with his pillow. That was no better. It was worse. Gasping for breath like a fish out of sea, about to shout out—*George, go away!*—there began something new. A new sound. It started as a rumble. A low and menacing rumble. A sound that, in no time at all, was a roar.

Kicking off his blankets and sitting upright in bed, he desperately wanted to hear now. He listened hard, seeking to understand, wanting to know what was happening and what to do.

Will felt it then. He felt the sound. He sensed its presence: it was very near. The sound was movement, movement itself, a shaking, a shambling, a tossing. This sound, this movement, it was steadily worsening, as if there was no limit to its fury and power. From another room there came the noise of something toppling over, something heavy crashing to the floor, of glass smashing into untold shards, bits, and pieces.

Earthquake!

The thought screamed at him, demanding to be heard over the thunder, the horrible clamor, the might of a thousand plunging locomotives.

The very ground cried out as it was torn asunder. As it

was shoved aside from the sheer momentum and might of the engines of the Bogart Cruise Lines dream ship, s.s LAUREN, as her hull plowed through the sea grasses and the kelp, the unctuous brown bay mud and its many mollusks and vertebrates, simple organisms and complex. Her bow, thrusting like a battering ram, slicing neatly through the boardwalk and up the fogged-in beach, slowing, slowing at last as she met resistance in the steadily shallowing path.

Coming to rest finally.

Just past Will's bed.

Epilogue
Years Later...

OUR STORY OF SAUSALITO AND ITS EARTHQUAKE Shack—no longer a refuge but itself a poor damaged thing—continues to this day. Will Dumont's story, however, is over. Or I should say his need for the shack's sanctuary and all that implies is at an end. For my father's story has become mine. It has been a labor of love to tell you how it happened—much easier than fitting together the pieces of those maddening Rubik's Cubes all the rage now.

Most who took part in that amazing year are still near our waterfront. Mephisto, as usual, being the exception. It was only after the LAUREN was hijacked that we found out his real name: Sheldon Shulman. He did nine years in San Quentin. Since then he's become a very close associate of the Reverend Jim Jones, and presently he is in Guyana with others from the People's Temple. Despite everything we wish him no ill.

Many of the particulars concerning my father's past, especially as they pertain to me, were in his letters. It was shortly after I turned eighteen that I first read them. They arrived in mysterious fashion. A woman arrived unannounced at my dormitory at Bowling Green, where I was in my first year. I remember being struck by her most incredible hair, wild beyond description even for those times. Of course this was Maggie. She introduced herself as a close friend of the father I barely remembered, whom I had neither seen nor heard from since

he left Ohio. She held out the packet—miraculously intact!—
that she said was unearthed beneath a scrapbook of yellowed
newspaper articles collected by Grandma Nadine in the ruins
of the cottage where he lived. She said to me, "He wrote these
to you when you were too young to read." Imagine my state
of confusion. I was stunned beyond words. I may have mum-
bled my thanks as this surprise visitor exited with the parting
comment, "You need time alone." She promised to be back the
following day. Nodding dumbly, I did not even think to ask if
my father was alive or dead.

My own love affair with Sausalito began soon after. Just
as my father had, I fell for her outrageous charms almost the
moment my hitched ride rounded the curve on the road into
town that reveals her cascading homes on flowering hills and
the high drama of the blue-green bay. I became our newest
Water Rat.

You're wondering about Will, my dad. My mother told me
he was dead. She told everyone that, and Grandma Nadine
backed her up. My Uncle Ben would have told me the truth
when I was old enough, I'm certain, but then he moved to
Guanajuato. It was after Aunt Abby died in the freak accident,
when I was six. I remember Uncle Ben taking it hard, blam-
ing himself for the tree overhanging the house like that. Poor
Aunt Abby. She always hated the winters, but how could anyone have foreseen that old maple splintering and crashing onto
the roof under the weight of frozen rain and wet snow? But it
set Uncle Ben free, and off he went and never looked back.

So it was left to my Aunt Grace to issue the first whiff of
truth.

We never saw Aunt Grace, whom my mother referred to as
"the dyke sister of your dead father." I knew she was an actress
in New York—actor, I guess would be the better women's lib
word today. I did not know she was just as estranged from
her upbringing as my father. I did think it weird Grandma

Nadine never spoke of her, that I knew her only from short notes on cards with the gifts, usually the lives of famous women like Madame Curry or Joan of Arc from Scribner & Sons. On my tenth birthday I was handed a box by the mailman who brought it to our door. I recognized the handwriting but not the Florida return address. My aunt had given up the struggle of Manhattan and moved to Key West. "From Aunt Grace!" I blithely announced. My mother raised an eyebrow and watched me tear through the brown paper to pry at the cardboard lid. My mouth fell open. Inside, encircled in tissue like an Egyptian mummy, was the largest, most perfect shell. A conch shell, its pink mouth smooth and delicate-looking as porcelain. I held it up, fascinated. To this sheltered Ohio girl, it was the Rosetta stone, my first intimation into another way of life. My mother, never much impressed by nature, turned on the sarcasm reserved for anyone in my father's family except Grandma Nadine. "How special," she sneered. It was then I noticed a corner of pink stationery tucked into this beautiful vessel. Wriggling it free, I unfolded the note and read.

> *Dear Ariel,*
>
>   *On this birthday, can you appreciate that strong as this beautiful home is, it didn't save the creature that lived in it? Life is to be discovered—and it's my hope you learn to live without hiding from it. Also, this shell reminds me of growing up with your father; for it was he who taught me to swim; and he who imparted in me his own sense of wonder about the oceans and the seas. As I write this, the turquoise Caribbean is in my window, and I think of him. He is looking out at his own sea, wishing he could leave his shell and swim with you.*
>
>   *Love and happy birthday from your Aunt Grace*

That is close to what it said anyways. As I was reading it for the third and final time, my mother snatched the paper from my hands. That note disappeared forever, as did Aunt Grace's new address. No amount of pestering would make my mother answer the questions my father's sister had put into my head. But from then on, I knew there was more to learn than what I had been told.

He does look longingly at his sea. From the day bed he has a clear view through the doors at DHARMA's stern, and One-Eyed George, now ancient in pelican years, manages to drop by and peer back at him in his cockeyed way. My father looks directly out onto the very spot where, so long ago, he popped to the surface and first laid eyes on his Maggie. When he returns his gaze in our direction, at the three of us, he always smiles. He reminds us he is content, that his life is far richer than it ever could have been in his old fantasy of roaming and wandering. He says he's even fine with trading "my mental health" for "my body's health." He says he never has dreams anymore. But Maggie tells him he hums in his sleep.

If it's under water he wants to see, he can turn his head toward his burbling aquarium or at the vivid canvases of silvery squid, brilliant anemones, and other sea creatures, personal favorites culled from Maggie's works created to peddle to tourists. She has set aside, for his sake and for Lauren's, her dislike of repeating herself. Her paintings fetch good prices, but the bills for his care and medicines keep coming, plus there's no end to the expense of raising "the miracle baby," my little sister. I still tease her by calling her that, though she's taller and stronger than me and could beat me up easily if she tried. Lauren smiles instead. "It's very Zen to love your enemy," she teases back.

Unfortunately, Fifa's son Malcolm doesn't heed that bit of wisdom, so often he will hiss at scrawny old Marilyn Macaw (whom we've inherited) before dozing off on my father's chest. Will smiles at Malcolm, too. He says he welcomes another guy around the place. That's lucky, for there's not much he can do about Malcolm's choice of a napping spot.

"Where are my angels?" he asks whenever he needs something.

The three of us share the tasks of caring for him. Feeding him, washing him, changing his clothes and the bed sheets. The more unpleasant duties. We believe we are all blessed. Maggie's own injury did no permanent damage to her or their child inside her. Her parents love her so. So do I, as do I my father and dear Maggie too.

Another thing's for sure, and that's that Will Dumont's no cruise line tycoon. As soon after the accident as he was able, he informed Sausalito the ships he inherited would never dock at the new pier. But Uncle Lyle, the only member of our family *certified* crazy as a coot, hadn't spilled the whole truth. There was more reason than he let on to take his leap—though Dad thinks he did it for the noblest of reasons and chooses to ignore the rest. Uncle Lyle's company and everything in it was wagered on the runaway success of the fledging cruise ship industry. He had run the stakes too high. Even had Dad wanted to, he could never have made a go of it. The creditors claimed the pot.

Not that the town escaped completely. In the fullness of time, what does? Sausalito has become a big tourist draw after all. And it has grown. Our beats and bohemians were joined—all but supplanted—by the flower children and drop-outs of the Sixties, and the Water Rat population grew with our worldwide reputation. Our houseboat community flourishes still and so does our famed colony of artists. Yet to this day no giant cruise ships dock on our waterfront. We—I include myself, because after these many months of assembling this saga, I feel I was there all along—won that battle. The long pier is a stroller's and fisherman's delight beloved by us Rats and many others, including the ageless Chinese who fish and crab off its sides, as well as remaining a reliable source of controversy whenever some Hillclimber decides it should become the next Santa Cruz Boardwalk or other lame-brained thing. After what we've been through, we will never let it happen. Besides, you know how things go around here. That the pier ever got built in the first place was a miracle: more than any Bible Belt® of the Buckworthys (long since moved on, presumably to Orange County).

And what of the Earthquake Shack? It, too, is no less loved for being somewhat diminished. Let's just say that after all the Water Rats of Sausalito went through, we are not about to allow it to go completely to rot—once the U.S. Corps of Army Engineers finally gets around to moving the rusting remains of the hulking ship off our beach. Is it not fitting that our battered old shack looks out onto what used to be called Whalers Cove, where Sausalito's ill-fated patron, *Señor* Richardson, once supplied sweet spring water and other vital stores to the anchored whalers readying to hunt the leviathan? Things definitely do move in whale time around here. Less gets changed that way, which is usually how we like it.

Speaking of which, a doctor at Stanford has informed us a new procedure is being tested that might reawaken parts of Dad's body that have been asleep—like Maggie was asleep—for all these years. It will be terribly expensive, of course, so it seems out of the question. But who knows? One of these days I might round up Varda and some of the others and we'll raise the cash with another great Water Rat blowout. Stranger things have happened, as you have seen for yourself. Dad says he just knows he doesn't like my idea of calling it S.O.D. (Save Our Dad) or S.O.W. (Save Our Will).

Oh, one thing more …

Dad says he never believed those ghost stories. The ones about the shack being haunted. Mostly not, anyhow.

SEE NOW, DIDN'T I tell you? We should never have bothered. Malachy, you are wise ... for a barbarian.

THE END

ACKNOWLEDGEMENTS

THE AUTHOR'S THANKS to all keepers of Sausalito's torch, and especially those who unselfishly shared their own remembrances of the woolly, bygone times. Special and heartfelt thanks to Rebecca Archey, Roger Archey, Ray Diedrichs, James Dalessandro, Phil Frank, Christopher Gortner, Susan Littwin, Lanny Jones, Margie Mason, Linda Joy Myers, Blaze Nash, Richard K. Rein, Stephen Schlatter, Mark Shulman, David Spurgeon, Susan Trott, Roland Wahl, Linda Wahl, fellow members of the Marin branch of California Writers Club, and the Sausalito Historical Society.

Printed in the United States
118500LV00002B/601-624/A